**"My lord, there's been an error,"** Triona began.

It was too late. The coach was moving. Triona glared at MacLean's shadowy form. "My lord, I am not who you think I am."

"What?" Amusement and disbelief colored his voice. "Then you are not Miss Hurst."

"No. I mean, yes. I *am* Miss Hurst, but *not* the Miss Hurst you think me."

Even in the gloom, she could make out the flash of his teeth as he smiled. "I see," he said politely. "You *are* Miss Hurst, but then you are *not*."

"I am Miss *Caitriona* Hurst. Caitlyn is my sister. My twin, in fact."

"Of course she is."

Triona relaxed a bit. Thank goodness he was a man of reason! "This has been a horrible mistake. Oh dear, this is so indelicate—"

He reached across the coach, his large, warm hands closing about her waist as he lifted her and placed her in his lap. He grinned, his handsome face within inches of her own as he said in a low voice, his breath warm on her cheek, "Since I caught the little bird, she is mine to enjoy. But first, let us agree to dispense with story time."

"My lord, you don't understand! I'm not Ca—"

It was then he committed an even more unthinkable act than holding her in his large, warm lap, as scandalous as it was. In the semidarkness of a luxurious coach as it dashed madly through a snowy night, MacLean bent his head and kissed her.

*Turn the page for rave reviews of*
*Karen Hawkins's romantic storytelling . . .*

**Sleepless in Scotland is also available as an eBook**

Also by Karen Hawkins

Available from Pocket Books

Look for the next sparkling Hurst Amulet novel

*Scandal in Scotland*

Coming soon from Pocket Books

# Sleepless in Scotland

## KAREN HAWKINS

POCKET BOOKS

New York   London   Toronto   Sydney

Pocket Books
A Division of Simon & Schuster, Inc.
1230 Avenue of the Americas
New York, NY 10020

This book is a work of fiction. Names, characters, places, and incidents either are products of the author's imagination or are used fictitiously. Any resemblance to actual events or locales or persons, living or dead, is entirely coincidental.

This Pocket Books paperback edition May 2011

POCKET and colophon are registered trademarks of Simon & Schuster, Inc.

For information about special discounts for bulk purchases, please contact Simon & Schuster Special Sales at 1-866-506-1949 or business@simonandschuster.com.

The Simon & Schuster Speakers Bureau can bring authors to your live event. For more information or to book an event contact the Simon & Schuster Speakers Bureau at 1-866-248-3049 or visit our website at www.simonspeakers.com.

Front cover and stepback illustration by Alan Ayers, hand lettering by Ronn Zinn.

Manufactured in the United States of America

10 9 8 7 6 5 4 3 2 1

ISBN 978-1-4516-0773-4
ISBN 978-1-4391-6434-1 (ebook)

I wrote parts of this book while staying at my in-laws house as my father-in-law fought his last few days against cancer. It was there, at his bedside, that I learned the true meaning of character, both from him and in watching the stream of caregivers who stood by his side.

To Hospice of St. Francis in Titusville, FL.
Thank you for taking such beautiful, compassionate care of my incredible father-in-law who was able to die as he had lived—strong, proud, and loved.

www.hospiceofstfrancis.com

# Acknowledgments

For Nate . . .

Thank you for the perfect wedding—
peaceful, joyous, and loving.
I love you more every day.

# THE MACLEAN FAMILY TREE

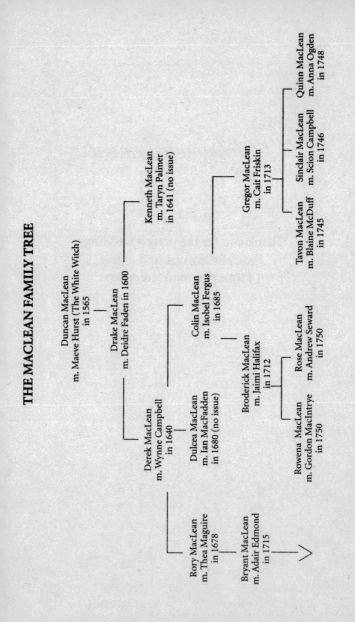

Duncan MacLean
m. Maeve Hurst (The White Witch)
in 1565

Drake MacLean
m. Deidre Faden in 1600

Kenneth MacLean
m. Taryn Palmer
in 1641 (no issue)

Derek MacLean
m. Wynne Campbell
in 1640

Colin MacLean
m. Isobel Fergus
in 1685

Gregor MacLean
m. Cait Friskin
in 1713

Tavon MacLean
m. Blaine McDuff
in 1745

Sinclair MacLean
m. Scion Campbell
in 1746

Quinn MacLean
m. Anna Ogden
in 1748

Rory MacLean
m. Thea Maguire
in 1678

Dulcea MacLean
m. Ian MacFadden
in 1680 (no issue)

Bryant MacLean
m. Adair Edmond
in 1715

Broderick MacLean
m. Jaimi Halifax
in 1712

Rowena MacLean
m. Gordon MacIntrye
in 1750

Rose MacLean
m. Andrew Seward
in 1750

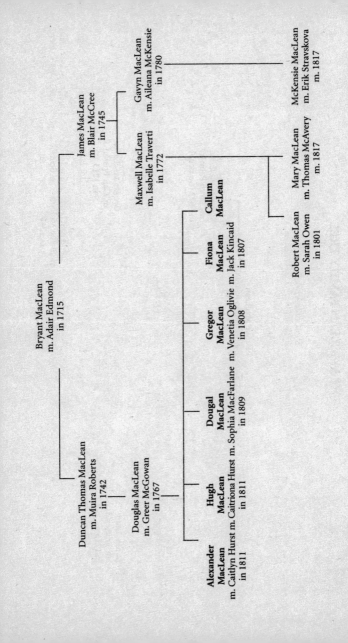

Bryant MacLean
m. Adair Edmond
in 1715

Duncan Thomas MacLean
m. Muira Roberts
in 1742

James MacLean
m. Blair McCree
in 1745

Douglas MacLean
m. Greer McGowan
in 1767

Gavyn MacLean
m. Aileana McKensie
in 1780

Maxwell MacLean
m. Isabelle Traverti
in 1772

McKensie MacLean
m. Erik Stravskova
m. 1817

**Hugh MacLean**
m. Caitlyn Hurst m. Caitriona Hurst
in 1811        in 1811

**Dougal MacLean**
m. Sophia MacFarlane
in 1809

**Gregor MacLean**
m. Venetia Ogilvie
in 1808

**Fiona MacLean**
m. Jack Kincaid
in 1807

**Callum MacLean**

Robert MacLean
m. Sarah Owen
in 1801

Mary MacLean
m. Thomas McAvery
in 1817

**Alexander MacLean**
m. Caitlyn Hurst
in 1811

# Chapter 1

*"There's naught worse than a man who thinks he's always right—'cept a woman who always is."*

Old Woman Nora to her three wee granddaughters on a cold winter's night

*I* forbid you to go." Though merely twenty years old, William Hurst thought himself in charge of Wythburn Vicarage when his father was away. "Be warned, Triona," he added in his deepest voice. "I will do everything in my power to halt this madness!"

His oldest sister didn't even look up from digging out a worn portmanteau from her wardrobe. Caitriona—Triona to her family—placed the case on her bed and snapped it open, then began packing.

"Did you hear me?" William said more loudly, "I forbid—"

"What? Oh, yes, I heard you. But *someone* has to go to London and talk some sense into Caitlyn."

"Yes, but—"

"Since Father and Mother are visiting Uncle Traveres for two more weeks, and you are in the midst of preparing for your exams, that someone will have to be me."

William scowled. A handsome young man possessing considerable height, he was used to being paid more heed. Everyone in the county deferred to him, except his own family, even when he wore his high-collared coat of blue superfine, his cravat tied in an impressive array of knots. "You are not Caitlyn's keeper."

"But I *am* her twin sister, so it falls on me to help her out of this mess she's made."

"William, leave Triona be." Eighteen-year-old Robert stood by the door, his arms wrapped around a huge tome, and smirked at his older brother. "Father expressly placed Triona in charge when he left. I heard him."

William scowled. "Father didn't intend her to go running off to London. As I'm the oldest male, that should be *my* job."

Triona adjusted her spectacles more securely on her nose and laughed. "Ah! I see; you don't wish to miss out on the fun. Well, I promise I won't stay long enough to have any." She crossed her fingers and held them up, saying primly, "Promise is as promise does."

William sighed. "I don't mind you having fun. I just don't wish you to find yourself in an awkward situation. A female—"

"Who is twenty-three years of age."

"—traveling alone—"

"Nurse is going with me."

"—to the most licentious city on earth, a den of iniquity and vice—"

"Ooh! *Very* well said!" She looked him up and down in admiration. "Is that from one of Father's sermon books?"

William couldn't stop a sheepish grin. "You know what I mean."

"I do, and I promise to be careful. But I'm the only one Caitlyn will listen to, so I must go."

"Yes, but—"

"William!" Seventeen-year-old Mary dropped her knitting with a huff of irritation. "This is an *emergency*! Caitlyn is acting so badly that poor Aunt Lavinia was forced to write for assistance!" Her lips quivered. "After this, Aunt Lavinia will *never* invite any of us to stay with her for a season!"

William sighed. "I'm not saying we shouldn't rescue Caitlyn from whatever mischief she's bent on; I just wish we could ask Father's opinion on how to deal with it."

"No, you don't," Michael said sharply from beside the fire, wrapped in a blanket to ward off the room's chill. Thin and pale and given to a weak chest, he possessed a sharp wit and a sharper mind that outstripped his fifteen years. Having caught the same ague that had kept Triona from enjoying a season in London with Caitlyn, he had not yet recovered, with an unnatural flush still coloring his thin cheeks and a wretched cough that lingered. "Father is the last person to notify about this. If he knew how badly Caitlyn has been behaving, he'd never allow another of us to visit Aunt Lavinia."

Mary chimed in, "It took *months* to get him to agree to allow Caitlyn and Triona to go, and when Triona became ill and couldn't travel, he tried to cancel the entire trip and Mother had to intervene and—"

"I know!" William said, clearly exasperated. "I was here, too."

"Then you should know that telling Father anything negative would be a colossal error."

Michael nodded. "Mary's right. Father would—" He coughed, a long, racking effort that sounded as if his toes might curl inside out.

Triona paused in folding her silver-threaded shawl and gave him a worried glance. The vicarage at Wythburn was a rambling, drafty house given to mysterious creaks and leaks. Besides the uneven stairs that leaned to one side and warped floorboards that no amount of nails could hold flat, cold gusts rattled the doors and windows and kept damp corners from drying out properly.

She frowned at her youngest brother. "Are you taking your medicine?"

Michael grimaced. "No." Before she could protest, he added sullenly, "It makes me too sleepy."

"Sleep would be good for you."

"All I *do* is sleep. I'm rested enough as it is."

William frowned. "You can't tell me you slept well last night, for I heard you coughing well into the morning hours."

Triona pointed to the bottle at Michael's elbow. "Take it."

"But—"

She set her hands on her hips. "Michael John Hurst, don't make me sing."

William turned to his brother. "Michael, take that medicine!"

"*Please,*" Mary pleaded fervently.

Clutching his book, Robert pointed to the bottle. "For all our sakes!"

Michael gave a weak laugh that turned into another racking cough. When he could breathe again, he picked up the bottle and a spoon. "Fine, but only because I feel sorry for all of you. I don't mind if Triona sings to me."

"How can you not?" Mary asked.

He grinned. "Because this ague has stopped up my ears. You all sound like you're very far away."

Triona waited to make sure he took a full dose, then turned back to her packing. "If all goes well, I should be back from London before Father returns. And if I can secure Aunt Lavinia's silence, he need never know."

Mary brightened. "Then he might not protest if she invites another of us to visit her for a season!"

Triona nodded. If Mary didn't eat too many crème tarts, she might well rival Caitlyn in looks one day. Meanwhile, Caitlyn was in full bloom, and it was difficult to imagine a more winsome beauty.

Although Triona and Caitlyn were twins and enjoyed some similarities, there were many more differences between them. Caitlyn was small and slim with golden hair, tilted dark brown eyes, a heart-shaped face, and a mesmerizingly graceful way of floating across a room that left men standing mouths agape, their eyes glued to her. Triona was tall and more rounded, her hair more brown than gold, her hazel eyes hidden by spectacles and lacking the tilt that made Caitlyn's so compelling. And no matter how Triona tried, she couldn't float across the room any more than she could trim a few inches off her ungainly height.

But it was more than that. It was the way Caitlyn laughed, and charmed, and . . . oh, Triona couldn't define it. Neither could the dozens of besotted young men who'd attempted to describe Caitlyn's charms in laughably bad poetry and gushing conversation.

"Before Triona leaves, we must all do one thing," Michael said, his tone unyielding. "We must all vow not to tell Father about Triona's trip. *All* of us." He gave Robert a pointed stare.

"Yes," William said immediately, his gaze locked on Robert as well. "We must *all* vow to keep our mouths closed."

Robert turned a dull red. "I won't vow any such thing! Father wouldn't wish us to keep secrets from him."

Robert had won Father's approval by applying himself to his studies in a way that left his siblings glaring at him from their respective corners of the dinner table, especially when he smugly answered one of Father's more esoteric questions in flawless Greek or Latin.

"Perhaps you don't understand the situation." Triona picked up a letter from the bed and handed it to Robert. "Aunt Lavinia is at wit's end to know what to do. As much as I esteem our aunt for her good nature and generosity, we all know how Caitlyn can be at times."

Mary nodded. "No one is more stubborn."

"Or impulsive." Michael's voice was faintly slurred, the medicine beginning to take effect.

Robert read the missive, then gave a snort of disgust. "Aunt Lavinia can't think ordering Caitlyn about will help things! It will only make her more determined to do worse."

William sighed. "It doesn't matter how badly Caitlyn mulls things—none of us have the funds to visit London, anyway."

"But just think," Mary said earnestly. "If Caitlyn makes an advantageous marriage, she can invite us to stay with her in London and take us to balls and plays and all sorts of events!"

Triona smiled dreamily, placing two books into her portmanteau. "I should like to see the British Museum."

Robert brightened. "By Jove, that would be something! I heard the Elgin Marbles are on display."

Michael said, "I'd like to go see Tattersalls auction house."

On her way to fetch her half boots from the wardrobe, Triona paused by the settee to muss Michael's hair. "That would be lovely," she agreed.

William's eyes shone. "I'd like to see that, too! And

Gentleman Jackson's Boxing Saloon, and Vauxhall Gardens, and—"

Triona laughed. "Caitlyn had better marry a man with a very, very large house so we will all fit."

"And she would certainly let us stay with her, for she's very generous," Mary said.

"And foolish," Robert added. "And impulsive and—"

William balled his hands into fists.

"Well, she is!" Robert eyed his older brother's fists and added hastily, "Not that it's her fault. Caitlyn's behavior is evidence of the decadent influence of London society—"

"Oh, please." Triona folded a night rail. "Caitlyn was just as impetuous and unthinking while here in the country."

"She wasn't such a flirt," Robert insisted.

"Yes, she was," Triona said in a regretful tone. "Poor Mr. Smythe-Laughton went into a decline when she left for London, and then there was Mr. Lyndon, and Lord Haversham's eldest, and—oh, more than I can count."

"There were dozens," Mary agreed enviously. "Father warned her of it several times, though I heard him telling Mother that Caitlyn didn't realize her effect on men and that, in general, he thought her flirting very innocent, though he couldn't help worrying that it might be her undoing."

Robert sniffed. "Father has been much too indulgent."

"I'll be sure to tell him you said that," Triona said dryly.

"Please don't!" Robert said so fervently that Triona laughed. He grinned in return. "Maybe I am being a bit harsh, but you must agree that London has had an unfortunate effect on Caitlyn. She might have flirted more than was seemly here, but she wasn't so lost to decorum as to declare in front of an entire ballroom that she was going to marry someone before the end of the year, 'one way or another.'"

"Not unless she was goaded," Michael pointed out. "Caitlyn's quick to take umbrage, so perhaps it was due to something Alexander MacLean said or did."

Triona wrapped a pair of shoes in brown paper and placed them in the portmanteau. "Grandmother is forever telling us about the MacLean pride; sometimes I think she would do better to warn us about the Hurst pride. It is just as formidable."

"Mam loves to talk about the MacLean curse," Mary said with a delicious shiver. "An entire family, cursed to cause storms whenever they lose their tempers! Just imagine!"

William's eyes twinkled as he curled his hands into claws and hunched his shoulders, saying in an old-woman brogue, "Don't ye be forgettin', me dearies, the MacLeans were cursed! Cursed, I tell ye, by the mysterious white witch. Now when they lose their tempers, the storms do fly!"

Everyone chuckled except Mary. "You shouldn't

mock Mam. She's a very wise old woman. Father says half the village wouldn't be alive if not for her knowledge of healing and herbs. Besides, who's to say that there's no such thing as a curse?"

"Father, for one," Robert said. "He says it's all nonsense. And as Mam is his mother, I'd think he'd know."

Michael moved restlessly on the settee. "Whatever the truth about MacLean, he can't be happy with Caitlyn making such a spectacle of him."

"It sounds as if *both* Caitlyn and MacLean have been misbehaving. Fortunately, we are not responsible for MacLean." Triona placed her portmanteau by the door, then gathered her cloak, scarf, and good bonnet. "I hear the carriage at the front door, and I daresay Nurse is waiting for me."

Michael smiled sleepily. "Good luck, Triona. Remember, Father is due back a week from Friday."

"Which is why I plan on being home at least two days before that, at the latest. Father will never be the wiser if we *all*"—she looked at Robert—"keep our mouths closed."

"And if you don't," Mary said smugly, "I shall tell Father who spilled milk all over his favorite copy of *The Odyssey*."

Robert started. "How did you know—" At Mary's amused gaze, he colored.

"So either hold your tongue, or face Father's wrath," she warned.

Robert flung up a hand. "Fine! But if some ill comes

of this trip, I will tell Father I attempted to warn Triona against it."

Triona pulled a pair of old gloves from her cape pocket and put them on. "Oh, Robert, stop being so gloomy. Nothing ill will come of this. Besides, Father said I could visit London once he returned. You could say I'm only going earlier than planned."

"Father wanted to escort you himself."

"And so he shall—next time." Triona glanced in the mirror and tucked a stray strand of hair into her bonnet. "Time to go."

William bent to collect her portmanteau. "If I didn't know that Mr. Olson would inform Father if I missed a tutoring appointment, I would go with you."

Triona smiled at her brother. "It does my heart good to know that you're willing to make such a sacrifice."

William grinned. "It *would* be a grand lark."

Triona laughed, then turned to Robert. "Stop glowering and give me a hug good-bye. I shall miss you!"

His stern expression softened and he complied.

Next was Michael. She bent and gave him an especially big hug. "Stay inside and make sure you take the medicine Dr. Felters left for you."

Michael scrunched his nose, his brown eyes large in his thin face. "If I must."

"You must."

She looked at Mary, who hugged Triona and whispered, "I'll keep an eye on Michael. Don't worry about a thing."

"Thank you." Triona smiled at her younger sister

and, with a grin, said loudly, "You're in charge, Mary. Make sure William meets with his tutor, and Michael gets his medicine, and Robert doesn't pour milk on any more books, and—"

Over the protests of her brothers, Mary laughed. "I will."

"Excellent! Good-bye, my dears. I will return as soon as I have cooled Caitlyn's spirits a bit." Triona went downstairs, William following with her portmanteau.

Smiling, she greeted Nurse and continued to the carriage, her mind already leaping ahead to London. Despite her cheery words to her siblings, she couldn't help but worry.

Triona's earliest memory was of watching Caitlyn trying to climb the banister to slide down it, though they'd been expressly told not to. Later, her leg in a cast, Caitlyn had told Mother and Father she was glad she'd done it, because it'd been such fun.

Even at age five Caitlyn had been a handful, while Triona had dutifully gone about life, never giving her parents a moment's fear. Her parents never knew how often Triona intervened to keep Caitlyn from falling into worse scrapes, either. Triona understood her twin sister better than most; she knew how Caitlyn's restless spirit made her yearn for excitement. There was little Caitlyn loved better than the chaos that magically appeared everywhere she went. She didn't exactly start it, but she rarely did anything to halt it once it began.

Triona, meanwhile, prized order above all things. And as the oldest, she was frequently called upon to provide exactly that for her many siblings. So rescuing Caitlyn now from yet another scrape was nothing new, and yet, somehow, Triona couldn't shake the feeling that this time something was different.

*Caitlyn, what are you into now?*

# Chapter 2

❦

*"Och, me lassies! Ye dinna know the trouble a man can be—especially one who ignores ye, no matter what ye do."*

OLD WOMAN NORA TO HER THREE WEE
GRANDDAUGHTERS ON A COLD WINTER'S NIGHT

What do you mean, she's *eloped*?"

Aunt Lavinia pressed a handkerchief to her trembling mouth. Seated on her overstuffed pink-fringed settee, her equally overstuffed figure encased in mulberry silk, her feet bulging over the edges of her black satin slippers, she looked as if she were about to pop.

"It's tragic!" she wailed. "I went to Caitlyn's room a little while ago and—I put her in the blue chamber, you know, as it has the prettiest views, and—"

"Aunt Lavinia, *please*."

"Yes, yes, I'm sorry." Aunt Lavinia's eyes, usually a merry blue, filled with tears. "I went to see if Caitlyn preferred mutton or cold sliced beef for dinner. Cook has both, you know, for she always goes to the market on Wednesday, and—"

"Aunt Lavinia!" Triona silently counted to ten.

"Sorry, my dear. As I was saying, I went to her room and discovered"—Aunt Lavinia took a shaking breath—"*she was gone!*"

Triona waited. "And?"

Aunt Lavinia blinked, looking disappointed with this prosaic reaction. "Nothing more. She was just *gone,* and I have no idea where she might be, so I came here to repose with my smelling salts and try to think what to do."

"And then?"

"I must have fallen asleep, for when I awoke, you were here."

Nurse harrumphed her displeasure.

"But . . . how do you know she eloped? Couldn't she just be out with friends?" Triona queried.

"Oh, no! I asked and no one had called for her. Nor did she take the coach, nor ask for a horse to be saddled—nothing!"

Triona mentally reviewed the many letters she'd received from Caitlyn over the last few weeks. "She loves shopping. Could she have gone to that milliner's shop off St. James's? Or perhaps to the British Museum? She loves the portrait hall."

Aunt Lavinia sighed. "Oh, dear, I hadn't thought of looking for her. I suppose I should have, but since the note said—"

"There's a *note?*" Triona's voice cracked on the last word.

Nurse made a noise between strangulation and disgust.

"Of course there's a note," Aunt Lavinia said, blinking her confusion. "How else could I know she's eloped?"

"How else indeed," Triona said through gritted teeth. "May I see the note, please?"

Aunt Lavinia waved a plump hand bedecked with an astonishing assortment of rings toward the gilded escritoire in one corner of the crowded drawing room. "It's over there somewhere. I couldn't *bear* to look at it anymore! Ah, how ill your sister has used me! And after I was so generous as to sponsor her for a season! I wish you had been able to come with her, Triona. I'm sure *you* could have curbed your sister's spirits!"

*I would have at least tried.* Triona managed a small smile. "Perhaps there's a clue to her whereabouts in the note." She crossed to the small desk, aware of an ache in her legs and back. They'd ridden to London with only the briefest stays in posting inns, sleeping on lumpy beds. The trip had taken more than two days, and every bounce of the carriage, every jolt over a poorly kept road, had rocked her and Nurse through and through. They were exhausted beyond thought, so arriving to find Caitlyn nowhere in sight was disappointing, to say the least.

Triona reached the small desk and saw, on a pile of notes and invitations, a folded paper bearing a familiar spidery script.

*Dearest Aunt,* Caitlyn's excited scrawl read, *forgive me, but by the time you read this, I will be gone. I can't explain except to say that when I return, you will be very happy to see me and we shall laugh together at my foolishness.*

Triona's heart sank. Caitlyn seemed to think running off was nothing more than a lark. Had she sunk so low in good sense and behavior?

*Rest assured that when I return, all will be well.* Caitlyn had underscored "well" so heavily that she'd torn the paper. *Until then, yrs etc, Miss Caitlyn Hurst.*

The "Miss" was underscored as well. Was that because when she returned, she would no longer be a "Miss"?

Triona handed the note to Nurse, who glanced through it before saying sourly, "It doesna say where she is, but it also doesna say where she's not."

Aunt Lavinia moaned and waved the smelling salts beneath her nose.

"We're too late," Nurse added. "Miss Caitlyn's gone and ruined hersel—"

"Don't say it!" Triona's stomach roiled at the thought. "We must find her before any real damage has been done. Where is Uncle Bedford? He'll know what to do in this situation."

Aunt Lavinia sniffed noisily. "He's at White's. I sent a message, but I vow those doormen hold on to notes from wives so the men will stay and spend more funds on—"

"Fine. We'll start the search ourselves. How long has Caitlyn been gone?"

The older woman looked at the small ormolu clock on the mantel. "Two hours."

Triona relaxed. "Only two hours? That's not so long!"

"We ate a late lunch and had a pleasant discussion about her latest plan before she went up to take a nap."

"Plan?"

"Oh, yes. I told her it was chancy beyond words—it never would have worked."

Triona sat on the settee and took her aunt's plump hand between her own. It took a good deal of self-control not to smack it. "Aunt Lavinia, if we're to find Caitlyn, you must tell us about this plan. What was she trying to do?"

"Why, to trick Alexander MacLean into proposing marriage, of course!"

Triona opened her mouth and then closed it.

Aunt Lavinia nodded, her soft brown curls bouncing under her lace cap. "I must have looked just as shocked as you when she first told me. But then she explained it was because of a wager MacLean made her, that no matter what, he would never offer her marriage."

"All of this for a *wager*?"

"She doesn't like to lose, as you know." Aunt Lavinia sighed heavily. "I vow, having your sister here has been an amazing amount of work. The house is never quiet, and people are forever coming and going. And don't get me started on the flowers! The bell never stops ringing and has quite destroyed my nerves, and—"

"Aunt Lavinia, about this wager?"

"I was getting to that." Aunt Lavinia glanced at

the open door before she leaned forward and said in a loud whisper, "Your sister wanted to learn when MacLean was leaving town, so she could hide in the seat locker of his carriage."

"*What?*"

"Ha! That's exactly what I said! Once they were well under way, she was going to pop out of the seat box and surprise him. If she stayed hidden until he was so far away that he could not return her before nightfall, her reputation would be ruined and MacLean would *have* to propose to her, and then she'd win the wager."

Triona gaped. "Aunt Lavinia, pray tell me that you urged her not to do anything so scandalous!"

Nurse snorted.

Aunt Lavinia cast an uneasy glance at Nurse before saying, "Of course I did. Although I must say that, as plans go, it was a very good one." She suddenly giggled. "Can you imagine Alexander MacLean's surprise when he found Caitlyn in his seat box? Lud, we had such a merry time discussing how shocked he would be. He's such a proud man that—"

"Lord, save me fra' the fools o' the earth!" Nurse exploded.

Aunt Lavinia flushed. "I never thought she'd actually *do* it!"

Nurse turned to Triona. "Yer sister's been an impulsive one since she were a bairn. What I dinna understand is how she thinks this mad plan o' hers will work. MacLean could just send her back to London on the mail coach and continue on his way."

"Oh, no," Aunt Lavinia said in a voice of surety. "If there is one thing the MacLeans are, it's honorable. But . . . Caitlyn didn't plan on accepting his offer of marriage. She just wanted to win the wager."

"But she'd be ruined!"

"I *did* point that out, but Caitlyn was sure she could keep everything quiet. I told her to be sure she did, for she's been invited to the Devonshires' rout and those invitations are *very* hard to come by."

Nurse harrumphed. "That's madness, 'tis!"

Triona agreed. Not only did it show a distressing lack of propriety, but Caitlyn obviously had not thought her plan through. Besides thinking she could keep her hijinx a secret, she hadn't considered the logistics. Though some carriages had storage beneath the seats for blankets and cushions and warming pans, even in the most luxurious carriage the space was quite small. Triona shuddered to think of being trapped in such a place.

Nurse shook her head. "Caitlyn will come to a bad end this time, mark my words. Ye dinna play with fire an' no' expect to get singed."

Aunt Lavinia's plump face folded with disapproval. "I can understand Caitlyn's behavior completely." At Triona's surprised look, she continued, "You would, too, if you'd seen how rude Alexander MacLean has been to her since she arrived. And she the belle of the season, too!"

Triona sighed. She supposed she shouldn't be surprised. Caitlyn was ever ready to rise to a challenge, real or not. "I thought she'd be so busy enjoying the season that she'd stay out of trouble."

Aunt Lavinia brightened. "We've been inundated with invitations! Dukes and earls and viscounts and barons—everyone wants to be seen with your sister. Beau Brummel himself walked with her the length of Bond Street and called her 'charming'!"

There were no words to describe the rapture on Aunt Lavinia's plump face; her aunt had clearly been living vicariously through Caitlyn's successes, Triona realized. "Even Brummel's good word will not be enough to save my sister if she's ruined herself."

Aunt Lavinia's smile faded. "I suppose not. Things were going so well before Alexander MacLean arrived in town. Your sister hasn't been the same since."

"What did he do?"

"He took her into instant dislike when they first met in Hyde Park! Her horse got away with her—she *would* ride your uncle Bedford's prize mare, though Caitlyn is just learning—"

"So she met Lord MacLean and he wasn't impressed."

"It was more than that. He barely acknowledged her, and told several people—horrible gossips, all—that despite her beauty, he thought she had no character."

Triona frowned. "How rude."

"Exactly!" Aunt Lavinia said eagerly. "Then his brother Hugh came to town, and things got worse. Where Alexander was cool, Hugh was frigidly cold, not acknowledging her at *all*."

"He cut her?"

"Yes! People began to talk, and then laugh. Naturally Caitlyn couldn't stand for that! I told her to pay him no mind, for he's always cold to women." Aunt Lavinia glanced at the open door again before saying sotto voce, "Hugh MacLean has no regard for females at all. They say he has over a dozen illegitimate children!"

Nurse clacked her tongue. "That's the MacLeans fer ye. Cursed they are, and the devil's own way with women."

Aunt Lavinia eyed Nurse with a cautious eye. "So it seems. Anyway, Caitlyn was infuriated and foolishly allowed it to show, which made Alexander laugh openly at her, and they had words about it—at one of the biggest balls of the season! Both of them said things they shouldn't have, and then he told everyone he knew that she couldn't attach him if she tried."

"Good Lord! Caitlyn wouldn't take that very well."

"No woman would," Aunt Lavinia said hotly. "Naturally she had to retaliate, so she wagered that she could bring him to his knees—literally."

"Did you try to talk her out of such a silly notion?"

Aunt Lavinia sniffed. "I told her to be discreet, though the child was well within her rights to demand satisfaction."

Wonderful. Just when Caitlyn had needed a calm, logical head to guide her impulsive thoughts, she'd received outraged encouragement.

Still, Caitlyn's actions seemed extreme—even for

Caitlyn. Triona frowned. "Aunt Lavinia, Caitlyn's not in love with Alexander MacLean, is she?"

Aunt Lavinia blinked. "Lud, no! She bristles every time he's near."

"Sounds like love to me," Nurse said glumly.

"Oh, no, not at all. It's just foolish pride."

Triona sighed. "I wish I could speak with her. I'd be worried about that note, but from what you say, so long as MacLean hasn't left town, she's still here in London and there's no need to worry."

Aunt Lavinia pressed her handkerchief to her mouth.

Triona frowned. "He *is* still in town, isn't he?"

"He was to leave this afternoon. Your sister told me at lunch. At the time, I didn't think—I hadn't thought . . . who would have foreseen? But now that I think on it—"

"Then they're gone," Triona said flatly. "Be that as it may, I'm not giving up! I'll find Caitlyn before it's too late, if I have to follow her to the gates of hell and back."

Outside the MacLean town house in fashionable Mayfair, Hugh MacLean pulled on his gloves. "Did you leave the stables unsecured as I requested?"

"Aye, m'lord," his groom replied in a low voice, sending a nervous glance at the carriage. "And I pulled the laird's favorite carriage into the center o' the drive so it wouldna be mistaken for another."

"Thank you. You've done well."

Ferguson leaned forward to whisper, "I sprinkled sawdust around the doors as ye suggested, and there was a footprint in it this afternoon."

Hugh smiled grimly. He would enjoy teaching the brazen chit a lesson. Ever since she had announced that she was determined to have Alexander in her court, Hugh had been leery. Alexander might laugh her off, but Hugh knew a thing or two about scheming women that Alexander did not.

So Hugh had paid a servant to keep an eye on the busy Miss Hurst, which was how he'd discovered her plan to stow away in Alexander's carriage and force an offer of marriage. Hugh's jaw tightened at the thought. The woman had no shame. None at all.

Without notifying Alexander of his intentions, Hugh had urged him to visit their property outside Stirling to wrap up a lucrative land deal. The night Alexander had left, Hugh put his plan into effect. He'd gone to a dinner party and said well within Miss Hurst's earshot that his brother was preparing to leave on the morrow and would, of course, travel in his favorite carriage.

Thus the trap was set.

Ferguson sent an uncertain glance toward the carriage. "M'lord, ye willna be a-hurtin' the lass, will ye?"

Hugh smiled, though not nicely. "Miss Hurst will get what she so richly deserves, but no more."

"That isna reassuring."

"Rest assured, I merely wish to frighten her."

Ferguson looked dubious. "I just hope ye dinna get caught in the parson's trap yerself."

Hugh snorted. "The last thing Miss Hurst wishes is to be saddled with a younger son. She will demand to be returned to town immediately, which I will gladly do once my point has been made."

Ferguson's expression darkened. "I dinna blame ye fer takin' a stand, m'lord. She's a rare handful, she is."

Hugh nodded. Many people considered him the most easygoing among the MacLean brothers, and he usually was. He saw no reason to inflict his problems and issues on others and he rarely lost his temper—which was a good thing, considering the family curse.

It had long been rumored that a white witch had cursed the MacLean family so that whenever they lost their tempers, the heavens above would open. Unfortunately, the curse was more than mere rumor. Hugh had conquered his temper and it took huge provocation to rouse it, but his brothers were not so fortunate. They were passionate men who fought as hard as they loved, leaving a trail of broken hearts and fierce storms in their wake.

Except Alexander. His answer to the curse was to keep everyone at arm's length, even his own brothers. Only Callum, their youngest brother who'd died under suspicious circumstances years ago, had been able to penetrate Alexander's rock-hard exterior. After Callum's death, Alexander had retreated even more. Though he spoke of business and discussed common family matters with Hugh, rarely did another word pass between them.

Hugh had attempted to warn Alexander about the Hurst chit, but Alexander had only shrugged and changed the conversation. Alexander didn't understand the danger as well as Hugh did, which was why he was forced to act. He hoped his brother would appreciate his efforts, though Alexander was more likely to be angered by the interference. Too bad. Hugh was decided on this action, though it would have been helpful had Alexander been more forthcoming about his feelings on the matter. *Callum would know how to tease Alexander into confiding his feelings about the Hurst chit. But only Callum.*

The memory of his youngest brother, so full of laughter and charm, weighted Hugh's heart. Callum had been the heartbeat of their family and they each felt his absence keenly, though none more than Alexander. Indeed, the weeks following Callum's death had been dark and bitter as the MacLean curse roused a stormy madness that had slashed the earth with wind and rain.

After Callum's death, their sister, Fiona, had tried hard to draw Alexander from his dark ways, and in some ways it had worked. But now that she was married and involved with her own husband and children, Alexander was more alone than ever.

It made Hugh's heart ache to know his brother was so isolated, yet there was no way to reach him. Hugh's jaw tightened. The least he could do was keep schemers like Caitlyn Hurst out of Alexander's way.

Ferguson looked up at the sun. " 'Tis getting late. Shall we go now, m'lord?"

"Yes. And to teach the 'lady' a lesson, hit every rough spot in the road from here to Stirling. No sense in making her trip pleasant."

Amusement twinkled in the groom's eyes. " 'Twill make a rough ride for ye as well."

"Yes, but I will have a cushion beneath my arse while she will be cramped in her boxlike prison." Cheered at the thought, Hugh headed for the carriage.

"Aye, m'lord!" The groom threw open the carriage door.

The interior of Alexander's coach was as luxurious as the exterior. While the outside gleamed with black lacquer and silver, the family crest discreetly mounted behind one window, the interior was all plush red velvet and rich wood accents with silver trimmings.

Hugh glanced at the floor and saw a trace of sawdust beside the forward-facing seat. The latch was also twisted to one side. The woman was boringly predictable.

He settled on the thickly padded seat and told the groom in a loud, clear voice, "To Stirling."

"Aye, m'lord!" Ferguson gave a broad wink and, still grinning, closed the door.

Hugh settled back against the thick cushions as the carriage set off. Trust Alexander to have a coach the Prince would lust after. Hugh was more about efficiency and simple comforts, so his coach was much plainer, though well sprung and with wider wheels that guaranteed a most comfortable ride. He was a man who knew his value and didn't wear his wealth on his sleeve. Alexander, as laird of the clan, was expected to make a statement, and he wore his wealth with a natural arrogance and elegance that made every dying-to-wed female pant.

Hugh received plenty of attention when he wished—and he'd garnered far more than his fair share—but his being a younger son kept most desperate females from pursuing him. Which was just the way he liked it.

As the carriage rattled down the cobblestones at a brisk pace, Hugh imagined the discomfort Miss High-and-Mighty Hurst must be feeling, and grinned. He hoped that by the time they reached Cadesleeds, she'd be hungry, thirsty, and thoroughly jounced about.

No one took advantage of the MacLeans. *No* one.

Thoroughly satisfied, he tugged his hat over his eyes, settled back in the seat, and drifted off to sleep.

Nurse hung on to the leather strap with both hands and moaned, her face green. "Does that coachman have to drive like a crazed man?"

Triona leaned out the window, the delicious wind tugging her hair. "We have to catch up with Cait. She has a good hour on us; MacLean's footman said the carriage left at four."

"Och, I know, but—" The coach hit another huge

hole in the road and Nurse bounced, her head hitting the low ceiling of the ancient coach.

Triona lost her hold on the window and fell across the seat, her head smacking the wood side panel. "*Ow!*"

Nurse settled back into her seat, her pale face grim. "The road is cursed by the devil himself."

Triona scooted across the seat so she could look out the window again. They were just approaching a small inn. Though the footman on the roof was supposed to watch for MacLean's distinctive carriage, she didn't trust him to remain vigilant. She stared at the innyard as they whizzed on by, but no fancy coach could be seen. She sighed.

"Did ye see it?" Nurse asked.

"No, but Aunt Lavinia's coachman said there are several inns favored by the gentry along this stretch." Triona peered through the darkening afternoon at the lights of an upcoming inn, and gasped. "There it is!" She stood and banged on the ceiling with her fist.

The carriage immediately slowed and pulled off the road into a low copse, an innyard visible through the trees. "There's the coach! I can see the crest, just as Aunt Lavinia described!"

"God be praised!" Nurse closed her eyes for a quick prayer.

Aunt Lavinia's coachman came to the door. "That's the coach, all right, miss! I saw it just as ye did!"

"Can you tell if MacLean's inside?"

Fletcher squinted through the trees. "Looks empty

to me . . . ah! I see MacLean standing by the inn with his man."

Nurse looked at Triona. "Shall we confront that beast in his lair?"

The sun was already below the horizon, its lingering beams casting long shadows. Triona regarded the coach with a narrow gaze. She could almost feel Cait's presence.

"Seems mighty quiet," Fletcher said. "Miss Caitlyn must not have revealed herself."

"We're still close enough to London for the laird to return her. She wouldn't show herself until they were farther away."

Nurse shook her head. " 'Tis a poor example o' womanhood who tricks a man like that and—"

"Look!" Fletcher nodded toward the inn. "They've begun to change the horses, miss. They won't tarry much longer now."

Triona unlatched the door and hopped out onto the soft, damp ground. The scent of the decaying leaves under the thin layer of fresh snow tickled her nose. "I wish I could speak to Caitlyn while the carriage is empty; I know I could make her see how foolish this plan is." What should she do? Caitlyn was within reach, and she couldn't let the carriage pull away without trying something. But what?

"I have to get inside that coach."

"Ye'll do no such thing!" Nurse said.

Fletcher shook his head. "That's a risky thought, miss. You could get caught."

She shrugged. "MacLean doesn't want anything to do with Caitlyn. If I told him that she was in his carriage, preparing to trick him into an offer of marriage, he'd thank me." She regarded the coach with a considering gaze. "If I weren't so determined to leave this place with Caitlyn's reputation intact—which requires MacLean not knowing about her plan—I'd do just that. I must convince her to leave his carriage while the horses are being changed. No one will be the wiser, and we can return to London and set things right with my aunt."

"I suppose ye're right," Fletcher said.

"I dinna like it!" Nurse snapped.

"It's all we can do, considering the circumstances." Triona turned to the servants. "Stay here. I'll slip through the woods and get close enough to the carriage to speak with her." Triona shivered as a sudden breeze swirled her cloak and skirts about her boots.

Nurse and Fletcher exchanged glances, but reluctantly nodded.

Triona pasted a hopeful smile on her face. "I'm off, then. Keep watch." Cloak clutched tightly, she quickly set off toward the inn, her heart pounding. *Ohhh, Caitlyn, you will owe me for this one!*

# Chapter 3

❧

*"The Hursts are known fer their honest souls and their hot, impetuous natures. And let me tell ye, lassies, 'tis that and naught else as led yer entire family down many a poorly chosen road."*

OLD WOMAN NORA TO HER THREE WEE
GRANDDAUGHTERS ON A COLD WINTER'S NIGHT

*W*hen Triona reached the edge of the woods, she saw MacLean's coach was pulled up to the inn door, the side facing her in the shadows.

Excellent. She could sneak up to the carriage and slip in with no one the wiser.

From the other side of the coach, the coachman's hoarse voice asked, "M'lord, are ye sure ye wish to go on? 'Tis coming on snow. I can taste it."

MacLean's voice was cultured and colored with a hint of a brogue. "Taste it? Next you'll be telling me you can smell it, too."

Triona almost closed her eyes to savor the man's voice. Deep and rich, it wrapped around her and warmed her skin in the most amazing way. She could see Caitlyn responding to that voice—Cait's love of pretty things would make her a pawn under the spell of a velvety-rich voice like that. And if the man matched it . . . Triona shivered. Her sister wouldn't have stood a chance.

She, however, was made of sterner stuff. Though a voice like rough silk might make her heart flutter, it wasn't temptation enough to make her toss her reputation to the winds.

As Triona prepared for a crouched dash across the innyard, a stableboy appeared with a leather bucket of oats and went toward the front of the coach. She gave a frustrated sigh, which fogged her spectacles. Using the edge of her cloak to dry the lenses, she examined the innyard again and saw that the stableboy was now beyond the front of the carriage. She could just make out one of the footmen helping a stable hand harness the fresh team, their backs toward her.

Now was her chance! Bent low, she scurried across the dark yard to the coach. She reached the door and easily pulled down the door latch. The click was loud in a sudden pause in the commotion, and she froze. Had they heard it? Her fingers grew cold on the brass handle, her ears tuned for every noise.

In the forest behind her a tree branch snapped, then fell to the ground, scattering chunks of snow across fallen wood and rock. Triona started, and her spectacles slipped off her wet nose and fell to the ground.

*Blast it!* She quietly released the door handle and scanned the muddy ground, but could not see them.

A noise from the front of the carriage made her realize how vulnerable she was.

Gritting her teeth, she reached for the door again. She'd look for them *after* she rescued her sister.

As she pulled the door open, she heard MacLean on the other side of the coach: "We'll have to watch for falling snow on our way. That could cause some problems."

"Aye, especially when we get that new foot o' snow me achin' knee is predicting."

"Perhaps. Let's check the lead horse's hock. He seemed to limp as they brought him from the stables, and I don't want him drawing up lame in this snowstorm of yours."

Their voices faded as they moved to the front of the carriage.

Triona cautiously slipped inside the coach, careful not to rock the well-sprung vehicle.

The inside was as opulent as she'd expected. The seats were covered with thick velvet, the walls a deep oak with heavy silver lamps adorning each corner. The window curtains were fastened down and a foot warmer rested on the floor, its gentle hiss evidence that it had just been filled with hot coals.

Triona bent down against one of the seat boxes. "*Cait?*" she whispered.

There was no answer. She must be under the other seat. Triona moved over, pressed her cheek to the seat and whispered as loudly as she dared, "*Cait? Can you hear me?*"

Silence loomed. She reached for the seat latch, her ears locked on the sounds around her—the occasional jingle of the harnesses, the faint wind whipping through the trees. Over that, she heard something that made her blood run cold—the coachman's voice growing louder, MacLean's deep voice answering.

They were returning! She struggled to open the latch, but it was stuck.

Directly outside the door, the coachman's voice seemed unnaturally loud. "Scoff if ye will, m'lord, but I can smell the snow. 'Twill be eight, nine inches at least."

MacLean laughed softly, and Triona shivered again at the velvet brush of his low voice. "Ferguson, that's more snow than they've had here in the last five years combined."

"Trust me bum leg, m'lord. 'Tis never wrong."

The latch finally gave with a faint scrape of metal on metal. Triona lifted the seat and peered inside. No Cait. Her sister had obviously been here, though, for her favorite thick muff sat in one corner beside a bandbox and a silver opera cloak lined with ermine.

Triona frowned. None of it looked disturbed. If Caitlyn had stowed aboard the coach, wouldn't the cloak have been mussed, the muff flattened, the bandbox bent or crushed? There would have been barely enough room for Caitlyn herself, with so much baggage.

Triona closed the lid and crossed to the other seat. She slid the hook open and carefully lifted it, the latch creaking the tiniest bit. Outside there was the faintest pause in conversation; then the two men continued to talk, this time about the best route to take.

Breathing easier, she peered inside. The box was filled to the brim with thick blankets, extra cushions, a leather desk box, and a traveling chess set.

Frowning, Triona silently lowered the seat and sat back on her heels. *Cait, where* are *you?* She had to have been here; *someone* had stowed the cloak, muff, and bandbox inside the—

"We're ready, m'lord!" called one of the footmen from the front of the coach.

"Let's go, then," came MacLean's voice. "Ferguson, bring my horse. I'm going to ride a bit before it grows too dark."

"Yes, m'lord." The groom called to someone; then Triona heard the sound of approaching footsteps crunching in the packed snow.

*Someone's coming!* Triona reached for the door to escape, but just as she touched the handle, the coach lurched forward and threw her into the door, her knee hitting the floor hard. She gasped as pain lanced up her leg.

Tears clouded her vision, but she swiped them away and crawled to the seat as the coach rolled on.

*Dear God!* What could she do? Exposing herself would be horribly embarrassing. How did one explain one's uninvited presence in a coach?

Gritting her teeth, she held onto the strap and stood to knock on the roof of the coach.

Nothing happened.

Frowning, she did it again, much harder. Maybe the coachman couldn't hear over the creak of the coach, which had picked up its pace.

"Blast, blast, blast!" Still holding on to the strap, she lowered herself to the seat and undid the leather curtain to look out. They careened down a narrow, snow-covered road in the settling darkness, white-capped trees blurring by. The carriage was moving so fast, she couldn't leap out if she wished to.

As she started to replace the curtain, a golden horse rode into view. The horse's color was unusual, but the sight of the rider completely wiped the horse from her mind.

He was tall and broad-shouldered, and even in the dim light she could see the lines of his face: the firm jaw, the sensual mouth, the faintly aquiline nose. All of it bespoke power and masculinity of a sort Triona had never encountered before.

As he galloped by, he should have been surprised to see a stranger sitting in his coach. Instead, the look he tossed her was one of lazy insolence, as if he'd known she was there, could see her worth, and deemed her below his notice.

Triona's hands fisted about the window. "Stop the coach!" she shouted, but the wind and the rumble of the carriage whipped away her voice. Though he must have seen her attempting to speak, her captor rode on with a mocking smile.

Unbelieving, Triona sank back onto the seat, resting her feet on the warming box. She didn't understand. MacLean had looked at her as if he knew her, as if he'd *expected* to see her there. But how—

The truth hit her with sickening quickness. *He thinks I'm Caitlyn.* Triona covered her face. He *knew* Caitlyn was supposed to be here, in his carriage.

She dropped her hands and stared ahead unseeingly. *But if that's so, then why is he continuing away from London?* If he'd expected to find Caitlyn hiding in his coach, wouldn't he be anxious to return her home? He would—unless . . . Triona blinked. Was this not a trick, after all, but an elopement? Or worse, a trick turned on Caitlyn? Did MacLean plan on *seducing* her?

Triona rubbed her forehead shakily. What a coil! Cold blew in around the flapping leather curtain. Teeth almost chattering, she closed it and attached it to keep in what little warmth remained, then opened the seat box and pulled out her sister's cloak to wrap about herself. The wild pace of the carriage hindered her and once she was even tossed onto the other seat, twisting her already pained knee.

Triona finally wedged herself into a corner with one foot pressed against the edge of the opposite seat, both hands clenched about the door strap. As the chill increased, she realized how unsuitable her sister's cloak was. "Trust Caitlyn to bring such a useless piece of clothing," Triona muttered. Taking her life in her hands, she tossed the cloak to the floor, opened the other seat box, and pulled out two thick blankets. Grateful for their warmth, she bundled into them.

Trying to stay calm, she took stock of her situation. Nurse must be frantic by now. Would she and Fletcher try to follow the coach? No, there was no way Father's old carriage could keep up this mad pace. Not only were their horses older and far from fresh, but the equipment wasn't made for speed.

Undoubtedly, Nurse would return to Aunt Lavinia's and put out an alert. Help would be on the way soon, so all she had to do was wait.

She touched her throbbing knee through her skirts and frowned to find it unnaturally warm. It was swelling, too; she could already feel it. Gritting her teeth, she gingerly lifted her leg and settled her foot on the cushioned seat opposite.

That was all she could do for now. One good thing about springing the horses was that they couldn't maintain this pace for long—not without changing the animals.

The thought calmed her somewhat. As soon as they stopped, she'd explain her presence to MacLean. Once he realized she wasn't Caitlyn—a strong light would reveal that—he'd arrange for her to be returned to London. She might even arrive at Aunt Lavinia's before Nurse, who was traveling in Father's decrepit old coach.

Outside, the light faded until Triona was sitting in near darkness. *Surely we'll stop soon. We can't keep—*

The carriage swung abruptly to one side, throwing Triona across the carriage, her sore knee striking the edge of the seat. She cried out, tears springing to her eyes.

The coach halted. Triona blinked back her tears and heaved a relieved sigh as the door opened, moonlight spilling inside.

MacLean climbed in and slammed the door behind him, enveloping her once again in near darkness. She heard him toss his hat beside her as he sat on the opposite seat.

"My lord, there's been an error," Triona began. The coach lurched forward. "*No! Wait—*"

It was too late. They were moving, returning to their original pace.

Triona grabbed the door strap once more, glaring at MacLean's shadowy form. He seemed even larger inside the confines of the carriage.

Indeed, at this close distance, everything about him was *more*. He seemed to fill the entire space, his long legs pressed against hers. Though she couldn't see his expression, she could feel the seething danger that warmed the air about them. "My lord, there has been a horrible mistake."

No answer came.

Triona took a calming breath. "My lord, I am not who you think I am."

"What?" Amusement and disbelief colored his voice. "Then you are not Miss Hurst."

"No. I mean, yes, but not the one— What I mean to say is that I *am* Miss Hurst, but *not* the Miss Hurst you think me."

Even in the gloom, she could make out the flash of his teeth as he smiled. "I see," he said politely. "You *are* Miss Hurst, but then you are *not*."

"No, no, no. I am not Miss *Caitlyn* Hurst, I am Miss *Caitriona* Hurst. Caitlyn is my sister. My twin, in fact."

"Of course she is."

She relaxed a bit. Thank goodness he was a man of reason! "This has been a horrible mistake. You see, I thought Caitlyn would sneak into your coach and try to . . . Oh, dear, this is so indelicate—"

He reached across the coach, his large, warm hands closing about her waist as he lifted her and placed her in his lap.

"*Ow!*"

He stopped immediately, holding her in place. "What's wrong?"

"My knee," she managed through clenched teeth. "I struck it on the seat when the coach jolted to a start, and it's swollen."

"Can you move it?"

"Yes, but it hurts."

He grunted and settled her more firmly in his lap, the muscles of his thighs hard beneath her skirts. "We'll have a look at it once we stop."

Triona's jaw tightened. "*We* will not do anything. *You* will unhand me and *you* will stop this carriage as soon as possible."

"Really?"

"*Yes*, really. If you do not, then when we finally do stop, I will demand your arrest."

"Arrest? Arrest for what?"

"Abduction."

His powerful arms tightened about her, and she could feel the irritation coming from him in waves, a deep heat that replaced her shivering with another kind. "Once we stop, I *will* look at that knee. As for the rest, you can call for whatever help you wish."

"I shall!"

He grinned, his handsome face within inches of hers as he said in a low voice, his breath warm on her cheek, his sensual cologne tickling her nose, "Since I caught the little bird, she is mine to enjoy. But first, let us agree to dispense with story time."

"My lord, you don't understand! I'm not Ca—"

It was then he committed an even more unthinkable act than holding her in his large, warm lap, as scandalous as it was. In the semidarkness of a luxurious coach as it dashed madly through a snowy night, MacLean yanked her closer until her breasts were pressed firmly to his chest. Then, his smile gleaming in the semidarkness, he bent his head and kissed her.

# Chapter 4

*"Whilst ye may not be as strong as a braw hulk of a man, ye're infinitely smarter. And smart will get ye further than ye might think."*

OLD WOMAN NORA TO HER THREE WEE
GRANDDAUGHTERS ON A COLD WINTER'S NIGHT

The kiss seemed to last forever, absorbing and enveloping her. The complete, utter devouring was nothing like the idealized, gentle kisses of her imagination. And nothing had prepared Triona for her body's willful reaction to the warmth of MacLean's seeking hands and mouth, for the way her heart pounded and her body softened as if welcoming him, soaking in the heated warmth of him, the heady scent of his cologne, the wild and almost out-of-control way his hands molded her against him, making her breasts tingle and her legs tense with the desire to move closer.

It wasn't until MacLean's hot tongue brushed over her bottom lip that she was shocked into reacting.

Suddenly freed from the fog that had held her in place, she pressed her hands against MacLean's chest for all she was worth. He reluctantly lifted his head and released her.

Triona scrambled off his lap to the seat opposite, gritting her teeth at the pain in her knee. Her body quivered with anger and something else, something so potent that she dared not attempt to define it.

"You are no gentleman!" she said, her voice trembling furiously.

He chuckled, the sound low and husky in the dark. "I never said I was, and you would be wrong to think I wish to be one."

She clenched her hands into fists. "I am done with this! There has been a horrible mistake."

"If there has, it would be your planning to trick a MacLean into marriage."

She swallowed a flash of temper. The man thought she was Caitlyn, and her sister's brash words and actions were reprehensible.

"My lord, allow me to introduce myself once and for all. I am Caitlyn Hurst's sister, Triona Hurst."

His deep laugh was not pleasant. "Yes, the convenient mystery twin. Really, is that the best story you can come up with?"

"It's the truth. I realize Caitlyn's behavior has been terrible. I, too, was shocked when I discovered her plan to trick you into—"

He laughed, the sound rolling over her like a dash of cold water. "Come, Miss Hurst, we both know there is no 'sister Triona.'"

"It's the truth," she replied in a waspish tone,

clenching her hands. "If you'd light a blasted lamp, you'd see for yourself!"

Still chuckling, he settled into the corner of the rumbling coach. "There's no need for such games, my dear. I am master of this trick now." He yawned. "Because of your silly plan, I had but an hour of sleep last night and was up with the sun. You may entertain me with your faradiddles when I awake."

Triona ground her teeth. The wretch was going to *sleep*? "Look, MacLean, I refuse to just sit here while you—"

"You don't have a choice," he replied, an edge of impatience to his voice.

"I'm *not* going to accept this simply because you—"

"*Enough.*"

His dangerously low, flat voice doused her irritation with cold reason. She was alone in a dark coach with a man she knew very little about, and what she *did* know wasn't promising. Her grandmother's tales about the MacLeans' storm-inducing temper and Aunt Lavinia's warning about the man's pride told her challenging him directly would be a poor decision.

To some extent, she was defenseless—though a woman of intelligence could always find some sort of weapon. She flexed her foot, thinking that her pointed boot could be used to good effect. It wasn't much, but it replenished her sense of calm.

If she wished to escape this little adventure unscathed, she must use her wits. She'd have to make her move when the carriage was still and there might be other people nearby—decent people, she hoped, who would help a woman in distress. "My lord, I suggest we find the nearest inn and repair there to discuss this unfortunate happening."

"There is no inn on this stretch of road, but I plan to stop within the hour. Meanwhile, I've ridden all day and I'm tired, so I am going to sleep." His voice deepened as he added, "Unless, of course, you are offering to entertain me with more than senseless babble?"

"Entertain? How could I—" Realization dawned, along with a flood of heated embarrassment. "I'd rather eat mud!"

He chuckled, the sound as rich as it was unexpected. "Then hush and let me sleep." He shifted deeper into the corner, though his long legs still filled more than his fair half of the space. "Sleep, Caitlyn or Caitriona or whatever you call yourself. Sleep or be silent."

Fuming, Triona hoped the lout would be in a more accommodating mood once he'd slept. She tugged the blankets around her from neck to toe and settled into her own corner.

As soon as they reached some place with a lantern, MacLean would realize his error and send her home. Meanwhile, all she could do was rest. The mad race to reach London, then the disappointment of failing to find Caitlyn twice over, had exhausted her. Her body ached from the roughness of the ride, too.

She turned toward the plush squabs, slipped her hands beneath her cheek, and willed herself to relax.

Yet she found herself listening to the deep breathing of her captor and wondering dismally where Caitlyn might be. Had her sister changed her mind at the eleventh hour? Or had something befallen her?

Worried for both Caitlyn and herself, Triona shifted, exhausted yet unable to rest. Her knee ached, her body still thrummed from MacLean's kiss, and her lips felt swollen and tender. She lifted a hand to her mouth, shivering at the way it tingled.

No one had ever dared kiss her before. Father's stern presence had protected her from many things, she realized, and in a way, it was rather sad. She was twenty-three years of age and had never been stirred by passion.

Triona frowned, realizing she was sorry for her lack of experience; a moral woman should be scandalized. She couldn't dredge up a bit of outrage, though.

The kiss had been . . . interesting. MacLean had been thorough and expert, a trait even an inexperienced kisser could recognize, and she thought she might enjoy kissing under different circumstances. She might enjoy it a lot, in fact. After all, what harm could come from a simple kiss?

She yawned. The rocking coach and the deep, soft cushions cradled her as they raced through the night, MacLean's deep breathing soothing her. Soon, sleep claimed her and hugged her into blissful nothingness.

*  *  *

Triona awoke, slowly becoming aware of the rocking of the coach, the creak of the straps overhead, and the incredible warmth engulfing her. She stirred, rubbing her fingers against the rough pillow beneath her cheek. She frowned at the roughness; then her fingers grazed something hard. She opened her eyes to find herself in a carriage, enveloped in dim light from a dim lantern, and blinked at the object at her fingertips.

It was a button. A mother-of-pearl button.

*On a pillow?*

Bemused, her gaze traveled from the button upward, to another button, to a wide collar and a snowy white cravat, and farther—past a firm chin covered with black stubble, over a sensual mouth, to a pair of amused green eyes. *MacLean!*

Triona gasped and bolted upright, leaving the warmth of the arm that had been tucked about her.

Hugh, who'd been enjoying the many expressions that had flickered over her face, chuckled. "Easy, sweet. You'll hit your head on the ceiling."

His mussed companion hugged herself, her gaze sparkling with anger. With a sniff, she moved to the farthest corner of the coach. "What were you doing on *my* seat?"

He shrugged, enjoying her discomfort. "You began to fall over. I merely gave you something to fall against."

Her brows lowered, her eyes flashing her irritation. Hugh was very glad he'd lit the lamp, though he'd kept it very low so as not to awaken his captive. In the faint, shadowed light, it was a testament to the strength of her expressions that he was able to read them at all.

It was odd, but in the few times he had met Caitlyn Hurst, he'd missed several important things about her—mainly because he'd made a point of not paying her the slightest heed. He hadn't spoken to her, looked directly at her, or even acknowledged her presence. He knew it had piqued her, and he'd enjoyed that immensely. Now he realized what he'd missed by his endeavors.

For one thing, he'd mistakenly thought her a slender, rather pixieish creature, but her face was softer, more curved than his memory had led him to believe, which made him wonder even more about what was under her cloak.

He'd remembered her voice as being higher-pitched, too. He'd certainly never realized that the troublesome chit possessed a voice that dripped over his senses like warm honey.

He also hadn't been aware of the thrum of physical attraction she exuded that made him . . . restless, eager to engage her in some way. Having seen his older brother's reaction to her seductive powers, he should have expected it. Perhaps he'd been immune before because he hadn't been in such close proximity. It was purely an imp of devilment that had made him slip onto her seat and pull her head to his shoulder, and her reaction hadn't disappointed him.

It was his *own* reaction that had astonished him. Having drawn her close, he'd been hard pressed not to touch her in other ways, and only the fact she'd been fast asleep had saved them both. Not that he really needed to worry. Her behavior had been wanton from the beginning, and she'd never squander her attention on a younger son. She'd be as anxious to end this farce as he was, probably more so.

A surprising twist of regret surged through him at the thought.

By Zeus, he needed to tread carefully. This woman was as false as her smiles. He'd suffered the hidden barbs of a woman's wiles before, and he'd not suffer them again.

She'd even attempted to convince him she was an innocent, with her refusal to respond to his kiss. She'd done very well at playing the shocked virgin, he thought grudgingly. Fortunately, he knew just who and what she was, and innocence had nothing to do with it.

Her gaze suddenly focused on the lamp and she turned toward him, looking eager. "Now you can see my face!"

He raised his brows. Was she looking for compliments? "So?"

She said impatiently, "Now you can see I'm not Caitlyn!"

His gaze raked over her honey-gold hair, mussed into curls about a distinctively heart-shaped face. "Still playing me for a fool, Hurst?"

She fisted her hands. "Blast it! You, my lord, have made a mistake."

"Not as much of one as you." The coach slowed and he turned to lift the corner of the curtain. As he did so, she gasped.

He glanced back at her and found her gaze locked on his hair. She stammered, "Y-y-you're not Alexander MacLean! You're his brother, Hugh!"

She'd seen the streak of white hair that brushed back from one brow, a relic of a dark time that he never dwelled on. "Stop playing the fool; it doesn't become you. You knew damned well who I am."

*"Oh!"* She fisted her hands and pressed them to her eyes for a moment before she dropped them back to her lap. "You are going to drive me mad! You don't believe a word I say and—"

Her lips thinned, her gaze narrowed, and he could almost see the thoughts flickering through her mind. *By Zeus, I've never seen such an expressive face before.*

Her lips relaxed, and then a faint smile curved them as her gaze traced the white hair at his temple.

"There is nothing humorous in this situation."

She lifted her brows, a genuine twinkle in her fine eyes. "Ah, but there is. I thought you were someone else while you now think I'm someone else—" She chuckled, the sound rich as cream. "The situation may be untenable, but the irony is delicious."

*But not as delicious as you.* He scowled, startled at his own thoughts.

"Stop this nonsense," he said impatiently. "I refuse to—" The coach slowed, then turned a corner. "Ah, the inn. It's about time."

Her eyes, large and dark in the dim light, sparkled with amusement. "Once we're in the stronger light, you'll see your error." A chuckle broke free, and she regarded him with such lively humor that Hugh was tempted to grin back.

Almost.

Finally he understood why Alexander had pursued her, even though he knew the dangers. There was something incredibly taking about the curve of her cheek, the way her thick lashes shadowed her large eyes, and the fascinating display of emotions across her expressive face.

It was a damned shame she was layered in two cloaks, for he couldn't see her figure. He knew what to expect, yet she seemed more rounded now, and oddly . . . taller, perhaps?

A chill rippled through Hugh.

Good God, had he seen what he wanted to see? What he'd expected to see? Surely he hadn't been so—

The coach rocked to a halt, but Hugh was only distantly aware of the cry of his coachman, the sound of another carriage drawing up beside his.

Then the door flew open and Hugh turned, only to meet a fist as it plowed into his chin.

The blow did little more than stun him for a second. He rubbed his chin and glared at his attacker, a smallish older man wearing a fashionable multicaped coat. "Lord Galloway," he said curtly.

"You cur!" Galloway's face was a mask of fury.

Hugh's companion lurched into the man's arms. "Uncle Bedford!" she cried. "I am so *glad* to see you!"

"There, there, my dear," Lord Galloway said, fixing a very stern gaze on Hugh. "This ordeal is over, Caitriona."

*Caitriona—not Caitlyn.* Hugh's heart thudded sickly as he closed his eyes and faced the truth. God help him—he had the wrong woman.

# Chapter 5

❦

*"Every once't in a while comes a moment that hits ye so hard it instantly changes yer direction. When one o' these come, ye can duck all ye wish, but it'll hit ye just the same. And usually right betwixt yer eyes."*

OLD WOMAN NORA TO HER THREE WEE
GRANDDAUGHTERS ON A COLD WINTER'S NIGHT

Over Triona's head, Lord Galloway's gaze suddenly widened. "Good God! You . . . you're not Lord MacLean! You're his brother, Lord Hugh!"

Hugh rubbed his chin. "So I've been told."

Galloway glowered. "Whoever you are, how *dare* you abduct my niece!"

"I did nothing of the sort! She was in my carriage of her own free will. God knows I didn't put her there myself."

"I know you didn't," Galloway said in a testy voice. "She caught up with you when you stopped to change the horses. In a vain attempt to rescue her sister, she slipped into your carriage, hoping to convince Caitlyn to give up her folly. Of course, Caitlyn wasn't there, but poor Triona had no way of knowing that." Galloway's mouth tightened. "You know what happened after that."

Hugh's chest ached as if someone were sitting upon it. He did know; she'd told him the truth and he'd dismissed her. Worse, he'd treated her as if she were a common woman of the street. *God, what a wretched, horrid mess.*

Lord Galloway seemed to follow Hugh's line of thought. "Triona's nurse returned to London post haste to tell us how the carriage drove off with my niece caught inside. Fortunately for Triona, I knew of a shorter route and was able to intercept you."

Fortunate for Triona, perhaps, but not for Hugh. There was nothing fortunate about this happenstance, not one bloody thing.

The door to Galloway's carriage flew open and two women climbed out. The first was short, round, and dressed in twelve shades of lavender, and he instantly recognized Lady Galloway. A second woman followed, heavily cloaked, her movements lithe and graceful.

The wind fluttered the hood of her cloak so that the bright light from the inn revealed her fully—a delicate heart-shaped face of breathtaking beauty framed in bright gold curls. *Caitlyn Hurst.*

Hugh turned his gaze back to the woman he'd captured. While her face was the exact shape as her sister's, her cheeks were fuller, her hair a honey blond and not gold, her thickly fringed eyes as large but lighter.

Lord Galloway slipped his free hand into his pocket

and withdrew it. "Triona, we found your spectacles." He glared at Hugh. "It's a wonder they weren't trampled."

Triona took a neatly folded pair of wire-rimmed spectacles from her uncle, snapped them open, and slipped them on. Through the frames, her hazel eyes regarded him condemningly. The prim spectacles sat in striking contrast to the sensuality of her rich coloring and silken hair.

Memory of the kiss flooded back, of her shock, uncertainty, and then resistance. The kiss of an innocent. *Bloody hell, what have I done?*

The older man's arm visibly tightened around his niece. "This is untenable. I'll have you know that Triona's father is a vicar!"

Despite the weight growing in his chest, Hugh gave a bark of sardonic laughter. "Of course. I suppose I should be glad she's not a nun, too."

Galloway's face turned deeper red. "This is not a time for levity."

"No," Hugh agreed heavily. "It's not. I just don't understand how—" He broke off, catching sight of the interested gazes of several footmen. Jaw taut, he said, "We should have this conversation somewhere more private."

Lord Galloway's gaze followed Hugh's. "I'll bespeak a parlor." He turned to give some orders to a footman, who took Triona's arm and escorted her away. She resisted, looking ready to speak, but before she could say a word she was swarmed by her aunt, sister, and another woman who'd just climbed from the coach. Hook-nosed and dragonlike, she glared angrily at Hugh.

So that was the nurse. It was a relief when the lot of them disappeared into the inn, Galloway herding them like a protective sheepdog.

*Bloody hell, how did I make such an error? And yet she looked so much like Caitlyn Hurst, especially when I saw her peering out the coach window.*

Hugh paused at the door to take one last, deep breath of the cold night air, trying to calm the sickening pound of his heart. His intentions had been so good, his purpose so clear—how could things have gone so wrong? Perhaps that had been his sin . . . the pride of certainty. And now he faced the bitter consequences.

"Och, m'lord!" Ferguson hurried up. "Should we stable the horses?"

"No, just walk them. I won't be long." Hugh's chest felt as if an iron band were slowly tightening about it.

"Aye, m'lord." Ferguson glanced about the busy innyard before leaning in to say, "If ye'd like, I can have the coach ready to move on a second's notice. We could be gone afore they even know it."

That was tempting. Hugh reluctantly shook his head. "Ferguson," he said in a heavy voice, "it appears the wrong lass ended up in our carriage."

Ferguson's mouth opened, then closed, then opened again, but no sound came out.

"That's pretty much what I have to say, too." Hugh rubbed his neck.

"But—I dinna understand, m'lord!"

"Apparently Miss Caitlyn Hurst has a twin sister."

"And that's who—" At Hugh's curt nod, Ferguson's eyes widened. He clapped a hand to his cheek, his mouth ajar. "*No!*"

"Oh, yes. And it's a damned shame for all of us."

Hugh glanced toward the front window. Wide and deep, it was now aglow with lamplight, shadowy figures crossing this way and that. Inside that room, a drama awaited. And if there was one thing Hugh MacLean disliked, it was drama. Worse, this particular scenario came complete with outraged guardians, a damsel in perceived distress, and promised histrionics of the caliber usually reserved for Drury Lane.

From inside the inn, Lady Galloway shrilly demanded something—probably Hugh's head on a platter.

He sighed. "There's nothing to be done but face it. Keep the horses ready, Ferguson. Once this meeting is over, I wish to return to London as fast as possible."

"Aye, m'lord." Ferguson eyed the window with a dark glance. "Are ye sure ye dinna wish to have someone with ye, m'lord? There's five o' them and only one o' ye."

"I can handle them. It's their morals that may overwhelm me." Hugh straightened his shoulders, and entered the inn.

A bowing and scraping innkeeper with a round figure and thinning brown hair rushed forward to take his coat and hat, handing them to a serving boy who reverently took them to the kitchen to warm them before the fire.

"This way, m'lord!" the innkeeper said in what he probably thought was a grand manner. "Yer friends are in the front parlor. I've laid them a nice fire and it'll soon be cozy and warm."

"Thank you." Hugh paused by the door. "You don't happen to have anything to drink, do you?"

"I brought the ladies some sherry, as requested, and the gent asked fer a pint of me best ale. Would you like some as well, m'lord?"

"I was hoping for something stronger."

The portly man's eyes twinkled and he looked over his shoulder before leaning forward to say in a loud whisper, "I might have a little something in me cellars that the tariff men don't know nuffin' about."

"What's that?"

"Port. The best ye've ever had!"

"Bring a bottle." Hugh paused. "No, bring two. One for here and one for the road. I fear I shall need them both."

The landlord beamed. "Aye, m'lord."

There was no more loitering; Hugh walked into the parlor.

As he'd expected, Lady Galloway, Caitlyn, and the forbidding old nurse were gathered around Triona, who sat upon the settee. Lady Galloway was beside her, patting her hand and saying in an angry tone, "—what a *horrid* thing to have happened! I vow, when

Caitlyn walked into the room, I could *not* believe my eyes! And then Nurse came in, positively *squalling* that you'd been abducted! Fortunately, your uncle arrived home from White's at just that precise moment. I was never so glad to see him in my life! He *immediately* knew what to do and decided that we would all set out after you and—"

"I wasna squallin'," the nurse said indignantly. She caught sight of Hugh and moved protectively to block Triona from his sight. "Och, dinna even *look* at her, ye rogue!"

"Your charge is safe from me." Hugh removed his gloves and went to stand at the far side of the fireplace, which was putting out nice heat. Observing Caitlyn and Triona so close together, he saw that Caitlyn was by far the more beautiful; her features were perfection, her eyes a deep brown, her hair golden, her movements graceful.

But it was Triona who held his gaze. Her face was fuller and more mature. Her eyes, a light hazel fringed with ridiculously long lashes and framed by those damned impudent spectacles, held intelligence and wit; her mouth was a plump plum that begged to be tasted. Whereas Caitlyn was pure beauty, Triona had an earthy sensuality that belied the prim way she sat and the stern line of the wire-framed spectacles.

She quirked a brow, as if asking why he was staring. She deserved a good stare, though he doubted she knew it.

He sent her a mocking bow, which made her color

and look away. Now that she was finally out of that damned cloak, he was oddly pleased to see that he'd been right; she had a lushly curved figure. Just looking at her full, rounded breasts pressed against her prim gown made his mouth water appreciatively. He'd always liked women who were shaped like women, not broomsticks, and Triona Hurst had more than her share of curves. In fact, she—

Lord Galloway walked forward to stand between Hugh and Triona. "My lord," the older man snapped, his color even higher than before, "we must speak about this unfortunate incident and what must be done to correct it." He glanced back at the women. "We cannot speak here. Join me by the window." Without looking to see if Hugh followed, Galloway marched to the far side of the room.

Hugh's jaw clenched. He wasn't used to people speaking to him as if he were an eight-year-old caught stealing pies from the kitchen.

"MacLean?" Galloway's voice rose imperiously.

Hugh clenched his hands, his anger rising. Outside the snug inn, a sudden wind rattled the doors and shutters. The horses in the innyard began to prance and whinny.

"Lawks!" Nurse screeched, looking up as blown snow struck the windows and the pine roof shingles clattered overhead.

"Good heavens! What's happening?" Lady Galloway's frightened voice warbled.

Caitlyn hugged her aunt, her eyes wide with fear.

Only Triona remained calm, looking at him with an accusing stare that made his thoughts stutter.

*Calm yourself, MacLean! This will only make matters worse.* Left unabated, his temper would feed the winds and they would grow. They would shudder the house and rip trees from their roots. They would make the rivers and streams flood roads and fields and villages. They would lift barns and houses from their stone foundations and toss them like toys.

Once the winds reached a certain level they became a force of their own, powerful enough to kill. That was why every MacLean struggled to maintain his temper. Legend said that if every member of a generation performed a deed of great good, the curse would end. So far, no generation had managed to perform deeds significant enough. Hugh wondered if there really was a way to end it. That was the problem with attempting to understand an ancient curse supposedly set upon the family by a mysterious white witch; after a few centuries there was no way to separate truth from myth.

The wind pounded against the windows. Lord Galloway sent a startled glance at Hugh, who clenched his jaw tighter. In all his life, only once had he allowed his temper to unleash completely—when his brother Callum had died. Seeing the devastation afterward, he'd vowed never to let it loose again, especially once he'd realized that his use of the curse was different from his brothers'—a secret known to only one other person.

Hugh closed his eyes and took deep breaths, letting them hiss through his teeth as he exhaled. In his mind, he imagined a small whirl of wind. He opened his hand and closed it tightly about the swirl and squeezed with all of his might, all of his concentration.

His heartbeat slowed, a dull pressure mounting behind his eyes. He squeezed tighter. Then tighter still.

His head pounded fiercely yet he continued past the pain.

His muscles ached with tension, sweat beading on his brow.

Slowly, the winds outside abated. When he could no longer hear more than a faint breeze, Hugh uncoiled his fist and allowed his muscles to relax. His head pounded sickly, a wave of nausea replacing the fierce power that left him as limp as a rag.

"It's going away, praise be!" Lady Galloway breathed.

"Of course it is," Lord Galloway stated. "It's a typical storm burst, nothing more." He glared at Hugh. "Come, MacLean! We have things to discuss."

Hugh swallowed a hot retort. He couldn't allow his temper to slip again; he didn't have the strength to control the winds a second time. He sent Triona a quick glance, but her gaze was fixed out the window. A faint breeze swirled about the carriages, stirring the snow with a weak finger. Triona's hazel gaze turned to Hugh, sure knowledge in her expression.

*She believes in the curse.* The knowledge surprised

him and, for a moment, calmed him. *She believes and yet she isn't afraid.*

If he hadn't felt as weak and ill as a kitten, he might even have smiled. But his knees were shaking and he had to sit down soon or make a fool of himself. He turned on his heel and joined Galloway by the window, then dropped gratefully into a seat, his knees buckling and tossing him against the cushions.

Lord Galloway scowled, no doubt thinking it would have been polite of Hugh to offer a seat to the older man first.

Hugh gestured to the chair opposite. "My lord?" He rubbed his temples, where a low, thundering roar seemed to have lodged.

Lord Galloway sat and turned a stern glare on Hugh. "You have much to answer for. Thanks to you, my niece has been compromised."

"I thought she was her sister or I would have returned her." Hugh wished the arse would speak more quietly.

"As you can see, she is not. Triona is an innocent. Though her actions may have been impetuous, they were completely innocuous." Galloway seemed to think Hugh would argue, for he waited, his mouth pressed in a challenging line.

Hugh managed a shrug. "As you say."

The older man's gaze narrowed. "You were alone with my niece in your coach for quite some time. I must ask"—Galloway leaned closer, his voice mercifully lowered—"*did you touch her?*"

He had, though not to the extent Galloway feared. Still, if Hugh looked at what had happened in the coach—pulling Caitriona into his lap, holding her there, kissing her passionately—the answer would have to be a resounding "Hell, yes."

And he had no remorse. It was a damned shame he hadn't touched her more, especially if this escapade turned out to be as expensive an error as it seemed it would.

Galloway frowned. "Your silence speaks for itself."

Hugh merely stared back, his chin lifted, his eyes half-closed against the pain shooting through his temples.

Galloway's mouth thinned. "Fine, then. I shall assume the worst. Though she's twenty-three years of age, I am still responsible for my niece's safety. She is still a maid, and you abducted an innocent woman!"

"That was not my intention."

"No, your intention was to abduct her sister, which is *just* as nefarious."

"I had hoped to frighten Caitlyn Hurst into leaving my brother alone. She was blatant in her attempt to trap him into marriage." Hugh met Galloway's gaze directly. "She announced on more than one occasion, before witnesses, that she would stop at nothing to do so. Furthermore, she intended to be in that coach, for I discovered her cloak and a bandbox hidden beneath a seat. So when I saw a blond woman in my brother's coach, I assumed Triona to be Caitlyn. Anyone would have done the same."

Lord Galloway nearly turned purple. "Caitlyn may have shown a want of decorum, but her sister should not be made to pay for that. Triona has been gently raised. I daresay she's never been more than twenty miles from the vicarage in her life."

Hugh found himself looking at her once more. Her face was turned away as her sister spoke to her, an earnest expression on both their faces. "They look remarkably alike."

Galloway's gaze followed Hugh's and the older man's face softened. "They *are* twins, though it is easy enough to tell them apart, especially when they are in the same room."

"Which they weren't."

"It doesn't matter. You had no business attempting to frighten a mere girl for nothing more than a few brash words."

"Caitlyn Hurst has been running wild since she arrived in London. *Someone* had to take her in hand."

Galloway's mouth turned white. "Her aunt and I were working to do just that, as was Triona. She had come to London to convince her sister to behave with more decorum."

Wonderful. The girl was sheltered, innocent, and a do-gooder. Word by word, he was being pushed toward the very edge of the cliff.

Hugh rubbed his neck, his eyes hot and aching. He wished for nothing more than the promised bottle of port and the peace and quiet of Alexander's coach, without a damned seductive innocent to tempt him.

"Well, MacLean?" Galloway said loudly, which caused the conversation on the other side of the room to come to a halt. "What do you have to say for your treatment of my niece?"

Damn it all, Lord Galloway would settle for only one answer—marriage. Hugh had no desire to be married. He'd almost made that mistake once before, and would happily swallow a hundred nails to avoid it again. "I will apologize to your niece for upsetting her, but I should point out that no one saw her enter my carriage, other than her nurse. If you and Lady Galloway will escort her back to London, no one will be the wiser."

Galloway suddenly looked uncomfortable. "I wish that were true."

Hugh's heart sank like a boulder dropped into an icy pond.

"Once Nurse realized that Triona had been taken in your coach, she raced back to London to inform us, and Lord and Lady Colchester and their daughter, Cassandra, were with us in the sitting room. They'd escorted Caitlyn from Bond Street."

"Bloody hell! Lady Colchester is a vicious gossip."

"Yes. By the time we return to London, everyone will know what has happened."

That was it, then. As much as he wished it otherwise, Hugh couldn't ignore the cold, hard fact that his arrogant action had led to Triona Hurst's ruin. He was doomed. Through gritted teeth, Hugh said, "I will come to your house tomorrow morning to make the arrangements."

"Do not look so angry, my lord. This is a mess of your own making."

"I did nothing but attempt to protect my brother. I will not apologize for that."

Lord Galloway's brows lowered. "I've met your brother on many occasions, my lord, and I can't imagine he either needed or wished for your protection." When Hugh opened his mouth to answer hotly, Galloway held up a hand. "Right now, I don't care a feather for Laird MacLean's opinion." He glanced toward the silent group of women, then turned his face away from them and added in an urgent undertone, "Miss Hurst has a younger sister and several younger brothers, not to mention that it is quite possible her father might lose his position when this scandal breaks. They will *all* suffer if her reputation is not quickly restored."

So he was now responsible for the future happiness of the entire family, was he? He longed to shove his fist down Galloway's throat.

Galloway straightened. "You will apply for a special license as soon as possible, and the marriage will take place three days from tomorrow. Do you understand?"

Hugh crossed his arms, refusing to answer.

The older man's lips thinned and he said crisply, "Good, then I shall expect you tomorrow at nine." He rose from his chair, and Hugh forced himself to rise as well.

*Damn the man!* Hugh longed to argue, to rail, to refuse to comply. Yet across the room Triona sat, her somber eyes locked on him, an ineffable air of sadness about her.

"We are settled, then. I bid you good night." With a stiff bow, Galloway turned on his heel and began to encourage the women to don their cloaks.

To Hugh's relief, the innkeeper appeared with the longed-for port. Hugh refused to look Triona's way again as the innkeeper poured a generous amount into a glass and held it out to Hugh.

Just as Hugh reached for it, the innkeeper noticed that his other guests were bundling back into their cloaks. He turned, the precious port still in his hand. "Leavin' so soon? I was bringin' in a side o' beef and some meat pasties fer the ladies—"

"Pack the pasties in a basket," Galloway said briskly. "We will eat on the way home."

Hugh captured the port from the innkeeper and drank it quickly, hoping the warmth might ease the tight band around his chest.

Lady Galloway, her gaze frosty as she watched Hugh, made an outraged noise as her husband herded her and the others toward the door.

Just as Triona reached the doorway, she paused. "Lord Hugh, I wo—"

"*Triona!*" Lady Galloway snapped. "I forbid you to speak to that man!"

"So do I," Caitlyn agreed, looking disdainfully at Hugh.

Triona's eyes flashed, but she said quietly, "I will speak to him if I wish to."

"Och, he's a devil, he is," Nurse warned.

"Triona," her uncle said firmly, "we are leaving *now*." He attempted to lead her from the room but she pulled free, her face a frozen mask of indignation.

Hugh recognized the flash of rebellion, because he felt the exact same way—frustration at the rules and requirements of society, mixed with a desperate desire for freedom. The pity of it was that Triona Hurst was as much caught by this little trap as he was. Fight though she would, there was no way out; her family would make sure of that.

Triona suddenly turned her fine eyes his way. "MacLean, my uncle is not responsible for my actions; I am."

Lord Galloway's mouth was pressed into a displeased line. "Triona, MacLean and I will deal with things. You need not worry your head over matters from this point on."

Hugh could see the irritation plain on her face, and something else. Was it . . . fear?

Hope flickered in his chest. She feared a union as much as he. If she cried off—

But no. Though he'd be free, she would still be ruined, and her entire family would be affected by it. Hugh wasn't capable of walking away from his responsibilities. He was many things, but a coward was not among them.

Triona now stood before him, her spectacled eyes dark with a myriad of emotions. She said in a low voice, "MacLean, don't let my uncle talk you into doing anything foolish."

A quiver of ironic humor tickled his lips. "Apparently I need no encouragement to do something foolish. I managed to do it quite well on my own."

"Triona!" her uncle called.

She grimaced but didn't look away. "We both erred. You were as concerned about your brother as I was about my sister. Neither of us should pay for what was obviously a simple misunderstanding. We can find some other way out of this that won't cost our freedom if we just—"

"No." Hugh was both touched and irritated, but it was time to speak plainly. "I thank you for your generosity, but as much as I wish to accept it, your uncle is correct about the cost of our comedy of errors. You would be ruined, and your family would pay the price as well. That is not acceptable."

Her brows knit. "Surely we can—"

"We can do nothing that society would accept, other than marry." He realized that his hand, clasped about the glass of port, was shaking faintly from fatigue. If he didn't get to his coach soon, someone would have to carry him.

Her lips pressed together. "I don't *wish* to marry!"

"We have that in common, at least." He forced his

weary legs to move and crossed to a chair by the fire. Though it was insufferably rude to sit when women were standing, he dropped into the soft cushions with relief. "Trust me, Miss Hurst, if I could think of another way out of this, I would do it. But I cannot, and therefore we are stuck."

"Triona, you have your answer," her uncle said coldly. "Now come."

She stiffened.

Though Hugh appreciated her spirit, he nodded. "Leave the details to your uncle and me."

"But I—"

"Good night, Miss Hurst," he said firmly. He turned away and refilled his glass, even that simple movement costing him dearly. He could feel Triona's presence there, but he didn't turn to see her expression. There was no need; he could feel the fury emanating from her as surely as heat seeped from the fire.

Footsteps crossed the floor. "Come, Triona. Leave the beast alone!" Caitlyn urged.

Naturally, Nurse had to add her two pennies. "Och, 'tis a sad day when an innocent bairn canna even enter a carriage without a rogue takin' advantage o' her!"

Hugh swallowed a mouthful of port, his gaze locked on a knot in the wood paneling. Outside the wind began to stir, but fortunately Hugh was too exhausted to grow truly angry, and it quickly died down.

"Triona, it is late and we must go," Lord Galloway said, sounding as tired as Hugh felt. "It's rude to keep your poor aunt out on such a cold night."

There was a moment of silence during which Hugh could almost hear Triona's voice demanding that he join her in protesting their fate. But though she might be ignorant of the ways of the world, he was not. Grimly, he kept his face averted and silently willed her away. Suddenly, with a whirl of her cloak, Triona marched from the room, the others following.

# Chapter 6

*"Listen closely, me lassies. The MacLean men can be trusted with yer funds, yer family, and yer future, but beware givin' one o' them yer heart."*

OLD WOMAN NORA TO HER THREE WEE
GRANDDAUGHTERS ON A COLD WINTER'S NIGHT

*I* would rather eat a raw toad!"

Aunt Lavinia blinked. "Triona, you have no choice. You're ruined."

"I don't care!" Triona whirled, pacing back and forth before the sitting-room fireplace. "I won't get married under these circumstances."

"But you must! And since you must, we should at least decide on the sort of flowers and laces and—"

"Aunt Lavinia, *please*," Caitlyn said from a chair by the front window. This was the first time she'd spoken all morning. "Triona has plenty to worry about without you pressing her whether to have lilies or roses for a bouquet!"

Aunt Lavinia looked crestfallen. "I just thought it might help her see the positive side of things."

Triona paused in her pacing. "Aunt Lavinia, this

wedding is not going to occur. Neither Hugh MacLean nor I should be forced into this situation."

"My dear, society is very clear in these instances and—"

"I don't give a damn what society says!"

"*Triona!* Proper ladies do not say such things!"

"Perhaps they should! Then more people might listen, and this must-marry silliness would be a thing of history."

"Lud!" Aunt Lavinia pressed a beringed hand to her bosom. "I'm having heart palpitations! Someone call Dr. Francis!"

Caitlyn turned to Aunt Lavinia, her eyes red-rimmed. "*Please* stop saying you're having heart palpitations. One day you will have them for real, and no one will believe you."

Aunt Lavinia's lip quivered, and her watery blue eyes traveled from Caitlyn to Triona.

Seeing the tears coming, Triona hurried to say, "Aunt Lavinia, I'm sorry I'm in such an ill temper this morning. It's just that when I awoke, it all piled in on me." She managed a wan smile. "I was so tired last night that I couldn't take everything in and I suppose, in some way, I thought it would all be back to right when I awoke."

Instead, she'd awoken with a distinct sense of dread, coming downstairs to an unusually early breakfast and finding Uncle Bedford already in his study waiting for MacLean. Meanwhile, Aunt Lavinia was in a flutter over "the coming nuptials" and talking gowns and flowers and so much nonsense that Triona had finally snapped.

Caitlyn had been oddly quiet this morning, her shoulders slumped, her face a mixture of regret and stubbornness. Triona knew that look well; Caitlyn always wore it when she was repenting one of her wild starts. "Cait, don't look so glum. It's not the end of the world."

Caitlyn gave a faintly hysterical laugh. "Triona, please do not be nice to me right now! I have made such a mull of things. If I could take it back—" A sob choked the rest of the sentence, and she covered her face with her hands.

"Caitlyn, don't!" Triona crossed the room to kneel beside her sister, pulling out her handkerchief. "Stop worrying, you goose. When MacLean comes this morning, I shall tell him I won't have him. No one can make me marry if I don't wish it."

Caitlyn dabbed at her eyes with the handkerchief. "Yes, you must!"

"Nonsense. I don't care if I'm ruined. I have no wish for a London season, anyway."

"It's not that simple, Triona. Word would spread, and it would get back to Wythburn. People will turn from you and talk behind your back. You have no idea how mortifying that would be! People will be so cruel to you and say such horrid things and— Oh, Triona, you mustn't let that happen!"

Aunt Lavinia cleared her throat. "You know, my dear, perhaps if you knew a bit more about your prospective husband, it might make things easier for you to accept. Caitlyn, what do you know about Hugh MacLean from his brother?"

Caitlyn bit her lip. "Well . . . Hugh looks like his older brother, a bit broader in the shoulders, if not so tall. And he smiles far less often."

"He has a sense of humor," Triona said absently. "It's just very dry." The few times he'd smiled had sent an astonishingly warm thrill up her spine.

Caitlyn said, "Perhaps he's like Alexander, who doesn't smile in public often, but in private laughs frequently."

Aunt Lavinia frowned. "When did you meet him in private?"

Caitlyn colored. "Just once or twice." She looked at Triona. "There are alcoves in many ballrooms, hidden by draperies and potted plants. They allow one to rest away from the noise and heat and—"

"Caitlyn!" Aunt Lavinia choked out. "People use those for assignations, and you should not have been in one of them at all! Lud, you'll be the death of me. When your mother and father find out about all that's happened . . ." She reached for her smelling salts. "Here I thought you were properly chaperoned, and you were meeting *privately* with MacLean all along!"

"Not very often!" Caitlyn returned hotly.

Triona regarded her sister narrowly. "Why meet him at all?"

Caitlyn's expression grew guarded. "No particular reason." Her voice was just a touch too casual.

Aunt Lavinia waved the smelling salts under her nose. "I am just glad you gave up your wild plan to stow away in that silly coach. You'd have been ruined, just like Triona!"

Caitlyn winced. "Had I known Triona would get involved, I never would have planned it. I didn't mean for anyone to get into trouble."

"Except yourself and Alexander MacLean," Triona pointed out. "Cait, you *do* know that if you had managed to win that proposal from MacLean, you could easily have ended up in the same situation I'm in right now."

"No, no! I was very careful about things, which is why I decided to abandon my plan to slip into his carriage."

"I wish you'd let Aunt Lavinia know that."

Caitlyn grimaced. "So do I. Triona, I vow to you that I was not going to risk my reputation. I was going to make *certain* no one knew about it but him."

Triona lifted her brows.

Caitlyn pressed her hands over her eyes. "Don't look at me like that!" She dropped her hands to her lap. "It was foolish of me to believe I could do such a thing without causing a scandal. I see that now. But at the time, I wasn't thinking clearly."

"If things hadn't gone as you'd planned and you'd ended up married to MacLean, he would have hated you for it and your marriage would have been a misery." Which was exactly what she was facing herself.

"I know," Caitlyn said quietly. "But when I came to London and met Alexander, I couldn't help myself.

Grandmama has been telling us about the MacLean curse all our lives, and I wanted to see it in action. Not a scary amount, just enough to know that it was true. Like last night—I could *feel* Hugh's anger." She shivered.

Triona remembered how the wind had made the building shudder, threatened the windows, and made the shutters bang furiously. *This is the man I'm supposed to marry?* She shivered, too.

Caitlyn's gaze locked on Triona. "Now you know why I have been teasing Alexander, although *he* thinks I'm merely flirting with him. I'd been trying for weeks to engage him in a wager he would lose, so that he'd be vexed enough to lose his temper. But he kept winning, which made him gloat horridly instead."

Triona frowned. "Caitlyn, when you were wagering Lord MacLean, what were the stakes? You have no funds."

She shrugged. "It was perfectly innocent."

"Thank goodness," Aunt Lavinia said.

"All we wagered were a few kisses."

"*Kisses!*" Aunt Lavinia shrieked.

"Well, there was a little more than kisses, but only once—" At Aunt Lavinia's moan, Caitlyn hurried to add, "After that, we went directly to the wager you know about: whether or not I could force him to propose." She scowled. "I had everything perfectly laid out, too. I was to hide in the seat box and then come out when he changed the horses at the first stage. He'd have to admit that I'd won the wager, then."

Aunt Lavinia blinked. "And . . . would you have married him?"

"As if I'd have a braggart like that for a husband!" Caitlyn scoffed.

"What if you were genuinely ruined?" Triona asked.

Caitlyn grew serious. "I didn't think that could happen until last night, when I saw Uncle Bedford with Hugh MacLean. I wish you hadn't come to London to save me."

"It's too late now." Aunt Lavinia fanned herself with her handkerchief. "Leave things to your uncle Bedford. Hugh MacLean should arrive—" She glanced at the clock and frowned. "He should have been here ten minutes ago. Your uncle will not be pleased he's late."

Triona came to her feet once more, resuming her pacing. "This is outrageous! I barely know the man!"

"Oh, child, I'm sure that once you and Lord Hugh marry, you'll find some commonalities and be quite satisfied. I barely knew your uncle Bedford before he proposed, and I have grown quite fond of him over the years." Aunt Lavinia smiled. "I couldn't have asked for a more gentle and kind husband. I was quite fortunate and you may be as well."

"What if we discover instead that we hate one another? That he hates the way I use my fork, or the fact that I'm a little grumpy in the mornings—"

"A little?" Caitlyn murmured, rolling her eyes.

Triona glared at her sister before turning back to Aunt Lavinia. "Worse, what if there is something seriously wrong with his character? Perhaps he's a-a thief!

Or kicks dogs, or hates living in the country? What if"—cold clutched at her heart—"what if he's in love with another woman?"

"He's not in love with anyone," Aunt Lavinia said with assurance. "If he were, I would know. Every time he and his brother so much as look at a woman, people talk. Hugh MacLean tends to avoid eligible females, and has made it plain he has no plans of ever marrying."

"Lovely. He's averse to marriage in general."

"As are you," Caitlyn pointed out fairly.

"I am not! I am in favor of marriage, just not this one and not under these circumstances!"

In the past, when she'd thought of marriage, it had been to wish for a relationship like her parents'. Mother and Father were supremely happy; it showed in the way they looked at each other, as well as the pride they took in sharing their lives with each other.

Aunt Lavinia said in a buoyant voice, "Yes, well, I'm sure Hugh MacLean will welcome marriage now."

"Oh, yes. Being forced to do something is such a pleasant way to change one's mind about it." Triona rubbed her forehead. "And what little I know of him—that he eschews eligible women and possesses a temper that could blow away an inn—indicates that he'd be a horrid husband."

Caitlyn frowned. "I've never heard anyone speak ill of him."

"Nor I," Aunt Lavinia agreed. "Indeed, the only negative talk I've ever heard toward Hugh MacLean is about his illegitimate children. They say there are scores."

"Scores?" Triona asked weakly, sinking back onto the settee.

"*Not* scores." Caitlyn shot a dark look at her aunt.

Aunt Lavinia shrugged. "I'm sure people are merely exaggerating. There cannot be as many as people say, for the man can't be old enough to have more than five or six. Unless there were twins, or if he was seeing more than one woman at a time, which I suppose is possible."

She finally caught Triona's panicked gaze. "Oh my dear, look on the bright side!" Aunt Lavinia said in a cheery voice. "They say he quite lavishes his children with affection, and spends scads on their well-being."

"So?"

"*So,* he must have excellent funding! Your uncle will of course discover more, but it is a very good indication that you will not want for pin money, or have a cold house because there isn't enough coal."

"So all we know about Hugh MacLean is that his financial situation is unclear, he has an unknown number of illegitimate children, and the family curse is true. I've caught quite a prize!"

Aunt Lavinia wrinkled her nose. "Do not look at it that way. Surely—"

"Pardon me, my lady," intoned the butler. "Lord Hugh MacLean to see Miss Caitriona Hurst."

# Chapter 7

*"Och, me dearies! Most men are worth the trouble when all's said and done, fer we all need challenges to keep us sharp."*

OLD WOMAN NORA TO HER THREE WEE
GRANDDAUGHTERS ON A COLD WINTER'S NIGHT

Triona sprang to her feet, hands fisted at her sides, her face hot.

*He came to see me, not my uncle.* Triona found that reassuring. Her thundering heart slowed a mite, and she managed to catch her breath.

Aunt Lavinia looked perplexed. "Bedford is waiting for Lord Hugh. Why is he coming here, I wond—"

Hugh's large form filled the doorway. Impeccably dressed in formal morning wear, his dark blue coat perfectly molded across his broad shoulders, his cravat a masterpiece of complication, he entered the sitting room and bowed.

Regarding him from beneath her lashes, Triona suddenly found herself unable to breathe. In the carriage and the inn, the dim light had hidden many things about Hugh MacLean.

The bright light from the windows played over his dark hair and caressed his strong jaw. Worse, it turned his green eyes to a deeper, mossier color that held her in place, unable to utter a single word.

The white lock that ran back from one temple shimmered silver, as if pulsing with power. His mouth, which he'd pressed on hers so indecently the night before, was thinned with displeasure, but it was the look in his eyes that gave her the greatest pause. He appeared stern and darkly angry, his emotions held in thin check.

Memories of the wind from last night made her shiver.

Aunt Lavinia began to push herself from her chair.

"Please," he said, his voice as rich and warm as melted butter. "Do not rise. I merely came to speak to Miss Hurst."

She lifted her chin. "I don't believe we have anything to say to one another."

His dark gaze flickered over her, reminding her suddenly of the way her bones had melted in his embrace, before he glanced indifferently at her aunt. "Madam, I would like to ask for a few moments alone with your niece."

Aunt Lavinia shifted uneasily. "I'm not sure I sh—"

Caitlyn grasped her aunt's arm and tugged the older woman to her feet. "Of course we'll leave Lord Hugh to speak with Triona." Caitlyn herded her aunt to the door.

"I cannot leave them alone; it would be *improper!*"

"Nonsense—Triona is already ruined." Caitlyn tugged her aunt out into the hall. "She can't get more ruined by a few moments alone with the man now."

"Yes, but your uncle Bedford—"

"Can attend them very soon." Caitlyn turned back and said in a breathless voice, "I can only promise you a few minutes. Once Uncle Bedford is informed that you're here . . ."

MacLean's gaze never left Triona. "Thank you."

Caitlyn nodded. "I'll do what I can to keep them away." She closed the door behind her, her voice raised as she assured Aunt Lavinia that it was perfectly proper to allow Lord Hugh some time alone with "his intended."

Triona's mind was occupied with a startling realization. In all the years since Caitlyn had come into her beauty, few people—especially men—ever paid Triona the slightest heed whenever her twin was about. Yet for some reason, Caitlyn's beauty had little effect on Hugh MacLean. He seemed far more disposed to look at *her* than Caitlyn, even when they were in the same room.

Triona rather liked that, and the realization calmed her nerves as nothing else this morning had. He might be supporting a houseful of illegitimate children and cursed with a storm temper to boot, but at least he *saw* her—and that was something.

Hugh crossed his arms over his chest. "I would rather we talk alone before this progresses any further."

"I would rather never talk about it at all, but it appears I must."

His lips quirked. "I feel the same, but your uncle will not rest until we've had many conversations—preferably over a breakfast table as man and wife."

"I'm certain that once some time has passed, no one will even remember this silly incident occurred and—"

Hugh reached into his pocket and handed a folded page to Triona. "This morning's *Post*."

Her heart sinking, Triona opened the paper.

An elopement scotched, or foul play? Last night, Miss H—, niece to Lord and Lady G— and sister of Miss C. H—, left London in the company of Lord H. McL—. Rumors of an abduction have been flying, especially since Lord and Lady G— raced off to rescue their wayward niece—

"Good heavens," she said weakly, sinking back onto the settee. "It's already all over town."

Hugh nodded tightly. "There is also a wager listed in the books at White's."

Triona pressed a shaking hand to her forehead. She became aware of MacLean's dark green gaze locked upon her face and she managed a faint smile. "I hope it is a positive wager, at least."

"Ten to one that I will offer to marry you." His lips twisted into a bitter smile. "I suppose I should be glad I'm thought so responsible."

Her heart thudding sickly, Triona forced her numb

lips to move. "There is no question of saving my reputation. I-I made the mistake. I will not have you pay for it."

"Miss Hurst, we *both* made mistakes. You were in that coach out of pure, though naive, motives. I was there not just to protect my brother, but also to exact revenge on your sister for making him the talk of the town. Of the two of us, I am far more at fault."

Triona pressed her hands to her cheeks. "My lord, there *must* be another solution. Marriage is so ... *permanent.*"

His deep laugh washed over her, and she looked at him, surprised.

His green eyes crinkled with genuine amusement, his face completely relaxed for the first time since she'd met him. *What an astonishingly handsome man!* The thought surprised her, and with difficulty she looked away. *Careful! I can't become muddled in my thinking. Handsome or no, I know nothing of this man but ill.*

For a brief moment she wondered what it *would* be like to be married to such a gorgeous man, to see him every morning over the breakfast table, to spend the day strolling on his arm, perhaps taking in an exhibit at the British Museum, and then going home to dinner and—

"Miss Hurst, I must ask you a question."

His face was still relaxed from laughter, his gaze amused and warm. Just one look made her tingle in the most unexpected places. "What's that?" she asked in a breathless voice.

MacLean walked toward her and stopped, his knees not quite brushing her skirts as he stood looking down at her. "Are you in love with anyone?"

Triona's thundering heart moved into her throat as she tilted back her head to look at him. "No. Are you?"

His lips twitched into a half smile that was as sensual as it was fascinating. "No. I'm not."

She hadn't realized how important those words would be, but a sliver of pure, unadulterated relief splintered through her. *At least we won't have to deal with that issue.*

"That was my one hesitation." He sat in the chair nearest her, his movements as fluid as a lion's, his broad shoulders dwarfing the chair back. "Miss Hurst, let me be plain. I don't believe in love. I never have."

Her cheeks heated when she realized she was staring at his muscular legs outlined by his well-fitted breeches, but she couldn't seem to help it. In all of her life, she'd never met a man who was so *physical*. Good God, she had to stop this. What had he said? Oh, yes.

"You may not believe in love, but I do. My parents love one another very much. Surely yours—" She forced her wandering gaze to lock on his.

"I haven't expressed myself well. I believe some people are capable of love, but I am not one of them."

"Why not?"

"My blood doesn't burn warmly enough for such emotion."

"Well, that is certainly plain speaking. Unfortunately, I always wished to marry for love. It's yet another reason we can't allow this situation to progress."

He frowned. "I don't believe you understand the seriousness of your position. That's not surprising, though, considering you have only your aunt, uncle, and sister to advise you."

She stiffened. "What do you mean by that?"

"However good your aunt's intentions, I wouldn't call her understanding strong."

Triona couldn't disagree. Even Mother called her sister "silly." "My aunt has a good heart for all of her faults. Furthermore, my uncle and sister are hardly empty-headed."

"Your uncle is a pompous ass, and I cannot imagine that he's taken the time to explain anything to you."

Triona hadn't even seen her uncle this morning, for he'd ensconced himself in his library to await Lord Hugh. That he'd done so without bothering to have a single word with her *had* been irksome, but she wasn't about to inform MacLean of that. "He said enough," she returned evenly.

MacLean flicked a skeptical brow. "And your sister hasn't displayed the best grasp of propriety, which is the crux of this issue."

"Caitlyn is usually not so mannerless, and you have your brother to thank for that. He *wagered* her that she could not wrest a proposal of marriage from him."

MacLean's brows snapped together. "Did he, indeed?"

It wasn't a question, but a wondering comment. "I was surprised, too. I can't imagine why he'd do such a thing, knowing the possible consequences. Meanwhile, my sister rose to his challenge and threw caution to the wind by publicly announcing—"

Hugh could see the exact moment it dawned on her that her words would confirm all he'd said about her sister's lack of decorum. Behind her spectacles, Triona's eyes darkened, her plump lips folded with disapproval.

Hugh smiled grimly. He'd take little satisfaction in winning this argument, but win it he must. "For the moment, let's leave them out of this. If there were another path I could take to defuse this situation, I would take it, but there's not."

Last night, instead of getting some desperately needed rest, he'd been awake most of the night, trying to find a better resolution. With dawn had come the *Morning Post,* and bitter acceptance.

He'd slept then for two hours and had awoken with a pounding head, his stomach refusing food, which was normal after a bout with the family curse. There was a cost for his ability to control the winds. Only once, years ago, had he attempted to halt the curse after it had grown full-blown, and it had almost killed him. He'd vowed never to do that again.

Of course, he'd also vowed years ago never to marry. Long ago, he'd paid dearly for allowing a woman into his life and he'd sworn never to repeat that mistake. Yet here he was, on the verge not only of allowing a woman into his life, but of making her his wife. Life had a cruel sense of irony.

Hugh regarded her from beneath his lashes, her hands clenched into fists, her face pale. She was resolute; every line in her body said so. "Miss Hurst, you have a sister—perhaps more than one?"

She frowned. "I have two. There's Caitlyn and my youngest sister, Mary."

"If you care for your sisters and their future, you won't return home until you are safely wed. If you don't marry, society will condemn you for what it believes has occurred, and them by association. Your sisters will be whispered about, then cut altogether."

"But neither of them did anything! Nor did I!"

God, she was lovely, especially when outraged. Her creamy skin flushed, her eyes sparkled behind her stern spectacles. Hugh had to force himself to look away from her just to recall his argument. "Society is a cruel mistress. She condemns by association just as quickly as for actual acts." He turned his gaze back to her. "You may not care about the whispers, slights, and cuts, but your sisters will, as will the other members of your family."

She didn't answer, though her lips thinned.

"And your father's a vicar," Hugh continued ruthlessly. "He will not be allowed to keep his living, once all three of his daughters are branded indecent women. Your brothers will be watched, their every move interpreted negatively. Then there is your mother: I can't imagine she'd deal well with—"

"*Stop!* I-I hadn't—" She shook her head, staring ahead with unseeing eyes. "It's so unfair."

"It's damnably unfair."

She slid trembling hands behind her spectacles to cover her eyes. "Surely not. Surely, surely not!"

"Why do you think your uncle is awaiting me in the library? Lord Galloway is determined that you and I sell our freedom to kill the flow of rumor with disinterest."

She lowered her hands. "Disinterest?"

"There is nothing less interesting than a married couple," he said dryly.

Triona stared at Hugh, her thoughts whirling. She imagined Father's disappointed gaze and Mother's hurt expression if, after years of seeing her daughters as the belles of the village assemblies, they were abruptly cut from the invitation lists and whispered about in public. Neither Father nor Mother had social aspirations; in fact, Aunt Lavinia's invitation for the season had almost been refused but for Caitlyn's impassioned pleas. Still, she couldn't deny the harm a scandal would cause her parents who treasured their family's reputation.

Triona looked down at her hands, tightly clenched in her lap. What choice did she really have? "Getting married would end all of this?"

"If we announce that yesterday we were on our way to meet my brother to announce our engagement, then yes. We'll say your nurse didn't understand the nature of our visit, and that your uncle, once he learned of our errand, not only joined us all later, but blessed the union."

"Will anyone believe that?"

"Some. By that time we will be married and on our way to the country, and it should become old news very quickly. If we don't marry, there will be nothing to counteract the rumor and it will grow."

Triona's knees ached with the need to run away. She stood and crossed to the window, looking blindly at the garden.

She *didn't* have any choice. None at all.

Hugh watched her closely. Her expressions were so vivid that he could almost follow her exact thoughts. The sunlight traced her stubborn chin and nose, glinting off her spectacles.

He'd never thought spectacles on a woman attractive, yet on Triona they framed her amazing eyes, enlarging them so that the flecks of gold in the hazel were bright and vivid. His gaze dropped lower to the smooth line of her throat, to the delicate hollows of her neck and shoulders, to the generous swell of her breasts. Damn, she was a warm armful, and he couldn't stop imagining her beneath him. Perhaps this marriage wouldn't be all bad, after all. A man's generosity could only go so far and he'd be damned if he agreed to such a stupendous sacrifice without getting something in return. He was many things, but a mealy-mouthed "gentleman" wasn't one of them.

She rubbed her arms as if cold. "There is really no more to be said, then. We must marry."

"I procured a special license this morning so that we can marry in three days' time."

"And after that?"

He shrugged. "After that, we'll go to my house in the country and live as the picture of domestic bliss until the rumors are forgotten. A few months should be long enough for society to forget us."

She bit her lip, her even teeth capturing her plump bottom lip in a way that made Hugh's body tighten unexpectedly. "What—" Her husky voice broke and she cleared her throat. "What happens after those months?"

"You may return to your parents' house and resume your life there, while I continue with mine."

"But we will be *married*!"

He shrugged. "You will be an honorable woman."

"But . . . what if a year from now I meet someone and fall in love?"

"Then you may have an affair. It wouldn't bother me, providing you are discreet."

She seemed to choke. "It wouldn't *bother* you? Not even a *little*?"

"Miss Hurst," he said impatiently, "you are making far too much of this. I, for one, never wished to marry."

"No?"

"No. I'm sure you did, for all women do, but we are both required to make sacrifices. Once this is over, so long as we both calmly go our own ways and act discreetly, I see no reason why we can't both have full and productive lives."

She appeared astounded. "Do you even *have* a heart?"

"Apparently not."

She gave a slightly hysterical laugh. "I don't know whether to pity you, or wish I could be the same."

"Pray don't make this an emotional issue," he replied calmly. "It's only fair that you know how things stand before we begin."

She twisted her hands in her lap. "MacLean, I know a divorce would be impossible without a public trial and an act of Parliament—"

"And we'd face an even worse scandal than we have now."

"Yes, but what about an annulment? Surely we could gain one once the rumors have died down."

"There are only three acceptable grounds for an annulment and every one would cause a scandal equal to the one we face now."

She took off her spectacles and rubbed the bridge of her nose. "I wish we could just pretend none of this happened and each go our own way."

"So do I, but it's not practical. We must make this look believable or the talk will not stop. Triona, once we embark on this path, we're committed. You will live with me at Gilmerton Manor in Scotland until the talk dies down, and then you'll return home and we'll be as we were before."

"But married." She sighed, her breath lifting her breasts against the fabric of her gown.

He watched, riveted. Damn it, what was it about her

that had him so on edge? If she so much as moved, he found himself watching her, waiting, wondering. . . . Ah, perhaps that was it. Soon she would be his, and he would have access to her plump lips, the slope of her white throat, the sensual thrust of her breasts—

"MacLean?" she snapped.

There was no doubt that she'd seen exactly what he'd been staring at. "We are settled then," he said promptly, his face warm. "I will return on Friday. Have your portmanteau packed and we shall leave alone for the church."

"Alone? What of my family? We'll need witnesses."

"I'm sure the church will provide what is necessary." He hesitated, then added, "I'd like to keep this information from your aunt and uncle. I have the impression they wouldn't accept our simple plan."

Triona hesitated, then nodded. "My aunt has done nothing this morning but talk about the wedding and how nice it will be."

He grimaced.

"My thoughts exactly," she agreed.

Hugh had to appreciate her sensible approach. Most women would have insisted upon the laces and trims; it was a good sign that she didn't seem to care for them. "Good, then. We will leave them a letter and be off on Friday." He hesitated. "What about your parents?"

"They are visiting my uncle in the Lake District. Aunt Lavinia sent word to them this morning, but it will take the messenger at least three days to locate them and another three or four for them to arrive in London."

"Then we shall marry without them."

"That is a good thing. My parents will be upset at this situation, and it would be better to leave them a note explaining that it has already been resolved." She slanted him a look of uncertainty.

"Yes?" he prompted.

"I would like to invite them to visit, if you don't mind."

"Of course. Gilmerton Manor will be your home, too."

Emotions flickered over her face, wariness foremost.

"I am an honorable man, Triona. You should know that."

Her gaze narrowed, her expression cool. "Your behavior toward me in the carriage was not that of an honorable man."

He wished he could say that he'd forgotten that kiss, but he remembered it all too clearly. She'd been soft and sweet, her lips ripe and succulent, and—for a moment—willing. Hugh's body burned with a sudden desire to repeat that moment. *Calm down, you fool. There will be plenty of time for that later.* He'd make sure of it.

Triona crossed her arms, unwittingly pressing her full breasts toward the demure neckline of her gown. "That kiss wasn't the action of an honorable man. You wanted to punish my sister, to frighten her."

He had, until his lips had touched Triona's and ignited that amazing heat. Then all he'd wanted was more.

A *lot* more.

He had to control that heat. Strong passions always burned themselves out, though, and he was certain that, once it was slaked in the marriage bed, he'd no longer have to fight this physical yearning for her. That was one advantage of marriage: enough contact would kill every vestige of attraction.

She wet her lips, a gesture that made him harden even more. "MacLean, this marriage of ours . . ."

"Yes?"

She lifted her chin. "It will be a marriage in name only."

*Like hell!* Hugh's gaze traveled from the dark gold sweep of her hair, to the lush line of her lashes, to her plump rosebud mouth, to the full breasts pressed upward by her crossed arms; then he lingered appreciatively on the generous curve of her hips. Her legs were hidden from sight by her skirts, but he could imagine . . .

"No," he replied firmly. "This will be a real marriage in every way, or it won't be a marriage at all. It would be foolish to take away the one thing that might make this marriage bearable."

"And what is that?" Her voice was low and breathless, and excited him.

"The physical pleasure, my sweet." He closed the distance between them, cupping her face with one hand, her skin warm beneath his palm. He ran his thumb over her moist lips, making her shiver, and he could almost taste the longing that simmered between them.

She tightly closed her eyes, and when she opened them her gaze was cooler and resolute. "I don't know that physical pleasure is all that important, if we're to separate afterward."

He remembered her innocence at their kiss, his body smoldering anew. "Ah, but it is. It is a very great factor." To prove his point, he slipped a finger under her chin and lifted her lips to his.

He meant only to show her how pleasant and sensual a kiss could be. But as his lips touched hers, and she hesitated a brief second before leaning forward and offering her sweetness to him yet again, something happened. The same thing that had happened in the carriage.

Hugh forgot where he was, what he was trying to accomplish, and why. All he knew was the feel of her warm lips beneath his, the pressure of her round breasts against his chest, the warmth of her as he wrapped his arms about her and pulled her against him.

But this time, the banked flames stirred to an even hotter, more dangerous level. Soon he would *have* this woman. In every way possible, she would belong to him.

The primitive reaction flooded him in a flash of passion so bright, so powerful, that he didn't even think of resisting it.

He ran his hands over her, exploring her curves, luxuriating in her fullness as he possessed her mouth, tasting her passion. She pressed against him, her skin seeming to burn through her thin gown, her movements insistent yet awkward. She didn't even know what she yearned for, but she wanted it badly.

Her wanton innocence set him aflame as never before, and only the sound of footsteps out in the hall made him realize the awkwardness of discovery. It took every bit of his resolve to lift his mouth from hers, and step away to keep himself from reaching for her yet again.

Her spectacles were askew, her lips swollen and parted, her eyes unfocused. "That was—" Her voice broke, and she had to take a deep breath and start again. "I concede your point, MacLean."

He almost laughed at her matter-of-fact statement. What a conundrum this woman was! Even while reeling from passion, she managed to state her position in a clear, sensible fashion. He rather liked that. "Please call me Hugh. We are to be married, after all."

She nodded jerkily. "Yes. Hugh, then. And I am Triona."

"I prefer Caitriona." He adjusted her spectacles so they were back to rights. "But I'll settle for Cait." He brushed a strand of her silky honey-colored hair from her cheek, marveling at the softness.

Her gaze met his and his hand froze, his fingertips grazing her cheekbone. She had the most fascinating eyes, hazel green with flecks of gold and brown.

She colored and pulled away. "I'm accustomed to Triona."

He dropped his hand and shrugged. "As you wish. I should leave now."

Triona glanced at the closed door. She wasn't sure how Caitlyn had kept their aunt and uncle away, but she was very thankful. "Yes, you should."

"I have a number of items to tie up before I leave town. Can you be packed and ready to leave by nine Friday morning?"

Triona nodded, her mind racing. "This is a bit embarrassing, but I have very few clothes with me, for I didn't expect to be in town long."

"We can order whatever you need once we reach Gilmerton. There are several talented seamstresses in town."

Triona sighed. "I wish I had Caitlyn's way with a needle."

"She can sew clothing?"

"Better than most modistes. I can sew, but I don't have her eye for it."

He glinted a smile at her that made her tingle all the way to her toes. "I have no doubt that you have other, more interesting talents."

Before she could ask him exactly what he meant, he said, "I must be off. I suggest you keep our plan private, unless you wish to defend it for three days solid."

"I won't mention it to anyone except Caitlyn. She can keep a secret."

"Good." He glanced into the mirror over the fireplace and adjusted his mussed cravat, then turned back to her. "I'll be quite busy, but if you need me, simply send a note to MacLean House and I will attend you as soon as I can."

"I doubt I will need to, but thank you." She hesitated, then added, "Hugh, I—" What? She hoped their marriage wouldn't turn out as horribly as she feared it might? That she wished she knew for certain that their decision was the right one? That at the end of their few months together, she hoped they'd both walk away unchanged and unscathed, with no regrets? That even as she burned to taste more of the passion he offered so easily, she also feared that same passion?

All of these questions and more trembled on her tongue and yet when she managed to speak, all she said was, "Until Friday, then."

He brushed his fingers over her cheek, the touch surprising her. "Until Friday." He gave her one last, hard, searching look, then placed a gentle kiss on her upturned lips.

Triona closed her eyes, leaning into him. The last few days had been so frantic that she savored his warm touch and the obliteration of all thought. Yet even as her emotions found respite, her body flared to life, thrumming with awareness. She wanted to step closer, to twine her arms about his neck, to press against him and hold him there until—

He lifted his head and moved away. "Good-bye for now, Caitriona."

She had to swallow a stab of disappointment in an effort to appear unconcerned. "Good-bye, Hugh."

He paused, one hand on the doorknob. "Don't let your relatives drive you mad."

"I shall do my best to remain sane," she managed in a credibly calm voice. "I'm sure it will be a battle, but I will persevere."

He chuckled. "I have no doubt. If there's one thing I know about you already, it's that you're every bit as hardheaded as I am. Good-bye, my dear." And with that he left, closing the door behind him.

# Chapter 8

❧❦❧

*"I've never found it helpful to treat fate with a gentle hand. Every time I've stroked, hopin' fer a favor, she's slapped me hand and laughed at me. If ye want something, take fate by the throat and shake it out o' her!"*

OLD WOMAN NORA TO HER THREE WEE
GRANDDAUGHTERS ON A COLD WINTER'S NIGHT

The next three days went by with agonizing slowness. Uncle Bedford was furious to discover that MacLean had spoken with Triona and not him. He'd stormed out of the house and had not returned until late, saying in a terse voice that "the damned scoundrel is nowhere to be found!"

It didn't help that rumors were swelling at a rapid rate, with the town's more brazen gossips calling in an effort to elicit information. Aware of his wife's inability to hold her counsel, Uncle Bedford had sternly forbade all of them to receive visitors or go out in public until the situation had been resolved. When the cream of society came knocking, Aunt Lavinia, often in tears, had to listen from the sitting room as Dobbins announced that she wasn't available.

Triona was glad for the mandate, for she was certain Aunt Lavinia wouldn't have been able to handle the waves of gossipmongers. However, her uncle was not spared the innuendos of his friends and acquaintances. Late one night, returning to the sitting room to retrieve a book, Triona overheard her uncle telling her aunt about some of the ruder comments. She'd been appalled to discover that she was being blamed for the entire incident while MacLean was held in some sympathy.

Furious, she'd retired to her room where she'd spent a satisfying thirty minutes pounding the stuffing from her pillow and cursing the whole of London society.

Uncle Bedford's disposition grew even more sour when, after he'd spent hours attempting to locate Lord Hugh, a note arrived on the second morning from that gentleman himself, announcing rather offhandedly that he was dealing with the situation and would contact Lord Galloway "in the none-too-distant future." Uncle Bedford had crumpled the note into a wad, tossed it into the fire, and stormed out.

Left with no visitors or amusements to distract her, Aunt Lavinia was more determined than ever to plan a grand wedding. She strewed laces and ribbons and even drawings of elaborate wedding gowns all about the house. Triona pretended not to notice, though it sorely tried her patience. Worse, Aunt Lavinia would darkly hint that she and Uncle Bedford were concerned whether MacLean even meant to "come up to the mark" and "do his duty." It was enough to drive Triona mad.

Had it not been for Caitlyn's sympathetic presence, Triona was certain she would have sent a note to MacLean and asked him to whisk her away well before Friday, the consequences be damned.

Of course, Caitlyn was not without her own opinion; she thought it dastardly that MacLean did not come to visit every day to reassure them all was well. To her surprise, Triona found that she couldn't share her sister's outrage. MacLean had said he'd take care of things, and she believed him. Though he'd agreed to follow the dictates of society, he would do it his way and no one else's.

She couldn't help but appreciate that, though it did give her pause. This time, they were of one accord. What would happen when they weren't? His calm disregard for the opinions of others was a good thing until he disregarded hers.

As the hours dragged past, Triona had more time to lament her situation. The idea of marriage was not horrible. Her parents had an ideal relationship: they were rarely apart, were respectful of one another, understood each other, and had the same values and morals. But it was that very knowledge of how true love should work that brought her spirits low. In agreeing to marry MacLean, she'd given up the opportunity to have a marriage like that. Ever.

She rubbed her temples where they ached. Perhaps things wouldn't be as horrible as she feared. Perhaps they could find some sort of middle ground or common interest. At least MacLean possessed the basic requirements of a decent husband. He certainly was handsome enough, and then some. He seemed well educated and was well-spoken. He carried himself with distinction and was obviously intelligent. She couldn't doubt his excellent breeding, either.

He also had the ability to turn her bones to butter with a simple kiss.

Still . . . was that a *good* trait or *bad* or was it just the way he treated all women? If so, did that make her soon-to-be husband a libertine? He'd told her he wasn't in love with anyone, that he didn't think himself capable of such an emotion, but she hadn't thought to ask him if he had a mistress. She wasn't the sort of woman to put up with being made to feel less. The thought weighed heavily on her.

Friday finally came, dawning as gray and overcast as Triona's spirits. She dressed with special care and wished she could don her best gown, but feared it would draw Aunt Lavinia's attention. She contented herself with wearing her favorite morning gown of pale blue muslin, banded beneath the breast and around each sleeve with dark blue and green ribbons. The color made Triona's hazel eyes appear greener, while the full skirts provided warmth against the chilly day.

Triona had just latched her portmanteau and placed it on the floor when a soft knock sounded on the door. "Come in."

The door opened and Caitlyn entered, her gaze

immediately finding the bulging portmanteau. She said in a brittle voice, "I can't believe this day has finally arrived. I didn't sleep a wink last night."

"Me neither. I kept thinking and thinking. . . ." And doubting and doubting.

Caitlyn frowned. "MacLean should have come to see you at least once these past three days."

"And risk Uncle Bedford discovering what we've planned? This was much easier for us both." It had been difficult enough to fight her own doubts without also having to deal with her uncle's and aunt's. Over the past three days, Triona's inner voice, which usually urged calmness and logic, had grown more desperate and now screamed at her to find a solution other than marriage. She'd stared at the ceiling every night until the wee hours, and not a single idea had occurred that wouldn't injure her sisters and family.

Caitlyn bit her lip, her eyes suspiciously bright. "Oh, Triona, if only I hadn't—"

"Shh!" Triona hugged her sister. "If I hadn't been so impatient to find you, and if Aunt Lavinia hadn't had guests when Nurse arrived, and if Nurse hadn't made her announcement in front of a gossipy old woman, and *especially* if MacLean hadn't been such an ass— oh, don't get me started!"

Caitlyn managed a watery giggle. "He's a proud one, isn't he?"

"I'm afraid so." She shook her head. "You'd think I'd know that much about him, from the stories Mam always told us."

Caitlyn sighed. "Our grandmother only *thinks* she knows the MacLeans better than they know themselves."

"Well, what's done is done, as she'd say herself."

"Mam would also tell us that haste is the quickest way to sure failure." Caitlyn took Triona's hands in her own, an earnest expression on her face. "Triona, I've been thinking . . . perhaps you should take more time with this, and have a wedding after all."

"Aunt Lavinia's gotten to you."

"No, she hasn't. Well, I suppose she has, in a way, though not how you think. Triona, marriage is special. Shouldn't you celebrate it at least a little? Buy a lovely new dress, put some flowers in your hair, wait for Mother and Papa so they will be here to see—"

"No, no, and no. I don't wish for a new dress—not for this. The few flowers to be had at this time of the year are far too costly. And I am quite happy with Mother and Papa learning about all of this while I am safely tucked away in Scotland. Papa would mope about my unladylike behavior in getting in the coach to begin with, and Mother would be snappish and upset—honestly, it's a blessing to marry and get out of town without dealing with all of that." She tried to smile, but couldn't quite manage it. "I know they would try to talk me out of this, even though it's in the best interest of the family."

"But what about you? I'm worried about you, and I wish—"

"Stop! This is the best course for us all, as you well

know. Now is not the time for cold feet." She hugged her sister, feeling better for saying it out loud. "Let's go down to breakfast. It will take an entire pot of hot tea to ward off this dismal weather."

In the breakfast room they found Aunt Lavinia sitting at the table, a flutter of lavender silk and deep sighs. She informed them that their uncle Bedford was out searching for MacLean yet again.

"He's done that for three days now," Caitlyn said, dishing eggs onto her plate. "Why doesn't he just wait for MacLean to come? He sent a note promising to do that."

"Your uncle doesn't trust that note and neither do I." Aunt Lavinia buttered her toast with vigor, sending crumbs across the satiny walnut table. "Nor do we trust MacLean! He's a reprobate, a rake, and a—"

"My future husband." Triona cocked a brow at her aunt. "Just last night, between debating the merits of pale blue over pale pink for a wedding gown, you told me that he was 'quality' and would make an excellent husband."

Aunt Lavinia flushed. "I'm sure he is quality! I just meant—perhaps 'reprobate' is too harsh, but the man has been remiss in not answering the many messages your uncle has sent requesting his attendance! Furthermore, he—" Aunt Lavinia straightened in her seat, her eyes suddenly wide. "Do you hear that? It's a carriage!"

Triona's stomach tightened into a knot. "Do I hear what?" she managed nonchalantly.

Aunt Lavinia stood, her plump stomach flipping her breakfast plate over on the table. She peered out the front window. "It's him! Hurry, my dear! To the sitting room!" She led the charge, almost bolting to the door. "Oh, I *wish* Bedford was home! What on earth shall I say to that man?" Her voice faded as she dashed across the foyer.

Triona and Caitlyn looked at each other and then hurried after their aunt, their breakfasts untouched. They'd just reached the sitting-room door when the front door knocker rapped peremptorily.

Caitlyn whisked herself into a chair by the fireplace, while Triona took a chair near the door.

Her skirts hadn't stopped swaying when Dobbins announced, "Lord Hugh MacLean to see you, my lady." He disappeared as another familiar form filled the doorway.

Aunt Lavinia began to rise.

"Please don't get up," MacLean said, his deep voice at odds with the dainty sitting room. "I won't be more than a few minutes. Is Lord Galloway at home?"

"No," Aunt Lavinia said regretfully.

MacLean frowned. "That's a pity."

"He's out looking for you!" Aunt Lavinia snapped with surprising asperity.

His brows lowered. "I sent him a note saying that I'd wait on him here when I could arrange it. Didn't he get it?"

"Yes, but he thought—wait a moment. Why will you only be here a few minutes? Surely you need to—"

"I have come for your niece. We are to marry this morning."

Aunt Lavinia's eyes seemed ready to pop from their sockets. "But—"

"The church is readied, so we can't tarry. The archbishop is to perform the ceremony himself, and is expecting us in thirty minutes."

*Thirty minutes.* Triona could neither speak nor swallow. *Only thirty minutes more.*

Aunt Lavinia blinked. "But . . . there should be a gown and lace and a ring and—why, to get married without those would be positively *barbaric*!"

A faint smile flickered over MacLean's face as he turned to Triona and held out his hand.

She looked at it for a moment, then placed her hand in his.

He pulled her to her feet. "Are you ready?" His eyes, so dark they appeared black, locked on hers.

"Yes. I will send a footman to my room to fetch my portmanteau."

Aunt Lavinia gasped. "You're *packed*? But—"

MacLean lifted Triona's hand and pressed a kiss to her fingers. "Then we are set."

"B-but . . . I don't . . ." Aunt Lavinia lumbered to her feet. "Triona, what is the meaning of this? I can't—"

Caitlyn took her aunt's arm. "Aunt Lavinia, for three days Uncle Bedford and you have done nothing but worry that Lord Hugh wouldn't come up to the mark. Well, you needn't have worried: he is doing exactly as he should."

"Yes, but your uncle will wish to speak to him about the settlement! And what about the *wedding*?" she wailed.

"I want no settlement," MacLean said quietly. "And the wedding will be private."

"But what about witnesses and—"

"That has been taken care of. After Miss Hurst and I marry, we will leave directly for my estate in Scotland."

Aunt Lavinia sagged back into her chair. "You have this all planned out! Ohhhh!" She pressed a hand to her forehead. "Someone please fetch my smelling salts! My head is about to explode."

Caitlyn patted her aunt's shoulder. "Aunt Lavinia, just think how nice it will be to tell everyone how Triona and Hugh fell madly in love and have already married and gone off to Scotland."

After a moment of silence, Aunt Lavinia peeped at Caitlyn from behind a plump hand. "Tell? We could tell people?" She dropped her hand to her lap. "But your uncle said we were to remain here and not see a single visitor."

"That was before Triona married. Now we must let people know. Clandestine romances are so much in vogue now, too. People will be eager to hear about it, and we shall tell them that Triona and Lord Hugh are madly in love."

"Oh, that *does* sound romantic."

"Yes. And naturally, everyone will want details, and will invite you places. I don't know what we'll do with so many invitations!"

"Heavens!" Aunt Lavinia said, much struck. "I hadn't thought of all that!"

"You'd be doing Triona a favor. We *must* give the impression that it was a romantic love match! In fact, since she and Hugh are off to marry right now, we could even find our best hats and gloves and visit some of your friends today."

"Right now?" Aunt Lavinia looked happier by the moment.

"Of course! The sooner we put this new turn of events about town, the quicker it will become old news and be forgotten."

Aunt Lavinia clapped her hands. "I know *just* who we should tell! That horrible Lady Oglethorpe is the world's biggest gossip."

"Yes—and if we ask her not to repeat it, you know she will."

Aunt Lavinia almost glowed. "When the word gets out, we will be inundated with invitations, for everyone will wish to know all about the affair!"

"We will be quite popular. At least until Mother and Papa arrive." Caitlyn grimaced. "I daresay I shall be returning to the vicarage then." She turned to Triona. "I'll ask the footman to bring your bag."

"Thank you, Caitlyn."

With a quick smile, Caitlyn left.

MacLean turned to her aunt. "Lady Galloway, I hope you and Lord Galloway will come to Gilmerton in the near future."

"Oh, yes!" Completely cheered, she rose and lumbered forward to envelop Triona in a fragrant hug. "My dear, you're about to become the mistress of a grand estate. How exciting! Be sure you write, and don't forget to tell me all about your adventures and whatnot." She blinked back sudden tears. "I'm so happy for you!"

Triona accepted her aunt's hug with a warm one of her own, and wished her spirits could be lifted so easily. "Thank you, Aunt Lavinia. I am trusting you to put things in a good light to Papa and Mother."

"Don't you worry about that, my dear. Your uncle and I will explain exactly how things were, and how happy you look to be marrying!"

Out in the hallway, they heard Caitlyn telling a footman to have the portmanteau strapped to the back of MacLean's carriage, and they all left the sitting room.

Saying good-bye to Aunt Lavinia hadn't been difficult, but it was far more daunting to say farewell to Caitlyn. Through it all, MacLean was there, solicitously offering his handkerchief even while encouraging their departure. All too soon, he was assisting Triona into his carriage and they were off to the church. The next hour was a blur—a round-faced clerk who fluttered about trying to find a pen, the gaunt figure of the archbishop in his flowing robe who beamed so much that Triona began to wonder what this hurried service was costing her erstwhile husband, all overshadowed by Hugh's somber impatience as he rushed through signing the required papers and then hurriedly repeated his vows. She tried to convince herself that it was all real—that she was, in fact, getting married—but it seemed too much like an odd dream for her rational mind to accept it. A scant hour later they were on their way to Scotland and MacLean's estate.

Huddled in her pelisse, Triona sat across from Hugh as the carriage rumbled out of town. She stared bemusedly at the huge ring on her finger. A large ruby surrounded by diamonds, it sparkled even in the dim light of the carriage.

This was it. They were married, their union sanctioned by the church, while her aunt made her rounds and spread the news.

She wondered what a new bride should say. It seemed imperative to say *something*, but she was unable to think of a single witty thing.

Hugh's gaze met hers, and for a long time, neither spoke. Triona couldn't believe this man—this gorgeous, handsome man—was now her husband. Her husband in name, and soon in other ways.

She cleared her throat. "I hope you won't take this the wrong way, but I don't really *feel* married."

A flicker of a smile touched his mouth. "What does married feel like?"

"I don't know. Older, perhaps? More matronly?"

He lifted a gloved hand and tilted her face until she looked up at him. His green eyes gleamed softly; his sensual mouth curved in a smile. "You look many things, but matronly isn't one of them."

"Thank you."

He laughed and dropped his hand from her chin. "I meant it as a compliment."

She offered him a smile. "This has all happened so quickly. I am sure I will feel more married once we're settled at your home."

MacLean shrugged, seemingly unconcerned. "I don't suppose it matters, as you'll only be there for a few months."

*That's right. We're married, but only for appearance's sake. Why am I having so much trouble remembering that?*

She didn't need to make a home at Gilmerton; she would only be visiting. Still, it wasn't in her nature to stay in a household and not become a part of it. Even at Aunt Lavinia's, she'd assisted in selecting menus, overseeing the placement of the linens, and other mundane chores Aunt Lavinia didn't like. She supposed she could do that much at Gilmerton as well. It would make the time pass more quickly.

She wondered what the house would be like, if it was situated on a hill or on a lake, if it was cold in the winter like the vicarage, and how many servants there might be.

Suddenly she remembered Aunt Lavinia's assertion that Hugh MacLean had several illegitimate children. Would they be there, too? If so, she'd at least have some companionship.

Hmmm. How could she turn the conversation in that direction? "So . . . tell me about Gilmerton Manor."

His gaze flickered, his brows contracting, but only for a split second. Almost immediately, his usual calm, inscrutable expression was back in place, but it was too late—Triona had seen that blazing look, though she was at a loss to know how to interpret it. *What did that expression mean? Did I say something wrong? Blast it, I have the* right *to ask questions!*

Before she could put her thoughts into words, he spoke. "Gilmerton's large and expansive. Most of it was built in the thirteenth century, which explains why every year we must address various roof issues."

"It's a ruin?"

His laughter, low and deep, washed over her. "No, although there are portions of it that are sounder than others."

"I look forward to seeing it. It sounds immense for just the two of us, though." She waited expectantly.

His brows lifted, his expression suddenly cool. "Most of the time."

She shivered at his chilly expression.

"You're cold. Where's that extra blanket?" He took her bare hands in his gloved ones and pulled her to his side. Then he opened the seat box she'd been sitting on and removed a thick wool blanket and tucked it about her. His hands brushed her neck, warm and gentle.

Triona had to fight the inexplicable desire to lean into him. Her new husband was a blend of cold and hot, coolly rebuffing her questions one moment and then thoughtfully tucking her in with a warm blanket the next. She wanted to believe the gentler aspects of his character were a truer representation, but couldn't. The real man had to be a combination of the two. How was she to ever understand such a conundrum?

She forced a smile. "I'm not used to such cold. Though the vicarage is north of London, it always seems much warmer there."

"If you think it's cold now, wait until we get farther north."

"How long until we arrive?"

"Four days, if we make good time. Much depends on the weather. Scotland doesn't have the roads England does, and a good rain or snow can make the going slow." He hesitated, then added, "If you don't mind, I thought we might press on this evening. It's a full moon and we should be able to do so safely. When you wish to sleep, there are pillows in the box and the seats are quite well padded."

"Of course. However you wish."

"Excellent." His eyes glinted. "I am anxious to get home. I believe you will like Gilmerton."

Her gaze dropped to his mouth and, out of the blue, she was hit with the memory of his kiss. Heat flickered through her like an actual flame, dancing along her skin, making her breasts tingle with warmth as if he'd touched her.

*All of this from a mere memory?* Her face felt so hot that it had to be afire, and for a horrid instant, she was sure he must know what she was thinking. A quick glance proved her right: his eyes glowed as if he, too, was remembering things he shouldn't.

He pulled his gloves from his hands and tucked

them into his coat pockets. "If you don't feel warmer soon, we can stop at an inn for a hot brick for the foot warmer." He nodded down at the metal pan that rested in the floor.

"No, thank you. We'll save it for later, when it's *really* cold." She snuggled deeper into the blanket.

Hugh almost laughed at the regretful look she sent toward the foot warmer. He was learning quite a few things about his new wife. For one, she was a good sport, uncomplaining when many women would be hysterical. Her instant agreement to push through the night had surprised him. It had also made him take a new measure of her. He had little doubt that willful, center-of-attention Caitlyn Hurst would have burst into tears at the thought.

He appreciated Caitriona's good spirits, which made him certain that this little escapade would have a peaceful ending. She would enjoy his hospitality at Gilmerton, then calmly return to her family's home and resume her life there.

Looking at her now, huddled beneath the blanket beside him, her pert nose pink with cold, her spectacles glinting in the afternoon light, he couldn't help but feel a twinge of regret. It was a pity life held nothing more for her than being a symbolic wife. She deserved more . . . only not from him.

She sneezed, her spectacles bouncing on her nose.

Hugh frowned. "You're still cold."

"No, no. I'm fine, really." She promptly sneezed again.

"Like hell." He slipped an arm about her, pulled her close, then tucked the blanket over them both.

"Hugh, I don't need coddling! If I'm cold, I'll tell you."

He settled back in the corner, keeping her firmly at his side. She might not need coddling, but he'd be damned if he'd allow her to grow ill while in his care.

She sat stiffly against him, her head turned away. Hugh had to smile at her willfulness, though it did afford him a good look at her.

There was something singularly sweet about her profile. He wasn't certain if it was the firm line of her jaw, though still delicate and feminine, or the curve of her bottom lip, but whatever it was, he found it intriguing. There was so much character in her face—intelligence, wit, and a calm assurance that fascinated him. He'd only known her for a few days, but he'd already witnessed her reactions under extreme duress—first in the carriage when he'd thought she was her sister, then afterward in the inn when she'd defied her aunt and uncle in order to speak out, and the next day when Hugh had gone to tell her of their options . . . or lack thereof. Each and every time, even in the face of insurmountable odds, she'd responded with spirit and intelligence and an almost stately calmness. She was no shrinking violet, nor a society chit bent only on her own amusement. Here was a woman of grace *and* wit, and more than a little beauty.

Hugh tightened his arm about her, turning so that his chin rested on her silken hair. After a tense moment, she relaxed enough to sink against him. For a while they sat thus, tucked together beneath the thick blanket, sharing their bodies' warmth, the rumbling carriage lurching from side to side.

Taking in her sweet fragrance, he closed his eyes, savoring the scent that made him think of the freshest day of spring. A low simmer of lust began to slide through his veins.

His hand slid over her shoulder and he bent to inhale her fragrance more deeply, her hair tickling his nose. She sighed and snuggled against him, turning her face into his shoulder and making his body ache with desire. For a long moment they sat savoring each other, and then, somehow, they were no longer sitting in one another's arms, but kissing passionately, even frantically.

Blood pounded through Hugh's veins as he devoured her, enjoying the feel of her soft body pressed against his. The simmer of passion fanned brighter and he lifted her to his lap.

Her arms linked around his neck as she pulled him closer, exciting him even more. She was an enigma to him, representing both passion and pragmatism, honor and lust, enslavement and excitement. He hardly knew what to think, and when holding her, he simply couldn't think at all.

Her arms tightened about him and he ran his hands over her back, exploring her as she moaned against his mouth. She was generously made, soft and pliant, making a man dream of sinking into her. The thought of teaching her the joys of the bedroom sent a quiver of excitement through him. He'd always had affairs with experienced women who enjoyed sex without any emotional entanglement. So this armful of delightfully passionate innocence was heady indeed.

He slipped a hand over her rounded hip and up to cup her breast. She gasped and broke their kiss, her eyes flying open. Her spectacles had fallen to the wayside, for nothing framed the rich hazel color but the thick, vibrant sweep of her sable lashes.

Hugh paused, his entire body racked with awareness. Slowly, without breaking her gaze, he gently rubbed her breast through her gown, his thumb finding her nipple with unerring accuracy. Her eyes widened yet more, and her breath sucked between her swollen lips.

"Do you like this?" He flicked the end of her puckered nipple with his thumb.

She arched against his hand, her eyes half-closing, her mouth opening in a gasp. She dropped a hand from his neck to grasp his wrist—and to his surprise, pressed it more firmly on her breast.

*Damn, she is a hot piece!* He devoured the sight of her passion-flushed face, her cheeks pink, her honey-colored hair falling loose from the pins. She appeared as wanton as a hothouse bird, though he knew she was anything but. The contrast was achingly erotic and he felt it in every part of his body.

He nipped at her lips, moving to her jaw, then her ear. She shuddered against him, squirming in his lap as she rubbed his hand over her breast. Giving her time to stop him if she wished, he slowly eased back the neckline of her gown, then undid the tie that held her chemise closed.

She stilled against him, her breath rapid. He continued to nip gently at her ear as he slipped his hand beneath her chemise to cup her bare breast. Full and warm, it filled his hand completely. He gently kneaded it, then flicked her taut nipple.

With a moan she arched against him, writhing even more, her bottom rubbing against his hard cock. He withdrew his hand and reached down for her ankle. Reclaiming her mouth, he kissed her thoroughly, his tongue slipping between her lips as his hand slipped up her stockinged leg to her knee, then higher still. He quickly moved aside the cumbersome skirts and chemise, and slid his hand up her bare leg. He gently stroked her thigh higher. Then higher still. His fingers brushed over her wetness—

She bolted upright, clenching her knees together, her hair wild about her shoulders, her lips swollen. "No!" she gasped, a frightened look in her eyes.

Hugh took a deep breath, closed his eyes, and fought off the passion that flooded his veins. *Bloody hell, this is no way to treat a virginal wife!* He was no crass lout who took his own pleasure without returning the same to the fairer sex. Attempting to initiate an innocent into the pleasures of coupling while careening down an uneven road in a trundling carriage was foolish.

She deserved better and, if it killed him, he'd see that she received the gentlest treatment. She might have been forced to marry him, but he meant for them both to enjoy their physical pleasures, and the seat of a carriage was not the right place.

For this seduction, he wanted only the best: the luxury of a large feather mattress covered with fine linen sheets, in a room warmed by a crackling fire that gleamed off his large brass bathtub. There, he'd show her the pleasures of intimacy. Not here; not this way. Not for her very first encounter. And not for his wife.

Why that mattered, he wasn't sure, but he couldn't ignore it. He gently disentangled his hand from her skirts and pulled them down about her ankles. Then he tugged her gown back into place on her shoulder. She assisted him with trembling hands, her face red enough to ignite a fire.

"Caitriona, we will do this, but not here."

She couldn't seem to look at him. Instead, she said in a husky voice that held a faint quaver, "I should find my hairpins."

He helped her. At some point the blanket had fallen off, though neither had noticed it. Hugh retrieved it and discovered her spectacles tangled in its folds. He handed them to her and she slipped them onto her nose, then repinned her long hair, the silken strands capturing his gaze.

"Here." He tucked her under the blanket and reached up to knock on the ceiling of the coach. It began to slow.

Triona huddled beneath her blanket, confused and embarrassed, yet still aching for his touch. "What . . . what are you doing?"

"I am going to ride my horse for a while. Shadow's tied to the back of the coach and could use the exercise." He smiled at her, a tight, almost pained smile. "I am not a man to do things halfway, and taking your innocence in a coach on the open road—no. It is best for us to wait, but I have to admit that I am very . . ." He rubbed a hand over his face, and she noted with amazement that it shook just as her own did. "The truth is that I need some cold, brisk air and some exercise, and—" He caught her gaze and gave a rueful grin. "You don't understand, do you?"

"You are tired of being in the carriage with me?"

"No, not at all! Caitriona, I'm very . . ." He caught her confused expression and winced. "Oh, blast it—here." He took her hand and pressed it to his lap. His manhood pushed against his breeches, long and hard.

She snatched her hand back, her face so hot it burned. "I see," she managed.

He laughed softly. "Don't look embarrassed; it's a compliment of the highest sort."

She tucked her hand back under the blanket. "Then—" She bit her lip.

The carriage rocked as the footmen climbed down. MacLean leaned forward to say quietly, "I didn't stop because you failed to arouse me; it is quite the opposite. I stopped because I don't wish your first time to be on a hard bench in a carriage."

Oh. Well. Since he was being kind, she supposed she should appreciate his thoughtfulness. Still . . . she'd enjoyed his touch so very much. "Does it matter? The seats aren't *that* hard and—"

He laughed softly, then gave her a quick kiss. "Trust me on this: you deserve better."

There was a sharp knock at the door. It opened and the coachman leaned in. "Aye, m'lord? Ye knocked?"

"Yes, Ferguson. Have my horse saddled. I wish to ride for a while."

"Very good, m'lord." The man withdrew and could be heard shouting orders to the others.

With a wink, MacLean climbed down, the cool air swirling into the carriage.

Triona cleared her throat. "Will you ride the rest of the way to Scotland?"

"Oh, no." His eyes crinkled with humor. "I just plan on riding until I am too tired to do more than stare at you longingly. An hour or two should do it."

At least she wouldn't be alone for long. She smiled. "Very well, then. I hope you enjoy your ride."

"I'm sure it will be wretched and cold, which is exactly what I need. Meanwhile, get some rest. We're days yet to go before we reach Scotland. Once we're there . . ." He gave her a heated look, then closed the door.

The carriage soon rolled back into motion and they were under way again. Triona peeked out the window and watched MacLean cantering alongside, the wind ruffling his dark hair beneath his hat. His eyes were as bright as the ruby that gleamed on her finger, and the firm line of his chin gave her pause. It gave her the distinct impression that he didn't negotiate—ever.

Triona sat back in her seat. At first she'd wondered about MacLean's insistence on the physical aspect of their marriage, but no more. Since it was highly unlikely she'd ever marry again, it was a good thing she would be able to experience lovemaking—at least for a short while. It would be a pity never to have that.

So far, she'd enjoyed it more than she'd thought possible. Smiling, she snuggled into the corner, the blanket toasty warm about her as she did as Hugh had bid, and fell asleep.

The next couple of days passed much as the first. MacLean began each day in the carriage with Triona, but the sexual tension between them became more and more palpable. After a short time he'd leave the carriage and ride beside it, staying there until he was so exhausted that all he could do was sleep once he was inside.

Of course, that did nothing for Triona's state of mind, and she discovered that one could lust after a man even while he was sound asleep, and even snoring a bit. Lust was a very, very mysterious thing.

After a while, Triona grew tired of sitting and being jounced in the carriage alone. Worse, as the terrain took on a craggier, wilder look, she began to feel homesick. She missed her brothers and sisters. She missed their noisy breakfasts, and their good-natured arguments, and everything else.

She also found herself worrying about how comfortable she'd feel at Gilmerton Manor. Would she ever feel as at home as she did at the vicarage?

Heart heavy, she wished she'd thought to bring a book, for she desperately needed something to redirect her mind.

They traveled through the first two nights, stopping only for a quick meal and, once, a blissfully hot bath. They were making good time because they changed the horses from Hugh's private stock along the route. On the third night, a cloudy sky kept them from pressing on and they stopped at an inn, for which she was profoundly grateful. Her back and legs ached from traveling, and even when they stopped, she felt as if she were still inside the rocking carriage, the earth moving beneath her feet. Exhausted, she fell asleep over her dinner twice and didn't even awaken when MacLean carried her to their room and tucked her into bed. She awoke in the early-morning darkness to a bed warmed by his body, though he had already risen and dressed. As soon as it was light, they were on their way.

Shortly after dark on the fourth day, they finally arrived at Gilmerton Manor. As they turned a bend in the winding country road, Triona caught sight of her future home, the moon lighting it in ghostly silver.

The manor perched on a treeless hill, three stories tall with a myriad of windows. Dark and menacing under the stark light of the moon, it seemed to glare down at her, and she shivered as she noted that only a few windows on the lowest floor were aglow with welcoming light.

Astride Shadow, Hugh looked at Gilmerton with an entirely different emotion. He was home. Finally.

Shadow clearly felt the same, for he kicked a bit and trotted smartly up the drive. Hugh laughed as he pulled the horse to a stop at the wide, red door, and swung down with a sense of pride. The house was spacious, well-built, and solid, the way Hugh liked things: a stately building of classic and simple design.

The door swung open and a tall woman dressed in a housekeeper's gown and apron came bustling out. Following her were the footmen, Angus and Liam, carrying lanterns on poles to light the portico.

Mrs. Wallis frowned. "Och, milord! We weren't expectin' ye fer another two weeks! 'Tis a good thing your bedchamber is already made up."

"I would have sent word, but circumstances hastened my return."

The coach came to a halt by the portico, and Ferguson hopped down and immediately went to help Triona out of the coach. Mrs. Wallis's eyes widened; Hugh never brought guests to Gilmerton.

Triona didn't seem to notice Mrs. Wallis's avid attention. Pale and wan, her hair half-pinned with long strands falling unnoticed down her back, her clothing wrinkled, she seemed too exhausted to take in her surroundings at all. Hugh's heart softened. She appeared so weary and, standing before the house, so very small.

Though she held Ferguson's arm, she stumbled a bit when her feet touched the ground. Hugh strode to her side, placed an arm about her waist, and helped her to the steps. "Mrs. Wallis, this is Lady Caitriona MacLean, your new mistress."

"Wha—?" Mrs. Wallis gaped while both footmen gawked. "La—ye mean—when did—I—" She flushed a deep red and sank into a curtsey. "Och, milady, 'tis very good to meet ye! Welcome to Gilmerton!"

Triona managed a smile, leaning upon Hugh's arm. "Thank you. I'm a bit fatigued from my journey, or I'd ask for a tour of the house." She gave a rueful grimace. "I fear that I couldn't manage all of the stairs just now. I've been sitting in the coach for four days."

"Only four days to come from Londontown?" The housekeeper pinned an accusing gaze on Hugh. "Ye didna stop fer nothin', did ye?"

"We were in a hurry."

"Aye, so I see. The poor thing must be exhausted! Why don't ye show her to her bedchamber, and I'll bring up a pot o' tea and some butteries."

"Butteries?" Triona asked.

"Aberdeen rolls," he explained.

She just blinked up at him, and Mrs. Wallis offered, "Sweet, soft rolls, milady. Ye'll like me butteries." She looked Triona up and down with a critical eye. "Ye London misses never eat enough, though ye seem better filled out than most I've seen."

"Thank you."

Hugh hugged her to his side and smiled. "Mrs. Wallis thinks we're all wasting away. It's one of her more charming flaws."

"Hmph. If ye'd eat when ye should, I wouldna have to say something! Never fear, milady, we'll have ye fattened up in no time." The housekeeper turned and marched inside. "Come, now! A little food and then it's off to bed with you."

Triona glanced up at Hugh. "I would like a bath, too."

"Of course!" Mrs. Wallis said over her shoulder as she headed across the grand hallway to the stairs. "Angus, off to the kitchen. Tell the staff we've a new mistress and she wishes a bath immediately."

Hugh and Triona climbed the stairs after the housekeeper, who explained the various pieces of weaponry and art that adorned the huge stairwell. Hugh could tell that Triona wasn't taking any of it in. Her face was pinched and pale, her shoulders slumped, and each step seemed to take her longer than the last.

As they reached the top of the first flight, Triona stumbled and would have fallen except that Hugh swung her up into his arms. She murmured a protest, her head resting against his shoulder, her arms clasped about his neck.

After a concerned glance back, Mrs. Wallis nodded her approval, then hurried to open Hugh's bedchamber door.

Hugh savored his role of "rescuer extraordinaire" as he carried his tired bride. He had an idea that such acquiescence was rare, and he'd best enjoy it while he could.

A gentleman would give his exhausted new bride some privacy on her first night in a strange house after a strenuous journey, but this was his wife, by God, and he'd already been more patient than any man he knew. If he had to put up with the aspects of being married that he didn't like, he'd at least enjoy the ones he did.

Mrs. Wallis plumped up a pillow on the settee by the huge fireplace. "I'll go and see to the butteries and the hot water."

"Thank you." The familiar large room was a welcome sight with its royal blue hangings, comfortable fireplace, red and green carpet, and heavy furnishings of rich, dark wood. Ignoring the settee, Hugh placed Triona on the bed. "Rest until food and the bath arrive."

She relaxed against the pillows and her lashes fanned her cheeks as she closed her eyes. Hugh's gaze drifted over her determined chin to the delicate line of her neck, then down to the soft rise and fall of her breasts—

A flash of lust slammed into him and he turned away, disgruntled that it took so little.

As her breathing evened out, her lips parted and her face turned to one side. She looked so young, snuggled there among his pillows, her hair tangled about her, faint purple smudges under her eyes attesting to her deep weariness.

Hugh found himself brushing her hair from her forehead. As his fingers slid over her smooth skin, something flickered in the region of his heart. *Sympathy,* he told himself. *She has to be exhausted and concerned for her future. I only hope that when she finds out how things really are here, she will not disrupt my life or anyone else's.* He hoped for that, more than anything.

He sighed, weary to the bone but wide awake. He would inform Mrs. Wallis that the butteries and hot water should wait while Caitriona rested. After an hour's nap, she'd be able to eat her dinner and bathe before settling in for a good night's sleep.

Perhaps, while he was downstairs, he'd retire to the library for some port before he came to bed. Otherwise he'd never sleep, and if there was the one thing he needed, it was a deep, unconscious sleep—especially with his innocent temptress of a wife within reach. In the morning, when she awoke . . .

He smiled and tucked the blankets about her. Then, still smiling, he quietly left.

# Chapter 9

*"If ye ever find yerself with a MacLean, avoid his green gaze. 'Tis said they've but to look at a woman to capture her heart, and 'tis always good to be careful."*

OLD WOMAN NORA TO HER THREE WEE
GRANDDAUGHTERS ON A COLD WINTER'S NIGHT

*A*n hour later as Hugh left the library, he noticed the sitting-room door was thrown wide, the lights inside softly glowing. He glanced in and stopped at the sight of a pair of boots stretched out toward the fireplace.

They were especially fine boots of soft Italian leather, shimmering with a polish not usually found off St. James Street. The heels were specially crafted and etched with silver, while ebony tassels hung from the white tops, the acknowledged footwear of a dandy. Judging by the sheen of the man's breeches, the rest of the man appeared to be just as well dressed.

Hugh strode into the room. "What are you doing here? What's wrong?"

The man in the chair sipped the port he'd been

cradling in a large glass. "Is that any way to greet a brother?" he asked in a languid voice.

Hugh frowned. "Where are the girls?"

"Abed, where they belong."

"Then nothing happened—"

"Your daughters are safe. Even now, they are guarded by seven of my best men."

Hugh sighed, raking a hand through his hair. "I'm sorry, Dougal. It's been a hell of a week, and I received that letter right before I left—"

"I know! It worried me, as well. That's why all of my best men are there. I would never allow anything to happen to my nieces."

Hugh managed a smile. "Thank you. Sorry to be so on edge." He glanced around. "Where's Sophia?"

"My lovely wife left for Edinburgh this afternoon to escort her father to see a specialist."

"Red is ill?"

"He merely has a case of gout, but Sophie fusses over him as if he were a baby." Dougal smiled, his gaze softening. "She won't be gone long; she is never happy away from me."

"Away from MacFarlane Manor, you mean. I never saw a woman love a house more."

"And who can blame her? It's not as impressive in size as this monstrosity, but definitely more elegant."

"And more expensive."

Dougal lifted his brows. "Oh? Are you suffering some sort of reverses? The last I heard, you were the wealthy one."

"Alexander has more than all of us together."

"He inherited his fortune; the rest of us have had to make our own money. You through your blessed horses, and me through my skill at the table."

"I never thought of card playing as a skill."

"Ah, but you've never played me."

"And never will."

Dougal smoothed the sleeve of his coat of blue superfine. "Don't trust me?"

"Not with cards, women, or my port."

"That's only prudent."

Hugh returned to the original subject. "If you are not returning the girls, why are you here?"

"I saw you gallop by and thought I would welcome you home."

"You couldn't have seen me; it was dark." Hugh went to the sideboard, retrieved an empty glass from a silver salver, and poured himself a goodly measure of port.

"It wasn't too dark for you to ride."

"I was on the open road with the moon overhead, while you had to peer through the trees that surround your house. You couldn't have seen me," he repeated.

Dougal shrugged and took a sip of his port. "Then perhaps I heard the coach."

"Or perhaps you're still paying that ramshackle footman of mine to spy for you."

"Liam is a good man," Dougal protested.

"To you." He'd have to talk to his footman again. The problem was, Dougal was so damned good at making things seem right even when one knew they weren't. When he and Dougal were younger, that had gotten Hugh in trouble time after time.

Dougal regarded Hugh from beneath his lashes. "If you were more forthcoming, I wouldn't have to hire a spy to learn things. Such as the interesting fact that my dear brother has returned from London with a *wife*?"

Hugh's jaw tightened, but he returned no reply. He'd just spent the last hour trying not to think about the woman currently gracing his bedchamber and he didn't welcome Dougal's prying attentions into that very situation.

Hugh had already downed a glass of port in the library in an attempt to soothe the edges off his lust and exhaustion—a bad combination on the best of days. He quickly finished off the rest of his newly filled glass and then refilled it.

Dougal lifted his brows. "Knowing you as I do, I could believe you returned dead quicker than wed."

"It's true." Hugh took a chair across from Dougal, planted his heels on the settee, and crossed his ankles.

Dougal looked at his brother's boots with disdain. "Heathen."

"Fop."

"But a well-mannered fop, at least." Dougal eyed Hugh with interest. "Liam seems to think you were forced to marry after getting caught in a compromising position with a vicar's daughter, no less. How close is he to the truth?"

Hugh took a deep drink of the port. "That's a crude version of events, but accurate."

Dougal lifted his brows. "You seem quite calm."

"I'm resigned. That's a different thing altogether."

"Hmm. What's her name?"

"Caitriona Hurst." Hugh paused. "MacLean."

"Hurst? Isn't that the chit Alexander was flirting with when I was in London last month?"

"No, that's her sister Caitlyn. My wife goes by Triona, but it doesn't suit her."

Dougal looked at Hugh curiously. "What name does?"

"I don't know, but Triona is too . . . plain."

"Ah, so she's a beauty."

"She's . . ." Hugh stared into his glass. "She's unique."

Dougal waited, but Hugh offered no more. Shifting in his chair, Dougal said cheerfully, "Hurst, eh? Good Scottish stock, then."

"She must be, though you won't detect an accent. Her family resides at the vicarage at Wythburn, north of London."

Dougal leaned forward, his elbows resting on his knees. "So, how did this happen?" he asked quietly.

Hugh rubbed a hand over his face. "I warned Alexander about flirting with the sister, but he just laughed. He left town for a week and I used your bribing-the-footman trick to watch the chit. I discovered that Caitlyn was setting a trap for Alexander to garner an offer of marriage, and I meant to thwart the scheme. Meanwhile, Caitriona was attempting to stop the plan as well—but somehow we both got caught instead."

"You could find no other way out?"

"I couldn't leave Caitriona to deal with the scandal on her own."

"There was a scandal?"

Hugh's expression grew grim. "It was all over town in a trice. Our names were even entered into the wager books at White's."

Dougal whistled silently. "And of course, being who you are, you could do no less than marry the chit."

"It was more my fault than you realize. If I hadn't been so intent on punishing the sister, I never would have compromised Caitriona. My temper got the best of me."

"Does Alexander know?"

Hugh shook his head.

"He will be furious that you interfered in his affairs."

"I have larger concerns at the moment."

"I suppose you do—such as what your daughters will think, finding themselves with a new mother."

Hugh's brows snapped together. "Those girls are *my* children. They are *my* responsibility and no one else's. Caitriona will stay here for a few months only, and then she will return to her family home."

"What?" Dougal's brows rose. "Does she agree with that?"

"I gave her no other option."

Dougal sighed. "Hugh, you cannot judge all women by Clarissa—"

Hugh was instantly on his feet, and outside a wall of wind slammed into the house, rattling the windows. "Don't speak that woman's name in this house ever again! I won't have it."

Dougal threw up his hands. "Very well! I'm sorry!"

The wind subsided as Hugh dropped back into his chair, his face grim. "Caitriona is nothing like her. If she had been, I wouldn't have married her, no matter the circumstances."

"I'm surprised you brought her here."

He shot a hard look at Dougal. "I had no choice. You know I dare not be gone for long."

"True." Dougal leaned back in his chair. "You are caught between hell and high water, aren't you?"

"Yes, I am. So . . . what do I do now?"

"Oh, no, you don't! The last time I gave you advice, it had to do with purchasing a certain mare that drew up lame. After abusing me for *months,* you told me you'd never ask for my opinion again."

"You know next to nothing about horses, but you have excellent taste in women. Sophie is a wonder."

Pride flared through Dougal and he couldn't help puffing out his chest. "I did well, didn't I?" Though to be honest, he wasn't so sure he'd picked Sophie as much as she'd picked him. "I'm not quite sure what sort of advice you want. If this woman is nothing like She Whose Name Shall Not Be Spoken, then what has you worried?"

Hugh stared into his empty glass, his expression dark. Finally, he said, "When I first met the girls' mother, I was besotted, wild for her. I couldn't eat, sleep, or think of anything else." His smile twisted with disdain. "I don't know how any of you put up with me."

"You were a youth, so of course you were annoying." Dougal shrugged. "We knew you'd come out of it, and eventually you did."

"Still, it disrupted the entire household, and for months none of us spoke." Hugh shook his head. "Now that my daughters are here and I am providing a home for them, I can't allow anything—or anyone—to disrupt our lives. They've had enough difficulties already; I can't be responsible for adding more."

Dougal poured more port into his glass. Damn it, he wished Sophia were here. She was a fount of wisdom about the human heart and its complexities, something Dougal didn't even pretend to understand.

Yet now Hugh—who rarely asked for help of any sort, except in keeping an eye on the girls when he had to attend to business in London—was asking for Dougal's opinion on that very subject.

Stalling for time, Dougal said, "Do you have reason to think ill of your new wife? What is she like?"

Hugh shrugged. "She's quite attractive and about this high"—Hugh held out a hand to his shoulder—"with dark blond hair and hazel eyes. And she wears spectacles."

"So far, I hear nothing to cause alarm."

Hugh smiled faintly. "She gives as good as she gets, and she's as stubborn as the day is long."

Was that grudging admiration Dougal heard in his brother's voice?

Hugh raked a hand through his hair. "Dougal, I need to ensure that when Caitriona leaves in a few months, we can all return to our normal lives without pain."

Without pain? "You expect to miss her?"

"Not me," Hugh said sharply. "The girls! I don't want them to grow fond of Caitriona."

"Ah! I thought—" Dougal frowned. "Hugh, are *you* attracted to this woman?"

To his surprise, Hugh turned red.

Dougal blinked. Hugh? *Blushing?* "I suppose that's a yes."

"She's a dashed pretty woman, so of course I find her attractive! To be honest, I'm looking forward to having her in my bed. But that does not blind me to the fact that, because of their mother's shortcomings, my daughters might be susceptible to Caitriona. They want a real mother, and I don't want them to grow fond of her over the coming weeks."

"And thus miss her when she leaves." Dougal shrugged. "Then don't let them grow close."

"How? If I tell the girls to stay away from her, they will become wildly curious about her, and if I tell Caitriona not to speak with them, she'll do it just to show me she can."

"That *is* a difficult situation." Dougal mulled this over. "Perhaps . . . perhaps you could just keep Caitriona busy."

"Busy?"

"Yes, too busy to entertain the girls and develop a relationship." Hugh immediately looked hopeful, and Dougal gave himself a mental pat on the back.

"That's a good thought. I could ask Caitriona to make certain that various chores are done—the big ones we usually do in the spring—and take the girls to work with me at the stables whenever possible."

Dougal leaned back and silently toasted himself. Sophia would be so proud he was helping Hugh; she was forever telling him how important it was that they talk to one another.

Hugh nodded thoughtfully. "I can do that."

"You train horses; women are not so different."

"That's a very good point," Hugh said, looking much struck. "Horses are skittish in nature, too."

"Emotional."

Hugh nodded. "There are parallels."

"Just don't tell your woman that, unless you fancy sleeping alone the rest of your life."

Hugh grinned. "Afraid I'll tell Sophia you suggested it?"

"Of course not," Dougal said in a lofty tone. "Besides, we were not speaking of me and Sophia. So, what are you going to tell this wife of yours?"

"I will give her a list of chores to oversee that should keep her, and the entire household, in a tizzy for weeks. The girls thirst for a real mother. Given even the smallest encouragement, they would latch on to Caitriona."

"Maybe she doesn't have to leave in three months," Dougal suggested.

Hugh frowned. "I have no room in my life for a woman, much less a wife. Furthermore, I vowed to protect my daughters from harm, and they would be deeply hurt if they grew to care for whoever I married and the relationship failed."

Dougal poured more port into his and Hugh's glasses. "What did Caitriona say when you told her about the children?"

Hugh was silent.

Dougal lowered his glass. "You *have* told her, haven't you?"

"No."

"Good God, why not?"

"At first because we were mere strangers, and I'm not one to discuss the children anyway. Then I was busy arranging things for the damned marriage, and . . . well, I forgot."

"What about on the way here?"

"It seemed such an awkward thing to blurt out." Hugh sighed. "Damn it, I never wanted to marry! If I could have found a better way to deal with the scandal, I'd have done it, but I had no choice. Then I spent the entire trip here trying not to—" He glowered. "I will tell her first thing in the morning."

"Good. See that you do."

Hugh finished his drink and stood. "I know what I need to do," he growled. "It's just damnably inconvenient."

"Consciences work like that."

Hugh made his way to the door. "Yes, well, I'd be better off without mine."

"Nonsense. The girls need your stellar example. Besides, it takes a lot of pressure off of me."

"Pompous ass."

Dougal just grinned.

Hugh reached the door and hesitated. "Dougal, thank you for the advice. You've given me something to think about."

"If Sophia had been here, I'm sure she would have told you the same thing." Dougal thought for a moment. "Except the part about training women and horses." He put down his glass. "Meanwhile, I suggest you find a gentle way to tell your new bride the rules of the house, including that you have three lovely daughters and she's to leave them alone. Be firm, but fair—you know how it's done. Your horses are the best trained in the entire country. Shall I return the girls in the morning?"

"After breakfast, if you don't mind. I'll need a little time to inform my new bride of everything."

"I shall be off, then." With a flourishing bow, Dougal sauntered out of the sitting room.

In the hall, he took his coat and hat from the footman, slipping the lad a shiny coin.

Liam beamed. "Thankee, m'lord!"

"You're quite welcome. Now that his lordship has a new bride, I may need your services even more."

Liam placed a finger beside his nose and gave Dougal an exaggerated wink.

Dougal chuckled. "Good lad! I shall expect to hear from you." He knew it wouldn't be all smooth sailing for Hugh. As Dougal well knew, any woman worth her salt would take a list of rules as a challenge. That was how he and Sophia had started their own courtship, after all—with a challenge.

His lovely wife had been a crack gambler and had brazenly challenged Dougal to a series of card games in an effort to win back the house her father had lost. Naturally, Dougal hadn't been able to turn from such a tempting offer, especially one with golden hair and the lushest mouth he'd ever seen.

Now he realized his hot pursuit had come from more than mere pride, but at the time he'd have sworn the whole thing had to do with Sophia's defiant attitude.

It would be good for Hugh and his Caitriona to face challenges; that was the true stuff of life.

Dougal walked out into the crisp night air where his horse awaited. At least there would be something interesting to do while Sophie was in Edinburgh. When he brought the girls home, perhaps he'd stay here for a few days, too.

The fireworks should be very entertaining.

# Chapter 10

*"Not all surprises are welcome, ye know. Some are hard, cold facts that run ye down and leave ye in shock."*

OLD WOMAN NORA TO HER THREE WEE
GRANDDAUGHTERS ON A COLD WINTER'S NIGHT

Triona awoke slowly, wonderfully warm and cocooned in fresh sheets. She smiled at the delicious warmth, moving her legs to untangle herself from the bedding. Then she realized that she wasn't just tangled, but trapped, almost as if—

Her eyes flew open and she realized she was securely tucked against Hugh MacLean, her back against his chest, his arm holding her against him, their legs entwined.

She'd thought they might have separate bedchambers; many married couples did. Still, she savored the coziness of feeling so protected. His arm was a comforting weight on her shoulders, his hand loosely curled over one breast, which caused her breath to quicken. But it was the feel of his legs, tangled with hers where her night rail had slipped up around her knees, that made her want to snuggle deeper in his arms.

His skin was so warm. She could feel the powerful muscles of his calves and thighs, and the rough hair on his chest—

Was he *naked*?

She sat straight up, scrambled from between the sheets, and jumped out of bed, her feet sinking into the plush rug.

MacLean pushed himself up on one elbow, his hair falling over his forehead. "What's wrong?"

As the sheet slipped down, Triona found herself admiring his broad, finely muscled chest and flat, rippled stomach.

He started to toss the sheets aside.

"*Don't!*"

He froze. "Don't what?"

"Don't get up! You . . . you don't have any clothes on."

After a startled moment, he gave a deep laugh. Still grinning, he dropped back against the pillows and tucked his hands beneath his head. "I always sleep in the nude."

Didn't he get cold? Perhaps not, for his skin had been as warm as if he'd been standing in front of a fire. Still, it seemed decadent and naughty.

He grinned, his gaze flickering over her. "I can see you believe in the benefits of sturdy nightwear. There's enough material there for two gowns. Maybe three."

She smoothed her night rail. "It's cold at Wythburn. The chimneys put out more smoke than heat, so we all wear sensible nightwear." The thought of her brothers and sisters made her throat tighten with homesickness, so she shoved the thought aside. "I was afraid to catch the ague."

He smiled slowly. "I haven't been ill a day in my life."

She'd wager that was true, for he certainly looked exceedingly . . . healthy.

He reached down and flipped back the sheet on her side of the bed, revealing a narrow strip of his muscular hip and leg. "Come back to bed; it's too cold to be up. Give Mrs. Wallis's troops a little time to light the morning fires."

It *was* a bit cold, even standing on the thick rug. And he'd felt so very warm.

Her gaze took in his broad shoulders, the way his chest tapered down to narrow hips that were barely hidden by the sheet.

Suddenly it was hard to breathe. Her heart pounded and her nipples tightened in the most unusual way.

"Come back to bed, Triona. It's too cold to be up."

She frowned. "No, really, I—"

Suddenly, the wind moaned—a dull, roaring moan that rattled the windows and stirred the curtains. Cold air whooshed down the fireplace with such force that a puff of ash blew out, and Triona shivered as her night rail fluttered about her.

She glanced suspiciously at MacLean. He was still in the same relaxed position, hands locked under his head, but there was a tension about his face—the look one got if one had a headache.

She eyed him. "You did that."

He laughed, though he rubbed one temple. "What if I did?"

"I've always heard that the MacLeans cannot control the weather; they just start it when they get angry."

"Hmm. Apparently you heard wrong."

She eyed him warily, crossing her arms over her chest against the swirling cold, not sure how she felt about this development. "Can the others do the same?"

He gave a smug smile. "No, just me. Now, come to bed, sweet. It's not even seven yet, and I refuse to give up a perfectly good morning. I get so few, because of—" He stopped suddenly.

She rubbed her cold arms. "Because of what?"

He lifted the blankets again. "Come to bed, and I'll tell you."

The bed did look tempting, and the wind had sucked all of the warmth from the room. It would take the fireplace hours to rewarm it. She hugged herself tighter, her teeth beginning to chatter.

Hugh's smile vanished. "Damn it, I didn't mean to make you freeze. Come to bed!"

She shook her head, her teeth clattering now.

With a muffled curse, he tossed back the sheet and rose. For one glorious instant, the light from the window by the bed highlighted him from head to toe.

Triona couldn't help but appreciate his fine masculine form. He was every nude statue she'd ever seen—

a wide and powerful chest, narrow hips, a flat, rippled stomach, and massive thighs.

She only had one second to look, because he scooped her up and carried her back to his bed, where he tucked her under the sheets and blankets, then climbed in beside her.

Triona closed her eyes, savoring his warmth as he wrapped himself around her.

"Stubborn woman," he muttered as he tucked her back against him, his hand once again cupping her breast, but not so loosely this time.

"Did-did it hurt you?"

"Did what hurt me?" His voice purred lazily.

"Raising the wind."

"No. Trying to make it stop after it's been stirred does, though."

She turned in his arms so she could see his face. They were now chest to chest, Hugh's arms loosely clasped about her waist. "But that's against the legend. If you can control it, it's not really a curse, is it?"

"If I lose my temper, the weather will roar just as it does with my brothers. But if I work hard, sometimes I can stop it. *Sometimes.*"

Something about the somber way he spoke made her ask, "At what cost?"

MacLean placed a warm kiss on her forehead. "That is for me to worry about."

She placed her hands on his chest and pushed him away. "I want to know more. My grandmother was forever telling us about the curse and how it works."

He chuckled, the rumbling noise making his chest vibrate against hers. "You are as curious as a cat."

She touched a finger to his chin. "How long have you known you're able to control your particular ... ability?"

His wolfish grin made her heart sputter. "I've always been able to control my ..." He slipped a hand around her waist and pulled her tight against him so she could feel his erection. "... ability. Would you like a demonstration?"

Triona leaned toward him, savoring the contact and relishing his good humor. "You are very different here, at your house."

"I'm home," he said simply. He cupped her face with a gentle hand and slid it down her neck to her shoulder. "I have a question for you: do you always talk this much in the morning?"

"Do you always touch this much in the morning?" she retorted. His hands had never stilled, stroking her back, her shoulders, down her side, grazing the side of her breasts in a way that made her stomach tighten and kept her from thinking about anything but him.

His eyes twinkled. "Sometimes I do even more." He kissed her cheek, then rubbed his cheek to hers.

There was something so ... interesting about the way his bare legs felt entwined with hers, the way her breasts seemed to tighten and swell as his fingers cupped her.

Her entire body warmed inside and out as restlessness grew within her. This was her husband and their marital bed, and it felt so *right*.

She tentatively trailed her fingers over his hard muscles, down his shoulder to his arm, then across his chest. Emboldened by her own daring and the way MacLean's eyes shimmered with growing passion, she continued.

Touching him excited her as much as being touched. She thrilled at the masculine beauty of his body, at the sensual feel of his skin gliding beneath her fingertips. She watched as her fingers brushed over his hip and then down his thigh.

She suddenly realized he wasn't moving. She glanced into his face and surprised a look of fierce determination. "What's wrong?"

He captured her hand on his thigh. "I must maintain some control, my love; I don't want this to hurt you."

"Hurt?" Her voice squeaked.

"The first time, it can—" He caught her expression and frowned. "Didn't your mother tell you anything?"

"She told me that it would be a pleasure to be with a man I l—" Triona clamped her mouth closed. "She said when the time came, my husband would show me what to do."

Hugh grimaced.

Suddenly feeling deficient, she added hastily, "I've seen animals mate, though, if you're worried I don't know the mechanics."

He looked astounded, then laughed as he kissed first one, then the other of her hands. "I am glad you know those, at least. That makes things easier." His expression softened. "I don't want your first time to be a sad shock, as I've heard it may be uncomfortable."

"Have you ever seduced a virg—"

"No," he said hastily.

"Then who told you that?"

His face grew red. "It doesn't matter."

"Yes, but who would—"

Hugh kissed her to silence the questions that were too awkward to answer, but as soon as his lips touched hers, all thought of anything was gone. She'd been driving him mad since he'd awakened to see her jump out of bed, all slender ankles and volumes of muslin floating about. As she'd moved, the material had caressed portions of her body with agonizing clarity—a long leg, her full breasts, the rounded curve of a hip—only to allow them to fade back into the soft folds. Now, holding her against him, he could feel every inch of her through the night rail, and it was driving him mad.

Oh, how he lusted for her! She was challenge and sweetness and something else he couldn't quite name.

He kissed her, moving from her sweet lips to her neck and then her shoulder. He pushed aside the maddening night rail and nuzzled her neck until she shivered with pleasure.

That was what he wanted! He slipped his thigh

between hers as he moved back to her ear. He found her breast and cupped it gently, rubbing his thumb over the nipple until it peaked and hardened.

There were so many things he longed to do, so many places he yearned to kiss—but now was not the time. He wanted to stir her senses, to raise her passion gently so as not to frighten her. He increased his ministrations, blowing softly on the delicate skin behind her ear. Her movements, growing increasingly restless, made him ache for her anew.

Finally she began to move against his thigh, her breath short, her hands grasping his arms as she strove to pull him closer. She was almost there . . . he could feel it.

Hugh gritted his teeth against his howling lust. He couldn't afford to let it loose, not yet.

He began to tug her night rail up and, to his surprise, she helped him, lifting her hips and yanking the material out of the way. Her face was flushed, her lips moist and swollen from his kisses, her hair tumbled about her in a cascade of curls. To see her so roused and so innocent was the most erotic moment Hugh had ever experienced. He had to rest his damp forehead against hers and halt his galloping imagination. *For her. This has to be for her.*

She writhed against him, her night rail now bunched about her waist, the tight curls between her thighs brushing his leg, damp and urgent.

Hugh positioned himself carefully, her legs opening for him naturally, then lifted up on his elbows so he could see her face. Slowly, inch by inch, he lowered himself into her. She was so tight, so sweet! His body pulsed with need and lust. *Don't frighten her,* he told himself fiercely. He sank deeper, the tight wetness almost undoing him. His body was drenched with sweat, his muscles screaming as he clenched them to hold off the building heat.

He paused as he reached the small barrier, holding himself there. She writhed against him, grasping his shoulders and pulling him. "Hugh!" she gasped. "Please! I want . . ." She locked her legs about his waist, and yanked him deeper inside her.

Her head jerked back and pain briefly flickered over her face. Hugh moved smoothly and quickly, caressing her breasts and kissing her deeply as he increased the tempo until she was gasping, her skin dewy with exertion and flushed a delicate pink.

She was so beautiful—so *his.*

Suddenly she arched, gasping his name and quivering. He shuddered as she tightened around him, stroking him with her heat and wetness. The moment seemed to stretch into infinity, his body aching with pleasure. Finally she stilled, gasping, her arms locked about his neck. Holding her close, he released his control and tumbled over the edge of pleasure after her.


A good deal later, Triona opened her eyes again, wincing a little at the tenderness between her legs. Mingled with that tenderness was a glow of sated passion that made her smile in deep contentment. *So this is what it feels like. No wonder so many poems are written about it!*

Beside her she could feel Hugh's deep, even breath, his arm once again over her, his body completely relaxed as he slept.

She smiled and looked around the room—*her* room now. The bedchamber streamed with sunshine, the rich, jeweled tones of the décor suiting her perfectly—the stream of golden sun as it fell on cobalt blue bed hangings, the bright green and red carpet adorning the floor, and the rich mahogany furniture.

Her favorite piece of furniture was the bed. She smiled again. Lovemaking was a wildly pleasurable affair, and she thought that she and Hugh had done it exceptionally well. The first time had been rather quick, compared to the final two, but she had no complaints other than a deep ache and a bit of stiffness, both of which were oddly pleasant.

She shivered at the memory and carefully extricated herself from the bed, sliding a pillow under Hugh's arm. He shifted slightly, snuggling deeper into the sheets.

He looked so boyish asleep, his lashes enviably long. And this man was her husband. Triona murmured the word "husband" several times, filling her mouth with the taste of it.

Feeling slightly silly, she pulled the covers over him and went to wash in the basin by the bed. To her delight, her clothes had been brought in while they slept and were brushed and pressed and were now hanging neatly in the huge wardrobe. God bless Mrs. Wallis!

Triona dressed, slipped on her boots, then found her spectacles on a small table beside the washbasin. She settled them onto her nose and took stock of her situation. This morning had been an auspicious beginning for her marriage.

She'd lived through the scandal, the wedding, and the trip to Gilmerton, and now she'd conquered her first few hours as mistress. Except for the faint homesickness, she was quite satisfied with her position. All she needed to do was discover how the house was run, so she could carve out a place for herself until it was time to return home.

*Home.* Back at Wythburn, her brothers and sisters would be crowded in the breakfast room, laughing and talking of the day's activities. Her parents would have returned and would know of her marriage, and perhaps be concerned about her. *I should write them a letter today, and one to grandmother letting her know I am here and arranging a visit.* Triona wasn't quite sure where Mam's house was in relation to Gilmerton, but they might be close enough for a day visit.

Feeling better, she glanced about for a desk, wondering where she might find some paper and a pen. Suddenly the skin on the back of her neck prickled and she turned to find Hugh looking at her, sending an immediate thrill through her.

He pushed himself upright, the sheet falling to his waist as he rubbed his face, then yawned. After stretching, he flashed her a sleepy smile. "Good morning, wife. I trust you slept well."

Triona found that she rather liked that title. "Good morning to you, too. I slept like a rock. And you?"

His slow, sensual smile sent a flutter through her stomach that had nothing to do with her hunger.

"Oh, I slept like a rock," he said with rich intimacy. "Because before I went to sleep, you made me as hard as one."

She flashed him a grin, though she suddenly felt all thumbs. She went to the settee where she busied herself with the laces on her half boots. "I know it's early, but I believe it would be beneficial for us to talk about our expectations."

His brows rose, his smile dimming. "Actually, I was going to suggest the same thing, because—" He glanced at the clock. "Good God, it's almost nine!"

"Yes." Her cheeks heated. "We are late rising."

He threw back the bedclothes, crossed immediately to the window, flicked aside the curtain, and looked out. Whatever he saw must have satisfied him, for he gave what sounded like a sigh of relief before going to wash in the basin by his side of the bed.

"Are you expecting someone?"

His dark green gaze flickered her way. "My brother Dougal is returning after breakfast."

"Returning?"

"He was here last night, but you'd already fallen asleep."

"I'm sorry I missed him."

"You'll meet him today. He visits often when his wife is out of town, and she's in Edinburgh for a week or so."

"I look forward to meeting him. Does he look like you?"

"Yes, except he's blond. In each generation, there is always one golden child among us." He tossed his damp hand towel over a rail on the side of the washstand. "I daresay he'll arrive in an hour or so."

MacLean crossed to the wardrobe, comfortable in his nakedness. Triona realized she was staring at her new husband's muscular posterior in an amazingly bold fashion. Cheeks hot, she hastily finished lacing up her half boots, hoping he hadn't noticed.

When she looked up she found, to both her relief and disappointment, that Hugh was nearly dressed. He'd donned brown breeches that tucked neatly into his black riding boots, and was pulling a clean white shirt over his head. A simple cravat hung over the end of the bed.

"Do you not have a valet?" she asked.

"No. I can't stand someone fussing about my things." He tucked in his shirt and slipped the cravat about his neck. With a few flips of the ends and an amazingly quick series of knots, he had it neatly tied. He put on a dark brown waistcoat and pulled a dark blue riding coat from the wardrobe. He caught her gaze. "Do you ride?"

"No. We never had any horses, except two to pull the carriage."

"Ah. We'll have to remedy that."

Triona heard disappointment in his voice. "I've always liked horses, and I would like to learn to ride."

"Good. I'll teach you myself. I ride every day. I must, for I raise horses. That's how I raised the funds to purchase Gilmerton. It took me almost ten years, but I did it. Now I own some of the most productive and coveted herds in Scotland."

Her chest tightened. She'd just been intimate with this man, yet here he was, informing her of the most basic facts about his life. The entire situation was ludicrous and awkward, and yet it was all they had. She forced herself to smile. "What kind of horses do you raise?"

"Beautiful ones. Expensive ones. And rare ones."

She considered this. "Arabians, racehorses, and . . ." She frowned. "What else?"

He chuckled. "That's very good. The rare ones are my herd of Akhal-Teke. They're Turkish horses bred by tribes. I have ten right now, with several mares ready to foal." He went to one of the large windows on the far wall, threw up the sash, and leaned on the sill to peer into the distant fields. "There they are now. The herd comes to the gates in the morning."

Triona came to stand beside him. In the distance, she could see a small herd of horses gathering by a gate. "Why, they're gold!"

He glinted a smile her way. "They are prized for their golden sheen. I saw one in Italy and decided to breed them. They are wonderful horses. They've carried Turkomen warriors for centuries, and are as agile as greyhounds."

Triona watched as a man approached the gate, pushing a wheelbarrow. The horses pranced and pawed. "They seem very hungry."

"As am I." Hugh looked down at her, his gaze raking over her face and then lower.

Triona was both flattered and disappointed in his perusal. She was flattered by his attention, but disappointed because she knew it was nothing more than pure lust. Of course, she wasn't sure she really wanted more than that since his plans for their marriage included shipping her off at the first reasonable moment.

Still, she had a few months in which to leave her mark on Gilmerton Manor and its owner, this incredibly sexy man standing before her. Yet in order to do so, she would need his support. She shot him a look from under her lashes. "Hugh, can we . . ." It was difficult to explain what she wanted, when she wasn't completely certain herself. "It would be nice if we were partners, as well as man and wife."

His expression lost some of its heat. "I'm not sure what you mean."

"Most couples know one another for a time before they decide to wed. We didn't have that luxury. I thought perhaps, to help us ease into this new relationship, we might begin as . . . I suppose I'd call it friends. People who support one another and help and—oh, I'm not saying this at all well."

"I'm not giving up my rights to you in bed."

She blinked up at him. "I didn't think you would. In fact, I rather enjoyed that aspect myself."

A smug, pleased smile tilted his lips. "I know."

Her cheeks warmed, but she managed a pert sniff. "As did you."

"Oh, yes. I enjoyed every delicious moment. So explain to me what you mean about being partners."

"I may only be here for a few months, but I want to learn as much about you as I can, be a part of this estate."

He crossed his arms over his broad chest, one brow arrogantly cocked. "No. We're here to do one thing and one thing only: establish your good name so that you and your family can go about your lives. I wish to do that with as little impact upon our lives as possible."

"I quite agree, but why shouldn't we at least enjoy each other's company?"

His brows rose.

She colored. "I mean, other than in the bed chamber. Why shouldn't I become involved in your business, too? I would like to know about you an—" She caught herself and amended the sentence. "I mean, *your* interests here. I want to see the stables and the horses and—oh, so many things! I want to help in any way I can. That's the way a marriage should work."

"Under normal circumstances, I would agree, but these are not normal circumstances. You will confine yourself to the household and nothing more." His tone brooked no argument.

Triona clenched her hands at her sides and fought a very real urge to begin an argument she was fairly sure they'd both lose. She couldn't shake the feeling that she was missing something, but she didn't even know what to ask.

Blast it, this conversation wasn't going the way she wished! She'd asked to be a part of his everyday life, of the estate and the horses he so obviously admired, and in return he was confining her to the house as if she was a potential nuisance to be contained within the house's four walls. She couldn't address this further without some advice. Fortunately for her, she knew just where to get it.

She forced her hands to unclench. "Fine, we'll discuss this more later. If it's possible, I would like to visit the modiste today to order some gowns, since I brought so few with me. I have a few pounds with me, and—"

"*I* will pay for what you need."

"MacLean, this marriage isn't *real*."

"Caitriona, you are my wife. As such, I have the right and *privilege* of purchasing you anything I please. I'll have Ferguson hook up the carriage after breakfast, and Mrs. Wallis can escort you. I have an account with the modiste, so you may order whatever you like."

Why did he have an account with the modiste? Did he . . . did he have a mistress? Her jaw tightened, and suddenly the last thing she wanted to do was order more gowns.

He turned from the window, adding over his shoulder, "I will be very busy for the next few weeks. As I said, several mares are ready to foal, and my men and I must monitor the herds closely. So while you confine your efforts to the house—"

"Confine?" She plopped her fists on her hips. "I don't know how things were for you, MacLean, but my parents run the vicarage *together*. What Papa can't do, Mother does. And when things are truly busy, like at Michaelmas or if there are many weddings, the whole family helps. I know how to keep accounts and such. I can also—"

"I don't need a partner." His green gaze flickered over her, suddenly cool. "Not even for a month or two."

She sucked in her breath. *I shouldn't be hurt. He's only reminding me of our situation, and I need to remember that.*

His expression softened. "I'm not an unreasonable man, Caitriona. I daresay there are many things that could use improvement in the house and elsewhere. The servants have had their way for a long time."

"Thank you so much," she replied sarcastically.

"You're welcome." He sent her a hard look from under his lashes. "There is one important matter we must discuss. While you have carte blanche inside these four walls, you will not interfere with my daugh—"

There was the sound of feet running up the steps, as if a herd of wild boar had been let into the house.

"What's tha—" Triona began.

The door flew open and three children appeared.

A thin young girl of fifteen or so entered first. She had lank blond hair tied back in a tight bun, her face wreathed in smiles until she saw Triona. Then she came to an abrupt halt. Hard on her heels was a younger girl, probably thirteen years of age, of astounding beauty with black hair and thick black lashes around eyes of the darkest brown. She was moving so quickly that she narrowly avoided running into the older girl. Holding her hand, eyes wide, blond curls framing her round face, was a little girl of no more then six.

The three looked at Triona with shocked expressions that Triona was sure were mirrored on her own face.

Then the girls looked past her and they all brightened, smiles blooming once again on their faces. "Papa!" they yelled as they ran forward, swarming Hugh with hugs and kisses.

# Chapter 11

❧

*"Och, lassies. Ye canna know the power o' yer own anger till 'tis burnin' in yer veins."*

OLD WOMAN NORA TO HER THREE WEE
GRANDDAUGHTERS ON A COLD WINTER'S NIGHT

*D*ougal followed his brother into the library. "You should have told her!"

Hugh scowled as Dougal found the most comfortable chair and claimed it. "I was in the process of doing just that when the girls came in. I thought you were going to keep them until after breakfast."

"I did! You're lucky I made them wait as long as I did, for once they knew you were home, they kept begging and begging." Dougal grimaced. "I was glad to return them."

Hugh sighed and rubbed his neck, dropping into the chair opposite Dougal. "Bloody hell. What a mess."

"I'm surprised you weren't already up. It was well past nine, so I thought I'd given you plenty of time—" Dougal's gaze narrowed on Hugh's red face. "Ah, yes. Newlyweds. How could I have forgotten? I take it you were both decent when the children burst in?"

"Barely."

Dougal grimaced. "I'm sorry. I just didn't think."

"If I'd had just ten more minutes to explain things to Caitriona, all would have been well." At least, he thought so. To be honest, their conversation hadn't been going the way he wanted it to before the girls had arrived.

He was beginning to worry that marriage—even this one—was more difficult than he'd suspected.

"What did your new wife say when she met the children?"

"Not much. She was silent throughout breakfast." Although she'd shot him an amazing number of dagger glances.

"And the girls?"

"They were just as quiet, but sulky." Hugh rubbed his face with both hands. "Damn it, everyone is unhappy now! I should have said something to Caitriona earlier, but I was so bloody tied up trying to explain my expectations for our marriage that I put off mentioning the girls. And I didn't even think that I should inform *them* about Caitriona, or how they'd react upon finding her here with no idea that I'd married." Hugh leaned his head against the back of his chair and closed his eyes. "Bloody hell, I've made a mess of things."

"Yes, you have."

Hugh glared. "I thought you were here to help."

"Me? I'm just hoping Sophie doesn't blame me for this mess. She has a tendency to think things are my fault even when they clearly aren't."

"We can talk about your marital troubles another time; I have enough of my own to worry about right now." Hugh grimaced. "I just didn't think they'd care so much. Females are such a pain! Dougal, if *you* had been forced into marriage and brought home your new wife, *I* wouldn't be upset. I'd welcome her into the house and do what was proper. Whatever happened after that would be between the two of you, and I couldn't care less, for that's the way men do things. But women . . ." He shook his head.

"Oh, they're very different. I don't care if you forget my birthday; I barely remember it myself. But Sophia never forgets it. And if I ever forgot hers?" Dougal shuddered. "I'd rather be tarred and feathered."

Hugh nodded absently. Damn it all—and things had begun so promisingly this morning! He wished he were back in bed now, wrapped around Caitriona. He'd been surprised by how delightfully responsive she'd been, how uninhibited. Imagining how bold she'd be in a few weeks, once she was more used to the marriage bed, made his heart thunder in his ears and—

"You aren't *listening*."

Hugh pulled his attention back to his brother. "I'm sorry. Did you say something?"

Dougal scowled. "I said that perhaps you should start with an apology."

"For what? I was going to tell her; I just didn't have time."

Dougal lifted his brows.

Hugh sighed. "You're right; I will apologize."

"What will you tell the girls?"

"The truth. They're even angrier than Caitriona, and—"

Dougal suddenly straightened, his gaze going past Hugh.

Slowly, Hugh turned. Standing just inside the door were his daughters.

Christina pinned him with her no-nonsense gaze. "Father, we'd like a word with you."

Dougal stood. "Perhaps I'd better—"

"Sit," Hugh ordered.

Dougal paused, his gaze flickering to the girls. Whatever he saw there seemed to decide him, for he resumed his seat.

Hugh faced his daughters. "I'm glad you're here; I wish to speak with you, too."

The girls exchanged glances. Then Christina nodded and went to sit on the end of the settee; Devon sat on the other. Aggie sat in the middle as they all three fixed their solemn gazes on Hugh.

"Well?" Devon asked, her dark eyes sharp.

"You didn't say anything about getting married when you left!" Christina charged.

"I didn't intend to get married. It was as much of a surprise to me and Caitriona as anyone."

Christina and Devon exchanged incredulous glances.

Hugh sighed. "Here's what happened. A young lady was attempting to trick your uncle Alexander into marriage, which is why I went to London. Unknown to me, Caitriona had also traveled to London for the same purpose."

Christina's gaze narrowed. "How did she know about it?"

"They are sisters."

"Aha!" Devon said, as if that proved something.

Hugh frowned at her. "There is no 'aha.' By *accident,* Caitriona and I ended up falling into the trap her sister had planned for Alexander, and we were forced to marry."

"How could anyone *force* you to do anything?" Devon asked in an incredulous voice. "You are even bigger than Uncle Alexander!"

Dougal smothered a laugh.

"Because of my rash actions, Caitriona's reputation was ruined. I had to marry her, or she and her family would have paid a very steep price."

Devon shook her head impatiently. "I'm sure that if you'd wished to, you could have gotten out of it."

"As a man of honor, I could do no less than I did," he said sharply. "Surely you wouldn't have me behave otherwise."

Devon's cheeks burned at his rebuke, her mouth tightening.

Christina said, "Of course not. If you say you had no choice, then we believe you."

"But we don't want her here!" Devon burst out.

Aggie, clearly feeling left out, nodded violently. "We don't need a mother!"

"We were perfectly happy the way we were, with just you," Christina said.

Hugh made an impatient gesture. "Sometimes life makes decisions for us. This is one of those times, and we must make the best of it."

Christina stiffened. "I will not treat that woman like a mother."

"No one asked you to," Hugh said, scowling. "But you *will* be polite to her for the short time she'll be with us."

Devon's gaze locked on to Hugh's face. "Short time? She won't be staying?"

"Only a couple of months, and then she'll return to her home. Meanwhile, you three will be polite. And no tricks, either. *None.* Am I making myself clear?"

Devon and Christina looked mulish.

Hugh's brows lowered. "Christina?"

She sighed. "Yes, Papa. I will be polite."

"Thank you." He glanced at Devon and Aggie. "You, too."

Devon mumbled, "Yes, Papa."

Aggie pushed out her bottom lip, but nodded.

"Good. Whether you like it or not, Caitriona is my wife and will be treated with respect. She will act as such during her time here, and will oversee the household."

Devon blinked. "But . . . Christina and I were doing that!"

"Now you'll have some help." Hugh looked at Dougal. "Perhaps the girls will have more time for their studies."

Dougal nodded, smiling a bit. "I'm sure they'll enjoy that. I suggest they learn Latin, as well as their Greek."

"Latin?" Devon squeaked.

Christina crossed her arms over her thin chest. "I don't wish to learn Latin!"

"Me neither!" Devon added.

Hugh ignored them. "Our lives will not be any different just because I married. In a few months, we won't even remember she was here."

"Do you promise?" Devon asked.

"I promise," Hugh said solemnly. "Have I ever broken a promise to you?"

Finally, Devon nodded. "All right, then."

Christina said, "We were just worried that it would be like when Mother—" Her gaze lowered to the floor, her expression strained.

"Though I have known Caitriona for a short time only, I know for a fact she is honorable. You can trust me on that."

Aggie asked, "What do we call her?"

"We are *not* calling her Mother," Devon said.

"You will call her 'my lady,' as is proper," Hugh said. "Now, stop looking like the three deaths! It's a beautiful day and we could be out riding, not sitting here moping about something we can't change." He looked at Aggie. "Are you ready to ride?"

She looked down at her morning dress and then back at him, astonished. "I don't have on my riding habit or boots or *anything*!"

He laughed. "I missed that completely. I hope your pony hasn't forgotten how to trot while I was gone."

Aggie grinned, showing a missing tooth. "I will ride *fast!*"

"Only if one of your sisters is leading."

"*And,*" Dougal added with a severe look, "you won't attempt a hedge."

Hugh frowned at his youngest daughter. "When did you attempt to jump a hedge?"

Aggie smiled sweetly. "I *might* have tried it when you were away."

"The next time you try something like that without proper instruction, it will be a month before you're allowed to ride again. You could break your neck doing such a foolish thing."

Aggie's smile dimmed. "Yes, Papa."

"Good girl. Now, I'm going to the stables. Change your clothes and meet me there. I need to ride through the herds, and you three may help me."

They came to him for a hug. Hugh gathered them to him, breathing in their sweet scent of soap, soaking in their presence.

Something tight inside of him released a little. His heart ached with the sudden infusion of warmth, and he couldn't imagine loving them more.

Dougal looked away, his eyes bright with unshed tears.

Finally, Hugh cleared his throat and kissed each of his daughters on her forehead. "Hurry and change."

"Yes, Papa." Christina took Aggie's hand and, with Devon trailing, left the sitting room.

As soon as the door closed, Dougal said, "They love you very much."

And he loved them. His life was divided into two parts; the time before the girls came to him and the time after. He barely remembered the time before. He'd enjoyed life, and always had. But now, when he awoke in the morning, it wasn't with the fuzzy uncertainty of whose bed he might be, but with a sense of peace and warmth and the knowledge that three very special smiles would be waiting on him over the breakfast table.

Those smiles made his day worthwhile.

Of course, in the beginning, it had been difficult for them all. It had taken time to get used to one another, to find the love that had gradually developed. The girls hadn't been willing to trust him at first, and he hadn't realized how special they would become. Over the past year, though, they'd carefully crafted their small family and he prized it above all else. He looked at Dougal and said simply, "They are my life."

"That's good . . . to a point."

He frowned. "What do you mean?"

"Hugh, you can't protect them from every little change life is going to throw their way."

"I can try."

"Then you'll fail." Dougal leaned forward, his expression earnest. "You must be careful what you promise the girls. They count on you. You can't protect them from everything, nor can you promise that nothing will change now that Caitriona has arrived. You're married; things are bound to change. That's just natural."

Hugh shook his head. "I will not allow anyone to set the household on its ear. The children need constancy. They've had so little."

"I hope your wife agrees to that."

"If she doesn't, then I will train her." He flicked a smile at Dougal. "Just as I would one of my prize horses. I will calmly state my wishes, and if she shies, I will firmly hold her in place. Soon she will understand who is in charge."

Dougal shifted uneasily. Last night, with the haze of surprise and port, his advice had seemed masterful. In the bright light of day, he wasn't so sure it could be called masterful. He wasn't even sure he would call it advice anymore, but rather a mistake. "Hugh, I don't remember exactly what I said last night, but you can't train a wife like a horse."

"Why not?"

"Because it's not done! And because it's wrong somehow, and . . ."

"Why is it wrong?"

Dougal wished with all his heart that Sophia were here to answer Hugh's questions. "I should have found a better way to explain myself. If she finds out—"

"Dougal, I'm not a fool; I won't tell her that's what I'm doing."

"She won't like being told what to do."

"Caitriona and I barely know each other, so I'm sure we'll get upset with one another over many things. But she'll be leaving soon." He shrugged.

"It doesn't work like that."

"It will for me." He'd make sure it did. Hugh remembered her sweetness this morning, and the way she'd put herself at risk to save her sister. Caitriona was nothing like the girls' mother; Clarissa was a cold, selfish creature.

Dougal rubbed his forehead. "I wish I'd never mentioned horses. Damn your port! My head still aches and I only had two glasses. Hugh . . ."

Dougal frowned as if searching for words, which surprised Hugh. His younger brother was known for his verbal deftness, if nothing else.

"Hugh, what if Caitriona is something more than you realize? What if she's *meant* to be in your and the girls' life?"

"Nonsense. We were perfectly fine before she arrived. Christina rarely has night terrors anymore, and Aggie has stopped wetting the bed. Devon isn't as thin, either. They are all healing."

"That doesn't mean there's no room for improvement. Caitriona might be good for the lot of you."

Hugh stood, suddenly restless, and strode to the window. The winter sunlight warmed the grass on which horses grazed contentedly, and glinted off the deep brook that wandered through the rolling hills.

The sight soothed him, as it always did. Everything was as it should be, and he would not give that up.

*Ever.* When he thought back to the dark terrors of a year ago— He closed his eyes. *Dougal doesn't understand because he doesn't know the entire truth. Perhaps it's time I told him.*

Taking a deep breath, he turned back to his brother. "Have the girls ever talked to you about their lives before they came here?"

Dougal shook his head.

"Clarissa dragged them through places no child should see, and left them for days at a time in tiny, rented hovels with little or nothing to eat. They went without heat in the cold, and without water in sweltering summers. She took them from dirty rooming houses to crumbling, moldy palaces to decrepit country estates, among people no child should associate with. Depending on whomever Clarissa was whoring herself out to at the time, they were shunned, hidden, or put on display like ponies."

Dougal's expression grew grim.

"They were in danger constantly, rarely had enough food, and were reduced to the lowest form of subsistence." Hugh ground his teeth. "I treat my horses better than Clarissa treated those girls."

Dougal nodded mutely.

"When they first arrived, Devon would hoard food beneath her bed. She still does, though less each month. Christina could neither read nor write, and the smallest quick movement made her jump as if she expected to be struck. I don't think Aggie had ever had a bath, for she screamed bloody murder when Mrs.

Wallis and the upstairs maid put her in a tub. They were thin, scarred, and bruised from head to toe." The lines about Hugh's mouth were white. "When they came here, I promised them that their days of uncertainty were over. We have adhered to a very simple schedule, a simple life, and they have blossomed."

Dougal's expression softened. "They love it here, and they love you. But I still feel that Caitriona might add something."

"I provide everything the girls need."

"Except a mother. They need a woman in their lives," Dougal said gently. "All girls do. Hell, all men do, too."

Hugh's jaw tightened. "They had a mother and she brought nothing but pain. My children come first, and always will." Outside, a carriage pulled up to the front door. "There is Caitriona now. She went to town after breakfast with Mrs. Wallis to purchase a few things."

Dougal sighed heavily. He'd known the girls had come from a bad life, but he'd never known the details. But then, that was Hugh; he'd always played things close to the vest. In public he was pleasant and jovial, but he never allowed anyone truly close to him. Until the girls had arrived—then things had changed.

Damn it all, something was lacking from Hugh's argument, but he couldn't quite put a finger on it. Dougal finally shrugged. "You'll do as you think best."

"Yes, I will." Hugh tamped down his irritation. Dougal was trying to help, however misguided his attempt. There were times when it was onerous to have so many family members living so close by.

A soft knock sounded on the door, and Caitriona entered, her cheeks pink from her journey to town, her dark gold hair wisping about her cheeks from pulling off her bonnet.

Dougal rose from his chair, and Caitriona's eyes widened behind her spectacles. "I beg your pardon. I didn't mean to intrude."

"You didn't intrude," Hugh said, and introduced them to one another.

Dougal bowed with his customary grace. "A pleasure to meet you. Welcome to the family."

She dipped a curtsey. "Thank you." Her gaze went to Dougal's gold hair, and she slanted a questioning glance at Hugh, who grinned.

"I know, he looks nothing like me."

"Actually, except for his hair, he looks *exactly* like you."

Dougal chuckled. "We may look alike, but I am definitely the better dresser. If you can get my loutish brother to improve his wardrobe, the entire family will be forever in your debt."

Caitriona's eyes twinkled. "I will see what can be done."

"Isn't it time you were leaving?" Hugh asked his brother pointedly.

"I suppose so." Dougal smoothed his sleeve, watching his new sister-in-law from beneath his lashes. She was not at all Hugh's usual sort. She was quite tall, and a bit plump, too. But her hair was shiny and dark gold, her skin milky white, her lips plump and red, and her eyes were an amazing shade of hazel behind those spectacles. Best of all, her expression spoke of calm good sense and a great deal of spirit. This was not a woman to be trifled with.

Dougal smiled. He had the feeling it would be an interesting few months. He took his sister-in-law's hand and pressed a kiss to her fingers. "I must take my leave of you now, but I shall return soon and tell you all of the family secrets."

She laughed and curtsied, rather liking this suave member of the MacLean family. "I'll have pen and ink ready to take notes. I'm sorry you must go. Do you live nearby?"

"Less than a mile down the road. My wife, Sophia, is in Edinburgh this week with her father, but will be most happy to receive you once she returns."

"So you are alone in your house? You must come to dinner! Hugh, tell him he must come."

Hugh snorted. "I will do no such thing. He comes to visit me far too often as it is."

Dougal grinned. "I shall return for dinner. Thank you, my lady." He bowed and headed for the door.

The door closed behind him.

His expression inscrutable, Hugh said, "Caitriona, I should have told you about the girls sooner. It was just awkward and I . . ." He grimaced. "I am truly sorry."

Triona hadn't expected that. After a moment, she said calmly, "I can imagine it would be a difficult topic to work into a conversation, especially as we've had so few."

"I was just making my grand announcement when they arrived home sooner than I expected." He hesitated. "I should have told you much earlier, but I wanted to wait until we were here, where we had some privacy and you weren't so exhausted. It's a lot to take in."

She gave him a cool look. "If you'd told me you had daughters, I would simply have asked to meet them."

His dark gaze remained locked on her for a long moment. Then, with a stiff bow, he said, "As I said, I'm sorry. There will be no more secrets between us."

"Thank you. I can see we need to spend more time getting to know one another. We lack trust, and that is lamentable."

"If it will help us avoid more difficult moments, I'm quite willing to do so. In fact—" He stepped forward and took her hand, his fingers warm over hers, and led her to the soft settee. Then he grabbed a nearby chair, placed it in front of her, and sat down, his knees almost brushing hers. "We should finish the conversation that was so abruptly interrupted this morning."

"I would rather talk about the girls. I don't know anything about them."

"They are my daughters. What more do you need to know?"

Triona placed her hands on her knees and leaned forward. "MacLean, if this is your idea of a conversation, then we're going to have many, many difficult moments."

He looked disposed to argue, but after a moment he sighed. "What do you wish to know?"

"Whatever you can tell me. They're lovely girls. I thought they were very well behaved at breakfast, though quiet."

"They were surprised."

"As was I. I'm sure that once they become used to having me about, they will warm to me. As their step-mother, I'll try to—"

"No."

She frowned. "No, *what*?"

"I don't consider you their stepmother. I'm very sure they wouldn't want that, either."

"But—"

"Our marriage is unusual."

"So? What does that have to do with the children?"

"With *my* children."

Her heart sank. It felt as if she stood in front of a huge door, but had no key. How could she get inside?

Worse, another thought reared its ugly head. MacLean had had three children over a number of years, and all had the same mother. He must have cared for this woman. There was only one way to find out. "Did you love her?"

His brows snapped down. "Did I love—oh. Their mother. I once thought I did, but no more."

His answer was so quick and natural that Triona relaxed. "I see. Is she . . . is she still alive?"

"Yes." He spat the answer. "When I was a callow

youth, I was captivated by her. But she is not a good woman. For years, the girls lived with Clarissa. As her life disintegrated, so did theirs. Until they came to live with me a year ago, they didn't know the meaning of the word 'home.' They'd never had one."

How difficult that must have been for them! Triona tried to imagine how her life would be without the familiar comfort of the vicarage, and couldn't. "Perhaps I can help—"

"*No.*"

She blinked at the harshness of his voice.

"Caitriona, you won't be staying more than a few months."

"Yes, but—"

"There are no 'buts.' It would make more sense— and be easier on the girls—if you kept your distance. I don't wish them to be upset when you leave."

Every word he said shut her out even more. This morning, she'd thought their lovemaking had signified something, that they were beginning life together as a couple, even if only for a few months' duration. Now she realized that what happened in the bedchamber was not necessarily reflected out of it.

Still, she couldn't fault him for wanting to protect his children. Though a sense of loneliness settled about her, she managed to say, "The children come first, of course."

"Thank you." He leaned back in his chair, some of the determination leaving his face. "It shouldn't be too difficult. You will see the girls at meals, but they will be with their governess and tutor most of the morning, and with me most of each afternoon."

She looked down at her hands, clasped in her lap. "Where is the girls' mother now?"

His gaze shuttered and white lines appeared down each side of his mouth. "You are determined to know it all, are you? I don't see how this will help, but her name is Clarissa Beaufort. She is the daughter of an obscure Irish baron. She is astonishingly beautiful; Devon will look just like her, I think. Clarissa was her father's only child and he raised her to think she was better than anyone, though the truth is far different. She uses her beauty to—" His lip curled, and it was with obvious difficulty that he continued, "No matter how horrid her behavior, or how inexcusable her actions, men flock to her in droves, and she welcomes them all."

"I see," Triona said softly.

"Years ago, Clarissa was launched into London society to great fanfare. She was courted by dukes, earls, even princes—at some time or another, every eligible man in London sat at her feet. That's when I met her. I thought we were . . ." He shook his head. "Needless to say, I was wrong."

"You cared and she didn't."

"I cared as much as a callow youth of eighteen can. Meanwhile, her father was ecstatic over her success and imagined her marriage would make the family's fortune. He didn't realize that Clarissa had no intention of marrying anyone; she was addicted to attention. As soon as she'd won one man's affections, she was off to the next. I was merely part of her court—a foolish boy whom she no doubt scoffed at, though I was too young to realize it. Fortunately, before I'd made too much of a fool of myself, I realized which way the wind blew and left town. A week later, she was caught with a footman in her carriage, and neither were clothed."

"Oh!"

"Worse, she was caught by the Duke of Richmond, who had come to propose. He told the world, and she was shunned. Her father was devastated and threw her out into the street. I don't believe he ever spoke to her again."

"What happened to her?"

"Oh, don't feel sorry for her; she always manages to land on her feet. She took up with a wealthy older man. When she'd used him up, she found another. And another."

"At least she was consistent," Triona said dryly.

MacLean managed a faint smile. "She was. But she chose a horrible, degrading way of life, and took the girls with her. They have been through—" His voice broke and he turned away, his eyes suspiciously bright. "They have been through enough."

Triona tucked away her own hurt. This situation was obviously deeper and far more complex than she'd realized. "You love your daughters, and they obviously love you. That's all I really need to know."

"Then you will do as I ask, and leave them be as much as possible?"

Triona thought of her parents' warm regard, of the teasing affection of her brothers and sisters, and her throat tightened. "I will do what I can."

The entire situation added to the swell of loneliness she'd been battling all morning. Suddenly, Gilmerton Manor seemed large and echoingly empty.

Some of her feelings must have shown, for Hugh leaned forward and took her hand in his large one. "You will have plenty to keep you occupied. Mrs. Wallis can instruct you in how things have been done, and I've no doubt you'll bring massive improvements to the place."

Which was something a normal wife *would* do. But a normal wife would also be welcome in all areas of her new household, not just the linen closet. Still, it was a beginning, a foothold on the first slope of a very tall mountain.

Fortunately for all concerned, Triona was very, very good at accomplishing tasks, even mountainous ones. While she was glad to spend some time organizing the staff and making the house run as efficiently as possible, she had another goal as well. She wanted her time here at Gilmerton to have value. When the time came to leave, she wanted to have been important enough that Hugh, at least, would miss her.

She regarded him from beneath her lashes. Could she engage his interest enough? It seemed a fair challenge, and heaven knew she needed something to occupy her so she didn't grow dismally homesick. The only real connection she had with this intriguing man had been between the sheets this morning. That, and the moments immediately afterward, had left her feeling close to him.

She couldn't allow him to regulate her out of all of the important affairs of the household, and yet neither did she feel that she could demand that right. It was obvious he loved his daughters very much and she could hardly fault him for such praiseworthy emotion. She'd have to earn his trust, win him over through her efforts, *prove* herself. Father had always said one action was worth a thousand words.

She smoothed her skirt over her knees. "I will do as you ask and remain aloof from the girls as much as possible, but I want a promise from you in return."

He frowned. "What's that?"

"I want us to continue to . . ." Her cheeks heated and she finished in a hurried voice, "Do what we did this morning."

A gleam entered his eyes and a slow smile curled across his face. "Ah, this morning. Yes."

"Yes?"

He laughed. "I should have said 'Of course!' " He stood and placed a finger under her chin, tilting her face to his, then bent close, his breath brushing sweetly over her lips. Triona closed her eyes for his kiss, eager to be swept away. Instead, he moved and whispered in her ear, "You will never lack for more of 'this morning.' " He rubbed his cheek to hers. "I promise."

Heat flooded through her and she instinctively leaned toward him, but he was already straightening.

He winked. "I will return for dinner, and we will resume our conversation then. Who knows?" He flashed a wicked grin. "We might even have some 'this morning' this very evening."

"You can do that?"

His laugh wrapped around her, and for a moment she forgot she was in a strange new house, filled with people from whom she was to maintain a distance, and servants she barely knew. Instead, for one warm, wonderful moment, it was the two of them, both smiling. It brought back instant memories of this morning, of the intimacy of lying in his arms, their bare legs entwined as their hearts slowed to a normal rhythm.

Oh, how she would like to savor that moment again! Her body tingled as a low thrum of excitement washed over her. She smiled back at him. "I shall look forward to it."

His eyes glinted, and for an instant, she thought he might pull her to him for a passionate kiss, but he turned toward the door. "I need to see to the horses. If you need anything, ask the housekeeper; I've left instructions you are to be granted whatever you wish."

"Thank you, but . . . when will you be back?"

He tossed her a warm glance. "As soon as I can."

"It's very difficult to plan dinner when you give out times like that."

He laughed and opened the door. "Very well, wife. I'll be home by six."

He left, closing the door behind him. She heard him collect his coat from the footman, followed by the swing of the front door as it opened. His riding boots marked his stride down the marble steps.

She raced to the window, pushing back the curtains carefully so she wouldn't attract his attention. She watched him walk down the path toward the stables until she could see him no more. Then she collapsed in the nearest chair, tingling all over at her own audacity.

Smiling to herself, she said aloud, "Just you wait, Hugh MacLean!" He might say he wanted her to stay out of his life, but he was wrong. She would win her position as wife both in his bed and out. She was a Hurst, by God, and Hursts never quit.

Yet Triona knew she needed help. And she knew exactly where to find it. She hopped up and swept out into the hallway to ask for pen and paper.

# Chapter 12

*"Och, 'tis kind o' yer father to send ye here each Michael-mas. It does me old heart good to bask in the light of such bonny lassies!"*

OLD WOMAN NORA TO HER THREE WEE
GRANDDAUGHTERS ON A COLD WINTER'S NIGHT

*I* thought Papa said she'd only be here a few days," Devon said disgustedly. Dressed in her chemise, she threw herself on her bed and stared up at the ceiling.

Christina pulled off her riding boots. "He said a couple of months, and it's only been one week."

Devon rolled over onto her stomach, her brow low-ered. "He was very quiet this afternoon during our ride."

"He barely smiled," Aggie agreed. "Until *she* came into the barn."

*She* was what they'd taken to calling Caitriona. "My lady" stuck in Christina's throat and wouldn't be uttered.

"He has a lot on his mind," Devon said darkly. After

a long moment, she added in a pugnacious voice, "I don't like her."

Christina shot Devon an annoyed glance. "Papa is the one who has to like her, not us."

Aggie sat on a stool, dressed in a round gown of blue that set off her eyes, her sapphire blue riding habit on a chair waiting for the maid to take it to be cleaned. She held a handful of hairpins and a brush as she waited for Christina to fix her hair. "She's been nice to us."

She had indeed been nice to them, but distant. Christina had expected that, of course. *She* was only interested in Papa, and couldn't care less about them.

Just like Mother.

Christina's stomach tightened.

Aggie, blissfully unaware, added, "Papa likes her more than he says. She is rather pretty."

Devon rolled to her side to stare at Aggie. "You can't mean that!"

"She has a nice smile," Aggie insisted.

"She wears *spectacles,*" Devon said with disgust.

"Yes, but her hair is very long and smooth." Aggie touched her own curls and said in a wistful tone, "I wish my hair was smooth like that."

"Well, *I* think she's dreadfully plain," Christina said. "I didn't get a good feeling from her at all."

"Me neither," Devon said, planting her elbow on the bed and resting her chin in her palm. "I think she tricked Papa into marrying her."

"I thought that was rather fishy myself." Christina combed out Aggie's hair. "I think Papa was taken advantage of."

"So do I," Aggie added, though it was obvious she was just trying to be included.

Christina looked across Aggie's head to meet Devon's gaze. "I wish there was something we could do to help Papa. She seems to be making herself at home."

Devon's expression darkened. "She's won over Mrs. Wallis, Liam, and Angus, as well as Annie and Moira."

"*Both* maids?" Christina asked.

Devon nodded. "This morning, Cook said she thought the 'new missus' was a right one."

This was much worse than Christina had thought.

"She has made the house nicer," Aggie said. "We've had better meals and the house is cleaner, and—"

"It was running fine when Devon and I were helping Mrs. Wallis," Christina said hotly. Although, Mrs. Wallis hadn't really allowed Christina and Devon to do more than select the menus. Still, it hurt a little that Mrs. Wallis and the servants seemed happy Caitriona was here. Christina was the oldest; shouldn't she have been running the house the way Caitriona was doing it now?

But even worse than the servants' defections, Papa was beginning to look at his new wife differently. The first few days, he'd been kind and pleasant. But lately there was a light in his eyes when he came home, which scared Christina very, very much. Mother used to get like that, too. She'd find a man and get that same look, and then she'd disappear. It would be days, sometimes weeks before she'd return. Christina had to breathe through her nose very slowly to keep the others from seeing how frightened she was.

Devon sat up, propped her elbow on her knee, and rested her chin in her hand. "That old witch tricked him."

Aggie's eyes widened. "She's a *witch*?"

"The worst kind," Devon said. "The kind who lures men away from their families—"

"Like us?" Aggie asked breathlessly.

"Like us," Devon said firmly. "Witches like her trick hapless men into marrying them."

Aggie's lips trembled. "But we just *got* Papa. We can't lose him now!"

Christina hugged her little sisters. "Don't worry, Aggie. We'll find a way to help Papa."

"Yes, we will," Devon said. "I just wish we could think of some way to—" She blinked. Then blinked again.

"What is it?" Christina asked. "You have an idea?"

"Oh, yes. A very good idea. One that will show Papa that *she* isn't who he thinks she is."

"Tell us!" Christina finished braiding Aggie's long hair, then twisted it into a neat, low bun.

"Papa has promised us that nothing will change, so I think he'd be very mad if she changed more than he wants her to."

Christina placed the final pin in Aggie's hair and stepped back to look at her work. "There you are, dear. Now, find that pretty sapphire hairpin Aunt Sophia gave you, and we'll pin it on." As Aggie scooted off the bench, Christina came to sit beside Devon on the bed. "I don't see how that will help us."

"If he gets mad enough, don't you think he might make her leave *early*?"

Which would give Papa less time to fall in love, as Christina feared he might. "I'd like that. Then we'd be back the way we were, just Papa and us."

Aggie, digging through a small jewelry box, glanced at them. "I don't understand, Devon. What's your plan?"

"Easy. We'll wait and see what she plans on doing to the house, and we just make it worse. Papa will grow tired of things always being wrong, and he'll tell her to leave."

Aggie grinned. "We can do that!"

"I don't know," Christina said, worry in her tone. "It doesn't really seem . . . fair."

"Was it fair that she trapped Papa into a marriage he didn't want?" Devon demanded.

"No."

"Then she is just getting what she deserves. Besides, the longer she stays, the more likely he will fall in love—and you know what *that* means."

Christina knew exactly what that meant. Every time Mother had disappeared, she'd been "in love." "I suppose you're right."

"Of course I am," Devon said. "We will just have to watch for our opportunity."

"Here it is." Aggie held out a beautiful sapphire hairpin.

Christina rose from the bed and fixed the pin at Aggie's temple. "There you go!" She winked and affected a droll, high-society tone. "My dear Miss Agatha, you look divine! Like a princess!"

Aggie giggled and threw her arms around Christina's neck. Christina hugged her sister fiercely. She remembered all too well the damp rooms and moldy bread of the old days, remembered hiding behind a locked door in a squalid boardinghouse while people screamed or fought or cursed or did worse. She remembered the hours she'd prayed for Mother to come home, hoping against hope that if she wasn't sober, she'd stay gone.

Guilt clutched at Christina's heart. She wasn't a very good daughter to feel so about her own mother, and she knew it. Especially when Papa had explained that Mother was ill and had made so many bad choices because of it. A good daughter would love her mother no matter what. Christina bit her lip as she hugged Aggie tighter.

Devon was right; they needed to get rid of Papa's new wife. It would be a betrayal of the worst kind if they allowed anyone to harm Papa after he'd made such a safe home for them. That was a debt that could never be repaid.

"Ow!" Aggie squirmed. "Stop hugging me; I can't breathe!"

Christina released Aggie. "I'm sorry. I was thinking about something else." She turned to Devon. "All
right. How do you suggest we begin?"

The butler held a large silver tray with two letters in the
center. "These arrived while you were out, madam."

Nora Hurst scowled. "Och, McNair! Why do ye
always use the silver tray fer two wee letters?" She
tossed her sewing into the basket at her elbow. " 'Tis
pretentious!"

"Yes, madam." McNair's stoic expression nonetheless managed to convey a long-standing adherence to
the proper manner, regardless of his mistress's views
on the subject.

Nora looked at the portrait over the mantel and
her expression softened. "John dinna put up wi' such
nonsense, and neither will I."

The butler's gaze followed hers, and for an instant
their expressions were remarkably similar, tender and
sad. "No, madam. He wouldn't." McNair set the tray
to one side and picked up the letters, then held them
out to his mistress. "Is this better, madam?"

Her thin cheeks folded with deep wrinkles as she
grinned. "Much better, ye scamp. Thank ye, McNair."
She plucked the letters from his hand with fingers
gnarled with age. "Why, they're from Triona and Caitlyn! Letters from me favorite granddaughters on th'
same day—'tis a good sign!"

McNair watched her fondly as she opened the first

letter. Forty years ago, Mr. John Hurst, the wealthiest man in the entire county, and related to half of the earls and dukes in all of Scotland, had shocked the entire countryside by marrying a commoner. At twenty-five, the woman was a full score of years his junior and possessed no fortune, no beauty, and very little formal education. It was even rumored that when she came to live at Hurst Hall, Mr. Hurst spent the first six months of their marriage teaching his new lady how to read.

Even before her marriage to John Hurst, Nora Macdonald was known for two things: her healing abilities and her hypnotic charm over the opposite sex.

There was something about Nora that drew men to her like flies, which was why by the time she married her beloved John, Nora had been married and widowed three times. This led to rumors of poisonings, even though two of her previous husbands had died in mining accidents, and the last one had been thrown from his horse and had broken his neck in full view of the village.

Still, there was a collective murmur of disapproval when Mr. Hurst married his Nora and took her off to live on the hill that held the jewel that was Hurst Hall. Upper and lower classes alike were offended at his marrying one of the commonest of the common, but none more so than his staff.

It is an odd truth that servants who work within the upper echelon of society tend to be snobbier and more sensitive to social position than their masters.

The seating order in servant dining rooms was often more hotly disputed than the succession to many a throne. So it had taken a while for their bluff and jovial new mistress to take with the servants. But over the years she had won their grudging respect, and finally their affection and undying loyalty.

Mr. Hurst called her his prized lass, and took great delight when Nora displayed not only an uncanny ability to heal the ill but a shrewd business sense as well. It was through her shrewd management that his lordship's mills had prospered even during the difficult years after his lordship's death.

One could say what one wished about her unfortunate beginnings and rough way of speaking, but though she brought neither wealth nor position to their marriage, no one could say that she didn't make the man blissfully happy all their days together.

As expected, Mr. Hurst left his entire properties and fortune to her, and she was as careful with his fortune now as she had been when he was alive. To no one's surprise, she continued to run the house so tightly that the servants were often reduced to counting candles and using leftover cuts of meat for soups. As she was fond of saying, there was nothing wrong "with a bit o' thrift." While the furnishings might grow a bit shabby over time, madam instantly replaced non-reparable items such as when the curtains in the front room finally grew too thin to darn. On that occasion, she'd chosen some very handsome red velvet drapes that had instantly polished the room and promised to wear well for at least a decade.

McNair just wished madam were a little more attuned to the dictates of fashion. She rarely wore anything other than plain gray gowns draped with a multitude of shawls, and the most sensible of boots. McNair and the other servants also missed the elegant dinners the master had once presided over, usually with madam ensconced at the foot of the table, genially holding court over the snobby and self-aggrandizing members of the local gentry. Those dinners had ended after Hurst's death at the grand old age of seventy-eight.

Though her accent was common, madam's manners were never poor. Never was her spirit less than bold, nor her understanding less than exceptional. Nothing got by those shrewd blue eyes.

"Och, dinna just stand there! Read it to me." Madam waved one of the letters in McNair's direction. "As soon as we're done, I'm to go to the village and help Mrs. Bruce wit' her sick bairn. She thinks 'tis an ague, but I've a mind it's teethin'."

Unfortunately, her skills didn't extend to curing her own failing eyesight.

McNair unfolded the letter. "This is the one from Miss Caitlyn."

Madam put down her teacup. "What does the lass have to say?"

McNair read, " 'Dearest Mam, I hope this letter finds you well. As you may know by now, I have been banished from London and—' "

"*Banished*? Are ye certain she says tha'?"

"Aye, madam."

"Och, wha' trouble has she stirred up now? She's a bonny lass, but has a temper tha' burns as hot as the sun. Read on, please."

McNair lifted the letter and cleared his throat. " 'I have been banished from London because of an error in judgment that I made. Worse, poor Triona has been made to pay.' "

"Good God! Wha' has the puir lass done now?"

He cleared his throat again. " 'It all began when I met Alexander MacLean—' "

Nora clutched at her chest. "Say 'tis no' so! I warned the lass no' to look into their green eyes, fer they'd bewitch her!"

McNair continued reading, " '—but before you say I shouldn't look into his green eyes, let me assure you that he ignored me completely.' "

Nora dropped her hands, her brows snapping low over her hooked nose. "The bastard! To ignore me granddaughter! I daresay she dinna take tha' kindly!"

"No, madam. Shall I read on?"

She nodded emphatically.

" 'I am quite upset because I allowed myself to behave in such a way as to bring embarrassment to myself and the family, and—' "

"Yes, yes, lass! So ye've said! Wha' happened next?"

McNair smiled and continued, " '—to cause Triona irreparable harm. I should have known better, for Mother and Papa have indeed raised me to—' "

"*Pssht!* I'll be dead and buried if the lass doesna

hurry wit' her story. Scan the letter, will ye, and give me the gist o' it."

McNair traced a long finger down the letter. "Hmmm. When Alexander MacLean ignored Miss Caitlyn, she decided to capture the laird's attention by trapping him in a compromising situation—"

"No!"

"Yes, indeed. However"—the butler frowned in confusion—"it says she had no intention of actually accepting his proposal, and that she just wished to make him ask. That cannot be correct."

"Och, she's makin' fine sense to me." She chuckled. "'Tis a woman's thought and no' one ye'd understand."

"Ah." McNair turned the letter over and continued to read. "She expresses a great deal of remorse about being involved in such a dangerous plan, and then— ah. Here we are. It looks as if—" McNair blinked. "It appears that Miss Caitriona came to her sister's rescue, and the laird's brother Hugh was caught with her instead, and—" His mouth dropped open. "Good God!"

Nora clutched the arms of her chair. "Spit it out, damn it! Wha's happened?"

McNair turned a stunned gaze toward his mistress. "Madam . . . they've married!"

"Caitlyn and Alexander MacLean?"

"Nay, madam! Miss Triona and *Hugh* MacLean."

Nora blinked. Then blinked again. "If that dinna beat all! Does it say where they are now?"

"Yes, madam. Gilmerton Manor."

"Why, that's no' but an hour's drive from here!"

"Yes, madam. Shall I read Miss Triona's missive?"

She handed it to him, taking back and folding Caitlyn's letter. "Ah, Caitlyn, I warned ye about tha' bloody Hurst temper, but ye dinna listen."

McNair unfolded Triona's note. " 'Dear Mam, I hope this finds you well. I would like to visit, for I'm in a difficult position and need your advice. I'm but an hour away, so send word to Gilmerton Manor and I shall come as soon as possible. Love, Triona.' "

"That's *all*?"

"Aye, madam."

"Fetch the coach!"

"Madam, it's too near dark. There's no way you could make it safely to Miss Triona's at this time of day. You'll have to go first thing in the morning."

She picked up the two letters and waved them in the air. "Damnation, I've a family emergency brewin', and neither o' me granddaughters can write a decent letter to let a person know wha's goin' on!"

Hugh pulled on his gloves and allowed Liam to help him into his coat. Across the foyer, dressed in one of her new gowns, Caitriona conferred with Mrs. Wallis about dinner. The light from the windows flanking the front door traveled over the gleaming wood floor to flicker over the blue folds of her dress and touch upon her golden hair.

Hugh buttoned his coat just as Caitriona glanced

his way. Their eyes met, and she flushed. He grinned, knowing just what she was thinking. Every morning since she'd arrived, they'd awakened in each other's arms and had thoroughly explored the delights offered by the marital bed. This morning had been no exception, and Hugh'd had the deep satisfaction of making her gasp with delight three times.

She was voracious, and he awoke most mornings with a smile, as eager for her as she was for him. Lust was a wonderful, delicious, simple emotion, and he welcomed it.

"Very well, m'lady," Mrs. Wallis said. "I'll tell Cook ye wish the roast lamb tonight." She left, and Caitriona crossed the hall to the breakfast room.

Hugh noted with appreciation the delightful sway of her hips beneath her gown. He must send a thank-you note and a bonus to the modiste. He'd never before realized how truly gifted she was.

Caitriona reached the breakfast room, where Angus was busy polishing candelabra. She inspected his work, encouraging him with a kind word, and returned to the foyer. She hesitated when she saw Hugh, then came forward with a smile. "Headed for the stables?"

"Yes. Two of the mares foaled in the night, and I'm anxious to see how they're doing this morning. When the girls come for their afternoon ride, can you have them bring some rolled bandages? Mrs. Wallis keeps a basket of them somewhere. I've used all of the bandages in the barn."

"Of course."

"Thank you." He hesitated, surprised by a sudden desire to kiss her once more. It had been almost reflexive, and he'd barely caught himself in time. He turned toward the door. "I should be back in time for dinner." With a quick smile, he left, leaving his temptations in the foyer.

The cold air chilled his heated body. He shouldn't be so quick to ignite after such a passionate morning, but one look at her mouth made him go hard like a sex-starved youth.

He laughed softly at his own foolishness. So far, to his cautious surprise, Caitriona's presence hadn't caused any huge disruptions in his and the girls' peaceful life. The house was cleaner, the floors polished to a new gleam, the fires laid more neatly, and dinner more varied and enjoyable, but other than that, there was no tangible sign that she was there. Well, there was one: his cock had never been so well-satisfied.

He grinned, his steps slowing as he looked back. Perhaps he should return and surprise her with a kiss. That would be—

A curtain moved in an upstairs window. His smile faded as he stared at the now-empty pane and realized that he'd forgotten to stop by the nursery and say good morning to the girls as he usually did. He'd been distracted by Caitriona's passion, then distracted by the changes in the house, then further distracted by the realization that he didn't want to go to the stables this morning. What he *really* wanted was to go back inside the house, toss Caitriona over his shoulder, and carry her back to bed.

Her passion was addictive. Not that he couldn't walk away if he wished . . . he just didn't wish to. What man would? She was innovative, sweet, playful, and threw herself into it body and soul. No man could ask for more.

Things were going very well. Caitriona had agreed to stay away from the girls and had done just that. Of course, the girls made it easy, for they did their best to ignore her. That was *one* change since Caitriona had arrived: the girls had become more and more silent. It was if they were huddled together against an impending storm.

He sighed. The girls would have to trust him. He glanced regretfully at the front door and then turned away, tugging the collar of his coat closer as the cold wind tried to sneak in. He didn't have time to return to the house; there were two new foals and two very tired mares to check on.

Inside the house, Triona sighed as Hugh turned away. He'd paused a second, and she'd thought he might come back. She didn't know why, but she'd been so certain that her heart had leapt—which meant it had that much farther to fall when he went on to the stables.

*That's what you get for wanting more,* she warned herself. *Learn to be thankful for what you have. That's the secret to happiness. You have this lovely house, and kind servants. The girls have been polite, while Hugh has been—* She shivered, rubbing her arms as she turned back toward the foyer. *I have no complaints at all. In fact—*

Triona came to a halt. There, standing across the top of the staircase, were the girls.

Devon, her dark hair falling about her face, frowned. "Where's Papa?"

"He just left for the stables to—"

"Before saying good-bye to us?" Christina asked in a breathless tone, her pale face tight.

"Perhaps he thought he'd see you after lunch, for your ride."

"He *never* leaves without telling us good-bye," Devon said, accusation clear in her tone.

"Maybe he was in a hurry because of the new foals," Triona offered.

Devon glared a moment, then gave a brittle laugh. "I'm sorry. It—it doesn't really matter."

"New foals?" Aggie asked eagerly, coming down the stairs at once. "How many are there?"

Caitriona had to smile at her eagerness. "Two."

Aggie clapped her hands. "Did he say if Satin had hers yet?"

"He didn't mention any of the horses by name." She chuckled. "*Do* they all have names?"

"Of course." Christina had also come down the stairs and eyed Caitriona cautiously. "How would he know which horses were which, if they didn't have names?"

"That's a good point. I'd just supposed he had too many to bother."

Aggie giggled. "He was running out of names before we came. He called one Old Spoonhead."

"Then he began naming them after items from his closet," Christina confided. "He called one Shoe and another Boot."

It was the first time Caitriona had seen the thin, serious girl smile, and the transformation was breathtaking. In the space of a second, she went from plain to an ethereal beauty that put Devon's more earthy looks to shame. Having had a sister who'd outshone her most of her life, Caitriona warmed to Christina. "I suppose Horse 1 and Horse 2 were already taken, or he wouldn't have resorted to footwear for names."

Devon reached the bottom step. "Papa is like that. Sometimes he seems very pragmatic, and then others—" She shrugged. "For example, he loves marmalade."

"Does he?" That was interesting. Perhaps she could find some on her next trip to town.

"Oh, yes," Aggie said. "He makes quite a mess when he uses it, too."

Christina wrinkled her nose. "He'll even stick his finger in the jar and get the bits the knife can't."

Triona smiled at the girls, glad they'd thawed a bit. She knew she wasn't supposed to engage them much, but a few conversations here and there couldn't hurt. Besides, she was feeling lonely. Hugh spent so many hours overseeing the horses that he was rarely inside. Meanwhile, she'd promised not to approach the girls, so she rarely saw them. At times the huge house seemed achingly empty. "Where do you ride when you go with your father in the afternoons?"

Christina shrugged. "Wherever he wishes. Sometimes he has to check on a certain herd, or we help him move them from pasture to pasture."

"You help him?"

"Yes," Devon said, sounding defensive. "We ride behind the horses and he rides in the front. I daresay we've ridden over every inch of this place."

"That's impressive."

Aggie hopped. "Yesterday we saw a fox!"

"No!"

"Oh, yes! And it was *very* red. Papa says that means it'll be a hard winter."

"Considering how frigid it is outside already, that's not surprising."

Christina added, "The millpond is frozen solid, too."

"Goodness, it *is* going to be a cold winter. I'll check the coal bins and see how we're faring, and order more firewood. I don't want us to run out." Triona glanced around the group. "I don't mean to intrude, but . . . aren't you supposed to be with your governess?"

Devon's expression couldn't have been more bland. "She has a headache and told us to conjugate our Greek verbs for the week."

"Which we did already," Aggie offered.

"As long as your father is happy."

Standing here now, noticing the air of desperation that hung about Christina, and how Aggie leaned toward one while talking as if wanting a hug, while Devon eyed all adults with distrust, made Triona regret her promise to Hugh. Surely there was something she could do to help these poor girls while she was here.

Devon crossed her arms, her accusing gaze pinned on Triona. "What have *you* been doing this morning?"

"Setting the menus for the week and organizing the cleaning duties."

"Christina and Devon used to do that," Aggie piped up.

"Really?" MacLean had never mentioned that! Good God, no wonder the children were cool toward her! She'd appeared out of nowhere and had taken over their position in the house. "I never knew anyone was in charge of those duties."

"Papa did," Devon said succinctly.

"Well, he forgot to tell me! Or more likely, he didn't think about it. He's a wonderful man, but he doesn't dwell on the niceties. When we married, I thought— well, never mind. I shall have a word with your father about this."

"Wait," Christina said. "What did you think when you were married?"

"Oh, suffice it to say that Hugh organized our wedding in a very precise, no-frills manner."

"That describes most everything he does," Christina said. "Papa's very—" She suddenly pressed her lips together. "I won't criticize Papa."

Triona chuckled. "It's not a criticism, dear. Just a comment on his style."

"Oh." Christina unbent a little, regarding Triona gravely. "In that case, he does tend toward the severe. It drives Uncle Dougal mad."

"Uncle Dougal is a fop." Devon sniffed. "Even Aunt Sophia says so."

Aggie giggled. "Aunt Sophia says it a *lot*."

Triona grinned, and realized again how much she missed her own brothers and sisters. Though she'd written a letter to each, it didn't replace being able to sit around the fire and talk. Her heart ached at the thought.

"Are . . . are you well?"

Finding Christina's gaze on her, Triona pulled her handkerchief from her pocket and dried her eyes. "Fine, thank you. I'm just thinking of my brothers and sisters—I miss them."

"How many do you have?" Aggie asked.

"Three brothers and two sisters."

Christina gaped. "There's a lot of you!"

"Oh, yes. We did all sorts of things together—we cooked and cleaned and—"

"Didn't you have any servants?"

"Very few. We didn't need many, for there were so many of us and we could do what needed doing. I make an excellent cottage pie."

Aggie gave a little hop. "Yum!"

"Oh, yes! And our house was always very noisy. It's very quiet here, and I'm not used to it."

Christina and Aggie exchanged glances.

Devon said, "I'd think you'd welcome a little peace and quiet. There are times I wish Aggie and Christina would stop talking."

Christina's cheeks bloomed red. "Devon!"

"Don't pretend you haven't felt the same; it's a perfectly natural reaction." Devon bent and retrieved a piece of paper from the floor. She glanced at it, then handed it to Triona. "I believe this is yours. It's the menu for the week."

"What are we having tonight?" Aggie asked eagerly.

"Roast lamb."

"Good!" Aggie patted her stomach in anticipation. "I hope there's no mint sauce. Papa hates that."

Triona took silent note of this tidbit of information. Never was it more apparent that she was married to a stranger than when she'd first attempted to set the menu. Based on the standard dishes served at Gilmerton, Mrs. Wallis knew some of Hugh's likes and dislikes, but she'd been unable to vouch for his opinions regarding some of the new dishes Triona had wished to add.

It was but one example of the many things she didn't know about her husband. It was rather nice that the children knew his tastes so well for it saved Triona from having to question him when he came home.

"Yes," Devon said. "He hates mint sauce as much as he loves carrots. Especially carrots baked into his cottage pie."

Christina blinked. "But—"

Devon pulled her sister back up the stairs. "We'd better review our Greek before Mrs. Appleton wakes up from her nap."

Aggie trailed behind her older sisters. "I don't want to do my Greek!"

"If you want to ride with Papa this afternoon, you have to finish. You know how he is," Devon said.

Shoulders slumped, Aggie walked slowly up the stairs after her sisters.

So MacLean loved carrots in his cottage pie, did he? Perhaps they'd have that instead of the roast lamb. If there was one dish Triona could make, it was cottage pie. She wondered if they had the ingredients already, or if—

A carriage rattled up to the portico, and Liam went to answer the door.

As Triona smoothed her gown, she heard a voice say, "Let go o' me arm, ye idiot! Do I look as if I canna walk on me own?"

# Chapter 13

❧

*" 'Tis a woman's right to change her mind, and a man's right to keep his."*

OLD WOMAN NORA TO HER THREE WEE
GRANDDAUGHTERS ON A COLD WINTER'S NIGHT

*M*am!" Triona hurried across the foyer to envelop her grandmother in a hug.

Nora blinked back tears. "Och, how are ye, me dear bairn!"

"Oh, Mam, I'm so glad to see you! Will you come into the sitting room? There's a nice fire there and I can have some scones sent up."

"Aye, I could use somethin' to warm me bones."

Triona sent word that refreshments were needed; then she assisted Mam into a nice, comfy chair in the sitting room. With a smile, she sank down in the one opposite. "You should have waited for me to visit you."

"How could I do tha' what wit' yer sister sendin' me a fat letter tha' dinna say a damn thing, and then ye sending me tha' sliver o' paper ye call a note? I'll know wha' is happenin' or I'll die tryin'!"

Triona had to laugh. "Caitlyn can write more and say less than anyone I know."

Mam turned a shrewd eye on Triona. "So, out with it. Wha' has ye in a dither?"

"Oh, Mam! There is so much—this all . . . it all happened so fast."

"I daresay ye're a bit confused, gettin' wed out o' pocket in such a way. Wha' was yer da thinkin'?"

"He wasn't in town. Uncle Bedford and Aunt Lavinia—"

Nora snorted. "Say no more! Those pompous fools couldna find their way out o' a sack o' potatoes, much less finagle a mess like yer sister set ye into."

"Caitlyn didn't mean to cause harm. The laird mocked her, and you know how she is."

"She's a sight too much like her mam, if ye ask me. I canna believe ye dinna write me. I'd have come and straightened out this mess."

"We didn't have time. People were saying horrible things, and not just about me. The entire family's name was being torn to bits, and with Papa being a vicar . . ."

"I see." Mam's shrewd blue gaze met Triona's. "So . . . how are ye?"

"I'm fine. I miss the family, of course."

"Aye, so did I when I first married. That's normal." Nora patted Triona's hand. "Now, tell me, me bairn, wha's sent ye runnin' to me knee? Wha's that husband o' yers doin' to upset ye?"

"It's more what he's *not* doing."

"Och, now! Dinna tell me he's no' laid hands on ye since ye wed, fer I've seen Hugh MacLean, and he's no' the sort to let a lass as bonny as ye slip away wit'out markin' her his own."

Triona blushed. "No, that's the best part, in fact. It's about my position. This isn't a normal marriage, so I don't know how—"

"Hold now, lassie. Ye're his wife, aren't ye?"

Triona's lips trembled in the beginning of a smile. "Yes, I am."

"And ye want to make his life better, and fer him to make yers better?"

"Well . . . yes."

"Tha' sounds like a normal marriage to me." Nora regarded her granddaughter shrewdly. "Or it will be, once't ye stop treating it like it's not."

Triona was silent for a moment. "I suppose you're right. So much of our trouble is that we don't know one another well enough. When I arrived here, I discovered that Hugh has three daughters."

"*Wha'?*"

"I was quite shocked, too."

Nora pursed her lips thoughtfully. "*Three,* ye say? When did that happen?"

"Well, one of them is about fifteen. The next is thirteen, and the youngest is about six. At first I thought Hugh must still have feelings for their mother, since he'd obviously been with her for a long time, but he said that was not the case. And he looks very angry whenever he says her name."

"Weel, then, what has ye so low?"

"When we married, MacLean and I agreed that when the rumors died down, I would return to Wythburn."

"No!"

"Mam, neither MacLean nor I wished to marry, so—"

"*Pssht!* Ye *are* married, so forget this wishin' an' wantin'. Ye made a promise to each other, and ye should honor it."

"He doesn't want me involved in his life—any more than I wish him involved in mine."

"Och, yer modern ideas are all hash."

Triona shook her head. "Mam, it's not a modern marriage. It's just that since we were forced into this situation, we should do what we could to"—she struggled to find the words, finally blurting out—"to minimalize the damage."

Mam turned red. "Damage? Since when has marriage been 'damage'?"

"That's not how I meant to say it."

"The problem with ye and Lord Hugh is tha' ye haven't yet faced the facts. Ye're married whether ye like it or not and the sooner ye both accept tha', the sooner ye can settle into a good, healthy marriage and no' this 'minimalizing the damage' bull."

"But what if we find we don't suit?"

"Then ye'll do as the rest o' us and *work* at suiting."

Triona wished it was that simple. "Mam, there is more to it than you think. Hugh asked that I remain aloof from the girls so they won't miss me when I'm gone."

"He's worried about the lassies?"

"Yes, and he's right. They've had a difficult life, and if I came to care for them and they for me, and then I left—well, it would be difficult for us all, but especially for them."

"Then dinna leave."

"That's not an option. We got married only to stop the rumors and save my sisters from ruin by association."

"Fools, the both o' ye." Mam cocked a brow. "What about now?"

"I know when the time comes to leave, I'll be ready but . . . I would like to get to know the children, to spend time with them. If they are plainly told that I'm leaving, I don't think they'll feel abandoned when I do. Afterward, I can keep in touch with them through letters, or have them visit at Wythburn."

"So, get to know the lassies."

"But MacLean has asked me *not* to."

"Lassie, listen to me. Many a time we make decisions, only to realize they're wrong. Ye must be brave enough to live yer own life, make yer own mistakes, and fix 'em by yerself. Ye're not fixin' 'em if yer sitting around all miserable, wishin' someone else would do the work."

Triona sighed. "Marriage is so difficult! I thought MacLean and I would have it easier, since we didn't marry for love."

"That is where ye're wrong. Love is wha' greases the wheels on the cart."

Triona smiled. "I'm beginning to realize that. It's difficult for me to settle for less than what my parents have."

"Aye, and in a good relationship, ye hand the reins back and forth when the time comes. Seems to me tha' no one is drivin' yer cart."

Triona considered that, then slowly nodded. "Perhaps I haven't taken my fair turn 'driving the cart' because I am too worried about being wrong, or hurting someone's feelings."

Mam blew out a gusty sigh. "Och, ye dinna know the times I've had to preach against such thinkin'. Women too often see themselves as the world's caretakers, which is a great pity if ye ask me. I say let some o' the men carry the burden! They're always goin' on about how braw they are. Use some o' tha' muscle on some real work, is what I say!" Mam shook her head in obvious disgust. "I think ye've let the MacLean magic weave a spell upon ye that ye're not thinkin' so clearly as ye should."

"There is no spell, just a curse. You know, I'd always thought you'd made that up, about the storms."

Mam looked surprised. "Why would I do such a thing as tha'?"

"I don't know. I suppose I just thought it was a fairytale." The only fairytale so far had been the one MacLean managed to create between the sheets. That sort of magic intrigued Triona far more than the storm-making. "I have to find a way to express myself better. Hugh is very logical and he makes so much sense and speaks with such authority and assurance that his way of doing things seems to be the only way; like this issue with the girls. He explained very calmly why he thought I shouldn't have anything to do with them and at the time it seemed to make sense, so I agreed. Later, after I'd had time to think through things, I realize I shouldn't have. The girls *need* me in their lives and, right now, I need them, too."

"Exactly! Ye must do wha' is right, or yer partner canna trust ye to make the tough decisions."

"So . . . if I decide our decision about the girls is wrong, I should let him know."

"Aye. It might irritate him, but think on it: he married ye because 'twas the right thing to do, so he's honorable."

"You're right. I'll speak with him."

"There's one more thing to consider. As soon as ye stepped foot in his house, he told ye ye're not to involve yerself. Perhaps this isna so much about the lassies as about MacLean. Maybe the *real* person he's protectin', but doesna even know it, is himself."

Triona frowned. "I don't know about that. He has an arrogant streak."

"All of the MacLeans do."

"So I've come to believe. I don't know how to convince him that I might be right about the girls. He gets very defensive whenever I mention them."

"It might take some time; ye'll have to build some trust first."

Triona sighed. "I know. I've been trying to show him that I am a woman of my word, but I'm not sure he really notices."

"Just be yerself and do as ye'd normally do. Ye build trust just by being there and no' goin' away. MacLean will come round eventually."

"I don't want to wait that long! I'm used to having my family about me. I-I'm lonely and . . ." Her voice quivered.

Mam squeezed her hand. "When ye're feelin' blue, ye can come visit me and we'll fill yer heart wit' scones and jam so ye've the strength to go back. Besides"— her eyes twinkled—"I dinna think he'll hold out long."

"I hope not."

Mam looked thoughtful. "I heard tell tha' MacLean's a horse breeder. I'd suggest ye take some ridin' lessons, lass."

She could do that. MacLean's head groom, Ferguson, would be qualified to teach her—and then she could surprise Hugh with her newly acquired skill. "I will, thank you. *And* I will talk to Hugh about the girls, though I don't think he'll listen."

"Find yer compassion, lass. He's like a rooster protectin' his flock, all puffed-up feathers and sharp beak. Once't he realizes ye mean him and his kin no harm, he'll see ye in a different light."

Triona managed a faint smile. "I wish I could be as certain about that as you are. Still, you've given me a lot to consider. I think I will learn to ride. That should prove I'm willing to make an effort to meet him halfway. And then, when the time is right, I'll broach the subject of the girls. Meanwhile, I'll start treating Gilmerton as if it is, indeed, my own house, beginning tonight. I believe I'll cook some of my shepherd's pie."

Mam beamed. "That's me girl!"

"Thank you."

"And then? Wha' about ye, lass? Ye canna give wit'out receivin'. What will ye ask in return?"

She thought about this. Finally, she said, "The right to decide for myself when the time has come for me to go."

"Tha's me granddaughter! Don't ye worry about MacLean: no man can stand alone fer long. 'Tis no' in their nature." Mam enveloped Triona in a hug that smelled of powder and lavender. "Just make sure ye visit me often. I might ha' a few questions fer ye myself. I've been wonderin' about the MacLeans, and now me granddaughter is wed to one! Who'd ha' thought."

"Who'd have thought, indeed." Triona smiled as Mrs. Wallis brought in a plate of scones and a pot of hot tea. "Mrs. Wallis, this is my grandmother, Mrs. Nora H—"

"Och," Mam interrupted, her gaze fixed on the housekeeper. "So ye're the one who's responsible fer the dust on the windowsills!"

Mrs. Wallis gulped and scurried to the closest window where she drew her finger across the smooth surface. Whatever she saw made her redden. "Why that lazy—" She bit off the sentence and turned to Mam and curtsied. "I'll send the girl to finish up her chores right away."

Triona wished Mam didn't try to fix *everything*. "Thank you, Mrs. Wallis. Also, for tonight, will you tell Cook that I'll be preparing dinner this evening?"

"You, m' lady?"

Mam scowled. "She's a good cook, she is. All of me granddaughters are."

Mrs. Wallis dunked a curtsey. "Sorry! I dinna mean to suggest— Of course I'll let Cook know she can have the night off. She'll be glad o' the chance to visit her sister."

For the first time in a week, Triona felt as if she knew who she was and what she should do. With a smile, she filled Mam's teacup.

Big wars were won with small battles, and she'd start hers with the best cottage pie Hugh MacLean had ever eaten.


Hugh handed his coat to Liam. "Where is Lady Caitri-ona?"

"I think she's a-gettin' ready fer dinner, as are the girls, m'lord."

Hugh nodded and made his way up the stairs. He'd just reached the landing when he met the girls, dressed for dinner and dashing to the dining room. Their sashes were half-tied, their hair ribbons askew. "Hold it!" he ordered.

They skidded to a halt. Devon shoved her hair from her face and frowned. "Yes?"

Behind her, Christina was trying to tie her sash behind her back, her elbows sticking out, while Aggie hopped on one foot and adjusted her stockings.

"Where are you going?"

Christina finished tying her sash. "Down to dinner."

He glanced at the clock on the landing. "Early?"

Devon frowned. "You told us not to be late again."

"I've told you that a few times, but I've never seen you come down *early*."

"We're just excited," Aggie said.

Devon shot her a hard glance and the younger girl turned pink.

"Not excited, really," Aggie amended. "Just hungry."

"That's right," Christina said. "We're starving. We did ride with you for over two hours this afternoon."

"*And* played with the new foals," Devon added.

He eyed them again. Something was going on, but the three gazes that met his told him nothing. He stepped aside. "Go ahead, then. But have yourselves put together by the time dinner is served."

"Yes, Papa!" They were gone in a flash, their slippers pounding down the stairs.

Hugh smiled as he went to his bedchamber. There was plenty of time for ladylike behavior later, when they were older. It was good that they were relaxing so much.

He opened his door and looked around, but the

bedchamber was silent. Every time he'd come home for the last week, Caitriona had been here, dressing for dinner. He was surprised at the sudden rush of disappointment that had swept over him on realizing she wasn't here.

Damn it, he was getting spoiled. Still, as he washed and changed for dinner, he wondered where she was. He wasted no time in getting ready, and soon headed down the stairs.

As he entered the dining room, he heard Devon say, "It won't be my fault! I'm not the one who thinks she can just walk in and—" She caught sight of Hugh and stopped.

Christina and Aggie had an unmistakable air of guilt.

Hugh crossed to where his children stood and gazed at each one, saving Devon for last. "What won't be your fault?"

Devon's cheeks pinkened, but she tilted her chin. "I was saying—"

Caitriona walked in, Liam and Angus following. Both footmen carried large trays, and they began to place dishes on the table.

Hugh watched Caitriona as she greeted the girls and took her place at the opposite end of the table from him. She was dressed in another new gown, this one light yellow and very simple. On another woman such a gown might have appeared plain, but hugging Caitriona's generous curves, it was gorgeous.

Liam removed the covers from the dishes.

"Ah!" Hugh said, grinning. "Cottage pie. My favorite."

"Miss Caitriona made it," Aggie piped up.

Hugh looked at the thick pie, inhaling the savory steam rising from it. "You *made* this?"

Her cheeks flushed and she gave a pleased smile. "Caitlyn may be the seamstress in our family, but I am the cook. I already knew the recipe and I made sure to add c—"

"Papa!" Devon said. "Please tell Aggie to stop kicking me under the table."

Aggie's eyes widened. "Kicking you? I can't even *reach* you from here!"

"Both of you stop it." Hugh helped himself to a large amount of pie, the rich scent making his mouth water. As soon as he placed the first bite in his mouth, he closed his eyes and relished the savory flavor.

"This is wonderful!" Christina's voice broke through his reverie and he opened his eyes to find the girls looking at their plates, surprise and awe in their expressions.

Catching his gaze, Caitriona lifted her brows, a small smile curving her lips.

He smiled back, and they shared the moment over the girls' heads.

Aggie chuckled. "Miss Caitriona fixed everything else, too, for she gave Cook the night off. Cook's not really visiting her sister, though. She's in the village drinking gin."

Devon frowned. "How do you know that?"

"Moira told me when she was cleaning the fireplace in our room."

"You shouldn't gossip with the maid," Christina said softly.

"Especially Moira." Caitriona smiled. "She told me yesterday that she saw a troll climbing out of a cart by the kitchen door, but later she discovered it was only Ferguson."

"Ha," Devon scoffed. "Moira only said that because she likes him, but he won't have anything to do with her."

Hugh noticed the hesitant smile Christina flashed Caitriona, misgiving beginning to bloom. She'd been keeping her distance as she'd promised, but the girls seemed to be warming to her anyway.

He frowned. Should he put a stop to it? *Could* he?

"Here, Papa." Devon took his plate and served him more pie. "There's only more for one person, so you might as well eat it."

As he did so, Hugh tried to shrug off a faint itch between his shoulders. Perhaps he'd talk to Caitriona about the girls tonight.

"Papa, are you . . . are you angry about something?" Aggie asked.

Hugh rubbed his arm. "No, why?"

"You look red."

He lifted his shoulder, a nagging itch on one shoulder blade. "I don't—"

"Hugh!" Caitriona's gaze was fixed on his face. "Aggie's right—you're turning bright red!"

He rubbed his hand over his face, where a solid itch seemed to spread. Good God, what was wrong? It felt as if a hundred ants were crawling over him. His lips felt swollen, too.

His gaze fell on his empty plate. "Caitriona—the cottage pie. Were there carrots in it?"

"Why, of course! I—" Her gaze flickered to Devon, who was busy eating.

"Damnation!" He sprang from his chair, rubbing his neck and one shoulder at the same time. "I can't eat carrots. They make me break out in a rash." He turned toward the door. "Liam! Bring a cold bath to my room immediately!"

Christina watched as her father disappeared out the door. Already his face looked splotched, and his mouth was swollen. She saw Liam race to the kitchen, Angus following.

"Well."

Christina peeked at Caitriona and then wished she hadn't.

Caitriona pinned her blazing gaze on all three of them. "I know it can't be truly dangerous, or you all wouldn't have suggested I add carrots. You care too much for your father to harm him."

Christina lowered her fork, awash in unexpected guilt. "He will be fine."

Devon tasted her bread pudding. "He'll itch for a few hours, but he'll be fine in the morning." She smirked. "But I don't suppose he'll want you to cook again."

Christina sneaked another look at Caitriona, expecting fury. Instead, Caitriona merely regarded Devon with a long, level gaze.

Christina gripped her fork tighter, her chest tightening. While she agreed with Devon that something must be done to protect Papa from the woman who'd tricked him into marrying, there were dangers in upsetting an adult. Christina knew this fact all too well.

"I see how it is." Caitriona stood, and her hazel eyes seemed greener than ever. "Well, ladies, you leave me no choice."

Aggie blinked, but said nothing.

Christina put down her fork, her heart beating wildly. "What do you mean?"

"I don't appreciate being made a fool of, but I must admit your little plot was masterfully done." Her lips curved into a faint smile. "The problem is, I come from a large family."

Devon glanced at Christina before looking back at Caitriona. "So?"

Caitriona placed her hands on the table and leaned forward. "So if I were you, for the next week or so, I'd walk very, very softly."

When Caitriona swept from the room, Christina felt like they'd started a fight they were sure to lose.

Devon was more nonchalant. "What can she do to us?"

Aggie bit her lip. "She could put snakes in our beds."

"That's for children," Devon scoffed. "She won't dare do anything, or we'll tell Papa."

Christina remembered the gleam in Caitriona's eyes and wasn't so sure. One thing was certain, she wasn't going to climb into her bed without checking for snakes, spiders, and ants. *What have we started?*

# Chapter 14

*"When I was a wee lass, e'ery mornin' I would carry water all the way from the well at the bottom of the hill to our stone hut at the top. While carryin' tha' water, I learned tha' be there one step or twenty, ye can only take 'em one at a time."*

OLD WOMAN NORA TO HER THREE WEE
GRANDDAUGHTERS ON A COLD WINTER'S NIGHT

Satin dinna come back." Ferguson sounded worried.

Hugh looked at the golden horses gathered about the fence and frowned. "You think she's had her foal?"

"If she did, she's early. Could be a problem."

Hugh patted a stallion named Kashmir, admiring the golden glisten of the sun on the horse's shoulders. Of all the breeds Hugh raised, he had a soft spot for his Akhal-Tekes. He loved that their hides had a slightly metallic sheen and how their almond-shaped eyes showed their spirit and intelligence. He also admired their athleticism. Their sloping shoulders and thin skin reminded him of greyhounds, all muscle and fast action with incredible endurance.

Sheba, a palomino mare, shoved past the much larger Kashmir for a pat on the shoulder. If any other horse had been so bold, Kashmir would have nipped at it. But he and Sheba had a long-standing relationship, so all he did was whinny his annoyance and give her a playful nudge.

Sheba bared her teeth, then turned contentedly back to Hugh.

Hugh laughed and gave her a fond pat. "Kashmir lets Sheba get away with murder."

"I dinna blame him; she's been his faithful consort fer years. She's had seven o' his colts and will likely have more."

Hugh noticed that Sheba looked over her shoulder as if to make certain Kashmir was still there. She might have wanted the stallion's place at the fence, but she didn't want him to leave.

Hugh could understand that double-edged sword—to want someone nearby and yet wish them elsewhere. He'd been fighting the same double dose of desire himself, and over the last two weeks it had grown stronger.

He absently rubbed his chin, where an itch still lingered from the carrots in the cottage pie. It had been two days before the rash finally faded, though he still itched now, a whole week later, as if in remembrance. Caitriona had appeared so shocked and had been so concerned for him afterward, he knew it for the innocent mistake it was. Yet he couldn't help thinking that there was more to it. At breakfast each morning since, the tension between Caitriona and the girls was almost palpable. *Something* was going on between them, though none of them would admit it.

He'd speak with the girls when he returned home. So far, whenever he questioned Caitriona, she'd given him a brief, firm smile and changed the topic.

"I hope Satin's foal is healthy," Ferguson said. "She's a good mum when all's said and done."

Hugh patted Sheba's neck. If the foal was healthy, it might be an excellent gift for Caitriona.

Ferguson stroked the nose of a little mare named Desert Flower. "Might be best if I saddle up and follow the herd. They usually stay at the end of Duncannon Glen, so I might find Satin there. She'd want to be in their home pastures fer foalin'."

"That's a good idea. I'll go with you. If we find her, we may need to stay with her until she's ready to move. There's a crofter's hut nearby if we need to stay the night."

"Aye, though we may have to stay longer if she's no' strong enough to travel. I'll pack supplies fer three days."

"I'll have Mrs. Wallis pack up some bandages, too. I've a feeling something's amiss."

"Aye, m'lord. When do ye wish to leave?"

"After my ride with the girls. They are due in an hour."

"Aye, m'lord."

Hugh also wanted to say a proper good-bye to his wife. He looked forward to that in many ways.

He patted Sheba's nose. It was a shame Caitriona didn't know how to ride. He'd offered to teach her, but she'd stalled, saying she might like that one day. Though she hadn't said no outright, he'd heard it in her voice. He wasn't a man to get upset over nothing, but her lack of interest disappointed him much more than it should have.

He was beginning to grow irritated with himself. He was perfectly free to ride when he wished, work with the horses when he wished, take his daughters for rides when he wished. Except for their morning bouts between the sheets, Caitriona made few demands of him and seemed perfectly content without him throughout the day.

He scowled. That should be what he wanted. Hell, he'd basically told her that. Yet he found himself distracted by thoughts of her, wondering what she was doing, what she was thinking, if she was content— and why she hadn't allowed him to teach her to ride, damn it.

He'd never met a woman who was so elusive. Even when she agreed with him and did as he requested, he felt thwarted in some way. But while she might be withholding herself in some areas of their life, she never denied him in bed. Her passion and enthusiasm there was entrancing.

Every morning, he woke up to find her curled next to him, her long hair silky on his shoulder, her soft breathing almost mesmerizing. And every morning, he made sure she knew he was there as well, usually in a very lascivious manner. She responded to him with such glowing, natural passion, welcoming him every time and with such breathless urgency, that he was often left in astounded wonder. Even more interesting, she was learning from each encounter. Just this morning, it had been she who'd started their lusty beginning of the day.

The memory made him instantly hard, and he was glad his long riding coat covered his reaction. He couldn't help it. Just the thought of her, of her expression as she shivered beneath him, her legs tight on his hips as she—

"M'lord?"

Hugh jerked around.

Ferguson was frowning at him, a look of concern on his broad face.

Hugh managed to say with credible calm, "Yes, Ferguson? I was just thinking of the supplies we'll need for Satin."

"Aye, m'lord." There was a note of disbelief in Ferguson's voice.

Hugh quickly continued, "We'll need oats, bandages, and that tonic you used on Hariam's fetlock."

"Och, I'd forgotten that! There's a mite left."

"Let's return to the stables and pack what we can before the girls arrive."

"Aye, m'lord." Ferguson emptied the last of the oats from his bucket, then followed Hugh back to the stables.

The stables were as well built as Gilmerton Manor.

Hugh had personally overseen their construction and was as proud of them as of the house. The stables held forty separate stalls, three tack rooms, two large stalls for birthing and treating serious ailments, and room overhead to store a year's worth of hay for the entire herd.

Hugh threw open the door of the main tack room and entered, assailed by the scent of leather and sweet oats mixed with the tang of iron. Along one wall ran a series of shelves. He found the tonic and turned to come back into the stables.

"Ferguson!" Caitriona's voice sounded clearly through the barn. "There you are. I was hoping we coul—"

"Shhhh!" Ferguson's hiss made Hugh stop in his tracks.

"What?" Caitriona asked.

*What, indeed?* Hugh, hidden by the tack room door, bent to one side and peered out through the hinge crack.

Her hair in a bun, her spectacles perched on her nose, Triona stood in front of Ferguson. The groom was wildly gesturing for her to be quiet, pantomiming toward the tack room.

Caitriona glanced there and back, her gaze widening. "Oh," her lips formed. She nodded and pointed to a small watch pinned to her pocket, held up one finger, then pointed toward the first stall door.

Ferguson sent a nervous glance toward the tack room and shook his head.

Triona's expression fell, but she mouthed, "Thank you."

Ferguson nodded even as he gestured for Caitriona to leave quickly.

She turned, wincing as she did so.

Hugh frowned, suddenly remembering that she'd winced this morning, too, when he'd slid between her thighs and lifted her leg to his hip. He'd asked her if she was well, and she'd said she was just a bit sore from climbing so many steps.

Hmmm. Hugh stepped out of the tack room and came to stand beside Ferguson.

"Och, there ye are, m'lord. I see ye found the tonic. I'll pack up some rags and—"

"That first stall, isn't it where we keep Bluebell?"

Ferguson's expression froze.

Hugh walked toward the stall and looked over the door. A smallish mare stood quietly snoozing. "Aggie rode her when she was first learning to ride."

Ferguson stood as if rooted to the floor.

"And there's a saddle on the rail, as if it just came off her."

"Aye, but that saddle's been there a whole day, m'lord. Besides, I canna remember every person who rides."

"You can remember this one. I'm sure of it." Hugh crossed to lift one of the stirrups. "I'd say this was rigged for a rider about . . . oh"—he held out his hand a little below his shoulder—"this tall." He dropped the stirrup. "Now, who do we know who is this tall?"

Ferguson closed his eyes.

Hugh leaned an elbow on the stall door. "Ferguson, you are teaching my wife to ride."

Ferguson laughed nervously. "The ideas ye get, m'lord!"

Hugh lifted his brows.

Ferguson's shoulders slumped. "Och, I dinna want to do it, but she was desperate, wishin' to learn! I tried, but I couldna tell her no."

"I should be the one to teach her, not you."

"And so I told her, m'lord! But she said she dinna dare learn in front o' ye and the lasses, fer 'twould be too embarrassing."

Hugh frowned. Embarrassing?

Ferguson sent Hugh an apologetic glance. "She's taken a few spills, she has."

"Was she hurt?"

"Nay! She took some good uns the first few days, but she's riding better now. She's showin' a good deal o' promise."

"How long has she been practicing?"

" 'Tis six days or more." Ferguson nodded eagerly. "Och, she's as pretty a seat as ye can imagine. She's a hard worker, m'lord. She rode fer two hours yesterday! I moved her from Bluebell onto Old Winston, and he's a stubborn one."

"How did she do with him?"

"Nary a falter. 'Keep 'is head up,' I said, and she did. Just like tha'."

No wonder she'd winced when he'd lifted her leg. Her thighs must have ached.

"I hope ye don't mind, m'lord, but I think she did it to impress ye."

"To impress me?"

"Aye. She said once she was good enough, she was goin' to surprise ye."

Hugh scowled. "She didn't need to worry about being good enough. I would never mock her."

"Nay, but—" Ferguson bit his lip.

"But what?"

"I dinna mean to be disrespectin', m'lord, but ye canna be so certain o' the lassies. They ride better than most men, they do. And they don't seem too fond o' their new mum."

"What makes you say that?"

Ferguson's face turned a deeper red. "Nothin'! I'm sure I'm just imaginin' things. They just—I heard the lassies sayin'— Och, don't ask me to say more."

"What did you hear?"

Ferguson sighed. "I heard Miss Devon say tha' if greasin' the steps would get rid o' the new mistress faster, she'd grease every one herself."

Hugh's shoulders felt like a millstone had settled on them. Was this the result of his request that Caitriona keep her distance? Had they come to despise and disrespect her because of his edict?

Damnation! Hugh handed the bottle of tonic to the groom. "Pack for the trip. I will be back in thirty minutes and we'll leave then."

"But ye haven't taken the lassies fer their daily—"

Hugh walked out of the stables and strode toward the house.

Damn it, she should have asked *him* to teach her to ride! He would never have mocked her and he damn well wouldn't have allowed the girls to do so, either.

He entered the house and saw Liam. "Where's the mistress?"

"She asked fer a hot bath, m'lord. Angus and I just carried it to her room, and she said she was goin' to soak in it till lunch."

Hugh's gaze narrowed. "Has she been requesting a lot of hot baths this week?"

"Every day, m'lord. Says they make her aches disappear."

Hugh nodded and headed toward the stairs, pausing when he heard the girls' voices in the sitting room. He walked to the door and stopped, one hand on the knob.

He heard Devon giggle. "She's taking yet *another* bath!"

"No wonder," Christina said, her voice alight with amusement. "She has to be black and blue. Did you see her land in that mud puddle this morning?"

"She splashed!" Aggie was giggling so hard Hugh could barely understand her.

"Yes," Devon said, obviously brimming with delight. "I wish I could paint a picture of her there, with mud in her hair and—"

His jaw hard, Hugh threw open the door.

Three startled faces turned toward him. The girls were pictures of perfect horsewomen, dressed in matching habits of varying colors, tall hats perched on their heads, their hair braided and neat. Their feet were shod in comfortable riding boots of the finest cut. He couldn't help but feel proud of them, and he had to deliberately remind himself of his purpose in coming here. One lesson this past year had taught him was that as sweet as the girls looked, they had their own measure of willful independence and weren't above breaking the rules now and then.

"Papa!" Her face bright, Devon jumped to her feet. "If you wish to leave early, we're ready to go now."

Christina nodded, putting aside her book of fashion plates. "We were just waiting for you. Shall we come?"

He walked farther into the room, eying them one by one.

Their smiles faded.

"Papa," Christina asked, "wh—what is wrong?"

Hugh crossed his arms. "I heard you talking through the door."

There was a moment of shocked silence. Christina's cheeks turned red and Aggie's head drooped, but Devon didn't flinch.

She lifted her chin. "So? We said nothing wrong. We were talking about how Caitriona was trying to ride but can't." She smiled. "A bear would ride a horse better."

Hugh turned his gaze on his middle daughter. "What did you say?"

Devon smirked. "I said she's *trying* to ride. We saw her this morning from the window."

Aggie's grin revealed her missing tooth. "She fell, too. Four times."

Hugh took a deep breath. "She fell off her horse, and you all found that funny."

Christina nodded, smiling uncertainly. "It was quite funny to see her . . ." Her voice trailed off when Hugh looked at her.

"You all seem very pleased by this."

Devon jutted her chin. "We are, for she's been quite mean to us this past week!" Devon's hands fisted at her sides. "That—that *woman* put honey in our pillows!"

"*What?*"

Aggie nodded. "We had to take an extra bath to get it out."

"She also turned the sheets on our beds sideways!" Devon continued in a hard voice

He frowned. "To what purpose?"

"So that when we went to bed, our feet stuck out the end. We had to remake the beds."

"And it was cold, too," Aggie added.

Christina remained suspiciously silent.

"I find it hard to believe Caitriona would ever do those things."

"She did," Devon said, visibly outraged. "And this morning, when we put on our pantaloons, we discovered that she'd sewn all of the legs together! I almost ripped mine, before I realized what was wrong with them."

Hugh looked from Devon's outraged face to Aggie's sulky one and then to Christina, who was looking down at her hands in her lap. "Christina?"

She peeked at him, her cheeks pink. "Yes, Papa?"

"Why would Caitriona do these things? None of them are harmful, but they certainly smack of revenge."

Christina swallowed with difficulty. "It's . . . it's because of something we did." Devon hissed, but Christina continued doggedly, "We told Caitriona you liked carrots."

Silence filled the room as Hugh took this in. So Caitriona had been duped—and rather than come to him, she'd decided to handle things her own way. Though his disappointment with his daughters was strong, he had a sudden urge to grin. "And you thought I'd be angry with her over the carrots."

Christina nodded. "Or at least not trust her cooking. Papa, I-I'm very sorry we did that."

"I'm not," Devon said, sniffing. "She's not welcome here, and the sooner she leaves, the better we'll all like it."

Hugh's heart was heavy in his chest. Now he knew why Caitriona had decided to learn to ride without his knowledge. And the reason was of his own making. "Come here, all of you."

Devon's brows lowered. "But—"

"On the settee. *Now.*"

They sat, Devon arriving last.

"I am going to say this but once: Caitriona is not

your mother, but she *is* my wife and you will treat her with *every* politeness. Is that clear?"

"Yes, but—" Devon began.

"There are *no* 'buts.' You will show her the same respect and politeness you show your aunt Sophia, only more so."

Christina and Aggie slowly nodded, but Devon crossed her arms over her chest.

"Devon, have I not made myself clear?"

Her mouth in a mutinous line, she finally nodded.

"I will hear no more of this mockery. Christina, when you came here you'd never ridden before, and you fell more times than I can count. And you, Aggie, have only been off leading strings for four months. I remember some of your more spectacular falls as well."

Both girls hung their heads.

Hugh locked gazes with Devon. "As for you, I remember a ride we once took to Uncle Dougal's where you fell—"

"That wasn't my fault!"

"—and landed right in the middle of a stream."

Her cheeks burned bright. "My horse stumbled."

"A good rider would have held her mount better. You let the reins go slack at a crucial time."

Her jaw set, but she offered no reply.

"I have never laughed at any of you for making mistakes, because that's how you learn. A rider who tells you she's never fallen off her horse is one who never rides at more than a walk."

Christina and Devon didn't meet his gaze, while Aggie's bottom lip quivered.

"Caitriona is trying to learn," Hugh said softly. "That is what matters the most." And it did matter. His heart warmed at the realization of what Caitriona had done—both in learning to ride and in dealing with his daughters in such a spirited, but gentle way. He almost grinned to think of their reactions as she turned the tables on their trick.

"Yes, but she isn't one of *us*," Devon said, her voice tight with anger. "She can barely ride at all!"

"At least she is working to improve her skills—unlike other young ladies I know, who'd rather gallop madly without regard for the health or safety of their mounts!"

Devon's and Aggie's faces glowed red, while Christina sent them a surreptitious glance.

"Another young lady I know cannot seem to keep her heels in, without being reminded every single moment."

Now Christina's face matched her sisters'.

Hugh scowled. "This is our house, and while she's here, Caitriona is part of our family. I should have made this announcement weeks ago, but I didn't realize—" He bit off the rest of the sentence. "We will talk about this more later. I am leaving for two or three days to find a missing mare."

They all looked up.

"You will stay at Uncle Dougal's while I am gone."

Devon planted her hands on her hips. "We want to stay here."

"And have your pantaloons sewed shut every morning?" He quirked a brow. "I can't trust you three to behave yourself with Caitriona. Since I can't stay and monitor you more closely, you'll go to Dougal's. When I return, we'll discuss this situation further."

All three girls slumped.

Hugh lifted his brows. "You like staying at Uncle Dougal's, so do not act as if I've just sentenced you to death."

Christina sighed. "Aunt Sophia's been away for weeks."

"Uncle Dougal is getting very cranky about it," Devon added.

Aggie sniffed. "He's lovesick."

"I am sure having the three of you with him will make him feel better."

"I don't know about that," Devon muttered.

He gave them each a hard stare. "If Uncle Dougal invites Caitriona to dinner while I am gone, as he will likely do, you will be on your best behavior. If I return to find that you were anything other than perfectly polite, there will be consequences. Do I make myself clear?"

All three nodded.

"Good. I am going to pack. You will return to your room and change. There will be no riding today."

Christina and Aggie nodded, but Devon's lips were pressed into a solid line.

Hugh's gaze narrowed. "I mean it. Now, go and pack." He turned on his heel and walked to the door.

"Papa?"

He turned to find Christina on her feet, a few steps behind him as if she'd run to catch him. "We-we didn't mean to make you angry."

He looked at her, irritation still roiling through him.

Her large eyes filled with tears, and just as suddenly as his temper had arisen, it was gone, and in its place was disappointment. He sighed and pulled her to him for a hug. "Lass, I know you didn't mean any harm, and nothing was done that can't be undone. But I expected better of all of you."

Christina moved back. "Please, just don't be angry."

"I'm much angrier at myself than at you."

Devon's brows lowered as if she couldn't puzzle this out, and he smiled, feeling as tired as if he'd spent the day in the saddle. "We'll settle all of this when I return. I'm going to speak with Caitriona right now. Change your clothes, and I'll come see you before I leave."

He gave them each a hug, then left. As he climbed the stairs, he mulled over what he should say to Triona.

Not once, in all of the intimate moments they'd shared, had she mentioned her problems with the children. She'd done as he'd convinced her to do and had distanced herself from them, to the point where the girls saw her as a permanent outsider. *Which is what I wanted, fool that I am.* And then the children had taken things too far. It irked him that she had needed something, but hadn't felt comfortable enough to ask for it.

That could not continue. He reached their bed-chamber and halted outside as he considered his options. Should he begin with an apology? Was one even necessary? Would she rather know he'd discovered that Ferguson was training her to ride, or should he allow her to surprise him? In a way, what she was doing was a gift, and he had no wish to lessen the importance of it.

But how did he convince Caitriona to be more open with him, without giving up something himself? They had worked out a delicate balance of power and he was loathe to upset it.

Inside the room, a faint splash reminded him that Caitriona had called for hot water. His wife was inside, naked, and soaking her lovely limbs in a scented bath. With a determined expression, he turned the knob and entered his room.

# Chapter 15

*"If ye wish to give, do it with yer heart and hands open. 'Tis shabby to give any other way."*

OLD WOMAN NORA TO HER THREE WEE
GRANDDAUGHTERS ON A COLD WINTER'S NIGHT

*T*riona closed her eyes and rested her head against the edge of the huge, high-sided copper tub. At Wythburn, their tub was merely a fourth the size of this one, only large enough to stand in. Once, several years ago, Mary had tried to sit in it and had gotten stuck. Caitlyn, Caitriona, and Mother had tried everything to get her loose. Finally, they'd had to throw a sheet over her and call in William to pull her free. Triona chuckled at the memory.

Mary would love this tub. Triona wondered if she could invite her sister to come and stay for a while. Mam had suggested it a few days ago, and it seemed like a good idea. Caitriona shifted in the tub, wincing. She'd never been this sore, but it would be worth it. Not only would she have something to share with MacLean, but it might also help bridge the gap between her and the girls.

Just this morning, she'd caught sight of them in an upper-story window as Ferguson provided her daily riding lesson, and they had laughed hysterically whenever she did something wrong. Caitriona smiled. She was sure they felt quite superior to her and found her inability to ride a cause for mockery, which was even better. It was hard to be suspicious and angry with someone when you thought them incompetent.

Being laughed at was a small price to pay for breaking through the barriers the girls—and Hugh—had set.

All in all, Triona thought she was making excellent progress, especially after their little stunt with the cottage pie. Just this morning she had made Aggie laugh, and once she'd surprised a genuine smile from Christina. Devon was the most suspicious and resistant to her, qualities Triona was sure the girl had inherited from her father. MacLean was many things, but trusting was not one of them.

It was slow going, but Triona felt things were improving. It had only been a few weeks, after all. She sighed and fished around for the soap, hidden beneath the thick layer of bubbles on top of the water. Mrs. Wallis's lavender soap was quite the nicest, frothiest—

The door suddenly opened, and Triona turned. Hugh entered the room, closing the door behind him. He was devastatingly handsome in his riding clothes, his black boots to his knees, his knit breeches stretched over his muscled thighs. The simplicity of his clothing highlighted his powerful masculinity.

As his green gaze lingered on her, it took all of her

will not to cover herself. This was her husband, and she enjoyed looking at him. How could she deny him the same opportunity?

To keep from feeling awkward, she soaped her washcloth and glanced at the clock on the mantel. "I'm surprised to see you. The girls will be expecting their daily ride soon."

"I'm not going riding with them today."

"Oh—they will be so disappointed."

"It will be good for them. Perhaps they will appreciate it more when I return."

Her heart sank. "Return?"

"I have to leave for a day or two. One of my horses is missing and we think she may be ready to foal, or has already."

Surprised at her disappointment, she managed a brief, "I see. Will she be all right?"

"More than likely, although I have a bad feeling."

She looked at him curiously. "Another of your MacLean abilities?"

His eyes crinkled. "I think you know most of my abilities by now."

Her cheeks heated at the images he roused, and she was suddenly hot, shivery, and restless all at the same time.

It was a feeling she was beginning to welcome. Even now, stiff and sore, she felt the familiar stirring deep inside, a restless hunger for his touch. She lifted the washcloth to her shoulder, and her lower back twinged in protest.

MacLean must have seen her grimace, for he plucked the cloth from her hand. "Allow me." He slipped off his coat and tossed it over the settee, knelt beside her, and rolled up his sleeves.

"Oh, no! You don't need to—"

He dunked the washcloth into the tub, wrung it out, and rubbed her arm in lazy circles. His eyes gleamed warmly. "How's that?"

"Fine," she squeaked. "Although I-I can wash myself."

"I've noticed." He gently pushed her forward so he could wash her back. "I've never seen a woman take so many baths." He rubbed her back in slow, even circles, unknowingly massaging her sore muscles.

That was *divine*.

She closed her eyes, wincing now and then when he hit an extra-sore spot, yet blissful as the muscles slowly relaxed beneath his magic touch. She sighed her contentment.

He chuckled, the sound low and devilish. Then he rubbed her shoulders, his long fingers lingering on her neck, as wet and warm as the cloth.

She shivered at the touch, her breasts tingling as if they, too, had received his attentions.

He kissed her ear, sending a shiver through her. "Lean back," he whispered.

She did so, sinking deeper into the hot water until it reached her shoulders.

He soaped the cloth again, regarding her with a mischievous expression. "You know, I believe there's room for us both in that tub."

"I suppose we could both fit."

His eyes glinted. "If I didn't need to leave soon, I'd spend an hour or two in there with you."

"The water would grow cold."

He leaned down and whispered, his breath warm on her cheek, "We could reheat even the coldest water."

Her face grew so warm, she knew it had to be as red as the rug.

He straightened and dipped the cloth into the water. Looking into her eyes, he placed the cloth on her breast, his fingers brushing over her bare skin.

Triona bit her lip, holding back a moan.

Hugh moved the cloth in small circles, teasing her nipple and sending shivery pleasure sparkling through her veins.

She closed her eyes, shifting restlessly. It felt heavenly and naughty at the same time.

"Caitriona," Hugh said, his voice deep and rumbly. "Lift your leg and rest it on the edge of the tub."

Normally, Triona could have done so easily. Today, however, her legs were sore from her ride and quivery from MacLean's touch. It took all of her concentration to do as he said.

The cool air chilled her wet leg and she shivered. Suddenly, she realized that the soap bubbles had thinned a great deal, and raising her leg had left her exposed in a very embarrassing way. She started to pull her leg back into the water, but MacLean stopped her.

"Keep your leg on the edge of the tub."

He dipped the cloth into the water and massaged as he washed, beginning at her ankle and working his way over her calf . . . past her knee . . . to her thigh. Each stroke was agony and ecstasy. She gripped the tub, caught between delightful dread and delicious anticipation.

His hand dipped lower, the cloth brushing between her legs.

She gasped, her entire body quivering. His wicked, make-me-stop grin made her heart pound madly.

He dipped the cloth beneath the warm water and again ran it between her thighs. She bit her lip, and he did it again. And again. Faster, and faster.

His eyes gleamed with a deep green heat. "Let me pleasure you," he whispered.

How could she stop him, when she couldn't even stop herself?

"This seems so . . . naughty."

His lips quirked. "That, my love, is why I like it."

*My love.* The words were meaningless, but they warmed her nonetheless.

He kissed her ear, making her shiver as he continued to stroke her. At some point, she realized he was no longer using the cloth, but his talented fingers.

He lightly bit her ear, then nuzzled his way down her neck. Each kiss made her explode with passion.

His hand never stilled, stroking and teasing. She squirmed, urging him on. It was so decadent, being naked in the tub before a dressed man, her legs splayed shamelessly, her breasts bouncing in the water, the air filled with the sound of her gasping desire as he brought her to the brink of heaven.

Each touch was driving her mad, and answering her deepest need. She panted, straining against his hand, arching and lifting her breasts out of the water.

He immediately captured her nipple between his lips, laving the turgid peak until she cried his name and cupped his head firmly to her. The moment seemed to stretch until she could hold back no more. Just as she fell over the edge, he leaned forward and captured her lips with his, as if to swallow her cries of passion whole.

Triona fell back, MacLean catching her to him. Her entire body quivered with aftershocks as she slowly regained her senses.

When her thundering heart returned to normal and her mind began to function again, she pushed back from his chest and met his gaze, blushing. "I-I-"

He grinned. "Yes?"

"Your shirt is wet."

"My breeches, too, for we lost a good deal of water out of the tub." His eyes twinkled. "I will have to change before I leave."

Oh, yes. He was leaving. Her heart sank, but she refused to let him see it. "Thank you for . . ."

"You're welcome. The next time I have a bath, you can repay the favor."

Oh! What a wonderful thought! "I'd like that!"

He laughed at her obvious enthusiasm. "Not as much as I will."

When he stood, she saw that his shirt clung to him like a second skin and his breeches were dark where the water had splashed out. "You really *do* need to change."

"I'm just glad I removed my coat and waistcoat before I assisted you in the tub." He pulled a fresh shirt and a pair of black breeches from the wardrobe, tossed them on the settee, and began to undress.

Triona watched as he peeled off his shirt, his rippled stomach and chest gleaming damply in the light, a scattering of black curling hair gathering to form a line down to his breeches.

She loved his chest hair and had trailed her fingers down that line many, many times.

He tossed the wet shirt to the floor and undid his breeches, which soon landed on the shirt.

Triona couldn't help but stare. "That," she said, pointing, "will *never* fit into your breeches."

He laughed. "*That* came out of my breeches, so it will fit back into them."

She frowned. "Won't that hurt?"

"No. Although if you think it might help, you could kiss it."

Her lips quivered. "You'll have to bring it over here. It's too cold out there for me."

"Under normal circumstances, I would take you up on that lovely offer. But I must go."

She tried not to look disappointed but must have failed, for he added in a warm tone, "I will come back as quickly as I can."

She nodded and watched silently as he finished dressing, forgoing his cravat for a simple neckcloth. He then found a serviceable waistcoat of heavy wool and buttoned that over his shirt before putting on his coat.

"Will it be cold where you're going?"

"Yes. The horses range up the mountains to a particular valley, and it's much higher than here."

"Ah." She leaned on the edge of the tub, watching him take several clean shirts from the wardrobe. He bundled them together and tucked them under his arm.

"Aren't you going to take a portmanteau?"

"Just a saddlebag. It will keep out the weather." He raked a hand through his hair and turned to face her, his expression suddenly somber. "Caitriona, I must ask you a favor."

"You wish me to watch after the girls! Of course I will. In fact, I'll—"

"No. That won't be necessary."

Triona's smile faded. "Not necessary? But—"

"The girls are going to Dougal's. I spoke to them about it before I came up here."

Triona frowned. "You don't need to ask your brother. I will keep them and—"

"No. And that's that."

Triona stiffened. "Why not?"

"I overheard them talking this morning. Something about their pantaloons being sewn shut."

"Oh. That." She sighed. "I should explain—"

"You don't need to. They've already told me everything, which is why they're now packing to go to Dougal's. I don't have time to sort things out right now, but . . . Caitriona, I owe you an apology. My request that you remain aloof from the girls—I didn't mean for it to cause more problems than it solved. They resent you and think of you as an outsider, and have taken it into their heads to chase you away."

"I know."

His frown deepened. "They've behaved abominably."

"Hugh, they're spirited girls and they're just being protective. I don't think less of them for that." She managed a grin. "Besides, I've been holding my own. Wait until they go to put their hair up tomorrow."

His lips quirked. "You took their hairpins?"

"Don't be an amateur! I put starch on their hairbrushes."

He laughed. "Giving them a taste of their own medicine."

"Yes, but . . . it's more than that. Hugh, I can't be here and not be a part of their lives. I've been thinking about it, and—" She took a deep breath. "I just can't do that anymore. I am either here, involved with you *and* the girls, or—"

The laughter was completely gone from his face. "Or what?" he asked harshly.

"Or I need to leave now."

Hugh clenched his jaw, and he had to force himself to speak calmly. "It's too soon." He wasn't sure how he knew that, but he did.

"It was never meant for me to stay more than a month or two. It hasn't quite been a month yet, but—"

"*No.*" He glanced at the clock. "I don't have time to go into this right now. We'll discuss it when I return." He gathered his things and headed for the door, an odd hollowness in his chest.

"Hugh?"

He paused by the door. "Yes?"

"Please don't send the girls to Dougal's. Leave them with me. I'll take care of them; I promise."

However he felt, he was not immune to the pain in her voice. "Caitriona, whenever I have to leave, I always make sure the girls are with Dougal. It's not because of you, but because of their mother." He saw the confusion in her face and hesitated. If he left without explaining, she'd think the worse. While he had no desire to examine his own feelings right now, she deserved to know why he was so concerned for the girls' safety. He sighed and returned to place the bundle of clothes on the bed. "Just before I went to London to stop your sister, I received a letter from Clarissa."

"What did this letter say?"

"The same thing all of her letters say—that she wants the girls back, and will come and get them."

"Do you really think she'd do such a thing?"

"She's tried before. She knows how I feel about them, and that I'll do anything—*pay* anything—to keep them."

Triona had never seen such a bleak look on anyone's face. Her heart ached with it. "That's blackmail."

"Yes. I made the mistake of letting Clarissa see how much the girls meant to me. At the time, she thought it was quite funny. Later, she saw it as a means to increase her wealth."

"How could she think your feelings were a matter of laughter?"

"I was a confirmed bachelor and had no interest in children. But then I ended up with the girls"—he shot her a hard look—"with *my* girls, and it changed things."

"You grew to love them."

He nodded. "I suppose it was quite ironic. Clarissa offered to leave them here if I paid her two thousand pounds."

Indignation made her blood boil. "Has she asked for other sums?"

"Several times. Once I refused, and she arrived with a solicitor, ready to claim the girls." His lips thinned. "It took ten thousand pounds to get her to leave."

"You must stop paying her!"

"She is prepared to take it to court, and I am not willing to do that."

"As the father, you have more right to them than she does. Any court would support you."

"It's a complicated situation."

"How?"

He picked up her towel. "Let me dry you."

She rose and he wrapped her in the towel, then carried her to the bed. Her sore muscles thanked him when he gently set her on the mattress, then gave her his dry robe.

"Thank you."

He winked and opened the wardrobe, then brought one of her new gowns to her.

She took it, but remained on the edge of the bed, wrapped only in his robe. "So you wish to leave the girls with your brother in case Clarissa returns?"

"Yes. At some point they will be too old for her to threaten, and then nothing she says will matter. Until then, I must be cautious." He paused, then added in a quietly agonized voice, "A lawsuit aside, she's not above abducting them. She knows I would pay anything to have them back."

"She's heartless."

Hugh nodded, his expression grim. "Which is why the girls must be watched. Dougal has men who protect his house because he worries about Sophia. She and her father are known gamblers, and sometimes have a great deal of wealth on hand."

Triona nodded. "Of course they must stay with Dougal. Thank you for explaining things to me."

"You're welcome." He collected his clothing once more. "I informed the girls that if Dougal invites you to dinner, they are to be polite to you. Tell me if they aren't, and I will deal with them on my return."

She frowned. "Thank you, but I wish you hadn't ordered them to be nice to me. I was handling things my way, and it would have worked. Now they'll be upset, thinking I put you up to it, just as I was making such good progress."

His gaze narrowed. "Progress? Then you've been *trying* to win them over?"

"I've been giving them the chance to trust me." Her gaze sparkled with irritation.

So she hadn't been following his directive to stay away from the girls after all. Exasperated at her defiance, Hugh allowed his gaze to drift over her face. Her eyes seemed to glow a deep hazel green, swirled with sparkles of gold and flecks of deep brown. Her hair, wet from the bath, had darkened to light brown. Her face was freshly scrubbed, her eyes large in her face.

It suddenly dawned on him that in a few weeks, she would be gone and this moment would be only a memory. His chest ached at the thought, and he realized with shock that he would miss her.

She met his gaze. "I would never hurt those children."

"Not intentionally."

"Not in any way whatsoever." Her voice was soft, but the intensity of her emotion colored every word.

If he was going to miss Caitriona this much after only a few weeks, how much more would the girls miss her? He hardened his heart. "I know what's best for my children."

She shot him a hard glare. Distracted by their disagreement, she'd let go of the robe and didn't seem to realize it was gaping open, revealing one of her breasts and her sweet, bath-flushed skin.

Suddenly leaving was the last thing he wished to do, and he wondered if he should let Ferguson take one of the stable hands to find the missing mare. But no—if something was wrong with her, no one knew better than he how to tend to an ill horse. "I will return soon." His voice had a harsh edge, lust tightening his cock until he couldn't think.

"Take your time," she sniffed. "I am sure we will all thrive without you."

"Caitriona, you must understand—"

"No," she said, grabbing the robe about her and standing. "*You* must understand. I am a part of this household, whether you like it or not. You made that happen when you married me. You can't expect me to meekly agree to everything you say. I have opinions, and some of them are better than yours."

He scowled. "I've never expected you to meekly do anything."

"Yes, you have. Every time you speak, it's an order. You never *ask* anything. And I, trying to be polite, have allowed you to do so far too often. But no more. I am not one of your children to be cowed by your pompous manner."

Hugh clenched his fists, and outside, the low moan of a cold wind rattled against the windows. "I have explained my position to you."

"And I've explained mine. This isn't about the girls. It's about you. You don't allow anyone close to you, do you, MacLean? Not me. Only the children, really." She said quietly, "I'm glad they haven't been as lonely as I've been."

He'd opened his house to her, introduced her to his children, and welcomed her into his bed. How *dare* she blame him if she felt lonely? "This conversation is getting us nowhere. We'll talk when we're not so upset."

She threw her chin up. "No, we'll talk about it *now*. You, Hugh MacLean, are the biggest coward I've ever met."

Hugh stiffened. "I am not a coward."

"You are when it comes to being a proper husband."

The words settled in the room between them like a wall. He couldn't believe she'd said such a thing and looking at her wide eyes, he realized she'd shocked herself, too.

His jaw tightened until it ached. "You don't mean that," he said firmly.

She lifted her chin and regarded him as if she were a queen holding court instead of a bath-soaked lass wrapped in a robe three times her size. "I do mean it. A proper husband would welcome his mate as an equal in all ways and not just the bedchamber."

"If this is about the girls, we've had this discussion before and you agreed with me!" In the distance, a low rumble of thunder echoed, punctuating his thought.

"We were wrong. I should never have agreed to stay away from the girls. They know I'm going to leave so they would be neither surprised nor upset."

"They would be if they'd come to care for you!" *Like I have.* The thought caught him, froze him in place, shocking him more than her words had. Through a fog he dimly heard her continue.

"Hugh, people come and go in our lives, but that doesn't mean they don't love us. The children need to know this, to understand that just because someone can't be with them, doesn't mean they aren't cared for."

Hugh clenched his hands at his sides, his blood simmering, his heart aching. He was filled with such a myriad of emotions he didn't know which to address first—uncertainty at his own reaction to the thought of her absence, irritation that he had to leave soon and couldn't truly do this argument justice, or pure fury that she dared question his decisions for his own daughters. His jaw tightened and the rumble of thunder grew closer still.

She cast a glance at the window, then returned her gaze to him, her brows lowering. "Don't threaten me with your storms. *You're* the one who has to travel in this mess, not me."

"I'm well aware of that fact," he snapped. "I would appreciate it if you didn't say such asinine things as force me to lose my temper!"

Her eyes sparkling with ire, her plump lips pressed in a straight line. "If what I said makes you lose your temper, then that's an excellent sign that it's the truth and you know it."

Fury roared through him, but she continued. "You are miserly with your emotions, and a coward with your love. You spend all of your life afraid of this and that. It's not enough, MacLean. The girls and I deserve more."

Hugh's vision went red. The fire flickered wildly, smoke puffing into the room. The windows creaked and groaned as cold suddenly flooded the room like an invisible layer of ice.

Caitriona kept her gaze locked on his, her face pale, a shiver racking her as she marched to him to stand toe to toe. "Well? What do you have to say for yourself?"

"Don't ever question my love for my children. *Ever*."

Her chin came up and she said through teeth that were beginning to chatter, "You may l-love them, but that doesn't mean you're sharing yourself with th-them. Those are d-d-different things."

"They have everything they need."

Her gaze didn't waver, and he clenched his teeth. His gaze dropped to her hand where it clutched the robe. He concentrated on her hand, picturing a wind blowing the robe away. Slowly, the bottom of the robe rippled. Then the low breeze grew and tugged at it harder. Overhead, thunder rumbled, rain slapping the roof.

The pain in Hugh's head increased, and with a flick of his fingers, he let the wind go. It roared through the house.

Triona's heart pounded as the vicious wind buffeted her, threatening to knock her off her feet. She flexed her knees and held tightly to the robe, coldness numbing her skin.

Hugh's lips thinned; white lines appeared at the sides of his mouth; his hair whipped around his face. A sudden surge cracked through the room as the icy wind ripped the robe from her grasp and sucked the air from her lungs. She gasped for breath, hugging herself in the frigid swirl, her teeth chattering uncontrollably.

A thick mist flowed across the floor and the air grew damp and icy. The wood beneath her bare feet grew freezing cold as the wind sent a delicate vase crashing to the floor. A row of books on a shelf flew off as if a hand had shoved them. One of the chairs by the fireplace flipped over and the settee blew to a crazed angle.

Triona hugged herself, dropping her head against the wind. It battered against her, pushing her back, back. She stumbled and fell onto the bed.

All over the house, vases could be heard breaking, chairs toppling over. Outside, lightning cracked as thunder roared. Someone gave a muffled shout, and then—

Just as suddenly as it began, it ended. All that could be heard was the steady beat of rain on the roof.

Hugh's eyes glowed an odd green and his lips were almost white. Strain showed in every line of his face.

"I-I h-h-hope you're h-h-happy n-now," she said through chattering teeth, furious and freezing. The robe had blown around one of the bedposts and she scrambled over the sheets to retrieve it. She pulled it on, glaring at him.

Hugh rubbed his furrowed forehead, deep lines tracing from his nose to his mouth. "Caitriona . . . I don't know why I did that. I-I've never done that before and I—" He passed a shaking hand over his face, his expression stricken.

"Go."

He took a step toward her, but she quickly moved away.

Something flickered deep in his eyes. "I'm sorry."

She didn't answer, unable to put all of her feelings of hurt, disappointment, anger, and fear into words. She felt everything and yet nothing but her chilled soul, as if all of those emotions weren't enough to warm her.

"Caitriona, I—"

She shook her head and sank down on the bed, clutching the pillows to her.

Finally, with a pained expression, he left.

Caitriona listened to his footsteps receding, waiting until she could hear no more. Then she buried her face in a pillow and cried.

Hugh stopped at the bottom of the steps, opening and closing his hands. What in the hell had he done? He *never* lost his temper. Not since his youth, when his younger brother had been killed, had he allowed his temper to get the better of him. This time, he hadn't just lost his temper, but he'd directed the wind, and he had nothing but a sickening headache and a painfully hollow feeling in his chest to show for his efforts.

He looked around the foyer at the fallen portraits and the ripped curtains. A large vase had shattered in one corner. Worse, Angus and Liam were staring at him, uncertainty in their faces. Their uniforms were askew, disarrayed by the storm he'd unleashed in the house.

Regret choked him. "Liam, fetch the girls and their luggage. They will be staying at my brother's for a few days."

"Right away, m'lord." Liam took the stairs two at a time, obviously glad to leave.

Angus stood rigidly at attention.

"I will need the coach brought around."

"Aye, m'lord." He sprinted off as if he couldn't wait to get away.

Hugh felt queasy, his head pounding as if he'd spun in a circle too many times. He would feel like this for several days, more if he didn't rest.

He hadn't meant to get angry. It had just infuriated him when Caitriona accused him of not being capable of sharing himself with his daughters. He loved Christina and Devon and Aggie with a love that had no bounds. How *dare* Caitriona question him!

But she did. She dared question him, just as she dared to give the girls a taste of their own pranks. Exhausted, he looked up the stairs and wondered what she was doing now. She'd appeared stricken. Should he go to her? Talk to her?

*Why? You don't even know how you feel.* He shook his head and walked to the door to wait outside for the children.

He needed some time and space to untangle the welter of lust and emotions Caitriona caused. A lot of time, and a lot of space.

Thank God he knew where to find both.

# Chapter 16

❧

*" 'Tis a sad day when ye ha' t' pinch yerself t' see if ye're awake or in th' midst o' a night terror. 'Tis a really sad day when ye have t' pinch yerself twice."*

OLD WOMAN NORA TO HER THREE WEE
GRANDDAUGHTERS ON A COLD WINTER'S NIGHT

*M*rs. Wallis bent down and squinted into the gloom. "I'm not sure which one 'tis, but . . ." She frowned. "Maybe 'tis no' here, after all. But I remember it bein' here, so . . ." She squinted again.

Triona, standing behind Mrs. Wallis, waited patiently. Outside a cold wind blew, a remnant of Hugh's fury, occasionally rattling the windows and leaking in around the sills.

Her stomach tightened at the memory of their argument two days ago. She hadn't slept well since. If she was honest, part of the reason was that she was so used to having MacLean's warm body in the bed, which seemed colder and even huger without him.

Mrs. Wallis straightened, her head barely missing the rafter overhead.

"Careful!" Triona warned, holding the lantern higher.

"Aye, the beams are low."

"And solid." Triona looked around. "Even this part of the house is exceptionally well built. The attic at Wythburn is the size of a closet and leaks dreadfully."

"Aye, the master has done wonders. When the journeymen finished wi' the house, he sent them to the laird to work on the castle. They've done amazin' things there as well."

Triona had seen the castle plenty of times. Huge and imposing, it was perched on a ridge across the valley from Mam's large house. As a young child visiting her grandmother, Triona had imagined the two edifices— the ancient castle of the cursed MacLeans and the new manor house where Mam always kept cookies for her wee granddaughters—were keeping watch over the sleepy town nestled by the river below.

"Hold tha' lamp over here. I'm thinkin' the trunk we need might be in this corner after all."

Triona did as she was told and was rewarded with a glad cry from Mrs. Wallis. "Aye! There 'tis! I'll send Liam to fetch it." She smiled at Triona. " 'Tis a sweet thing ye be doin', makin' the lassies new wool petticoats fer their ridin' habits. His lordship doesna think o' the cold, and he has those poor bairns ridin' in the worst weather. 'Tis a wonder they have no' died o' the ague!"

Triona had some thoughts on his lordship, too, but none of them were fit for public airing.

Mrs. Wallis took the lantern and headed back downstairs. As Triona followed, she groaned. "I'm so sore from riding. Does it ever get better?"

Mrs. Wallis chuckled. "Look how long ye rode this mornin', and withou' Ferguson, too! I was a bit worried fer ye, since ye were gone fer two whole hours."

"I'm regretting every minute of it now."

Mrs. Wallis sent her a beaming smile. "Well, I think 'tis a good thing ye're doin'. His lordship will be so pleased. Horses are his life—he lives and breathes them." Mrs. Wallis tsked. "Worse, he's raisin' those three young wild things to do the same. He takes 'em riding every day, rain or shine."

*Because he loves them.* Since Hugh had left, Triona had relived their argument over and over. Everytime she came to the part where she had accused him of not being able to care, she winced.

That was grossly false, for he dearly loved his girls. She'd spoken in hurt and anger, and her words had achieved their purpose—she'd made him just as upset and angry at her as she'd been at him.

Triona's throat tightened, and she had to clear it before she asked, "Why do you call the girls 'wild things'?"

"Spoiled, they are. If they were my lassies, I'd give 'em a good switchin'. His lordship doesna see the trouble they cause. Good as gold they are, when he's in the house, but let him be gone ten minutes . . ." She scowled. "Just last week, one o' them put salt in the sugar bowl but I discovered it before 'twas set on the table!"

Triona smiled. "My brothers have done much worse than that. William especially can be counted on to think of new ways to get into trouble." The thought made her momentarily homesick. What were her brothers and sisters doing right now?

Her feelings must have been evident, for Mrs. Wallis's expression softened. "Aye, children will be children."

"Except William is twenty years old and should know better." She would write her brothers and sisters another letter today. She was due one from them, too. Caitlyn was a horrible scribe, as were William and Robert. But Michael and Mary could be counted on to send her long, detailed accounts of all that went on at Wythburn.

She could picture them now, sitting about the small fireplace. Mary would be knitting or embroidering, for she never sat without keeping her hands busy. Robert would be reading some tome he thought might endear him to Father, while sneering at Caitlyn, who read nothing but the ladies' magazines and fashion plates. William would be lounging against the mantel talking about horses or hunting or whatever new hobby he was pursuing, while Michael, if still feeling poorly, would be on the old red settee bundled against the cold.

She even missed Robert's complaining! But with Gilmerton so empty, the halls seemed to echo. And the fact she and Hugh had parted on such difficult terms made things worse.

"Will ye be visitin' yer grandmother, m' lady? Liam will be goin' to town on some errands fer Cook today and won't be about to drive ye, since Ferguson is gone."

"No, she always visits town on Wednesdays, so I'll go tomorrow."

"Very good, m' lady. 'Tis nice tha' ye visit yer grandmother."

"She's been a great help to me. She might know what to do about these sore muscles, too."

Triona followed Mrs. Wallis down the grand staircase to the foyer. Liam and Angus were polishing silver in the dining room, close enough to the front door to hear if someone knocked.

" 'Tis a boon yer grandmother knows her herbs," the housekeeper said.

"She's been a healer for most of her life. She also runs the mills my grandfather left her."

"Och!" Mrs. Wallis's eyes grew round. "No' the Hurst mills?"

"Yes."

"Never say tha' yer grandmother's Old Woman Nora from Hurst House?"

"Yes, that's her."

Mrs. Wallis beamed. "If I'd only known yer grandmother was Old Woman Nora! I've always wish't to meet her but never had the privilege. She delivered two o' me granddaughters. Me Mary had a horrible time wit' the last one, but she said she knew when Old Nora arrived tha' she and the bairn would survive, no matter wha'."

"I'm sure she'll be pleased to know she's remembered."

Mrs. Wallis shook her head, smiling. "To think tha' his lordship runs off to Londontown and ends up marryin' the granddaughter o' Old Woman Nora! 'Twas fate as brought the two o' ye together."

Triona wished she could believe that; it would be nice to have fate in her corner. She'd alienated Hugh and she needed all of the assistance she could get, divine and otherwise. She stifled a sigh. "I wish to write a letter to my family and shall need more ink. The well in the sitting-room desk is dry."

"Aye, m' lady. I'll see to it right away." Mrs. Wallis shot a glance at Triona and said, "My, tha' was quite a storm we had the other day."

"Wasn't it?" Triona said politely.

"Aye, it scared poor Cook nigh to death. An entire rack of knives came flyin' at her as she hid under the workbench."

"I'm glad no one was hurt." If someone had been, she'd have felt responsible for she'd goaded Hugh.

It was a good lesson. If she wanted a reaction out of him, anger was not a viable option. Besides, she much preferred his unbridled lust.

They reached the sitting-room door and the house-keeper said, "I'll bring some ink straight away."

"Thank you, Mrs. Wallis. I appreciate your assistance."

"Och, think nothin' o' it! Ye've been ridin' and climbin' stairs, and that's just this morning. I can tell ye've been raised in the healthy country air. Moira says ye were out of yer bed this mornin' a full hour afore me!"

Oh, Triona had been up much longer than that. She'd awakened with the dawn, cold and alone and missing being tucked against Hugh's warm, naked body. Each morning as she'd stir sleepily, he'd tease her to a passion to match his own.

But she missed him for more than their lovemaking. Over the past few weeks, he had become a part of her life. She enjoyed their conversations over breakfast before the girls were up, about their childhoods and their expectations and even nothing at all. Added to their physical bond, it was a beginning.

If only she could convince him to unleash some of his passion out of bed as well . . . but after their argument, he'd be even more determined to keep her at arm's length.

Worse, she was just beginning to realize the effect his actions had on the girls. They were resisting her not because they resented her position in the household, but because they could sense their father's reluctance and feared her influence over him. If they only knew the truth, that she not only had no influence over their father, but she'd been completely unable to engage him in any way except on a physical level. Well that, and she apparently possessed the dubious talent of stirring his temper to boiling heights.

She rubbed her arms, suddenly restless. Since Hugh had left, she'd been having the same thoughts over and over. Left alone in such a huge house and filled with regrets over her final words with her husband, was beginning to take its toll. She needed a project to keep her busy, something that would leave her good and tired when the sun sank below the horizon and the empty house suddenly seemed bigger and even emptier.

"Will there be anythin' else, m' lady?" the housekeeper asked.

"Mrs. Wallis, how many years have you been with Lord Hugh?"

"Fifteen," she said proudly.

"So you know MacLean very well."

Mrs. Wallis's gray eyes met hers steadily. "Aye. Well enough to know when one o' them has lost his temper."

"It would be difficult to miss," Triona said dryly.

"Why did ye wish to know?"

"Because I'm of a mind to make some changes. Nothing drastic, but it would be nice if I could add something—something of myself—to Gilmerton." *Before I leave.*

"That seems a fair idea. Wha' is it ye have in mind?"

"I would like to surprise his lordship by making the house better in some way. But everything is so well run that there's really no room for improvement."

Mrs. Wallis beamed. "Thank ye, m' lady. I dinna know if this is what ye had in mind, but I've thought fer several years tha' perhaps we should move the furniture. If ye keep it one way too long, it mars the wood floors as people walk just one way through the room."

"A wonderful idea. Perhaps we can do that after lunch—"

There was a loud knock on the door, and Liam came out to open it.

Mam swept in dressed in her Sunday finest, a lavender gown with a sober gray cape, her sober brown boots peeking out from beneath the hem. Her iron gray curls were tucked beneath the largest flowered bonnet Triona had ever seen.

Leaning upon her cane, she looked Triona up and down. "Well? Are ye goin' to offer me a drop o' tea? I traveled a whole hour to get here, and me bones are creakin' wit' a powerful thirst."

Mrs. Wallis dipped a curtsey. "I'll fetch ye some tea right away. By the way, Mrs. Hurst, I'm sorry I dinna know before tha' ye were Nora the Healer or I'd have thanked ye fer helpin' me bairns."

Mam lifted an interested brow. "Oh? An' who might yer wee ones be?"

"Mary Wallis and Lara Kirkland."

"Och, I remember them both! How are yer bonny daughters a'doin'?"

Mrs. Wallis flushed with pleasure. She spent several minutes telling Nora about her daughters, then scurried off to fetch tea and scones.

"Don't forget the marmalade!" Mam called after her. "I do love some nice marmalade when I'm out visitin'." She sent a guilty glance at Triona. "I don't like to serve it meself, as 'tis mighty dear."

Triona laughed and hugged the old woman. "You are just the woman I was hoping to see."

"I figured ye might could use an ear." Mam cocked a silver brow as Triona escorted her into the sitting room. "I suppose ye could say the thought came a' me in a rush."

Triona sighed. "The wind?"

"Aye. Tha' had to be his lordship and no one else." Mam sat on the settee by the fireplace and patted the cushion beside her. "Come, child, and tell me what's happened."

Soon Triona was pouring out her heart to her grandmother. Mam listened to it all, asking shrewd questions along the way. They stopped only when Mrs. Wallis brought in a tray of scones with marmalade and tea.

Finally, long after Mrs. Wallis had departed, Triona finished.

Mam sat in silence for a moment and then tsked. "Ye both lost yer tempers."

"I was so frustrated."

"I can see tha'." Mam took a noisy sip of her tea. "Lassie, wha' do ye want from MacLean?"

"I want him to fully accept me as his wife."

"Ah. So ye wish fer a commitment of the heart." She patted Triona's hand. "Ye wish him to be in love wit' ye."

"No, no, no. I just want him to . . ." What *did* she want? Acceptance? Yes, of course, but she wanted more, too.

Was Mam right? *Did* she want a commitment of the heart? Could she ask for such a thing?

"Easy, now! Yer head will explode if ye keep thinkin' so hard. 'Tis no' a complicated matter. From wha' ye said, it sounds as if ye were both barin' yer teeth at one another. Ye each owe t'other an apology."

"I was afraid you'd say that."

Mam patted her hand. "La, lassie! Is tha' so bad?" Her bright eyes locked on Triona's. "Tell me—and this is important, lass—do ye love him?"

Good God, what made her ask such a thing? "No! Of course I don't. I mean, I care for him, but—" She blinked. Finally, she said slowly, "It's possible, I suppose. But I surely hope not."

"Why?"

"Because I don't want to be the only one," Triona said softly.

"Ahh. Tha' could be a problem indeed."

"I think about him a lot, and I can't help but remember how kind he is and how much he loves those girls." A wistful feeling twisted in her heart. "I just wish he'd share some of that with me."

"He will, lassie. He's just no' a person to absorb changes quickly." Mam frowned. "One o' the problems with the curse is tha' it teaches those involved to guard their emotions carefully. Think o' it, child: if getting angry could raise the ocean and sink ships, ye'd be a mite cautious about feeling anything at all."

Triona nodded thoughtfully. "I hadn't thought of that."

" 'Tis a terrible responsibility. One tha' can shape a person, and no' always in a good way." Mam patted Triona's knee. "Before ye decide how to react to MacLean, ye need to walk in his boots."

"You're right. I've wanted to ask him about that, and other things, but I keep tiptoeing around, trying to find my place."

"Och, that'll never do! Wha' did ye do when MacLean lost his temper and tried to blow ye head o'er heels?"

"I told him I was angry."

"Good. And then?"

"And then . . . he left."

"Wha'? Ye didna make him stay to listen to yer complaints?"

"I did at first, but then I was angry, too, and I just wanted him gone."

"Then tha' was a good idea, as ye were both mad as hornets. Wha' are ye goin' t' do when he returns and ye're no' so mad?"

Triona thought about this. "I am going to ask—no, *demand*—that he allow me some say in all parts of our household, including the children."

"And if he forgets ye're the apple o' his eye and foolishly says no?"

She smiled. "Oh, I've already let him know that he's not the only one who can shake the house when he's upset."

"Good fer ye, lass! That's the spirit!" Mam's grin creased her weathered face. "A fight is no' always a bad thing."

"I've never seen my parents fight."

"An' ye never will. Yer mother canna stand fightin', which is a pity—they'd be happier if they'd clear the air sometimes. Fightin' lets ye both say wha' needs to be said. Just be sure ye fight clean, and dinna bring up old hurts or blame one another. That's never a good thing."

"But won't it make MacLean angry?"

"Tha' depends on wha' sort o' fight ye have. MacLean has more control over his powers than his brothers."

"He does, indeed." Triona looked curiously at her grandmother. "Do you know how much?"

"La, lassie, o' course I do."

"How?"

"There is another MacLean they dinna speak of—Lord Hugh's younger brother who was killed in cold blood. When he died, the skies shook and roared fer days." Mam's gaze darkened at the memory. "The valley flooded, lightning snapped till the air was thick with sulfur, and icy winds roared. A good bit o' the village was washed away or burned to the ground. The villagers were huddled in their homes, frightened to death. One day, I saw yer man upon the castle roof. He stayed there fer two hours straight, and when he left, the storms were gone.

"His brothers came fer me to help him. He was too weak to walk, and they almost lost him, so they'd sent for me to tend him. I knew wha' had happened, but he didna wish me to tell a soul—not even his own kin."

Mam frowned. " 'Tis the nature of a curse to punish those who find ways around her. So when he puts his will against her, she pushes back. I think it could kill him, if he pushed too hard."

Triona found that she couldn't swallow.

"Och, dinna look so scared!" Mam patted Triona's hand. "He's a good man, and ye need to know it. But dinna look fer a man to tell ye ye're right. It takes a true love to tell us when we're in the wrong."

A true love. Triona had never thought of herself as a romantic, yet . . . perhaps she had idealized her parents' relationship. There had always been some tensions between Mother and Mam, and Father had to have felt caught in the middle. Yet never had she heard him say so. It made Triona wonder what other issues she didn't know about.

Perhaps the truth was that there were no perfect marriages, just some really good ones. And that was what she wanted: one of the *really*, really good ones. Suddenly, Triona realized that somewhere along the way, her goal in this relationship had changed. She no longer wished to leave her mark upon Gilmerton when she left. Now she didn't wish to leave at all. What she really wanted was a full-fledged, normal relationship with Hugh and his daughters. She didn't know if she could convince her husband to take such a chance, but she was willing to try.

"Thank you, Mam." Triona hugged her grandmother. "You've given me a lot to think about."

"Good. People dinna think as much as they should anymore. Always doin' this, and doin' that—if ye never think, how do ye know what ye're doin' is what ye ought to be doin'?"

Triona agreed. It was far too early to tell whether she and Hugh could find love. But by living well day to day, including one another more and having frank—maybe even loud—discussions, they could work their way in that direction.

Mam grinned widely. "Now, lass, on to more important matters."

Triona leaned forward. "What's that?"

"If ye're not goin' to eat tha' scone, could ye put it on me plate? I've a long drive home, and I dinna wish to starve along the way."

Triona laughed and put the last scone on Mam's plate, smiling as she watched the older woman slather it with marmalade.

"There she is," Devon whispered as she peeked in the sitting-room window. "She's with an old lady."

Christina moved beside Devon. Caitriona was sitting beside a woman who had to be over a hundred years old. Her face was a mass of wrinkles and lines, her nose large and crooked, her gray hair wispy. "She looks like a witch!"

Devon dropped back to her hands and knees. "We need to go to the other side. They're sitting closer to those windows."

Christina nodded and whispered, "Through the rose garden, then. And be careful you don't tear your dress. Uncle Dougal will be suspicious if we go home all mussed."

Devon led the way, bent almost double as she crept through the shrubbery to the window closest to the settee. She took a position on one side, Christina on the other. But they were too late to overhear Caitriona and her guest, for the old woman was leaving.

They heard Caitriona say good-bye, and then Mrs. Wallis entered the room. "How nice to see yer grandmother!"

"Yes, it was."

"Shall we move the furniture now?"

Devon scowled.

"Oh, yes!" Caitriona said. "What do you have in mind?"

"First of all, I have a mind to get Angus and Liam to do the work fer us!"

Devon peeked over the edge of the window to see the two women talking and laughing. First they moved the escritoire to a place where the sun warmed it, and then the settee so that it faced the fireplace instead of bordering it. From the looks of it, nothing—chairs and tables, candelabra and rugs—was to be left untouched.

"What's she doing?" Devon hissed, her lips almost white with fury. She whirled away and angrily scrambled through the bushes.

Christina hoped the women inside were too busy to hear, for Devon's movements were far from quiet. Shaking her head, she followed.

They made their way through the garden and out the gate to the clearing hidden by a stand of trees. There, the horses were tethered to a low limb as Aggie contentedly munched an apple.

As soon as they reached the trees, Devon wheeled on Christina. "Did you see that? She's doing just what I said she'd do—she's *changing* things!"

Christina frowned. "She's only moving furniture."

"That's where she'll *begin*." Devon's hands fisted. "But it's not where she'll stop!"

Christina didn't answer. She'd agreed to this little jaunt because she'd been curious about what Caitriona had been up to since Papa had been gone. She wasn't sure what she expected, but hoped they might have seen Caitriona doing something really bad. That would be nice, because then Christina wouldn't have this sinking feeling that perhaps they weren't being fair to Papa's new wife.

Not that he wanted her—his actions had made that clear. Or had, until he'd gotten so angry with them for laughing at Caitriona's lack of equestrian skills. Even now, Christina could see Papa's face. Some small part of her wondered if perhaps, just perhaps, Papa *did* care for Caitriona, but didn't want anyone—maybe not even Caitriona—to know.

Christina hadn't liked that at all. Worse, Devon had felt humiliated by Papa's scold and had been burning to get her revenge on Caitriona.

Christina sighed unhappily and joined Aggie on the ground.

Devon paced angrily, her skirts swishing with each step. "I can't believe she'd do such a thing!"

"What was she doing?" Aggie asked around her apple.

"She was just moving furniture," Christina answered.

Aggie paused. "So?"

"That's what I said," Christina said. "But Devon thinks it's an act of the devil."

"Of a *she* devil," Devon retorted. She stopped in front of her sisters. "Perhaps we didn't find Caitriona doing anything horrible, but we only watched her for a few minutes."

Christina sighed. "I don't know. I get the feeling that maybe we're making things worse. Maybe we should let Papa handle this. There have been times when I thought he might enjoy being with her. And he *did* ask us to be polite to her."

"Yes, and he'd never asked us that before, had he?" Devon stooped in front of Christina. "Do you see what's happening? She's slowly pulling him into her way of thinking and doing things. In her life, there are no children. We're interlopers and in the way."

Christina's heart sank. *Did* Caitriona see them that way? Were they just in the way for whatever life Papa and his wife wished to have?

"She'll push us away," Devon continued, her voice raspy. "She'll make Papa think we're doing bad things, and then, when they have their own baby, there won't be room for us any longer."

Christina's chest ached as if someone were sitting on it.

Aggie blinked. "You . . . you really think that's what she wants?"

"I'm sure of it."

Suddenly unable to sit still, Christina sprang to her feet and turned to look back at Gilmerton Manor. Alone and splendid, it rested on the crest of the hill like a jewel set on the curve of a ring. The sun glistened off the windows and the mellow stone looked warm and inviting, ivy trailing up two sides. It was the only place she'd ever called home. A lump grew in her throat. She didn't totally believe Devon's line of reasoning, but one thing had rung true: What would happen when Papa and his new wife had their own child? Would there be room for her and her sisters then?

She bit her lip hard to fight back the tears. The memories returned of lonely, bad-smelling rooms. And waiting for Mother, who sometimes came home but just as often didn't. Of a two-week period when Christina, driven to desperation by her sisters' cries of hunger, had ventured out into the cold streets of Paris to steal some food. It had taken her hours, but she'd managed to scour enough for a few days. She'd returned wet and dirty, her gown torn by a man reeking of liquor who'd tried to drag her into an alleyway. She knew what he wanted, and her desperation had given her the strength to break free and run as fast as she could back to their cold attic home.

Now she had Gilmerton. She looked down at the house, admiring the way the sun glinted off the mullioned windows, the strong line of the stone walls, and the thick solid doors. *This* was home, and she would do anything to keep it. She couldn't leave Gilmerton, *couldn't* lose Papa.

A sob broke through, and immediately Devon's thin arms pulled her close in a fierce hug. Aggie's rounder arms followed. They stayed so for a long time, until the memories faded and Christina stopped shaking.

When Devon released her, Christina wiped her eyes and forced a smile. "We should get back. Uncle Dougal will notice we're missing."

Devon swiped at her own eyes with the back of her hand. "We'll take the loch path. It's quicker."

The path went around the small loch at the end of the valley before branching off in two directions. One led to Uncle Dougal's elegant house, the other to MacLean Castle. Papa had said that at one time the path had been a major route to and from the castle, but that now, because parts of it had been washed away and the slope into the loch was so steep, no one used it. He'd warned them to avoid it, but it was such a convenient shortcut that when they were on their own, they'd begun to use it more and more. Christina thought that Papa had overstated the danger. As long as they kept their mounts calm and went slowly through the narrow parts, they were all very comfortable with it.

"Come, Aggie." Devon led Aggie's horse to a low stump and waited for her sister to mount. Then she did the same for Christina. When it came time to mount her own horse, she grabbed a short rope on the saddle and swung herself up.

Christina watched with envy. Devon was fiercely, hotly independent and refused to need anyone. Christina wished she could absorb some of her sister's spirit. If they were turned out on their own again, she would need it.

Heart heavy, she pulled her horse beside Devon's as they started out. "What do we do?"

Devon pursed her lips. "We have to keep Caitriona and Papa from growing closer."

"How do we do that? So far, everything we've done has only done the opposite."

"Let me think about it."

Christina nodded, guiding her horse down the path while Devon mulled her options.

As they reached where the path narrowed, Devon pulled her horse level with Christina's, a sly look on her face. "Ha! I know what we're going to do."

"What's that?" Christina asked.

"Papa's supposed to come home very late tonight. Uncle Dougal sent one of his men to find out exactly when."

"So?"

"So, before he arrives, we'll slip out and come back to Gilmerton. It will be after dark but we know the way well, so it shouldn't be a problem. Then we will rearrange the furniture."

"How will that help?" Christina asked.

"You'll see." She set off down the narrow path.

Whatever Devon's idea was, if it delayed the inevitable for even one hour, Christina would be a part of it.

Feeling better, she hurried to follow her sister.

# Chapter 17

❧❧❧

*"Love is a curious thing, me dearies. At times it gallops up on a white horse and sweeps ye off yer feet like a grand story from times past. Other times, it steals in wit' th' quiet o' a raindrop and whisks awa' yer heart afore ye even knew 'twas at risk."*

OLD WOMAN NORA TO HER THREE WEE
GRANDDAUGHTERS ON A COLD WINTER'S NIGHT

There!" Triona rubbed her back wearily. It had taken almost two hours to arrange the sitting room to their liking. "I like it this way. Much brighter and more cozy."

Mrs. Wallis nodded her approval. "So do I, m'lady." She told Liam and Angus, "Take that extra table to the breakfast room and put it in the corner. It can hold the teapot in the mornings. Och, look at the time! I'll ask Cook to serve dinner—"

"If you don't mind, I'd prefer a tray in my bed-chamber." The last thing Triona wanted was to eat by herself at the long table in the dining room. "I'm rather tired." *Thank goodness. I hope I sleep better.*

"Goin' to bed early, m'lady? I don't blame ye.

Besides, his lordship will be back soon along wi' the bairns, so yer days of peace are nigh over."

Triona laughed. "I hadn't thought of it like that. Maybe I should have a hot bath as well."

Mrs. Wallis chuckled. "Right away, m'lady." She surveyed their work one last time before giving a satisfied nod. "Much better! If his lordship doesna like it, the man's daft."

Triona smiled. Tomorrow things would return to normal. She hadn't realized how much she'd come to enjoy having everyone around until she was alone in this big, magnificent house. She'd come to look forward to the morning trysts that seemed to set the day with a special glow, their solitary breakfasts before Hugh left to see to the horses, the way his eyes crinkled when he laughed, the girls chattering as they came downstairs for their afternoon rides with their father, Hugh's deep voice answering them with love and laughter, her rides with Ferguson as she increased her skills, and the talks with Mrs. Wallis that usually involved laughter.

Life was strings of simple moments, and they were weaving together to form a strong strand. Even making the sitting room more homelike increased her sense of belonging.

After having her tray of cheese and bread, sliced apples, and a large orange, Triona soaked in her bath. Afterward, dressed in her night rail, she relaxed on the settee before the fireplace with a cup of freshly brewed tea. Hugh would be home soon, and she could barely sit still.

To distract herself she tried reading a book, but she couldn't concentrate. Her gaze kept wandering to the bed and then to the window, as if Hugh might miraculously appear in the dark, climb through the second-story window, sweep her up, and take her to bed. She shivered at the thought.

Though Hugh had been upset when he'd left, surely he would be calmer when he came home. After all, she'd gotten over the insults he'd tossed at her.

Honestly, marriage wasn't quite what she'd thought it. For one thing, she hadn't realized how much compromise was involved: between what he wished to do and what she wished to do; about dealing with the girls; about how to run the household; about their places in each other's lives.

She'd often had to find compromises to keep the peace among her brothers and sisters, but it seemed that *she* was the only one compromising now while MacLean stubbornly held to his pre-marriage ways.

Mam was right; that could not continue. She wished she could ask Caitlyn's advice—if anyone knew how to get men to listen to her, it was Caitlyn. She always seemed to know just what to say and how to say it to get exactly the response she wanted. Triona's gaze flickered to the desk. Well, why not write to Cait now and ask her? It might be a week before she responded, but it would be worthwhile if Caitlyn had an idea that would help.

Triona went to the desk, dipped a pen into the ink. First Triona asked after the family's health, especially Michael, whose cough was supposedly on the mend. Then she asked if Father was still angry about the London fiasco. Next she told Caitlyn of her efforts these past few days since Hugh had left.

As she wrote, her homesickness returned. Missing the warmth and camaraderie of Wythburn, suddenly she was writing about Hugh and how she wished with all of her heart that things were different, and how she was at a loss to know how to make them so. She wrote and wrote, the pen scratching swiftly over the paper.

When she finished she felt drained but focused, ready to have Hugh and the children back home.

A distant thud made her pause. *That sounds like the garden gate. But Hugh wouldn't come into the house that way.*

Suddenly, she remembered his concerns about the girls' mother. Could someone have come to the house to do the girls mischief? Triona's heart sped and she ran to the window. The full moon streamed over the garden, lighting the white stone path. Beyond the path, the gate was securely closed. Movement caught her eye, and Triona saw two figures scurrying up the hill behind the garden. The one in front turned slightly, and Triona saw a dim lamp that had been shielded.

She gripped the window casement as the light disappeared behind some trees. *Blast it, the servants are asleep on the far side of the house. Should I run outside and see what direction they go?*

Triona whirled and raced to the wardrobe. She found her heavy cloak and shoved her bare feet into her boots. Within moments she was running down the back stairs, holding her cloak and night rail up so she didn't trip.

When she reached the back door, she threw back the lock and slipped into the garden. Hugging herself against the cold, she quickly went to the gate.

She peered up the hillside but could see nothing. *Which direction did they go?* She silently swung the gate open and stealthily began to climb the hill, staying hidden in the brush. When she heard the low murmur of voices, she paused and frowned. The voices sounded feminine—two women? The cloaked strangers *had* looked small.

As she neared the small cluster of trees that hid her quarry, Triona could make out the outlines of two people atop their mounts. She slipped in closer.

"Devon," came a low voice, "hold that lantern higher."

*Christina! What is she doing in the woods at night?*

"I can't." Devon spoke so quietly that Triona had to strain to hear. "Someone might see it from the house."

"No one is awake to see it."

"There is a light glowing in Papa's bedchamber. *She* might be awake."

Christina made an exasperated noise. "Don't be silly; it's far too late. She probably fell asleep while writing letters or something. Mrs. Wallis says she's never seen anyone write so many."

"She can write all of the letters she wants tomorrow. It won't help." Devon's voice held unmistakable satisfaction.

Triona frowned. What did she mean by that?

"We'd better hurry," Christina said.

"We'll be at Uncle Dougal's before you know it. There's a full moon and the horses know the path."

The voices grew fainter as the girls walked their horses through the copse. Triona, shivering from the cold, hugged her cloak closer. Should she follow them and demand to know what they were doing? She doubted that Dougal realized the girls were out of their beds. At least they'd had the sense not to bring Aggie.

The lantern flickered as the girls moved farther down the path. Triona hesitated only a moment, then hurried after them. When the girls reached the edge of the copse they extinguished the lantern, hooked it to Devon's saddle, and then turned the horses east. In her rides with Ferguson, he'd said the wide road to the west was the way to Dougal's house. Was this path a shortcut?

Soon they were out of sight. What on earth had they been doing? They had to have been up to some mischief, but what?

When Triona got back to the house, she took a lamp from her bedchamber and carried it upstairs to the girls' room.

Nothing seemed different. They could have taken something with them, but Triona wouldn't know.

She made her way downstairs to the foyer, which was eerily silent and dark. Triona paused at the foot of the stairs. Every door was closed, the lamps neatly hung, the faint scent of wax hanging in the air.

Everything looked exactly the same.

She sighed. She didn't even know what she was looking for, and the girls could have been anywhere—the kitchen, the wine cellar, the library—who knew? All she knew was that the house was cold and she didn't relish searching it alone in the dark. She would discover whatever ill the girls had planned tomorrow anyway, so she might as well go to bed now. In the morning, she'd search the house from attic to cellar.

In her bedchamber, Triona placed the lamp beside the bed, hung her damp cloak over a chair, removed her shoes, and grimaced at the damp, dirty hem of her night rail. She removed it and looked fruitlessly for her other one. It must have been collected for laundering.

Sighing, she dashed across the cold floor to the bed, blew out the lamp, and slipped between the cool sheets, yanking the blankets over her head.

Slowly, the bed grew warmer. Triona snuggled in deeper, wishing Hugh were here to warm her. Finally, with a yawn, she went to sleep.

An hour later, Hugh shut the door to the stable, glad to be in its bright warmth. "There. Safe and sound." He looked at the mare standing in the fresh straw, her foal leaning tiredly against her legs. "We're going to call this one Trouble."

" 'Tis a good name." Ferguson hung the lantern on the wall. "I dinna remember when any mare has hid so well. I'd never have thought o' lookin' fer her up on the ridge."

"I'm glad we found her when we did. A few more hours and they would have died." The foal had been breech, and it had taken all of Hugh's and Ferguson's knowledge to save them both.

Hugh found himself looking out of the open barn doors at the house, his gaze seeking out a set of windows. *She'll be asleep. Will she be glad I'm home?*

It had been harder to leave than ever before. While he'd expected to miss the girls, he hadn't expected to miss Triona so much. Everything reminded him of her: the snow-fresh scent of the wind made him think of her silken hair, the curve of a hill reminded him of how her breast filled his hand so well, the sound of the grass beneath his horse's hooves echoed the whisper of her skirts about her long legs, tantalizing him to madness.

He couldn't see the wild beauty of the hills without wondering what she would think of it. He couldn't stop thinking about the way she smiled, shy and so sexy when he kissed her awake. About the feel of her legs entwined with his in the early mornings. About the lavender scent of her baths. The way she'd determinedly worked with Ferguson every morning to learn how to ride.

She was a fascinating woman, unlike any he'd ever met. And, when not furious at him, she was steadfast and calm, forthright and plainspoken. There was quality to her, but also a strong, sweet passion.

Every morning he'd been away, he'd awoken hard and ready, having dreamed of Triona naked beneath him, of the taste of her, the feel of her. It seemed that the more of her he had, the more he wanted. Though they'd parted on the worst of terms, he found that his desire was undiminished, which surprised him. He'd been so angry, but though he hadn't agreed with Triona, he shouldn't have lost control of his temper. Even now, he had to fight a twinge of guilt when he thought about the havoc he'd caused.

Sighing, he turned to help unload the wagon.

Ferguson waved him off. "Go on wit' ye, m'lord. I'll wake one o' the stable hands to help."

Hugh glanced toward the house. She'd be in bed now, smelling of sleep and the sweetness of lavender, her night rail wrapped about her legs, her skin warm and—

Within moments, Hugh let himself into the house. He undid his coat and tossed it over a chair in the foyer, rubbing his freezing hands together. Perhaps he should warm up before he went to bed, or his cold feet and hands would wake his wife unpleasantly.

His body tightened at the thought. Oh, how he wanted to wake his warm, well-rounded, hot-spirited wife. But when he did, he wanted to be warm—*very* warm, indeed.

A little port by a crackling fire should do it. In the morning, when things were more settled, he'd fetch the girls and things could get back to normal. Or it would if Triona could forgive him.

He opened the library door and walked into the darkness toward his desk to light the lamp.

"*Ow!*" Hugh tripped over something and staggered forward, reaching for the settee, but his hand whooshed through empty air. With a spectacular crash, he fell against a small table, glass shattering as something fell to the floor.

For a stunned moment he lay staring up at the ceiling, his ire rising. *What in the hell?* He gingerly rose to his feet, careful not to touch the broken glass. He managed to find the small table he'd knocked over and righted it, his boots crunching on glass. That was odd; this table used to be by the fireplace. Why was it in the middle of the room?

Hugh scowled, his toe throbbing, his jaw tight. He could barely make out the outline of the furnishings in the room, but none of them seemed to be where they should. *What has that woman done?*

He held his hands out before him and carefully made his way to his desk, bumping into another table and almost falling over a chair. He found the lamp and lit it. The golden glow beamed gently over the room.

He looked around, unable to believe his eyes. Every piece of furniture had been moved except the desk. The rest had been placed without regard to common sense, almost as if the perpetrator thought to drive him mad. Without another thought, he bellowed for the servants.

Soon, a noise sounded in the hallway and Mrs. Wallis stood in the doorway, a robe thrown over her night rail, a lamp clutched in one hand and a broom in the other as if they were weapons. Behind her, grasping what appeared to be a chair leg, was Angus.

Mrs. Wallis clutched at her chest. "Och, ye gave us a scare, m'lord! We dinna know ye'd returned and—" She blinked around the room. "Goodness! What happened in here?"

"Ask your mistress," Hugh said grimly.

"But we didna change the furniture in here. Only the sitting room. And a bonny job we did, if I say so meself."

He eyed the housekeeper. "You helped her?"

"O' course, m'lord. As did Angus and Liam."

Angus nodded.

Hugh rubbed his neck wearily. "She must have come back later to do this room."

Mrs. Wallis began sweeping up the broken glass, looking unconvinced. "I dinna know, m'lord. 'Tis an unlikely arrangement fer a library, and the missus is no fool." She glanced at Angus. "Fetch a dustpan, and be quick about it."

He nodded and left, the chair leg over his shoulder.

Mrs. Wallis tsked as she swept the floor. " 'Twas the candy dish yer sister, Fiona, gave ye fer Christmas. A pity." She paused, looking around and shaking her head. " 'Tis no wonder ye knocked somethin' over. There's no rhyme nor reason fer puttin' the furniture such."

Hugh crossed to the sideboard, stepping around two chairs that had been placed back-to-back, and poured himself a drink from the decanter. "It's a mess. Almost as if—" He frowned, the glass halfway to his mouth.

"Almost as if what, m'lord?"

He took a slow sip, then shook his head. "Nothing." Mrs. Wallis finished sweeping the broken glass into a pile. "Have the girls been here since I left?"

"No. And tha' surprised me, fer they usually make a point o' stoppin' by when ye're away."

It had to have been the girls. He couldn't see Triona doing such a thing, especially not to his library. But why would they have moved the furniture? They had to know it would anger him, and—

Was that it? They wished to make him mad? But at whom? Did they think he'd blame Triona?

He almost had, he realized with chagrin.

Angus returned with the dustpan and Mrs. Wallis finished cleaning up the broken glass. "I'll wake Liam and we'll get the room back to order, m'lord."

"No. Just leave it."

She and Angus exchanged a glance. "Leave it?"

"Yes." He put down his glass. "Off to bed with you both. It's late."

"But ye just arrived and—"

"I can put myself to bed. I'm bringing the girls back tomorrow, so we all need to get what rest we can tonight."

"Very well, m'lord."

Hugh waited until they'd left before he surveyed the dining room, and then the sitting room. The furniture had been moved here, too, except the heavier pieces, although only the sitting room arrangement made any sense. He tried the door to the breakfast room, but it was stuck.

"Little brats," he muttered, carrying the lamp up the stairs. He'd have a good talk with the girls in the morning. Meanwhile, he had a wife waiting for him in his bed. The thought urged him on until he found himself hurrying, moving faster until he was almost running.

He reached the door and paused to calm his racing heart. Then he took a deep breath, extinguished the lamp, and quietly opened the door. The moon's glow dimly streaked across the carpet to the bed. He placed the lamp by the fireplace, then stripped and made his way to the bed.

For a moment, he stood looking down at her. Her long hair was a fan of shimmering softness over his pillows. *His* pillows. He didn't know why that was important, but it was. She was in *his* bed, sleeping under *his* sheets, all because she was *his* wife.

He'd never understood the need or desire to marry. His sister was married and seemed happy; Dougal walked about with an annoyingly self-satisfied air since he'd found Sophia; and even his brother Gregor, who'd been a confirmed bachelor until he'd realized he was in love with his longtime friend Venetia, seemed to relish being married. But for Hugh, marriage had always been a distant concept—a place he might visit someday, but never today. Never *now*.

When he'd been forced to marry Triona, he hadn't understood how his life would change. And not just on the outside, though his house and life were livelier with Triona around. He'd changed on the inside, too.

Things he'd enjoyed before—his home, his work with the horses, even his feelings for his daughters— all seemed to be even more important, because now he wanted to share them with Triona.

She sighed in her sleep and stirred, curling her hand under her cheek. As she did so, the sheet slipped and her bare shoulder was revealed, the moonlight shimmering on her creamy skin.

Hugh's body tightened. With a hand that slightly shook, he lifted the covers. The moonlight caressed the slopes of her full breasts, limned the lines of her rounded hips, and traced along her thighs. She frowned in her sleep and burrowed deeper into the sheets. His heart racing, Hugh slipped between the sheets beside her.

As he pulled her to him her eyes flew open, dark and fathomless in the moonlight. For a long moment they stared into each other's eyes; then, with a smile that made his heart skip a beat, she slipped her arms about his neck. "Welcome home," she whispered. "You found the mare?"

He lifted up on his elbow and ran a hand down her arm to her waist, then up to cup her breast.

She gasped.

He grinned. "Yes, I found the mare. She and the foal are fine."

"Good." She placed her hand on his cheek and he turned to kiss the palm, biting the tip of one of her fingers.

Her eyes darkened.

He smiled. "Welcome home, indeed. Someone moved the furnishings in the library, and I almost killed myself stumbling in the dark."

"*What?* But we didn't change anything in the library!"

"Someone did."

"But who—" Her gaze narrowed in thought. "Oh."

"Exactly. We'll have a talk with them tomorrow. Meanwhile, someone must tend to my wounds."

She lifted up on her elbow, her face even with his. "Are you hurt?"

He shrugged, rubbing his thumb over her nipple.

She bit her lip.

He hid a grin. "I may have bumped my head."

She leaned forward and placed a lingering kiss on his forehead.

Hugh closed his eyes at her gentleness.

"Anywhere else?" she whispered.

His groin grew heavy with need. He touched his cheek. "Here."

She leaned forward to press her lips to his cheek, her silky hair tickling his arm.

"And here," he said, touching his bottom lip.

She slipped her arm about his neck and pulled his mouth to hers.

Hugh's control slipped, fell, and crashed into pieces.

Hot and sweet, urgent and passionate, he took her. Took her until he could no longer breathe. Took her because he wanted her, needed her, desired her. But most of all, he took her because she was his.

Much later, their skin damp from their exertions, his arms wrapped about her, her legs entangled with his, he gently kissed her brow and closed his eyes.

He slid into the warm embrace of sleep, realizing how vital she'd become to him, to his life and his happiness. He wasn't sure how he felt about that, but at the moment, replete and exhausted, he was just glad to be home.

For now, that was enough.

# Chapter 18

*"There's naught tha' love canna do."*

OLD WOMAN NORA TO HER THREE WEE<br>
GRANDDAUGHTERS ON A COLD WINTER'S NIGHT

"*Y*ou told him *what*?" Sophia looked aghast.

Dougal sighed. Until a moment ago, his beautiful wife had been all purrs and smiles, delighted to be back where she belonged—in his arms.

Now she was no longer perched cozily on his lap but was standing before him, hands on her hips, her blue eyes sparkling with outrage.

"Sophia, my love, I didn't mean it to sound quite like that, but—"

She whipped up a hand. "Wait. You *accidentally* told your brother that the best way to ensure his future happiness with his new wife was to train her like one of his *horses*?"

When she put it like that, it did sound rather bad.

Sophia's gaze pinned him to his seat. "That was your *best* advice?"

"Well, I—"

"How about telling Hugh that a happy wife is a happy home?"

"I suppose I could have—"

"Or that he should spend some time getting to know her, since they were thrown together in such a mad way?"

"That would have been a good ide—"

"Or that he should take care to make her comfortable in his home or she'll feel like an outsider?" Sophia's eyes flashed fire. "Did you think about that? Or did you perhaps forget it in your zeal to sound knowledgeable, which you obviously *aren't*."

Sophia's Scottish accent was becoming more pronounced, a sure sign he was in deep, deep trouble. He held his hands wide open. "Sophia, the second it was out of my mouth, I knew I'd made an error. But Hugh seemed to respond to it, so perhaps it's working well."

"Have you visited them lately?"

Dougal shifted in his chair, thinking of Hugh's solemn looks as the days had progressed. "Yes, though you can't always tell how people are feeling."

"Of course you can! Do Hugh and his new wife *appear* happy? Do they laugh? Smile at one another? Hold hands?"

Truthfully, Dougal had never known Hugh to look less happy. "Well . . . he looks at her a lot."

"What does that mean?"

"It means he's interested."

"I should hope so! He married her, didn't he?"

"He was *forced* to marry her. And not through any fault of hers, which he openly admits."

"How generous of him," Sophia snapped. "So he marries her and then brings her home to 'train' her. Call for the coach—we're going over there this minute."

"But Hugh sent word that he'd fetch the girls later—"

"We are leaving now, *with* the girls. You and I can undo the damage your little pearl of wisdom has caused." Sophia turned on her heel to march out the door, but Dougal was quicker.

He leaned out and grasped her by the waist, spun her about, and set her back on his lap. There he held her, though she remained stiff and unyielding. "Sophia, I didn't mean to cause any harm."

"How *could* you tell him such a thing?"

"You know how he is about horses, and I was trying to explain in a way he understood that you have to work at being a good—"

"*Don't* say 'trainer.'"

"I was *going* to say 'husband.'" Dougal sighed. "Sophia, I admit that I said it badly. What I meant to tell him was that if he'd just be patient and spend time with her, like he does with those damn horses, then perhaps he could build a relationship worth having. I know I've made a mull of it—but I just wanted him to have some of the happiness that I've found with you."

Her expression lost a touch of its severity. "You are a *very* fortunate man."

"The luckiest," he said honestly, savoring the feel of her in his arms. God, how he'd missed her.

He captured one of her golden curls and slipped his fingers through the silky length. "Oh, Sophia," he said in a low voice, "I'm sorry if I made you angry, but I've missed you horribly."

She sniffed.

He hid a smile and kissed her cheek, whispering, "I only wanted Hugh to find what we did. You mean the world to me, Sophie."

Her thick lashes dropped to her cheeks and she curved a bit into his arms. "We are happy, aren't we?"

He brushed another kiss across her creamy cheek. "More than I ever imagined possible." He nuzzled her neck. "I've missed you so much."

She shivered and leaned against him, her head on his shoulder, her blond hair tickling his neck. "I missed you, too. I'm sorry I was gone for so long, but the trip was so hard on poor Red."

"I'm glad your father is doing better now." He hugged her tighter.

Sophia was silent a moment; then she sighed and sat upright. "I'm sorry I was so mad at you, but that was horrible advice to give your brother."

"I knew that as soon as I said it. If you'd been here, you'd have known exactly what to say, but you weren't, and he was so miserable that I had to say something."

A thoughtful look crossed her face. "Miserable, hmm?"

"He's more taken with her than he realizes. And every day, he seems more so." Dougal frowned. "If he would just let her close to him, I think they'd discover their feelings are stronger than they realize. But he's afraid she'll hurt him—and the girls, too."

"Of course he is. He's been so busy protecting the girls from their mother that he's built a beautiful shell about them all."

Dougal captured his wife's hand and pressed a kiss to her palm. "Rather like someone else you once knew."

"Yes, but you were afraid of caring for me because you thought such strong feelings would cause you to lose control over your temper. That hasn't happened."

"If anything ever happened to you—" He clamped his mouth shut at the thought. "In some ways, I was right."

"No." She placed her warm hand on his cheek, her eyes shining. "If anything ever happened to me, you'd be sad, but you'd also know that I love you. That would help."

He covered her hand with his, his heart aching and tight. "I can't promise anything."

"Yes, you can," she said firmly. "And so can Hugh. Besides, I've never seen him worry about losing control of his temper."

Dougal was silent a long moment. "There was a time when we were all mad with fury and loss."

Sophia's eyes were suddenly somber. "When Callum died?"

Throat too tight for speech, Dougal nodded. His youngest brother, the darling of the clan, had died a senseless death, and his five remaining siblings had been furious and grieving.

Their collective rage had raised winds so strong they'd lifted houses from their foundations, rain so harsh that streams had burst over their banks and become raging rivers, carrying away houses, barns—whatever was in their path. Lightning and thunder had roared through the skies, striking every moving object, while deadly hail had rained from above.

Once the storm had begun, they'd come to their senses, but it was too late. None of them could control it. . . . During the worst of the storm, Dougal had found Hugh collapsed upon the castle parapet. That was what had brought the rest of them to their senses.

Dougal's chest ached at the memory of Hugh, crumpled on the roof, soaked by the rain, so pale that they'd thought him dead. Only the small quiver of heartbeat in his throat had assured them otherwise. They'd placed him in bed, fading fast, until Old Woman Nora arrived to tend him. With her knowledge of potions and herbs, she'd managed to bring him back, but it had been almost a year before he'd regained his strength.

Dougal rubbed his forehead. He wondered if Hugh had ever really been the same since.

Sophia tilted her head to one side. "How are the girls with Triona?"

"They haven't given her a chance. I've tried to talk to them, but that just seems to make them more determined not to like her." Dougal hesitated, then added, "I fear they're up to something."

"Why? What have they done?"

"I don't know, but they've been very secretive the last few days. I've caught them whispering, and when I ask what they're doing, they say 'nothing' in too innocent a tone."

"Then they're planning something for certain." Sophia kissed his cheek. "Come. We need to go to Gilmerton. I've a feeling that once we get there, things will become clearer."

Triona descended the stairs for breakfast, pausing to place the letter to her sister on the tray in the front hall. The butler would make sure that it was sent. Hugh hadn't even stirred when she'd arisen; he had to be exhausted. If the trip to find the mare hadn't done it, then their exertions in bed had. She smiled at the thought, but it slipped almost immediately. She and Hugh had a wonderful relationship in bed, but she so longed for more.

Heart heavy, she started toward the breakfast room, but Angus stood in front of the door. That was odd. "Is breakfast ready?" she asked.

A frown rested on his face. "Aye, m'lady. But 'tis a bit difficult to get into the room. Liam went to fetch two o' the stableboys to help move the buffet, but—"

A knock sounded on the front door.

With a mumbled apology, Angus dashed to answer it.

Mam walked in. "Och, there ye are, lassie! I came to see if—what's wrong? Ye look perplexed."

"I was just going to the breakfast room, and—"

Another knock sounded on the huge front door.

Triona hid her impatience and nodded for Angus to answer it.

Christina, Devon, and Aggie entered, their cheeks pink from the cold, while Angus kept the door open, waiting for Lord Dougal.

Triona's heart lightened. "There you are! I was wondering when you'd be back."

The girls stood together, Devon and Christina looking about uneasily.

"Has Papa returned?" Aggie asked excitedly.

"Oh, yes. He's sleeping right now."

Aggie's shoulders sagged. "Oh."

Dougal entered the foyer, and at his side was a very petite woman who was quite easily the most beautiful creature Triona had ever seen.

The woman smiled warmly and came forward. "My dear! I'm so sorry I was out of town when you arrived."

Triona politely held out her hand, but the woman enveloped Triona in a warm hug.

For a startled moment Triona simply stood there, but then she laughed and hugged the woman back.

"Sophia MacFarlane, is that ye?" Mam asked.

The woman turned, gave a delighted cry, and swept forward to hug Nora as well.

"Good heavens," Triona said. "The whole world has come to visit us this morning."

Mam's grin broadened as she returned the hug. "I thought 'twas ye! How is yer pa, rogue that he is?"

"Pardon me," Dougal said in a mock serious tone. "Sophia's last name is now MacLean, and has been for some time."

Mam *"pssht!"* him, and said to Sophia, "I never thought tha' rapscallion man of yers would make such a gran' husband, but I was wrong. He's takin' to it like a duck to water."

Dougal bowed elegantly, his hair glinting gold. "I am well under the cat's paw and happy to be there."

Mam cackled. "That's as it should be."

Triona watched wistfully as Dougal shared a look with Sophia, his expression both tender and loving. What did she need to do to have Hugh look at her that way?

Dougal turned to Triona. "You may not know this, but your grandmother once saved our sister, Fiona. In fact, she's had her hands full keeping the MacLeans well-mended over the years."

Triona caught sight of Devon whispering to Christina. "Oh, I hadn't thought of the children's breakfast. Have you eaten yet?"

"No," Dougal said promptly. "And we're starved."

Sophia laughed. "I was in such a rush to come meet you that we decided to throw ourselves on your mercy for breakfast."

"I'm sure there is plenty." Triona turned. "Angus, will you inform Mrs. Wallis we have guests for breakfast?"

Angus, who'd been helping everyone with their coats, took them, bowed, and scurried off.

Triona saw Christina staring at the breakfast room door, a frown on her brow. "Christina, have you eaten?"

The girl started, her face flooding with color. "No, no! I mean—I'm not hungry at all."

Christina and Devon exchanged a glance, and Devon asked in a challenging tone, "Where's Papa?"

"As I told Aggie, he's asleep upstairs. He came in very late, but I'm sure he wouldn't mind if you woke him up."

Devon's eyes flashed. "We don't need your permission to wake Papa."

There was a startled silence.

Sophia sent a disapproving glance at Devon, while Mam clicked her tongue.

Christina, her cheeks still red, said quietly, "If you don't mind, we'll just—"

"Papa!" Aggie cried. She flashed past them and was up the stairs before anyone could move.

Hugh had walked onto the landing. Without pause, he swooped the young girl into his arms. The other girls were not far behind and he laughed, hugging them all.

His face softened with love as he spoke to each of them. The girls laughed and chattered, alternately hugging him and pulling back to exclaim over this or that. Triona watched from the bottom of the stairs. She'd been a fool to challenge Hugh's love for his daughters. He did love them—it was evident in everything he did. Why couldn't he include her in that love? She curled her fingers into her palms against an onslaught of tears.

Suddenly Mam was at her elbow. " 'Tis a fine family ye have, lass."

"They're not mine." Every word burned through her, tears clouding her eyes.

"They're yers, dearie, whether they know it or no'." Mam put an arm about her shoulders. "Sometimes fate enjoys makin' ye wait fer wha' ye want most. But if ye're patient and dinna quit the journey, ye'll reach yer reward."

Triona nodded. Mam was right—and she was no quitter.

"Pardon me," came a soft voice.

Triona found Sophia at her other elbow.

She smiled. "I couldn't help but overhear. Your grandmother is correct; the girls will come around, but it will take some time. They're good children, but high-spirited. Honestly, it's good you're here. They need someone in their life." Her gaze went to the top of the stairs. "They all do," she added softly.

Hugh, hugging the girls, caught Caitriona's gaze and his smile disappeared. There was tension in her face, and he instinctively knew something had happened.

Devon pulled on his arm. "Can we eat? We are famished."

"We are!" Aggie said.

He looked at Christina, who shook her head. That was odd; lately she'd had a robust appetite.

Devon tugged on his arm again. "Uncle Dougal and Aunt Sophia are hungry, too."

"Well, then, we can't keep our guests waiting, can we?" Hugh went downstairs, the girls trailing behind. "We seem to have a large complement for breakfast."

"I hope you don't mind," Dougal said. "Sophia arrived home just this morning, and was determined to bring the children to you as soon as possible."

Nora cackled. "Gettin' rid o' them, eh?" She looked at the girls and winked. "Ye aren't causin' trouble, are ye?"

"No," Christina said in a breathless voice. "Of course not!"

Sophia came forward to give Hugh a sisterly kiss and hug. "I would keep them forever, as you know, but they're always so excited to come home that I brought them right away. Besides, I wished to meet your wife."

Hugh flicked a glance at Caitriona. "I'm glad you did." She looked especially adorable this morning, all prim upswept hair, her spectacles perched on her nose as if trying to disguise her beauty, but failing miserably. It had been a disappointment to awaken and find her gone. He must have been more tired than he realized, for he'd not heard a thing until Dougal had arrived.

Mrs. Wallis swept into the foyer. "We're havin'

breakfast brought up now. The room should be about ready. I had Liam and Angus climb in through the window."

A loud scraping sound caused everyone to turn toward the breakfast room.

Hugh frowned. "What in he—"

Triona cleared her throat and looked meaningfully at the girls.

The door opened then, and Angus and Liam grinned out at them. Mrs. Wallis smiled at the gathering. "Come eat. We've eggs and ham, porridge and butteries, and Abernathy biscuits!"

Hugh slipped a hand into the crook of Triona's arm and walked with her to the door. As they crossed the threshold, she came to an abrupt halt. Just as in his library, every piece of furniture—with the exception of the heavy table and the large buffet against one wall—had been moved. The chairs were lined to one side along with the smaller buffet, which, from the floor scrapes, had apparently been resting against the main door. Angus and Liam were putting things back to rights, but the disarray was obvious.

"Lord above," Nora exclaimed, "What's happened here?"

Dougal looked curious. "Were you cleaning the carpets or—"

"No," came a clear, loud voice.

Everyone turned toward Devon.

Head high, her face pale, she said steadily, "Papa told Triona she could do what she wanted with the furniture." The girl looked around the room with an expression of satisfaction. "I don't like it, though. I don't like any of it."

Mrs. Wallis shook her head. "The missus and I only changed the sitting room."

Hugh turned to look at Devon, who appeared ready for a fight. She stared back, defiant, while Christina avoided his gaze.

His irritation must have shown, for Christina paled and took a step back while Devon's hands fisted at her sides. He said sternly, "Girls, you have—"

Caitriona gripped his arm, pulling him toward her. "Hugh, let's talk about this after breakfast. No one has eaten yet."

He frowned.

"We can replace the rest of the furniture after breakfast. But since we have guests now . . ." Her calm hazel gaze locked with his.

Ah. So she didn't want him to upbraid the girls in front of their aunt and uncle. He reluctantly supposed she was right.

"I am famished," Sophia said brightly. "And I like the look of that small table by the window. It would make a lovely nook for more private meals."

"Aye," Nora agreed, eying the girls with a sharp gaze. "There's promise in the new arrangement. Some might like it better, if they'd a mind to."

Hugh nodded. He would wait to address this issue with the girls, but he would have plenty to say when he did.

He covered Caitriona's hand with his own and forced a smile. "Let's eat, then."

For all of the tension emanating from Devon and Christina, the meal was spritely with conversation, thanks mainly to Sophia and Nora. They bantered with one another, asked numerous questions of Caitriona, shared all the local gossip they could think of, and generally kept everyone smiling. Except Christina and Devon, who were mutinously silent.

Why would they wish him to be angry with his wife? He watched as Sophia urged Triona to tell a story about her childhood. Caitriona's face lit up as she revealed how she and her siblings had mistakenly used one of the good sheets as a curtain for a play and had accidentally spilled paint on it, and the madness that ensued trying to hide it from their mother. Everyone at the table gasped with laughter, except the girls.

Outside, the weather was cold and drizzly, but inside, bathed in the warm glow of brass lamps and Caitriona's musical laughter, all was warm and golden. That was what she had brought to his life.

As soon as they could, Devon and her sisters excused themselves from the table. Hugh quietly informed them he'd soon be up to speak with them. They exchanged glances, but nodded and said their goodbyes. He watched them leave, feeling guilty. He'd been so worried about protecting the girls that he hadn't thought about Caitriona getting hurt. But from now on, Gilmerton would be a peaceable kingdom.

Caitriona had made the effort, and the rest of them would as well.

The low fire in the nursery put off more light than heat. Christina shoveled a scoop of coal into the iron door, closed it, and locked it tight. The flames immediately leapt up, pouring forth warmth. She smiled at her sisters. "I like the new furnaces Papa installed."

Aggie, who occupied the far end of the settee, surrounded by three of her favorite dolls and tucked about with her favorite blanket, bobbed her blond curls. "It's much warmer."

Devon slouched at the other end of the settee, her arms crossed over her narrow chest, her mouth turned down in a scowl.

Christina's gaze narrowed as she regarded her sister. After a moment, she went to sit beside her. "Out with it, nuisance. Something is bothering you."

Devon sent her a sidelong glance, but didn't move. "Maybe."

"It's breakfast, isn't it?"

"Yes! We worked so hard, and Papa should have been furious!" Devon scowled. "That woman is a witch. She has put a spell on him."

"There are no witches."

"What about Old Woman Nora? Everyone says she's one!"

"They say she's a white witch. They're not dangerous."

"Well, her granddaughter is a dark witch, and she's *very* dangerous."

Aggie looked up from her dolls. "I don't think she's a witch. I think she's sad."

"What do you know about it?" Devon snapped.

Aggie said stoutly, "More than you! I know she has three brothers and two sisters, and that she's the oldest and has always taken care of everyone, which is how she ended up married to Papa! I know, too, that she misses her home."

Christina frowned. "How do you know all of that?"

"She doesn't," Devon sniffed.

"I do, too! I know lots about her—more than you do." Aggie eyed her sisters with a frown. "You two moved the furniture, didn't you?"

"What if we did?" Devon demanded. "She deserves it."

Aggie's brows lowered. "I don't think she does. I know you think she's been mean to Papa, but . . ." She fingered the lace edge of her doll's elaborate gown before lifting tear-filled eyes to her oldest sister. "Christina, what if our being mean to her has made her *lonely*?"

Surprised, Christina scooted closer, wrapped an arm about Aggie, and hugged her. "Why on earth would you think that?"

Aggie shrugged, her gaze locked on her doll.

Christina regarded Aggie for a moment, then withdrew her arm. "Fine. If you won't tell me what *you* know, then I suppose I don't have to tell you what *I* know."

Aggie's head jerked up as if pulled by a string. "What do you know?"

"Oh, something I overheard Papa say to Uncle Dougal. You won't want to know. It's just about"— she paused dramatically—"the *curse.*"

Aggie's eyes widened. "The MacLean curse? You heard Papa mention it?"

Christina nodded.

"He *never* mentions it."

Christina waited.

Aggie fingered the edge of her doll's gown again. "I suppose I can tell you how I found out those things about Papa's new wife. It's just that . . . I sort of stole it."

"Stole what?" Christina asked quietly.

Aggie reached into her pocket and pulled out a creased note. "Caitriona writes letters to her family almost every day. I saw this in the front hall, ready for the mail and . . ."

"You *took* it?" Devon didn't look as if she believed Aggie capable of such a thing.

Aggie nodded miserably, tears welling once again. "I shouldn't have, but I thought maybe she had written her plans to trick Papa so I started to read it, and then one of the footmen came down the hall, and I got scared so I stuck it in my pocket and—" Aggie's lips quivered. "Oh, Devon, I'm afraid we're wrong!"

Devon looked at the note. She slowly reached out, took it, and read it, her face paling.

Christina watched, her own throat tight. "What does it say?"

Silently, Devon held out the letter.

Christina opened it and read silently. After a long moment, she dropped her hands to her lap and stared into the distance.

Devon stirred restlessly, and Christina let out a shuddering sigh. "She's homesick."

Aggie nodded, her curls bouncing. "Just like we were, when we first came to stay with Papa."

Devon seemed to have trouble swallowing. "She doesn't want us gone at all."

"No," Aggie said, "she just wants us to *like* her."

A lump filled Christina's throat. "All this time she's been homesick, and we've been making things harder on her."

Devon's lips quivered. "I just wanted Papa to stay away from her. I never thought—" A tear spilled down her cheek. "I-I just didn't want to lose Papa. If he leaves us, we'll have to go back to Mama, and—" A sob broke from her.

"No!" Christina grasped Devon's shoulders. "No matter what Papa feels about his new wife, he's not going to stop loving us."

Aggie smoothed her cheek over her doll's hair. "Do you really think so?"

"Yes," Christina said firmly, though in her heart of hearts, she wasn't so certain.

Devon broke the silence. "I know Papa says that,

but Mama stopped loving us when she found someone new."

Christina thought this through.

"There is a big difference between Mama and Papa.
Mama was never very good at being a mother. She
wasn't good at the sort of love that lasts. Her love is
more like a quick, hard shower surrounded by days
and days of dryness."

"And Papa?" Devon asked.

Christina smiled. "He's like a nice, steady shower
that keeps the gardens green and fresh, but not too
much so." She tweaked one of Aggie's curls. "Mama
didn't know how to love us any better than she did.
And Papa has done the best that he could."

Aggie nodded. "Sometimes he yells, but doesn't
mean it."

"And sometimes he yells because he cares, but
doesn't know how to show it."

Devon thought about this. "Not very often, though.
He's usually in a good mood."

"He was, until Caitriona came." Christina thought
about this. "I thought it was because he didn't wish to
marry her and was mad that he'd been forced to do so.
Now, I wonder if perhaps it's like when we first came
to stay with Papa. Do you remember those times?"

"He was very quiet and cross."

"And so were we. We didn't know him well and—"
Christina rested her elbow on her knee and propped
her chin in her hand. "That's actually very interesting,

when you think about it. It makes one wonder . . ." She stared into the distance, her blue eyes unfocused.

Devon let her sister think. Christina was an excellent thinker, even better than Socrates, Papa said. If anyone could figure out the complexities of the odd ways adults acted, it would be Christina.

Christina jumped up and began to pace. "He acts as if he's angry with her, although it wasn't her fault they were forced to marry."

Devon shrugged. "So?"

"*So*, perhaps he doesn't know *how* to react to her and he just *seems* angry. Maybe what's really happening is that he cares for her, and it scares him."

"Nothing scares Papa," Aggie said stoutly.

"That's not true. He was a little scared of us, at first. I think Caitriona scares Papa even more, so he's trying to stay mad."

Devon stared at her hands.

Aggie lifted her gaze to Christina. "Do you think that's why Mama stayed away from us? Because she was afraid she might care too much?"

Christina sat down beside Aggie. "Yes. That's exactly what I think. She isn't a very strong person."

Aggie solemnly considered this. "It's not a very happy way to live."

"No, it's not. Which is why we need to apologize to Papa." Christina looked at Devon. "And Caitriona."

Devon didn't look up, though she knew her sister wanted her to. If anyone owed Caitriona and Papa an apology, it was her. She'd been the one to push things, to try to embarrass Triona before Papa. Christina had tried time and again to make her see the other side of things, but she'd refused. She wasn't a nice person. In that way, she was a lot like Mama.

The thought shot through her like a shard of glass, causing her stomach to clench. She gasped, and Christina leaned forward, concern on her face. "Devon, are you ill?"

"I'm fine," she managed. But she wasn't. She wasn't fine at all.

She was evil, like Mama. Of the three of them, she was the one who looked the most like Mama. Perhaps that was why she was so selfish.

Her heart ached. She'd caused Caitriona pain, but worse, she'd hurt Papa. Tears flooded her eyes, and she fought them back. She couldn't let Christina or Aggie see; couldn't let them know. Papa was going to be so mad.

She knew he'd guessed what had happened this morning, but had waited to say anything. That was a bad sign, for he never waited. Had she caused too much harm this time? Was he going to send them away because of their tricks?

*Oh, God. Not that!* He would send them all away, and they'd never have a home again.

Her gaze flickered to Christina, who was talking quietly to Aggie. Sometimes dark memories haunted Christina. Devon knew, because she slept in the same room and heard her talk in her sleep. How she cried out to Mama to come home, and how she'd begged people for food when they'd been young.

Whenever Christina had those dreams, Devon pulled her blankets over her head and wept into her pillow. As the months at Papa's had gone by, so had Christina's dreams.

And now, because of Devon's selfishness, Papa was hurt and would turn them all away and her sister's nightmares would begin again. Devon couldn't allow that to happen. *She* would go away, before Papa turned his anger on them.

"Christina? I have a headache and want to take a nap."

Christina looked surprised. "All right. I'll stay with Aggie until Papa comes to talk to us."

Her feet dragging, Devon left the room, glancing back for a final glimpse of her sisters.

Then within a few minutes, she changed into her riding habit, bundled some clothes into a pillowcase, and slipped down the back stairs.

# Chapter 19

*"When the light fails ye and 'tis too dark to make yer way, follow yer heart. Love is a light none can extinguish."*

OLD WOMAN NORA TO HER THREE WEE

GRANDDAUGHTERS ON A COLD WINTER'S NIGHT

"Weel, I should be goin'."

Triona followed Mam to the foyer. Her other guests had left and Hugh had gone upstairs to speak with the girls.

Mam hugged her. "Dinna ye fash about MacLean. He'll be gentle wit' the bairns."

"I hope so. He was very grim during breakfast."

"Aye, 'twas a sad trick they played on ye."

"William and I have done worse."

"Aye, but no' wit' such intent." Mam's shrewd eyes narrowed. "They wished to discredit ye and 'tis a talkin'-to they need. I'd ha' thought less o' MacLean if he didna realize it."

"I just don't want this to cause any more strain in my relationship with my stepdaughters. It's such a small issue; I could have dealt with it myself."

"Aye, but 'tis a family ye are, so 'tis as a family this

should be addressed. 'Tis proper fer MacLean to do the talkin' since it was his own behavior tha' set the bairns off."

Suddenly Hugh's bellow echoed through the house. *"Angus! Liam!"*

Caitriona whirled as Hugh came racing down the stairs, Christina and Aggie following, tears on both girls' faces. "What's wrong?"

"Devon's missing." He turned as Liam entered the foyer. "Saddle my horse and be quick about it."

"Aye, m'lord!" The footman ran off.

"Do ye have any idea where she's off to?" Mam asked.

Hugh shook his head. "She's run away from home. Some of her clothes are missing, and it looks as if she'd changed into her riding habit." His jaw tightened. "If one of my stable hands has been so stupid as to saddle a horse for her in this weather—" He left the words unsaid.

Christina wrung her hands, her face pale. Aggie choked back a sob. Triona hugged the younger girl, looking over her head at Hugh. "Why did she run away?"

He hesitated. "She left a note."

Christina lifted her hand, where a crumpled note dangled. "We-we moved the furniture. Devon thought Papa would blame us for—and it *was* our fault, but she—"

Triona reached out and pulled the older girl to her as well, hugging her tightly as the tears flowed.

"There was nothing to be sorry about! It was a joke and nothing more. My brothers and sisters and I did much worse, believe me."

Christina pulled back. "It wasn't a joke. We-we wanted you to go away. We didn't want Papa to send us away."

"What?" Hugh sounded confused.

"We thought you might not want us if you began to like Caitriona. We were afraid you'd have a child. Then we would just be in the way and—"

He placed his hands on her shoulders and bent until his eyes were even with hers. "Listen to me, Christina. No matter what, no matter who is in my life, I would *never* abandon you."

"And I would never let him," Triona added with asperity. "What sort of man would abandon his children?"

"But . . ." Christina's face crumpled. "We're not his children!"

Caitriona blinked, then looked at Hugh, stunned.

"I wondered about tha'," Mam murmured.

Hugh's heart was heavy. Had Devon really left for such a reason? "Christina, we've had this conversation before. You three *are* my children, because I have deemed it so and no one, least of all Caitriona, wishes it otherwise." He looked at her over Christina's head. "Am I right?"

He didn't mean to say it in such a challenging fashion, but every word echoed defiance.

Caitriona didn't flinch. Her eyes softened, her full

lips quivered. "They are your daughters, and now they are mine. They belong here, at Gilmerton, with us." She hugged Aggie tighter. "Christina, I come from a large family. There is plenty of love for all of us here. Even if Hugh and I had a dozen children, you and your sisters would be loved no less."

Her gaze met Hugh's, and in that second, he realized that she had created the one thing he hadn't been able to—a family. But not his warped view of a family. Rather, somewhere along the way, she'd taught him a better, more generous meaning of that word; one that wasn't focused on keeping people out, but on allowing people in. And she'd done it with patience and love.

Love. She *loved* him. The amazing realization washed over him with the power of a MacLean flood. He didn't know when it had happened; he only knew that he finally recognized it. And he did so because his own heart was filled with the same. He loved her, too.

As he opened his mouth to say so, the door flew open and Ferguson came in, wrapped in a dripping cape. "I've brought yer horse, m'lord, and mine as well. I only hope we can find her," he said grimly. "One o' the stable hands saddled her horse nearly an hour ago."

"That damned fool!"

"Aye, he'll be feelin' a strop afore the day's out, to be sure. Fortunately, it's still mornin'. We should find her well afore dark."

"We'd better," Hugh said grimly. "We'll need all of the men—"

"Already done, m'lord. I told Angus and Liam to fetch the stable hands and every man they could find."

"Good." Hugh hugged Christina and then gently pushed her into Caitriona's arms. "I'm going to fetch Dougal and some of his men, and follow the roads toward the village. She can't have gone far." He glanced at Nora. "Will you stay until we find her?"

"O' course."

Caitriona's gaze sought his, her eyes bright with tears. "Please find her soon!"

Hugh answered this with a hard kiss, hoping she could read his love in his eyes. "We won't return until she's safe."

He turned on his heel and went to the door. When he returned, he'd talk with Caitriona. It was time to set things right and begin anew. He pulled his collar higher, ducked his head, and walked out into the rain.

From the windows by the front door, Triona and the girls watched Hugh and Ferguson ride away. Outside, the wind whipped the rain in all directions, and all of the warmth seemed to follow him through the downpour.

Mrs. Wallis bustled in, concern on her face. "I heard about the lassie."

Triona nodded, and Mam said, "MacLean has gone to look fer her."

"He'll find her, dinna fash. Come. I've biscuits and

tea in the sitting room. Might as well fortify yourselves whilst we wait fer his lordship to bring her home."

"Tea is just the thing," Mam agreed. "Come, dearies. We canna help, standin' about the hallway."

Christina sniffed and pulled out of Triona's embrace. "Some tea would be nice."

Triona forced herself to smile. "Come, let's eat all of the biscuits so we can tease Devon when your father brings her back."

Aggie managed to smile in return. "I'll eat two extra ones."

Soon they were seated in the sitting room, uneaten biscuits and untouched tea before them. Outside, the rain slashed down even more heavily.

The minutes passed. Then an hour. Triona tried not to look too often out the window, but it was difficult. Christina kept glancing out, too, wincing at the thunder. Triona had to grit her teeth not to jump up and order the carriage. But what good would that do? She didn't know where Devon had gone, and a carriage couldn't always follow the path a horse might take.

Aggie poked at her uneaten biscuit. "I wish we could look for Devon ourselves."

"Me, too." Christina rubbed her hands together nervously. "She's not likely to go far in this weather," she said for the hundredth time.

"She'd take shelter," Triona responded yet again. "She'd find a rock ledge where it's dry, maybe even a little cave somewhere." She hoped that was true.

Christina stood and walked to the window, staring out as if willing Devon to appear. "The road can be hazardous in rains like this. Papa should have taken one of us with him. We know all of her hiding places."

Triona turned toward Christina. "You have others besides the copse of trees behind the garden?"

"How did you know about that?"

"I followed you last night after you moved the furnishings."

Christina's cheeks colored. "We have some places at Uncle Dougal's house. One is behind the barn, and another is an old gazebo by the lake." Christina said thoughtfully, "You can't see the gazebo from the house, and it's fairly large. It would be a good place to wait out this weather, and it's large enough to provide shelter for her horse."

Christina made sense. Devon wasn't foolish; she would sit out this weather for her horse, if not for herself.

Triona crossed to the window to stand beside Christina. Hugh needed to know this information, but how to get it to him? He'd taken all of the stable hands and the footmen with him in his search.

She bit her lip. She knew the path to Dougal's house, for she'd seen the girls take it. She'd have Mrs. Wallis help her saddle a horse and go herself. Once he knew where to look, he'd find Devon.

Decided, Triona announced, "I'm going to change into my habit."

"But . . . you can't leave!"

"I must. Your father needs to know about the barn and the gazebo."

"But Papa said—"

"He didn't know about your hiding places. I do." Mam nodded. "He needs to know."

Christina's eyes filled with tears. "I am worried."

"So am I," Triona admitted. "But we'll find her." She kissed Christina's forehead, her heart warming as the girl leaned against her. "I promise," she whispered.

Half an hour later, Triona bent her head against the rain, her hat brim barely shielding her eyes. The heavy rain seeped into her clothing until her riding skirt felt several stone heavier. Solid old Bluebell plowed on, head down.

The going was much slower than Triona had anticipated, and the afternoon light was fading fast. She'd taken the trail between Gilmerton and Dougal's house, but she hadn't been prepared for it to be so narrow. The rain made things worse, making it difficult to see the edge that disappeared in places down a steep ravine.

The thought of Devon slipping and falling down that steep slope made Triona's heart thud sickly. She continued grimly. When this was over and Devon was safe, she'd make certain they were never allowed on this trail again. What was Hugh thinking, anyway?

Something caught Triona's eye. In the center of the path lay Devon's riding hat, the sapphire blue scarf sodden and muddy. Bluebell saw it, too, for she skit-

tered on the narrow path, her eyes rolling wildly. Triona gripped her knees tighter as Ferguson had taught
her, and the horse settled down.

As soon as she had her horse under control, Triona
cupped her hand to her mouth. "*Devon!*"

There was no answer. The wind whipped and the
rain thrummed, but no other sound broke through.

Triona held the reins firmly and yelled again,
louder. "*Devon!*"

Still there was no answer. Just as Triona called out
a third time, lightning cracked overhead. Bluebell
jerked forward, but Triona was ready and calmed her
yet again.

Triona stared at the hat, noting that the trail's edge
seemed crumbled. Had Devon fallen? Had her horse
bolted at a flash of lightning? Or had she just lost her
hat and ridden on? There was only one way to find
out.

Heart pounding, Triona dismounted and brushed
water from her face. It was a useless motion, for the
rain just replaced every drop she wiped away. She
went to Bluebell's head and patted her nose. "We have
to find Devon." She looped the reins through some
brush, tied them tightly, and went to examine the
edge of the path.

Through the sluicing rain, she could see down a
rough ravine covered with jagged stones and thick
brush. To one side, a flat rock projected from the hillside, jagged and broken. Rain gushed down, making
streams that disappeared into the mist at the bottom.

The wind ripped over the hill above, blowing rain into Triona's face and lifting her hat. She barely caught it before it could fly off.

Was Devon down there? Triona called again and again, but there was no answer. *Dear God, don't let her be injured.*

An ear-splintering crack of thunder blasted through the air. Bluebell shied violently, yanking the reins from the shrub. Triona made a desperate grab for them but Bluebell was mad with terror, her hooves pawing at the air near Triona's head.

Triona ducked and stepped back toward the edge of the trail. It gave way beneath her boots and, with a gasp of terror, she went tumbling down the side of the ravine, landing on the flat rock.

All was silent, except for the sound of Bluebell's hooves as she ran back to her stable.

And the rain beat down on Triona's unconscious form, a rivulet of blood washing silently into the stream below.

"Home at last." Hugh swung down from his horse and reached for Devon. She slipped into his arms, quaking with cold and exhaustion. "You're lucky Uncle Dougal thought to search every outbuilding."

"I-I-I know," she chattered back.

Dougal tossed his reins to Ferguson and dismounted from his horse. "What a day! I'm famished. I hope Mrs. Wallis has something hot prepared."

"Me, too." Hugh hugged Devon tighter. "After you take the horses to the stables, Ferguson, come and eat."

Dripping water, Hugh carried Devon into the house, then set her down in the foyer and removed his wet cloak from her shoulders.

Nora was the first to arrive. "Ye found her!"

Mrs. Wallis ran into the foyer. "Praise be!"

"She needs a hot bath and some food," Hugh said.

"Especially some food," Dougal added.

"Right away!" Mrs. Wallis turned to Angus. "I've hot soup ready. Fetch some towels and bring a hot bath to the nursery right away."

Angus ran off and she turned back to Hugh. "Where was the lass?"

"Waiting out the storm in my brother's barn."

"I'm glad she had the sense to get out of the rain."

Devon's face crumpled. "I-I didn't m-m-mean to be so m-m-much tr-trouble. I-I-I am just sorry ab-bout—"

"Shh." Hugh kissed her cheek. "I'm just glad we found you. If something had happened to you—" His voice broke and he hugged her fiercely.

"*Devon!*" Christina and Aggie ran down the stairs, and Hugh released her so she could hug her sisters. They threw themselves at her, jumping up and down. "We were so worried!" Christina said, hugging her sister hard. "Where was she?" she asked Hugh.

"At your uncle's house."

"That's where I thought she'd be! I'm so glad Caitriona found you."

"Caitriona?"

Christina's smile faltered. "Didn't she . . ."

Nora stepped forward. "Caitriona went to find ye at MacFarlane Manor, to tell ye about the girls' hiding places there."

For the second time that day, Hugh's heart stopped.

The front door flew open and Ferguson ran in. "M'lord! Bluebell just returned without a rider!"

The floor tilted below Hugh's feet.

Dougal frowned. "Caitriona couldn't have gone to my house; we would have seen her."

"She wouldn't have taken the main road," Christina said.

Everyone turned to look at her.

"She saw Devon and me take the old trail—the one through the valley."

"I told you two never to take that trail! It's treacherous," Hugh said.

"We only use it when we're late or"—she glanced at Dougal—"in trouble."

"Damn it, if Caitriona took that trail—" Hugh turned toward the door.

"Wait!" Dougal grabbed his arm. "Eat first. It's already been a long day and we can't—"

Hugh jerked his arm free. "I have to find her."

After a moment, Dougal nodded. "We will find her. I only hope the storm lets up a little."

Nora glanced out the window. "It's a big one, I can feel it in me bones." Then her gaze narrowed. "It's no' of yer makin', is it?"

"No," Hugh said shortly. "Though I wish it were."

"Why?"

"When I fight the storms made by my brothers, I know they've stopped developing them. This one"—he glanced out at the swirling black clouds overhead, the lightning that was cracking ever closer—"is getting worse."

Dougal frowned. "What do you mean 'fight the storms'?"

Nora snorted. " 'Tis wha' he did when yer brother Callum died."

"When we found Hugh collapsed upon the parapets?"

"Aye. He'd given his all to stop the storms. " Her whizzened face puckered. "We almost lost him tha' night, we did. There's a cost fer such power."

Dougal turned to his brother, but Hugh was already gone, head bent against the storm.

Muttering a curse, Dougal pulled his coat closer about his throat, bent his head, and went after his brother.

The rain was falling harder now, lightning crashing overhead, a fierce wind blowing rain directly into their eyes. The horses were forced to walk slowly, picking their way along the treacherous trail, stepping over fallen rocks and slick muddy gullies. In two places the rain had freshly washed away the entire path, and they'd been forced to jump the horses.

Hugh's heart thudded sickly in his chest. *Caitriona, where are you? I have to find you.* Not to do so was a pain he couldn't describe, a thought he couldn't complete. He loved her.

*And I never told her. I never told her how she's made my life better. Never told her that there's no better way to wake up than to have her beside me.*

"There!" Dougal pointed ahead.

To one side of the trail was Devon's hat. Had Caitriona seen it, too? Had she stopped here and—

"Let's look down there!" Dougal pointed into the ravine below.

Hugh jumped off his horse, his boots sinking into the mud as he stepped to the edge and peered down.

At first he didn't see anything; then something caught his gaze. Squinting through the hard rain, he finally saw Caitriona on a flat outcropping, her skirts twisted around her, her hair streaming over the rock as the water washed through it.

His chest threatened to explode. He tossed the reins to Dougal.

"Hugh, let me get a rope. You can't just—"

But he was already scrambling down the steep hill. It was a miracle that the wet plants he grabbed didn't pull out by their roots, and the mud-soft hill didn't give way, but soon he was on the outcropping beside her.

She lay cheek down, muddy water giving her a brownish halo. The rain had filled an indentation of the rock, the puddle threatening to overtake her. He bent over her, shielding her from the rain. "Caitriona!"

She didn't move.

He touched her, searching for wounds. She seemed intact, but one arm was pinned beneath her in a crevice. Try as he would, he couldn't free her. The rain was pounding, the puddle growing deeper every moment. *She could drown!*

"How is she?" Dougal called.

"She's trapped! The rain is filling the indentation and—" He stared at his gloved hand, where he'd brushed her hair from her forehead. It wasn't mud that encircled her head, but blood. *Oh, God, no.* He ripped off his gloves and searched, finding a deep gash over her ear.

*So much blood—and so much water. She is going to drown while I watch! Oh, God, help me!*

The world seemed to stop. Though the wind roared about him and the rain poured down, he could neither hear nor see. All he could do was feel the wild, painful beating of his own heart. And somewhere, deep inside, he could feel hers, too.

In that moment, calm reigned and he knew what he had to do. He could not free her from this ledge with the rain beating so fiercely. To save her, he had to force the weather to his will.

He stood over her, arms outstretched as he lifted his face to the skies and fought the storm with every fiber of his being.

*"Hugh, no!"* Dougal took a step forward, halting as a huge chunk of the path crumbled and fell heavily

below, skittering down the ravine and narrowly missing the rock where Hugh and Caitriona were.

Dimly aware of his brother, Hugh focused on the blackness above, on the torrents of water, on the crackling heat of the lightning. He pushed. He pushed with every ounce of his soul. With every drop of his blood. With every beat of his heart. He pushed and pushed, and the storm fought back with all its strength. It was young and angry, and wanted to expend itself now. But he could not allow that. *Would* not allow it.

Pain lanced through Hugh's shoulders but he forced his arms to stay lifted toward the skies, taking in the power of the storm and fighting back, wrestling with the black, swirling mass with everything he had.

Lightning struck nearby, but he didn't waver. *Die!* he screamed at the storm. *Die and leave us alone!*

From the ledge above, heart pounding against his throat, Dougal watched as his brother fought the storm. Rain pounded on Hugh's upturned face, and lightning cracked so close that it made the hair on Dougal's neck rise.

Yet slowly, ever so slowly, the wind shifted. Then the rain began to abate. The lightning flashed less frequently, and the thunder rumbled farther away.

Hugh was winning. As soon as the rain had lightened enough for Dougal to get down the slope he did so, slipping and sliding, bruising his legs and hands.

He reached the ledge just as Hugh's arms dropped to his sides and, like a limp rag, he sank to his knees. His face was paler than Dougal had ever seen it, the white streak over his brow glowing silver and wider now than before, but he managed to smile. "Help me free Caitriona," he rasped. "Her arm is trapped."

Dougal bent to her side, seeing the mounting water around her head for the first time. "She almost—" He couldn't say it.

"She almost drowned." Hugh came to kneel beside her. "But she didn't." He lifted her shoulder. "Smear some mud on her arm. Maybe that will help it slide out."

Working gently, it took them quite a while, but they finally freed Caitriona. Dougal offered to carry her, but Hugh silenced him with a blazing look. As if she were made of the finest china, Hugh carefully lifted her and began the long, arduous climb to the road.

# Epilogue

*"Love doesna always mean burning flashes o' passion. Sometimes, it's jus' the warmth o' yer hearts as they beat yer day together."*

OLD WOMAN NORA TO HER THREE WEE GRANDDAUGHTERS ON A COLD WINTER'S NIGHT

"*Y*e can see him now," Mam told Triona.

"It's about time!" She started to rise from the settee where she'd been ensconced, then winced and pressed a hand to her bandaged head. "I know, I know. You warned me."

"And as usual, ye dinna pay me the least heed."

"It's just that it's been *days*—"

"Two."

"—since I've seen Hugh."

"He was no' awake. Besides, ye needed the rest yerself. Now ye're both on the mend." Mam gave Triona her arm and they made their way out of the sitting room. Weak-kneed, her head aching, she walked slowly.

"Caitriona?"

Christina, Devon, and Aggie were coming down the stairs.

Triona smiled. "Have you seen your father?"

They nodded.

"He's pale," Christina said. "But other than that, he looks well."

"He's fine," Devon said, smiling shyly at Triona. "Papa asked for you, too."

Christina chuckled. "Actually, he threatened to burn down the house if Grandmama didn't bring you right away."

Triona sent Mam a startled look. When had she become "Grandmama"?

Mam beamed at the girls. "Ye were good sickroom visitors, ye were. Ye didna hang upon him nor wear him down wit' nonsense."

"We took him presents," Aggie said. "Christina embroidered his old slippers so they look new, and Devon sewed him a sachet for the wardrobe, and I drew him a picture."

"I'm sure he loved all of them," Triona said.

Mam told the girls, "I know ye've lots to say to Triona, but she canna stand fer long yet. Let me get her settled wit' yer da' and then ye can come see them both."

Aggie's face lit up. "Now?"

"Soon. Give them a half hour together, first."

The girls smiled and turned to leave, then Devon hesitated. "Grandmama wouldn't let me see you, but . . . thank you for looking for me."

Triona leaned on Mam and took another step. "I did what any parent would do—you were lost and I went to find you."

Devon's eyes filled. "I'd hug you, but Grandmama would yell."

"So I would," Mam agreed. "There's enough time fer such maudlin going's on later. Now, off wit' ye or I'll change me mind about lettin' ye eat lunch wit' yer parents."

Devon gave a blinding smile and the girls left, talking happily.

Mam helped Triona up the rest of the steps. They reached the landing and, knees shaking, Triona leaned against the wall outside the door. "My hair must be a mess."

"Och, ye look like ye've been in a sickroom, which ye have."

Triona sighed. "I wish I had a comb—"

Mam opened the door and led her in. "Yer husband willna care if ye're a mess or not."

"No, he won't," came a deep voice from the settee by the fireplace.

Triona looked into Hugh's green eyes, drowning in a blaze of familiar warmth.

He grinned and patted the cushion beside him. "My nurse has suggested we are running her ragged by making her keep two sickrooms."

"Aye," Mam said. " 'Tis weary I am from traipsin' up and down the stairs over and over." Mam helped her to sit down.

Caitriona was immediately enveloped in Hugh's warm embrace.

"There," Mam said with evident satisfaction. "Now,

if ye'll excuse me, I've porridge to make fer lunch."

Hugh groaned. "No more porridge!"

"That's all ye're gettin' till ye've lost tha' last bit o' fever." Mam collected a small glass from the table. "I'll be back in twenty minutes wit' yer lunch. The bairns will be joinin' ye, I think." She paused by the door. "And try no' to fight, as 'tis bad fer a man wit' a fever to get excited."

With that, she was gone.

Triona looked up at Hugh. He was very pale, and thinner, too. The streak of white at his temple was broader and more silver, and she traced it with her fingers.

He captured her hand and placed a kiss on her palm.

"What was that for?" she asked breathlessly.

"It's for now." His eyes gleamed with a different kind of fever. "I'll show you what I have for later, but we're going to have to wait until our captor has gone to bed."

She chuckled. "You can't be ready for such exertions. Mam said excitement was bad—"

"Caitriona, my love, I adore your grandmother, but there are some things she doesn't know. *You* are the one we need to take care of." His gaze flickered to the bandage about her head, his eyes darkening with concern. "How is your head?"

"A few stitches and I'm good as new."

"No headache?"

"Just a little dizzy now and then. It's *you* I'm worried about. Dougal said you collapsed when you reached the house and didn't wake until yesterday. He . . . he said you made the storm stop, and—" A sob broke from her lips.

"Ah, Caitriona, no!" He pulled her close and kissed her forehead. "I'm fine!"

She fought not to cry, but couldn't seem to help it.

"Here, I'll show you how fine I am." Hugh pressed her hand to his lap.

Triona managed a watery laugh. "You're right; you are fine."

He grinned. "Give me a week and I'll be back to normal. Last time it took me months to recover." His lips curved tenderly. "Your grandmother seems to think it's because of you that I'm healing so quickly."

"Me?"

"Yes. This time, I had a reason to recover."

Triona's heart began to hum. "Oh? And what's that?"

His smile was devastatingly tender. "I love you, Caitriona. I'm sorry I was so blind to it before. I was just afraid of being hurt."

"Hugh, I love you so much. I would never hurt you, or the girls."

"I know that now."

She touched his cheek. "Do you know when I realized I loved you?" When he shook his head, she smiled. "When I met the girls. I knew then that you were the sort of man worth being with forever."

His eyes blazed, and he lifted her into his lap and

nuzzled her neck, breathing deeply. "How I've missed this! Your scent, the taste of your skin . . ."

She shivered and wrapped her arms about his neck, wincing a bit as she did so.

"Your arm?"

She nodded.

He pulled back her sleeve to reveal a bandage.

"It's just bruised."

His arms tightened about her, his voice rough with passion. "I almost lost you. I don't know what I would have done without you."

She leaned against him. "I know. I feel the same way."

Downstairs, they heard the rattle of dishes, Mrs. Wallis's lilting brogue, and the girls chattering excitedly to her as lunch was brought up the grand staircase. Elsewhere at Gilmerton, Angus and Liam polished the silver, and outside, golden horses gathered at a fence and waited for Ferguson.

All was as it should be. Smiling contentedly, Triona snuggled deeper into Hugh's lap and whispered, "Hold me. For as soon as Mam arrives, I will be told to behave."

His arms tightened about her and he whispered back, "I'll hold you forever, my love. And nothing will ever take you from my arms again."

Turn the page for a special look

at the next delightful

Hurst Amulet novel

from *New York Times* bestselling author

Karen Hawkins

Scandal in Scotland

Coming soon from Pocket Books

*A letter from Michael Hurst, explorer and Egyptologist, to his brother, Captain William Hurst:*

William,

I doubt this will reach you before you set sail, but letter writing is one of my few diversions while locked in this Godforsaken place. I shall endeavor to send this on the next English ship that sets sail and hope it reaches you.

I received our sister's communication that the artifact is now in your care. William, as soon as your ship is ready, please make haste. My captors are growing more impatient as the days pass and while I'm perfectly capable of dealing with their rude treatment, being forced to remain in such close confines with my assistant, Miss Jane Smythe-Haughton, has not made my captivity any more enchanting. She's removed all of my good brandy and has now implemented an exercise regime. I feel as if I've returned to boarding school.

I will not taste freedom until I deliver the object my captors have demanded. To be blunt: my fate is in your hands.

Sincerely,
Michael

*W*illiam Hurst strode onto the *Agile Witch*, the salty wind swirling his cape as he crossed the gangplank, his boots ringing with each step. He paused upon the deck and squinted up at the rigging, then gave a satisfied nod. Every brass hook and ring had been polished until they shone and every sail was freshly patched.

Good. An idle crew was a troublesome crew, and he had no time for such nonsense. He hadn't been captain for almost fifteen years without garnering a clear idea of how a ship should run.

"Cap'n!" The first mate hurried over, saluting as he came to a halt. "Ye're early."

William slipped a hand into his pocket, his fingers closing over the wrapped object there. "My sister was on time, which I didn't expect. I believe I have her new husband to thank for that."

"Do ye like him, Cap'n?"

"He seems to be well enough. One thing is for certain; my sister is enamored of him." Which had surprised William. Mary wasn't usually a romantic, something he'd always liked about her. But whenever she was in the same room as her new husband, the Earl of Erroll, she went from common sense to nonsense all in the flicker of an eyelash. It was ridiculous.

"Women," MacCready said with a note of disgust.

"Exactly." William took a last look about the ship. "She looks to be in fine fettle."

MacCready beamed. "Och, so she is. I put Halpurn in charge whilst I purchased supplies. He did a fine job keepin' the crew on task, except—" MacCready hesitated. At William's pointed look, the first mate added, "There was one item, but I've taken care o' it. It won't happen again."

"Excellent." William lifted his face to the breeze and eyed the distant horizon. "I taste a storm."

MacCready stuck out his tongue and then smacked his lips. "Ye're right. Do ye think it'll break tonight?"

"I think she'll take her time building, but when she comes, she'll be a worthy one. Plan on setting sail with the morning tide. Perhaps we can miss her altogether."

"Verra guid, Cap'n."

"Give Lawton a copy of the manifest. We make this journey at my brother's behest; he can damn well repay the expenses."

MacCready chuckled. "Aye, Cap'n! Consider it done."

William headed below deck to his cabin. Michael had gotten himself into quite a mess, and all over an object small enough to fit into a man's pocket.

But that was Michael. He'd been a sickly lad, and had only found his health and strength after childhood, which had made him far more reckless than the average man. Thank God he'd found the redoubtable Miss Jane Smythe-Haughton to keep up with his belongings and schedule and . . . William wasn't exactly sure of the woman's role, only that he'd never met a more capable—and frightening—individual in all his days, even when he and his crew had happened upon cannibals while resupplying ship at a supposedly deserted island.

Michael's recklessness had been somewhat curtailed by Miss Symthe-Haughton's iron rule until this crisis had occurred. *Where was Michael's assistant during all of this? Surely if there was a way for an escape, he and the redoubtable Miss Smythe-Haughton would have already found it.* William had to assume that there was no way out and thus the artifact in his pocket had to be delivered as soon as possible.

In his cabin, William removed the ancient Egyptian artifact from his pocket and placed it upon his desk. "Michael, you will owe me more than funds for this little favor," William murmured.

He withdrew a chain from his neck where a small golden key was hung, unlocked the desk, then placed the artifact inside and locked it away.

He returned the chain and key to his neck and tucked it out of sight before reaching for his map case. His fingers had just closed on the stiff leather tube when he caught a faint whiff of the purest essence of lily.

The scent was so real, so immediate, that it made him freeze in place, held there by a scrap of a memory—one he'd thought he'd forgotten years ago. A memory of exotic lavender eyes set with thick, black lashes; of hair that slid through his greedy fingers like black silk; of golden skin that held the sun's fragrant kiss; and of a lush mouth, ripe for kisses that—

"Hello, William."

The throaty voice yanked him from the memory. He closed his eyes, his hand still on the map case. The voice possessed an unusual resonance that made even a whisper clear. It was a rich voice, deeper than usual for a woman, yet feminine and richly wanton.

William knew the voice as well as his own. And it was the last voice he expected to hear coming from inside his own cabin.

"Aren't you going to return my greeting? Or are we still not speaking?" The voice lilted playfully, running up and down his spine, as sensual as a warm hand.

He gritted his teeth against his traitorous body and released the map tube before turning.

There, sitting in a chair at the head of the captain's table, was the one woman he never wished to see again. The one woman whose gut-wrenching betrayal had left him hollow, a fact he'd managed to keep her—and everyone else he knew and loved—from knowing by taking his ship to sea and staying away for more than two years.

He'd vowed to never, ever trust another woman . . . especially this one. He'd promised himself he'd never again lay eyes upon her.

Yet here she was, the fading sunlight caressing her golden cheek and tracing the line of her graceful neck. A black cloak was tossed over the back of the chair in which she sat, her red gown as wanton as her nature.

He removed his own cloak, turning away and breaking the spell of her beauty. He hung the cloak on a brass hook by the door, taking a deep breath as he did so. He didn't even bother to turn back around as he said, "Get out."

"You're not even going to ask me why I'm here?"

"I don't care why you're here. Just leave."

A faint rustling told him she'd stood. "William, I must talk to you. I had hoped you weren't still upset about us—"

"There was no 'us.' We were an illusion. A puff of fog in a long and cold winter." He turned to face her, his gaze pinning her in place. "That's *all* we were, and you know it."

She flushed, her creamy skin pinkening as if he'd slapped her. "I'm sorry. I was wrong to have acted as I did and—"

"Leave." He had to grit his teeth. There was something about her that was simply breathtaking, mesmerizing, that made it almost impossible not to watch her. *Damn it, I should be over this! It's been years . . .*

Her hands fisted at her sides and she sank back into her chair. "I can't go. I came all of the way here and I—" Her voice broke. "William, I am desperate."

Another man would have been moved by her tears, but he ignored her obvious manipulation. "Find another fool, Marcail. This one isn't available."

She gripped the arms of the chair. "You *must* hear me out. No one else can— William, *please.*"

"What could you possibly want from me? Has Colchester finally come to his senses and kicked you from his apartments?"

At the name of her protector, her gaze narrowed. "Of course not. Colchester appreciates me . . . as others never did."

"If by 'appreciate,' you mean 'give large sums of money,' I'm certain that's true. The marquis is a wealthy man."

She managed a smile, but it was strained, and he took pleasure in knowing he was testing the limits of her acting skills, considerable as they were.

That was how she earned her living: by treading upon the boards of Drury Lane. Marcail Beauchamp was beautiful, accomplished, and reportedly the finest actress England had ever produced. Her name and her beauty were spoken of with reverence in far countries. He knew what so many others didn't; that her beauty was not due to artifice. No, that she left entirely for her own soul.

His gaze flickered over her, noting that her elegant gown was a trifle too low cut for true modesty. *And that is the* other *way she makes her living,* he reminded himself harshly. *She gives herself to the highest bidder.* "Colchester can have you."

"Whatever you may say of the marquis, he is not involved in my coming here." She hesitated and he saw a flicker of uncertainty. But was it real? "William, I came to ask for a favor."

William gave a bitter laugh. "No."

"You don't even know what it is."

"I don't need to know. If it has to do with you, I want nothing of it."

Her smile was completely gone now. Not that her expression truly mattered, for she changed it as she changed hats, selecting them to augment whatever aura she wished to project. *What was I thinking, to believe the words of an actress?*

He knew only one fact for certain, and it was a damningly inconvenient one; she was just as beautiful as before, perhaps more so. Over the years her beauty had matured and ripened. Gone was her slender, almost coltish beauty and in its place was a seductive, mature woman, one who moved with an assurance that could not be faked.

It was fortunate that he was no longer under her spell.

"William, please, don't look so—" She waved her hand, the movement as graceful as she. "This is not easy for me, either."

"I don't care if this is easy for you." He pulled a chair from the table—the farthest one from her—and dropped into it. "I didn't invite you. How did you come here? The crew didn't alert me that I had a guest and they would have, had they known."

"I came onboard before it was light."

"There is always a guard by the gangway."

"He was asleep."

*So that was the issue MacCready had alluded to. I should have asked more questions.* "I sense some trickery here. I know you, Marcail Beauchamp, and you are not telling me everything."

"You don't know me. You never did." She spoke with such quiet dignity that he was almost taken aback.

Almost. "I suppose you'll eventually tell me what you want; I could use some merriment before I set sail."

She frowned. "You're leaving soon?"

"In the morning."

Her lashes dropped to obscure her true expression. "I see."

She leaned back in her chair, her deep red gown a perfect foil for her upswept black hair, the thin white ruffle at her décolletage pretending a modesty that was betrayed by the way her full breasts swelled above it. She was a master at looking innocent and wanton at the same time; it used to make him crazed for her. Fortunately, he now recognized the artifice written all over her beautiful face.

She caught his stare. "What?"

"You look older. What has it been? Six years?"

"Eight."

"A pity it wasn't eight more before we had to meet again."

His cool, harsh words didn't even cause her to blink. She merely shrugged. "I will make this short. William, I need your help in locating something that's been lost. It's— Oh Lord, this is difficult to say, and I—" She stood as if restless, her lush figure on display as she crossed to the port window. She peered out of it before turning to him. "I didn't wish to ask for your help, but I have no one else to turn to." Her gaze fell on the decanter and glasses that sat on a sideboard. She gestured toward it. "May I?"

He shrugged.

She went to the decanter and unstopped it. She took a delicate sniff, looking at him with raised brows. "Very nice. You didn't use to be so discerning in your port."

"I'm far more discerning in *all* of my likes now."

Her lips thinned, but she merely poured out two glasses.

"It's from Napoleon's private supply." William wasn't sure why he'd felt the need to mention that inane fact.

"That monster. I'd heard you were with the navy then."

"I've been many places since we parted."

"I shall enjoy the port all the more since it was taken from Napoleon." She replaced the stopper and brought him a glass.

He made no move to take it from her, so she placed it on the table before him, then carried her glass back to her seat. She sat and delicately swirled the liquid. "I wonder, am I wasting my time by coming here?"

"If there's one thing you taught me, it's to never trust an answer that is in fact another question."

"I taught you that?"

"Oh, you taught me all sorts of things—none of it good." He took a drink of the port, the sharpness clearing his throat. "Enough of this. What in hell do you want? You have two minutes to tell me and then you're going overboard."

She pushed her glass away. "Fine. I came to you because someone is blackmailing me."

"What does that have to do with me?"

Anger flashed across her face, so swift that he believed it real. "William, I am *desperate*. I don't know who is doing it or why or— They must stop."

"Ask Colchester for his help. Isn't that his place as your 'protector'?" William watched Marcail over the edge of his glass as he took another drink. At her closed expression, he lowered his glass. "Ah. You don't wish him to know this secret, whatever it is. What happened, Marcail? Did you stray? Is that the secret? That you can no more be true to a man than a dog can stop himself from chasing a squirrel?"

Her eyes flashed fire. "Dammit, this is important! If my secret were revealed—and no, it's nothing so tawdry as that—it wouldn't be I who would pay, but others."

"What others?"

After a moment's obvious struggle, she said, "It doesn't matter. You aren't going to help me, anyway. I should have known better than to ask."

"Yes, you should have. I am done with secrets and hidden lies." He pushed his empty glass away, suddenly tired of it all. Tired of the deceptions that had left him so beaten all those years ago. "I think you should go."

"I will. But first, I wish to tell you something." She rose and came toward him, pausing just shy of where he sat.

"Say what you will and then leave."

"Oh, I shall leave, but not until you've helped me."

"I've already said I wouldn't help you." Dammit, was he slurring his words? He looked at the glass of port. He'd only had one glass. Normally it took far, far more than that to—

He slowly looked up at Marcail. "You put something in the po—" His mouth wouldn't make the words, his vision suddenly wavering. He gathered every ounce of his strength and forced his numb arms to push him to his feet, where he swayed dangerously.

She frowned. "William, don't! You'll hurt yourself and—"

He toppled forward.

She tried to catch him, stepping into his fall and wrapping her arms about him, but he was too large. She managed only to keep him from buckling face-first into the table, her slight body only tilting him to one side so that he instead landed upon the hard floor.

*Why in the hell has she drugged me?* He was too numb to feel anything, his emotions as muted as his body. He watched with cool, unemotional interest as she took his cloak and made a pillow of it and gently placed it under his head, her hands warm and sure.

Then she gently slipped the chain from around his neck and took the desk key. The lowering sunlight cast her in a golden glow that made her seem ethereal, an angel of purity and beauty and such exquisite grace that it almost pained one to watch her.

It was that grace that had won him in the first place. Not her face nor her figure nor her rich voice, all of which had helped catapult her to fame from the boards. To him her crowning jewel had been her innate, unconscious grace. When she walked, she drew the eye and held it almost as if she were dancing to music that only she could hear.

She bent over the desk, her dark hair agleam with the golden haze of the final lingering rays of light. She unlocked his desk and reached in. He tried to remember how much gold he had in the cubbyhole. *Two hundred guineas? Three? Why does she need funds so badly? Colchester spoils her with his wealth. Has she garnered debts she can't tell him about? Perhaps she's taken to gambling or—*

She removed her hand, holding the ancient artifact that would free his brother. *God, no!*

Even in his drugged state, fury trickled through. *I must have that artifact. I cannot free Michael without it.*

She tugged open the sack and glanced inside, her brows lowering as she slid the slender onyx box free from its velvet pouch. She traced the tip of a finger over the edge of the box, her expression perplexed. Uncertain, she glanced his way and met his gaze.

Her cheeks darkened as if she were blushing and she hurried to tuck the artifact away.

William wanted to cut her to shreds in word and deed, but all he could do was glare at her with all of the force of his anger, which was burning through the drug's haze.

He suddenly realized he could move his toes, which had been impossible just two moments ago. The drug was already wearing off. Soon he'd be able to rise, and woe betide the wench then. He'd teach her a lesson she'd not soon forget.

She collected her cloak and tied it about her neck before she slid the onyx box into a deep pocket. She paused as she walked past William, the edge of her skirt brushing his hand.

Unexpectedly, she stooped and placed a hand upon his cheek, her dark gaze bright as if with unshed tears. "Don't try to follow me when you can move; I won't be where you can find me." Her long silky hair brushed over his cheek in a gossamer caress, the faint scent of her exotic perfume making his heart pound faster.

She lowered her lips to his ear. "I am sorry to do this, *mon chere*, but I have no choice." She brushed her lips over his, the kiss as gentle as sea mist. Then she brushed the hair from his forehead and said in a voice tinged with remorse, "To you, this is a trinket. To me, it is freedom."

With that cryptic statement, she rose and pulled the hood over her head, tucking her hair out of sight. "I must have the box. I wish it were otherwise, but—" She shook her head and stepped toward the door . . . but William's fingers had closed about her hem.

He held tightly to the skirt, but only his fingers and toes were capable of moving.

"Oh, William. You never let anything be easy, do you?" She gathered her skirt and with a quick yank, freed it from his grasp. "Good-bye."

She left the cabin, quietly closing the door behind her, leaving William in the growing darkness.